Sheri Holman

Sheri Holman grew up in rural Virginia and now lives in
Brooklyn, New York

S

SCEPTRE

Also by Sheri Holman

A Stolen Tongue

The Dress Lodger

Sheri Holman

SCEPTRE

First published in 1999 by Hodder and Stoughton
First published in paperback in 2000 by Hodder and Stoughton
A division of Hodder Headline
A Sceptre Paperback

10 9 8 7 6 5 4 3 2 1

A CIP catalogue record for this title is available
from the British Library

ISBN 0 340 71784 X,

Typeset by Avocet Typeset, Brill, Aylesbury, Bucks
Printed and bound in Great Britain by Mackays of Chatham PLC,
Chatham, Kent

Hodder and Stoughton
A division of Hodder Headline
338 Euston Road
London NW1 3BH

For my mother, my best friend.

ACKNOWLEDGMENTS

I would like to thank the city of Sunderland, England, which was delightful in winter and a far cry from its grim portrayal in this book; the librarians in the Sunderland Local History section, Dr. Lesley Gordon, special collections librarian at Newcastle University, Michael North at the New York Academy of Medicine, and the members of the VICTORIA listserv for their help and guidance in researching this period. Ruth Richardson's extraordinary book, *Death, Dissection, and the Destitute*, was an early inspiration and invaluable source. Special thanks goes to the incomparable Molly Friedrich, my agent and great friend; Elisabeth Schmitz, as passionate and marvelous an editor as anyone could wish for; the gang over at the Aaron Priest Agency, Morgan and all the people at Grove/Atlantic. I 'd like to shake a bone of thanks to my friend and early reader Dan Smetanka, and everyone else who suffered through early drafts: George Green, Julia Crowe, Bill Tipper, Lindsey Tate, my aunt Marilyn, and my mother who actually read things twice, just because she wanted to. Lara Farina and Matt Morgan kept me sane and well-fed through this process, Gary Morris, David Conrad, and Gini Sikes kept me maybe a little drunker than was absolutely necessary. Thanks too, to my father, Gene, and my sister, Shannon, for their constant support.

Like the book before it, and the books to come, The *Dress Lodger* owes everything to my cherished partner, Sean Redmond: bread maker, bird sitter, loving editor, and resident genius. I have my Eye on you . . .

The Dress Lodger

I
WORK
OCTOBER, 1831

"Grave: A place where the dead are laid
to await the coming of the medical student."
—Ambrose Bierce, *The Devil's Dictionary*

I

A GIRL AND HER SHADOW

The boys down on the Low Quay know a hundred ways to sell bad fish.

They'll mingle four dead eels with every one alive knowing full well the average man can't tell which is which tangled inside a cloudy tub. They'll polish up a stinking mackerel with a bit of turpentine and buff it with their shirttails until it gleams. Beneath the wharves late in the day, you can catch them blowing air into the bellies of cod to make their under weight catch look fat and succulent. Poor hungry family, to puncture those flatulent fish and find them more air than meat. But a boy's got to make a living, and when he is forced to feel around in the mud at low tide, scrambling after sprats dropped overboard from a trawler, he may have to take a little advantage to earn his daily wage.

You notice it most on Saturday nights when the markets are set up along Low Street. The orange sellers have secretly boiled their fruit to plump it up, though the practice causes it to turn black within a day; the cherry vendors have weighted their prepacked boxes with cabbage leaves to tip the scales. Not everyone is dishonest, but nearly every merchant prefers to sell his wares after dark when their imperfections are softened by candlelight and men's eyes are less discerning after a full day's work. Most workers are paid on Saturday night here in Sunderland, so they have money in their pockets for meat pies and jacket potatoes kept warm in barrel ovens; they buy two pennies' worth of greasy herring and a roll to go with it. The young sons of public house owners crisscross the market delivering trays of ale to wives who've ordered it for their family dinners, and are stopped along the way by so many thirsty men, they have to run back for more. On Saturday night, when the streets are extravagant with stacked purple cabbages, ruby apples, bright green leeks fringing stalls iridescent with oyster shells, everyone feels rich. There will be meat on Sunday, and when a favorite customer comes to buy his chops the expansive butcher holds out a newly slaughtered pig's heart like a present.

It is Saturday night; work is another two days away. Sunday, you may play cards or walk out on the town moor or, if you are feeling guilty about something, wash your face and go to church. Perhaps you'll just want to sleep, which is what happens most Sundays, when you take your tea on the stool by the fire and realize how good it feels just to sit and stare until your head drops down upon your chest and your cup slips from your fingers. But Saturday night you are alive and want some entertainment. Two new shows have come to town. One is about that disease everyone keeps talking about, the cholera morbus, but the second one sounds far more promising. The Spectacle Unique Les Chats Savants: Signior Capelli's celebrated menagerie of Sagacious Cats, well known in the principal cities of Europe, Whose Docility and Intelligence Never Fail to Astonish. You could certainly stand to be delightfully astonished, since the astonishment you'll receive tomorrow when you learn half the plums you bought tonight are rotted through will be decidedly less pleasant. You push your way between the stalls along Low Street headed toward the theatre on Sans. On your right, the River Wear makes a snaking black ribbon between Sunderland proper and well-lit Monkwearmouth on the opposite shore. There are fewer ships on the river because of the Quarantine, you think, and it is killing everyone, from the keelmen who load Newcastle coal to the potteries that need imported Dorset clay. Your back room matchstick factory is safe, at least, no matter what happens. For ten years you've painted phosphorus tips on little wooden splinters and you've never, for a day, done without supplies. The phosphorus is slowly rotting your jawbone and turning you into a freakish mess, you can't bear to look in the glass, but tonight, Saturday night, you want only to see some sagacious cats, and not think about how your hands and face glow in the dark.

Outside the cheap theatre, where children and domestics get in half price—as if life weren't easy enough for them anyway—you come upon a stampede. Housemaids leap squealing into coachmen; little boys stomp, stomp, stomp like Indians in a rain dance. It's those damn frogs. They've come up from the riverbed, where they've been fucking and spawning, fucking and spawning all this wet, warm autumn until they've overflowed the steep banks and invaded the town. Merchants along Low Street have found moist green frogs suffocated in their flour, the pastor of Trinity Church found them floating in the Communion wine. Just last night, your landlord cursed the chorus of frogs yowling in his basement and sent down his ferret to rip through them. Now it seems the frogs are headed toward the nicer part of town. They are advancing on Bishopwearmouth, the third and by far the most affluent section of Sunderland, built on higher ground to the south. Good, you think. Let a little of the river bottom come up in the world. Let a lawyer or two lie awake and worry, like you have on too many nights, that the Lord has sent a modern plague of Egypt to destroy this town.

How those dainty domestics and little children carry on, jabbing their umbrellas at flailing rubbery legs, frightening the frogs far more than they themselves are frightened! You roll your eyes and dig into your pocket for the 5 d. they extort from you at the box office, reach across to hand the rouged ticket vendor your money—but if you please, wait just a moment. . . .

Before you duck inside, dear matchstick painter, and disappear from view for what will be at least two hours, we beg leave to ask what might at first seem a frivolous question, but which will eventually make sense: if you were to compose your own story—forgetting for a moment the small fact that you cannot exactly write—would you choose this Saturday night, outside of this cheap theatre, through this veil of frogs in which to introduce your heroine? If you might have at your command the entire globe, any moment of historic confluence, if you might in the writing of a humble book bring back to life a Queen of Sheba or an Empress Josephine, would you strew her path with frogs here in dirty Sunderland when you might pluck from your imagination green emeralds to scatter before her in Zanzibar? No, we thought not. You are a personage of refined taste. Left up to you, who is to say this book might not evolve into a tender tale of a matchstick painter whose matches so delight the King of Sicily that he dedicates his palace to her private use, festoons it with pearls and causes the British royal family to hold her quartz and lapis phosphorus pots? If the story were in your hands, we might expect no unpleasantness, no murder or blackest betrayal, for you are not of a punishing nature. And yet, dear matchstick painter, your growing suspicions are correct—this is not your story. This is ours, and you have been summoned, led through the marketplace, encouraged to see this entertainment over the tedious play on cholera morbus down the street for solely that purpose: to provide us with an introduction to our true heroine, who, if you'll turn around, is walking down Sans Street toward you, carefully picking her way across the unctuous carpet of frogs.

Don't be upset, dear friend; we can't all of us be heroes. Though we met you first, we shouldn't feel compelled to follow your tiresome life. From the factory. Home. To the public house for a warm beer every third night—the whole process repeating itself ad nauseam. You have a purpose in the machinery of this book, and though it is not large, it is necessary. We have brought you here to describe her to us, we being too far away in time and space to form a clear impression. Please, dear friend, keep us in suspense no longer. Is she lovely? Plain? Young? Old? First impressions are difficult to shake, dear friend, so please, be precise.

Begin with her face.

It is thin, you say, but well formed? Has she not the snub nose and round cheeks of so many Sunderland girls whose raw ancestors tramped down from Scotland or washed ashore lo those many centuries ago from pork-fed Saxony? Oh, hers is a more Gaulish beauty—if you dare to use the term as a compliment barely fifteen years after Waterloo—with delicate arching brows, a reasonably straight nose, and large, dark, almost navy blue eyes. Her slightly sunken cheeks are drizzled with light freckles—hereditary, you would wager, for surely freckles coaxed out by a pleasant day at the shore would not sit so starkly against white skin. And she is very pale. Her face and exposed arms are the color of cooling milk, faintly blue in the bucket; they possess the sort of pallor that scatters light, the sort of luminescence that great ladies, it is rumored, take small tastes of arsenic to achieve. Hers is the skin of a girl who never sees the light of day.

And her hair, what of her hair? Such skin must set off a deep brunette mane or a fiery halo of red. No, you say? She is blonde? With hair almost as pale as her skin, worn in a complicated style (known in fashionable circles as an "apollo"); her tresses braided and wrapped into a topknot at the crown, while little blonde ringlets are left to frizz at her temples. An ornament which if decorating the tresses of a lady would be a gilt arrow to honor the slayer of Python but on our heroine is a pigeon-feather-dyed red, bisects the knot and completes the apollo.

But we are confused. Is our heroine not a lady? Are we to go through this novel in the company of some commonplace Sunderland slut—not invited to any fancy parties, fed on boiled potatoes and beer when we might, in some other novel, have prawns and champagne? You said she has the pallor of a lady, wears her hair after the fashion of the day. How is she dressed, pray tell? By her clothes, surely we will know her.

Her dress is blue. How descriptive. But of what color blue? Yes, of course in better years we too attended spectacles where nymphs and water sprites yearned for mortal men, where mermaids brushed their hair and admired themselves in flashing mirrors. You would have us picture, then, the backdrop of that theatrical Sea: the billows of cyan silk, the azure pasteboard waves, the ultramarine netting, tangled with sea horses and starfishes, flung to represent an aquatic paradise. We will close our eyes and do as you command. Ah, how cool they look while we sweat in the theatre of a hot summer's night, spying on their underwater world with its hierarchy and despot king and chorus of rebellious daughters; a world so rich and foreign, yet so happily fraught with the politics of our own. Now, to that cool, blinding blue, we are to add the color of our play's artificial sky, appreciating the scene painter's ability to reach back into his childhood and extract the extinct shade of cerulean that floated over the River Wear before the factories were built. Yes, we are old enough to remember that color. We are old enough, certainly, to remember a good many other things besides.

To the complex blue body of her dress, you would have us add wide blown gigot sleeves swelling from bare shoulders and a matching belt cinched at her narrow waist, creating the inverted-triangle look so popular among fashionable women of today. Festoon the entirety with tulle and white bouffant in three puffy tiers from knee to ankle-length hem. Tie her up with a handful of bows down the bodice. She is a sumptuous, fantastical wedding cake. A walking confection. A tasty morsel. And yet, still you hesitate. Certainly no one other than the finest lady might afford such a singular dress. So what is wrong?

She seems small.

Is that all? Dainty is the fashion, my friend. Long gone is the tall, lithe, neo-Grecian look made popular by Boney and his Court in France. Give us the fantasy of the Romantics, frothy faux shepherdess frocks and Oriental accessories! We are a global power, and yet we are pastoral! We have fought in Egypt, we are marching across India; we have the technology to replicate the entire world in our clothing, and we yearn for a simpler time. Anyone would look small against such an empire. But stop, you say. If we are to tap you for a description of our heroine, we must trust your evaluation. Daintiness is bred and daintiness is manufactured. This girl—for surely she can be no more than sixteen—has had daintiness thrust upon her. She seems to you stunted and underdeveloped beneath that dress; her shoulders are painfully thin and her belt hangs loosely at the waist. Her shoes, the universal giveaway of poverty, peek out from under the skirt, revealing themselves as mud-spattered, worn-heeled work boots.

Is it possible? Could we be mistaken in our choice of heroines? Perhaps we got the date wrong, or the address, or even the century. Is there no one behind her—one of her betters perhaps, coming to rescue our book from certain dullness? Look again, dear friend, leave the ticket booth and just peer around the corner to make sure we have not overlooked someone.

Why do you draw back? What? What is it there in the shadows you see?

Now you are rushing back to the theatre. Now you claim your duty is done? We have given you the opportunity to participate in our story, and you choose instead to hide yourself among the mass of anonymous theatregoers eating sandwiches from dirty handkerchiefs, pulling the corks from bottles of beer with their round yellow teeth. What is her name at least? Ask her name! But now the lights are come up, the first disoriented snow leopard bounds on stage decked in an alchemist's cape and black cone hat; and you, dear matchstick painter, for we can see you hesitating in the aisle, are wrestling with yourself. It is Saturday night. You only wanted to see some chats savants, you wanted nothing to do with this infernal business. But you knew her, didn't you? We could tell from your stricken face when you peered into the shadows, you recognized that girl. What is her name?

A lioness teeters on her back paws wearing a mortarboard. A gray tabby, mangy and naked, runs figure eights through her unsteady legs, and the crowd roars.

Gustine. Her name is Gustine.

Thank you, kind matchstick painter. We have a certain sight, you know, but the fact is, we don't always trust it for details. It's a strange ability we have that allows us to see more clearly those who are closer to us, who perhaps are only a few weeks or a few months separated in time. Like for instance you. Or the turnip-fleshed woman who is trailing our heroine. The one you pulled back from in the dark. Her we see quite clearly, though perhaps she appeared to you as only a malevolent shadow along the ground.

In front of us, Gustine and her shadow turn left onto High Street.

A greasy drizzle has picked up, slicking cobblestones already slippery with fallen oak leaves. She heads away from the theatre toward dark linen and woolen shops, bakeries, booksellers and stationers shut up tight against the raw night. Hackney cabs clatter by, not pausing to see why a respectably dressed woman might be walking alone in a closed neighborhood without a cloak or umbrella at half past nine at night. A few merchants, reluctant to go home and face another night of boiled onions and Bible lessons, linger over their locks, peering into their dark windows as though sure of having forgotten something very important. They catch a glimpse of her, reflected by gaslight in their plate glass, and stay just a little longer, to watch and wish that one night, they might be coming out at exactly the moment she passes by, and might, by accident, brush against her tight hot snatch. Gustine lifts her skirt and shakes a frog loose from the hem.

People are saying this explosion of river frogs is due to an atmospheric disturbance, the same that brought the lightning storms and unseasonably warm weather even through October. They say that cholera is certain to follow in its wake. Gustine looks up to where the atmosphere is supposed to be. She wonders if one night it will merely begin to rain cholera. She wonders if cholera could even make it through the heavy gray clouds on this moonless sky begot by Sunderland's hard-working chimneys.

Behind Gustine her shadow pauses, and it too cocks an eye at the sky.

"Damn it!" Gustine turns and yells at the creature behind her. "Will you please just sod off?"

The girl gathers her dress and sprints away down High Street. She takes a right and then a left and then another right, trying her best to shake the old woman who follows her every night. The old bitch who dogs her every bloody step. Truly, business is bad enough with the Quarantine. The last thing she needs is that hag on her tail.

The shadow does not run after her, for shadows need never run; they are, by their very nature, inseparably, inexorably pulled along in the wake of their objects. They do not think, they do not argue. They never worry they will be lost or shaken. A shadow cannot be paid off or given the slip like some commonplace retainer; it is with you from the hour of your birth to the day of your death and beyond, following you even where no one else will, into the wooden box as they hammer down the lid.

Wet blue rat.

The old woman walks with her head down as though scenting prey, and yet, she has almost no sense of smell, nor of taste, and she is so old she can barely hear. The rain has plastered her gray hair to her cheeks like whiskers, but she doesn't feel it. She walks with a bent head studying her own shoes, confident they will take her where she needs to go, and she walks quickly for a woman her age—which, depending on who you ask, is anywhere from sixty to eighty-three. She wears a loose-fitting brown wool dress with a dirty handker-chief tied over the bosom and her hair pulled back in that old-fashioned no-style style. Nothing about her, from her slightly hunched back to her hairy ape arms, would distin-guish her from any other old woman in the East End—until you looked into her slack-skinned turnip-colored face. With a single glance you would realize what makes this abandoned shadow so assuredly calm and confident. What keeps Gustine afraid. What made poor matchstick painter pull back in hor-ror outside the cheap theatre. You would see the shadow has an Eye.

Not eyes, mind you, but an Eye: a single gray carbuncle that has, over the years, siphoned from her other four senses every bit of potency, redirected the diffuse sensations of sound and touch and even smell straight forward into a sin-gle supreme ability; into an Eye so aware, so magnified it never tires, needs no sleep, misses nothing. No one may steal an apple but the Eye sees it. No one may pick his nose or slap his wife or feed his dog under the table, but that it is noted. How happy Jeremy Bentham would be to discover a living, breathing Panopticon moving through Sunderland's East End, kicking aside squabbling cats, splashing through black puddles of human waste and rotting food, its formi-dable sight turned upon a single prisoner only—that pretty young girl laced inside her bright blue dress.

The Eye takes in the rain eddying between the uneven cob-blestones of High Street, a lone green frog trapped on an island of brick, afraid to hop across the rushing gutter, and the slimy vegetable tops left over from the abandoned market closed two hours early because of the bad weather. She can detect the slightest disturbance in the puddles made by the mad splashing of Gustine's boots as she ran away.

Fast rat. Blue rat.

People have told a hundred different stories about how the shadow lost her other eye. Only the oldest in town ever remembered her having a matched gray set instead of that twisted flap of purple skin to the left side of her nose, and they are all dead now. Now people who weren't even born when she was grown imagine that her left eye was put out by a jealous boyfriend after he caught her looking at another man. Those less romantic say she caught an ember in the face during the New Theatre fire of 1781, but that it served her right for being there so late at night. People used to believe she sold her eye to the Devil for a bottle of gin, but now the dominant theory is that she had it gored out by a wild pig while making water on the town moor. No one knows for certain how she came to be the Eye, no one but herself, and she hasn't spoken in so long, most people suppose she does-n't know how.

All that *is* known of this woman—called Eyeball or Evil Eye or Gray Sister by boys who have read their Homer, but mostly called just plain Eye—is that she still lives at 9 Mill Street as she has since before the building was erected, and as she probably will long after it collapses around her; that her landlord suffers her to stay so long as she follows his expensive dress, making sure the girl inside does not steal it or pawn it; and that the night has never fallen these past two years which has not found the pair together—girl and her shadow, the dress and the Eye—plying the streets of Sunderland. All the other rumors, such as her having sold the recipe for human meat pies to the body snatchers Burke and Hare, or her being responsible for the Methodist Meeting House Panic back in '75 when all those children were crushed . . . well, that is nothing but idle gossip and everyone knows it.

Up ahead, Gustine slows down when she reaches the intersection of High and Bridge Streets. Gaslights follow one another on evenly spaced blocks, the lanes widen into avenues the farther west she pushes. Since the building of the great Wearmouth Bridge thirty-five years ago, the geographic center of the city has pushed west to meet it; not long ago this was all pastureland—now, it is booming with shops under construction. Men walking over the bridge from Monkwearmouth, their faces hidden by umbrellas, measure her carefully. Is she what she seems or merely someone's reckless younger sister caught in the rain without carfare? A paunchy mustachioed man in a green plaid woolen suit slows down and catches her eye.

"Are you lost?" he asks.

"I wonder, sir," replies Gustine with an apologetic smile. "Can you tell me the way to Silver Street?"

"Ach, you're far away from there," he says. "That's the other way, back in the East End."

"Oh," says Gustine, looking distressed.

"Are you certain of the address, miss?" The gentleman clears his throat, and finds his cheeks growing hot. "Tha's a rough part of town."

"Is it?" asks Gustine, now mightily distressed.

"Oh yes, miss."

"My brother," she falters. "My brother's friends are having a birthday party for him there at ten o'clock. I told them I was usually in bed by ten o'clock; we have church tomorrow, you know. But they insisted I come."

The man in green plaid peeks at his watch and glances up at the threatening sky. The rain is falling harder now and the pretty miss is without an umbrella. He should offer to walk her. Still, he too has somewhere to be. There's this new show in town featuring some awfully smart cats—he read about it in the newspaper—if he's not already too late.

"I'm sorry for troubling you," Gustine says, sensing his confusion. "Thank you for your help."

She turns right and begins walking down toward the dark riverbank.

"Miss!" shouts Green-plaid. "You are going the wrong way!"

She obviously does not hear him, for she appears to speed up. How can she not know she is about to walk straight down into the river? Green-plaid gives chase and catches up to her at the stone pilings, in the shadow of the great Wearmouth Bridge.

Every town in England is famous for something, whether it is a cathedral or a ghost or a blackberry jam recipe, and in 1796, a good twenty years before Gustine was born and thirty-five years before Sunderland became more famous as the first town in Britain stricken with cholera, we were drunk with love for our new cast-iron extension bridge, the longest and without a doubt the highest of its kind you'll find in all of England. Our town had been getting by since the days of the Venerable Bede, who swore his vows at Saint Peter's over in Monkwearmouth, but not until Napoleon reared his head had we come into our own. Suddenly all of England was on alert; ships were needed for the navy and men were needed to build them. In a matter of years Sunderland became the undisputed Queen of Shipyards—the river was clogged with every kind of ship, from worthy vessels to shoddily slapped together carracks destined to go down for insurance money. Our Sunderland keelmen shoveled coal from Newcastle and Durham onto barges that would circulate it among the machines of the new Industrial Age. Hammers bounced off pliant timber; drying hemp, festooned on the wooden skirders of Rope Walk, perfumed the still wealthy East End of town. The town sprang up on both sides of the Wear: in Sunderland proper, bounded by rich Bishopwearmouth, and in Monkwearmouth, on the other side where the natural docks cut in at Potato Garth. Surely, a bridge was needed—a spectacular modern bridge, for a booming, prosperous town. It took an Act of Parliament and a highly clever engineer to erect the 240-foot long, 80-foot-high cast-iron voussoir bridge, but now every child in Sunderland, including Gustine, can recite the famous pledge buried inside the foundation stone: "At that time when the mad fury of the French citizens, dictating acts of extreme depravity, disturbed the peace of Europe with an iron war; we the people of Sunderland, aiming at worthier purposes, hath resolved to join the steep and craggy shores of the River Wear, with an iron bridge."

Beneath the great Wearmouth Bridge, the man in the green plaid suit is pushing Gustine's pretty blue dress up around her neck and fumbling with his trousers.

"Don't tell anyone about this," he is saying. "It won't take a minute."

"Please don't," Gustine whispers, halfheartedly pushing him away. "I never have."

"You're a flighty little thing. It's bound to happen sooner or later." He pulls back the skin of his prick and jabs about her thighs. Behind him, the bottle-work furnaces fire; along the bank, the black, dead-fish sewer stink rises on the fog. He finds his mark and Gustine turns her head to watch the river lazily carry downstream a bloated sheep, the poor thing bobbing like someone's comfortable, upended ottoman, dead of the scrapie.

When he's done, he shakes his cock and wipes it on his linen handkerchief.

"C'mon," he says, "I'll walk you to Silver Street."

"I don't need to go to Silver Street," she says.

"Aw, come on now," he whines. "Don't be like that."

"I just need you to pay me so I can be on my way."

"I knew it!" Green-plaid spits and kicks the ground. "You haven't gone an' given me a disease, have you?"

"Pay up," she says, holding out her hand. "I'm not a charity."

"All dressed up like a lady," the man snaps, and feels in his trousers for his purse. "A person can't even tell who's who anymore."

Observe, friends, how a man of honor conducts his business transactions. If Gustine had come into his accounting office, say, and asked for an advance of an equally small sum as she now demands, Green-plaid with great gallantry would have counted it out, dropped each shiny penny into her palm, and sent her off with a pleasant little wink. He loves helping out pretty women, and if the door is shut and she doesn't mind a quick feel-up, well, he loves that, too, and has been known on occasion to count out an extra penny from his private pocketbook. But when a woman demands honest remuneration for an honest job performed, how does he then behave? Observe: he extends two dull coins churlishly, makes Gustine reach for them, and when she is off-balance, gives her a furious push that sends her reeling down the riverbank.

"I'll not be taken advantage of, you little slut!" he yells, scampering up the hill, soiling his green plaid knees each time he slips on the muddy slope. Damn these whores. All dressed and perfumed. How is a man supposed to know? He has almost made it to the road when a heavy shadow falls across his neck and stops him cold.

Sad, stupid rat to think he could escape the Eye. She saw plaid rat sink his teeth into blue rat's neck, mount her, and tear at her fur while he furously humped himself dry. Now he scurries away, back to his hole. Bad rat, thinks Eye. To run away.

The red flames of the furnaces hellishly light her face. Know, rat, she is warden and guard. She watches the dress. She watches herself grab you around the throat and shake you until you surrender your rat-skin purse. From it she takes four shillings, the dress's fee, no more, no less, and tosses the rest back to you. She watches you scamper up the hill, choking and coughing, humiliated, crying for the constable, for any bloody cop, goddammit, and she sees, just as surely, there is not one to hear you for miles.

Eye walks heavily down the bank. She spies a puddle of blue under the bridge, half in the water, half in the black mud. The dress is dirty. Their landlord won't like that. When she gets a little closer, she sees the blue rat is not hurt. She is staring intently at something laid out beside her.

A dead rat, about six feet tall, wearing a wool cap, brown

trousers, and a mud-stained white shirt. His wide sightless eyes are turned upstream, watching for ships trapped on the far side of Quarantine.

"Look what I found!" Gustine leaps up, clapping her hands. "Let's go tell Henry!"

HENRY

Henry says, though perhaps it's not strictly true, that he frequents the cramped pub on narrow Union Lane for no better reason than its name. Not long after he came to town, he accompanied his uncle, our illustrious Dr. William Reid Clanny, on a scarletina fever case. When they arrived at the flat, they found the young girl tossing in a caul of red rash upon a filthy bed she shared with four other siblings ranging in age from six to fourteen. Their parents and the youngest child slept on flea-infested ticking in the same claustrophobic room; only the day before the mother had given birth and was too weak to stand up. The walls, not having been whitewashed in years, were furred with soot from the clogged fireplace. They had no cupboards in which to store their food, so a month's supply of rotting potatoes was stashed under the bed. At least they have a floor, Clanny had whispered to his nephew; many here in Sunderland sleep on cold, pestilent earth.

They did what they could for the child with scarletina, who was delirious by the time they were called, and not likely to last the night. Henry ordered the new mother to drink beef tea and wrote her a prescription for tartar emetic that she could get free at the dispensary on Sans Street, knowing full well she would never go. When they finally left the sad, squalid house, Clanny suggested they treat themselves to a drink. A cheerfully painted sign for the public house next door invited them in, its emblem a shovel poised to dig up a smiling skull and above it, its moniker: the Labour in Vain. Henry thought the sentiment about summed up their evening, and in the course of the year he's been in town, he's realized the sentiment about sums up his life. Most nights find him here, at least for a pint, sometimes surrounded by his students, sometimes alone with a book. He often amuses Audrey with stories of the characters he meets at the Labour in Vain. She says she would love to come with him, but he's not that depraved. He doesn't need to sully the one pure thing in his life.

"Another round, Doctor?" asks John Robinson, the flat-faced, shaggy-haired, hulking proprietor of the Labour in Vain, reaching for Henry's glass.

Henry passes him the empty and watches the publican fill it with suds. Henry's bandaged hands, thick with cotton gauze, make it difficult for him to carry the full pint back to his table without spilling.

On a typical night, John Robinson pulls drinks for every sort here. Early on, most of the tables are taken up by good-natured day labourers headed home from the docks. Later, a few butchers might drop by in their crimson aprons and pick the dried blood from under their fingernails while they toss back a couple with friends. The night will wear on, the air will get hotter and the boasting meaner. Just when you've decided the room is too full of men and it's a sorry state of affairs for a Saturday night, a pair of pretty factory girls will switch in, or someone's Catholic daughter will come to drag her old man home. Then the fun begins. Men who were about to come to blows only minutes before are now show-ing off, rolling back their cambric sleeves and arm-wrestling

for love and honor. The factory girls applaud and are treated
to gin and sugar water, while the old man talks his shy
daughter into staying for just one more sip. On a typical
night at the Labour in Vain, when the hilarity swells and the
singing begins, the patrons never notice a couple creep in,
install themselves in the corner, and quietly order some
drinks. The woman is invariably pale with swollen eyes, gripping her glass of beer as if someone were about to pry it
from her; the man rests his elbows on the table, and studies
the round white water stains on the wood before him. They
will have come in via the Church Walk, like so many other
couples before them, leaving someone behind in Trinity's
overflowing graveyard. They will have a single beer and slip
out as quietly as they slipped in. It is getting late and the
Labour in Vain's hardworking, hard-drinking patrons will be
thinking it's time to leave. But John Robinson knew what he
was doing when he christened his pub. He knew there are no
patrons so happy to sit and drink as patrons who are given
something to gripe about. Inevitably, on their way out the
door, they glance up at Robinson's cheap wooden sign, the
painted shovel and its grinning skull, realize that yes,
dammit, they have been working their fingers to the bone,
their palms are bloody, and for what, they ask, what? The
sign works every time. They sit back down and order another
round.

Through their disgruntled midst carrying his sloshing
beer goes Henry Chiver, tolerated if not exactly welcomed at
the Labour in Vain. The men know he is a doctor, which
makes them suspicious, and they see how the factory girls
eye him—as if they were simply dying to run their fingers
through the disheveled young man's whorls of sable hair.
What could they possibly see in him? Sure, he's smart-look-

ing, dressed in his London fashions with choking collar and cravat, sporting those tight trousers all the swells are so fond of, when corduroy knee breeches have always done a workingman fine. But they couldn't say he is handsome inside those expensive clothes, for his nose is large and his dark eyes are set too wide apart and his overlapping teeth war each with the other for supremacy in his mouth. Worse than all of this, the doctor is possessed of a single trait that is almost unforgivable to the workingmen of the Labour in Vain: Henry is skinny. Everyone knows he could afford to walk into any restaurant in Sunderland and order the menu; yet he is thin by choice.

"Make room, boys," says Henry, and waits for his four students to adjust their chairs. He takes a seat himself and wipes his moist bandages off on his coat.

Little is known of the new Dr. Chiver beyond what the town gossips could collect, and we can tell you very little more. He studied at St. Thomas's in London with one of the nation's most acclaimed surgeons, Sir Astley Cooper. He graduated top in his class, and was handpicked by the even more famous Dr. Knox to teach anatomy at his extramural school at 10 Surgeons' Square, Edinburgh. About two years ago, Henry left under a cloud, which for all the town's expert seeding has not been made to precipitate the truth. Prominent wives have invited Henry's uncle Clanny to dinner and hinted at all the usual doctor disgraces: back alley abortions, drug addiction, a rich man dead on the operating table; but he, discreet soul, has calmly chewed his mutton and kept his silence. So no one knows for sure why Henry left Edinburgh two years ago. Though it does seem odd his exit coincided exactly with his mentor Dr. Knox's implication in the Burke and Hare murders.

So here he sits on another Saturday night, leaning on a rickety table whose broken legs are trussed with string, sipping beer that tastes brewed from old rags and soda bread. He has lived almost a year in Sunderland, rescued from his mother's house in London, where, for all of the previous year, from the time he left Edinburgh to the day his uncle called, he barely left his room. He is trying to start over in our town; his uncle found paying students for him and advanced him the money to convert his house. Audrey has been his saving grace, loving him so openly and unconditionally, he is almost embarrassed by it. It has been a healing year, a back-slapping-get-back-on-that-horse-my-boy year. He's immersed himself in teaching, helped his uncle in these anxious cholera-expectant times, even found a moment to get engaged, and yet, the only thing true about this year, he thinks, the only times that he has been completely honest with himself are on the nights he's spent here. Only among this crowd of the failed has he felt comfortable living inside his own defeat.

Uncle Clanny might not see him as a failure. Audrey certainly doesn't, but Henry's four students—Bishopwearmouth boys who have met him here tonight, as they do at least once, sometimes twice a week, looking always out of place no matter what old, don't-mind-if-it-gets-stolen jacket they've pulled out of the closet to wear—are, without a doubt, onto him. Oh, they pretend. Redheaded Bietler, mechanically reaching into his pocket and cracking sunflower seeds between his squared-off horsy teeth, pretends to read the *Sunderland Herald*, recently founded to champion Reform. Grose, the Tory, whose father is a vestryman, and who refuses to read such radical trash, subscribing instead to the musty *Sunderland Gazette*, where there is no talk of Reform except to bemoan it, pretends to read that. Short, bespectacled Coombs looks over Grose's shoulder, catches perhaps two or three words a page. Even gentle Mazby, who with his girlish complexion and long lashes is perhaps the brightest of the bunch, distractedly thumbs a month-old copy of *The Lancet*. They are staring at the words but deep down each is waiting for Henry to speak. Will tonight at last be the night? Will Dr. Chiver finally make good on his promises? Henry looks from boy to boy, dreading having to tell them that once again he has nothing for them, but annoyed that they have begun to assume it. They brought newspapers instead of their kits; at least, up until now, they have made a pretense of bringing their dissection kits.

Four paltry students, Henry thinks with a sigh—and they are far more difficult to handle than the huge crowds that came to 10 Surgeons' Square in Edinburgh. Before Burke and Hare, Dr. Knox was so popular he would draw on average five hundred students a session. His anatomy theatre held only two hundred, so he and his assistant, Henry Chiver, taught in three shifts a day: morning, afternoon, and just past dinnertime. How many evenings did Henry choke down a capon and a mug of beer in Dr. Knox's dining room, knowing their subject was laid out upon the table in the next room, just as Dr. Knox had left it at the end of the previous lecture; the abdomen opened first and viscera removed, as they decompose quickest; the torso opened next, the head removed and packed in ice for study the next day? How many evenings, as he ripped into his drumstick, would he imagine the ropy tendons of the body's dissected hand left pinned in place with the point of a compass, so that two hundred students might shove past and make a quick sketch before heading off to their own dinners? Some afternoons when Knox and Henry ran late, they would eat their cold sandwiches over the opened corpse while they argued a point of procedure: what to dissect next? Knox always lobbied for the brain, Henry was obsessed with the heart. The room was kept purposefully cold during the Winter Session to preserve the bodies, and Henry would stomp his feet to warm them, listening with his hands pressed against his armpits as crotchety, atheistic Knox went on about the glories of that most perfect human organ, the unknowable brain. It is the seat of all reason, he would say, the true heart of man, far more so than that muscle in the chest. It is mysterious yet desirous to plumb its own mysteries; it is the Grand Usurper to the throne of impotent old King Soul and its reign defines our modern age! Yes, but, would say Henry. Yes, but—Henry cannot forget the painting of Christ's Sacred Heart perpetually bursting into flame over his boyhood bed. Against a triumphant fire, bright, sentimental cherubim lifted high that red and blue holy pump; the aorta wide open like the mouthpiece of a trumpet, the four chambers shadowy beneath a venous pink pericardium. It was an anatomical heart, a scientist's heart, enlisted in the aid of Christ. He knew he was meant to see his savior's humanity in this isolated organ, and yet by the time he was old enough to enter medical school, the torso of Jesus that faith should have wrapped around it had never materialized; and Henry was left instead worshipping a deified heart. These students are not atheists like you, Henry would argue with Knox. What better way to demystify, what better way to put power into their hands and let them know they have a right to understand the human body, than to have them claim for their own the most ancient symbol of Man's very Self, his passionate heart? It is easy to intellectualize the body when you are able to take it for granted, thinks Henry, watching his four students fidget over their newspapers here in the Labour in Vain. Since Burke and Hare, he will never again allow himself to take anything for granted.

"Listen to this," says Bietler, who has the annoying habit of reading aloud every manner of trivial news. "They opened an Asylum for Female Penitents in Newcastle last month. It's already full."

Mazby glances at Henry to mirror his reaction, but their teacher is impassive.

"I went to a whore in Newcastle once," volunteers Coombs. "She was so grimed with coal she looked like a Negress."

No one encourages him to continue, but he does so just the same.

"I also had a whore in Paris."

Grose has shouldered Coombs away and now he can no longer even pretend to read. The student looks around the pub and lights on the staircase leading up to John Robinson's second story. A smirking keelman pulls a factory girl along by her wrist and disappears up the steps.

"I wonder if she's one," he says.

"Corn's up because of the Quarantine," reads Bietler.

"Do you think the Quarantine is doing any good?" Mazby asks, hoping to draw Dr. Chiver into a conversation. He's been so quiet tonight.

Yesterday, at his house on Nile Street, Henry had his students inject a pregnant dog with blue prussiate of potash, then extract and study her organs. Though they had made only one injection, the pancreas, the salivary glands, the kidneys all had turned blue. The prussiate turned the placenta blue, too, and through it, the veins of the fetus had absorbed the color, tingeing the puppy inside a deep hairless sapphire. One small prick here, and an entire body is conquered. A city is like a body, my boys, thinks Henry. It circulates, it shares, it absorbs. Let cholera but prick our pathetic Quarantine and you will soon witness the miracle of circulation.

"For what it's costing my father," sniffs Grose, "the Quarantine had better do the trick."

Have they learned anything? he wonders. They speak of holding back illness as if it were as simple as fencing out a curious pig. Did they give more than a passing glance to the shy girl who came in to retrieve her father tonight? Mark her too bright eyes, notice the dainty drops of blood blooming on the handkerchief she touched to her mouth? Over by the door, did they observe the once-handsome face craterous with smallpox, or his companion, the swine-eyed old man whose nose has been eaten down to a snout by syphilis? Disease is drinking in the bar with us. For all we know, Cholera Morbus is even now thumping the bar for a gin. I am wasting my time on these boys, Henry thinks. He looks down at his hands, wrapped in clean white bandages, the only thing about him that has remained clean. I nearly gave my hands in service to you, ungrateful boys. I am teaching you all the time and yet you have no eyes with which to see.

"Here's something," Bietler offers, flipping back a page so that Henry knows he's read the passage already but deliberately saved it. "Warburton has reintroduced the Anatomy Act. Soon we'll have all the bodies we need, and we won't have to wait for you to procure us one. Isn't that fortunate, Dr. Chiver?"

Poor Mazby looks woefully at his teacher. Oh, now I see, thinks Henry, looking from one young man to the next. They drew straws before they met me here, and Bietler won the

privilege of reminding me that eight months into their training, I have once more failed to produce the bodies I promised
for dissection.

"Soon we will have our pick of the workhouse dead, won't
we, sir?" asks Grose, seconding Bietler. "We won't need to
wait until the moon is new or the ground is soft, or whatever
it is you are waiting for."

"It must be better for us to get our bodies legally from the
workhouse than worry someone has murdered to sell to us,"
says Mazby softly, not looking at his teacher.

No, we must be able to trust our suppliers of corpses, and
what better pander, thinks Henry, than the British government? It will provide the bodies of the poor in heaps so that
we may learn from them how to save the rich. God, it used to
be so easy. A professional resurrectionist would appear at Sir
Astley's or Dr. Knox's back door, negotiate a price, and with
out further ado, the students would have a body upon which
to learn the art of kidney stone removal, of suturing, of
speedy amputation, so that they might save lives. No one
liked it, but the system had been in place for well over a hundred years. Then along came Burke and Hare and nothing
would ever be the same again.

"You told us Human Anatomy began in the winter. We are
two months into it already," says Coombs. "What is it you
are waiting for?"

What *am* I waiting for? Henry swirls his glass of flat
mahogany beer and watches the sediment sink like grave dust.
God damn Burke and Hare. He is waiting for absolution.

Outside, the rain has picked up. The patrons of the Labour
in Vain can hear it against the windows, and each new man
who comes in is handed John Robinson's towel with which to

dry his hair. The bar has a little rush when the theatres let out. One or two had taken in the new play *Cholera Morbus* and declared it a right frightening little melodrama. By far the favorite, though, was Signior Capelli's menagery, and all the men who saw it moan into their beers over their talentless cats back home, who if they only showed the least bit of initiative could make their fortunes.

Into this crowd slips a little bit of blue. John Robinson automatically hands over the towel, and then he sees who it is. His wide, flat face lights up.

"Gustine, my girl, what can I get you on this raw evening?" asks he.

"Not a drop," says she, frowning. "I'm working."

John Robinson reaches for his least dirty glass and pours into it a splash of gin.

"Just to take the chill off," he says, holding it out to her.

"No point in an expensive dress if I have liquor on my breath." Gustine waves it away, and scans the crowd. She sees a hundred brown heads and a hundred beefy red faces. Could he not have come tonight?

"Little hope anyone here could afford that dress," laughs John Robinson, following her eyes around the crowded bar. "Except maybe the good doctor . . ."

"Is he here?" asks Gustine.

The proprietor of Labour in Vain smiles fondly at the overdressed girl. Everyone thinks it's sweet that Gustine has a crush on Henry Chiver, and who knows—though he doesn't strike John Robinson as the type, maybe he'll keep her. With Clanny's money, he could certainly afford a cheap little flat somewhere, she could quit the pottery, move out of Mill Street. That is, if Whilky would ever let her go. He nods toward the far corner.

"Back there," he says, but Gustine has already spotted him and is pushing her way through the crowd. She is all business, this Gustine.

"It's a shame to waste such fine gin," John Robinson says to the counter, giving it a wipe with the hair-drying towel. "Madame Eyeball, won't you taste it?"

The old woman who followed in the slip of blue rolls her all-seeing eye toward the counter and spots a cloudy bit of juice. She smacks her lips and downs it in a gulp.

Before she can find him, Henry spots the dress making its way through the crowd. It is unmistakable against the earthen browns and rust blacks, a dress fit only for the fanciest ball or for the stage. He has not seen that dress for a month, was beginning to think the girl who had worn it was nothing more than a diseased dream, a blue and white laudanum hallucination. God help him, he wishes she were.

Mazby spots her first and stands up respectfully.

"Is this the gentle Miss Audrey Place we've heard so much about?" he asks gallantly.

The other boys quickly fold their newspapers and rise. Everyone stands but Henry, whose face is crimson.

"No," he says tightly. "This is not Miss Place."

Mazby hurriedly sits back down, blushing brighter than his instructor. Of course this is not Henry's fiancée. Why would she come to a place like this? On a wet night like this? Oh why doesn't he think before he speaks? Why? Why?

"Sir," says she, barely glancing at the students, "step out with me?"

Henry rises as if he had been waiting to do so all night long. Wordlessly, he follows her to the front door of the bar. The back of her expensive dress is wet and streaked with mud.

The rain is falling in great torrents now and sheet lightning, far out to sea, leaches the eastern half of the black sky indigo. They stand on the single step elevated from the flooded lane, sheltered under John Robinson's shovel and skull. Now that he looks at her sober, Henry realizes Gustine has much in common with her name. Except for a slight gutturalness in the first letter, her name would be almost musical, and if not for the unfortunate gutterishness that began her, she, the girl, might have grown up to be very pretty. The name suits her so well, he wonders if she made it up. Standing so close, he can smell butterscotch candy on her breath, mixed with the sickly scent of rotting teeth.

"I found one," she says. "Dead under the bridge."

"Gustine," Henry starts. "Forget everything I said."

"Snub Irish nose. Bloody bully and a drunk, I'd say."

"I've decided to teach from plates. I will make models. I can't do this."

"You told me to look for you."

"I know. I can't."

"I've been looking. For weeks. Keeping my ears open like you said. Asking after the sick. I've been working for you."

Why does his temperature drop ten degrees when she stands near him? Why does he feel infected by her, fluish, why do his teeth chatter? It used to be when he was in love he felt this way. Then, when he stood before the uncharted universe of his first opened body. Inept, hopeful, terrified. Like he felt a month ago, in the Labour in Vain, when drunk and floating on laudanum he poured out his soul to this girl; confessed his needs, his fear, his failure at the Trinity graveyard. They must have bodies, he told her. My teachers—Sir Astley, Knox— they provided bodies. I am afraid. Did he say it out loud? I am afraid.

"Who is Miss Place?" she asks.

"Gustine, go home," he says, a little sickened to hear his fiancée's name in her mouth. He knows he shouldn't be angry at her. She is only doing what he, in a moment of insane weakness, asked her to do. But he is embarrassed by her. She has no idea what it is she's doing.

"Dr. Chiver."

He hears her calling his name, but walks back inside. Did anyone overhear what they were saying? He looks around suspiciously, but the only person he sees regarding him is a hideous one-eyed woman standing by the bar. Someone did a bad job sewing that up, he thinks. Back at his table, four oblivious boys slouch in their chairs, their long legs imperiously stretched out before them. Four boys from among the best families in Sunderland, friends of his uncle Clanny's, paying students. Here in this out of-the-way town where he was to forget everything that happened in Edinburgh, where he was to begin again. With his own school. Under his own control. But he has taught them everything he can from charts. He has exhausted the illustrations from Albinus and Bichat. And he has seen firsthand the dangers of allowing a surgeon to operate when all he knows of the human body is the space it takes up in a book. Back in London his teacher's nephew, Bransby Cooper, was admitted into the Royal College of Surgeons with no better qualification than a kinship to Sir Astley. Henry witnessed him perform what should have been a routine bladder stone removal on a middle-aged man, the father of six children—a procedure any trained surgeon could perform in under eight minutes. Bransby took an hour, digging with his knife, then his clamp, finally groping with his fingers like a grocer fishing for olives. The patient, fully awake the entire time, bound, and screaming in agony, was so exhausted he died twenty-four hours later. Six children. Could he live with himself if he graduated four more Bransby Coopers?

Behind him, Gustine waits. She has someone for him. A drunk and a bully. Dead under a dark bridge. Who is to know? Burke is dead. Hare gave King's evidence and was transported. It is not the same, he tells himself. We have murdered no one.

"Dr. Chiver." Gustine comes up behind him. "I lost money coming to find you. My landlord is going to be mad."

And Gustine's landlord is going to be mad if he doesn't give her some money. There is no way around it. His students are slouching, again pretending to read their papers, but about to mutiny. Our teacher is afraid, he knows they are thinking. He is afraid to get us a body.

"Did you hear me?" she asks.

Henry strides to the table in the back and Coombs, who had taken his seat, jumps up. Henry knows they are wondering about the woman in the fancy blue dress. He can see the unasked question hovering on Coombs's lips like a smirk. He won't give him a chance to ask it.

"Be at my house in two hours," he says. "Sleep, eat, do whatever you need to do. Tonight, we will have a lesson."

It is midnight, and the Labour in Vain is closing up. John Robinson wipes the sticky beer from the tables with his fusty rag, sweeping the rain-soaked sawdust onto the street to clog up the gutters. He has blown out all the lamps but one to save on oil, leaving the public house shadowy and cold, robbed of the evening's fire and body heat. As he sweeps, he reunites the chairs with their tables, turning them over and setting them on top to discourage the rats from climbing up.

One by one, he wipes and sets the chairs. Here sat that shy consumptive young girl who came to drag her father home, waiting for Da to drink himself into a semblance of sobriety, or at least to get through hilarious and on to maudlin. She smiled at his jokes patiently, then with her soft gentle voice got him to crying with how he was breaking Ma's heart, and from there it was easy enough to help him from this chair— which John Robinson now turns over—and out the door for home.

Sweep, sweep. John Robinson moves on to the next table and collects the sugar-crusted gin glasses left by the factory girls. By the end of the evening each girl had a silk kerchief for her neck given to her by a keelman who had fallen madly in love. He's seen it a hundred times before. Each will wear her man's cloth like a lady wears an engagement ring, giving out the favors a hardworking fiancé has the right to expect. They will be madly in love until next Saturday night, when there is a row, and the next Saturday night, when perhaps there is a bruise, and then, John Robinson suspects, the smart factory girl will give her neck kerchief back, the stupid one will wear hers to the altar.

The proprietor of the Labour in Vain puts their glasses to soak in cold soapy water and moves on to the larger table in the back. Chiver's four students left their newspapers behind on the table; John Robinson collects them to read and to line the windows upstairs. They seemed more nervous than usual tonight, he thinks, sweeping up the hulls from the sunflower seeds Bietler obsessively fished out of his jacket pocket and ate. Usually, they swagger in with their teacher, act bluff and all hail-fellow-well-met like they belong in such a bar and not off sipping sherry at the Bridge Inn. When they think he's not looking, they wipe the rims of their pint glasses with their shirtsleeves. Usually, they last an hour, maybe two. Tonight though, he couldn't get them to leave. They switched from beer to rye and knocked back a bottle between them, looking grimmer and grimmer with each round.

Their four chairs he wipes and turns over.

Tired John Robinson leans against his broom and surveys his bar. Before he goes upstairs to bed, he must water the gin and correct the wine. He buys as cheaply as he can from a French sailor, mostly vinegared old casks, sweetened with a little packet of grayish-red oxidized lead got off the chemist. He knows he stands a chance of poisoning half his clientele, but most drink beer, so he doesn't sweat it.

Saturday seems to be his only solid night since the Quarantine. There was a time, before this cholera business, when any night of the week his bar was packed to overflowing, when sailors who didn't frequent the Life Boat or the Golden Anchor would walk the few blocks up to the Labour in Vain for a pint or six. Then the tap would flow, then the blood would fly! Most nights he'd have to toss out twenty brawny men instead of four sotted students. Ach, that it's come to this. A few keelmen, four nervous rich kids, lost without their teacher, and him off to get a little piece of Gustine. The proprietor shakes his head. He wonders if Whilky would look kindly on his dress lodger spending so much time downstairs in his brother's bar. She's dressed for the Bridge Inn and the Majestic Theatre; she's dressed to have a vestryman invite her up to his best friend's dark flat—oh, no, he's off on business just now, but he left the key under this mat. It's dangerous for a working girl to keep too much company with one man. And she is smitten. John Robinson saw that the night they sat here in the corner.

At this last table. Far back in the dark corner. That night

a month ago they sat at this same table for two bound by a broken chain of round, white water stains. Usually this table beckons those that come in via the Church Walk. Two came in tonight, a different two will come in tomorrow night. They can tell it's a table for hiding, it's a table where a glass can leave a stain from not being lifted and toasted of an evening. Back here it's dark enough for those that have just buried a loved one to cry a little more, or to hide dry eyes if not crying is what they feel bad about. With the Church Walk only two narrow alleys away, the Labour in Vain sees its share of burying customers. John Robinson got the chills the night Gustine sat down with the wild-looking, mud-spattered doctor. He always thought it foreboded something ill if an unbereaved couple picked that table to sit at; it was like courting certain death in the family, or at best a crippling accident, and he didn't like it. Of course, John Robinson couldn't know that that night they'd had a right to the burying table.

But back to work.

He turns over the chair that held an eager, animated Gustine. Sweeps beneath it. He lifts the chair upon which sat Henry, whose heart that night raced with fear and laudanum. John Robinson remembers serving him gin after gin, with sugar cubes for Gustine. He can still see them clearly: Gustine leaning in, her small pink tongue playing around the edges of the sugar cube clamped between her teeth; Henry taking suicidal gulps of gin, talking crazier and crazier, looking over his shoulder as if pursued by the Devil. John Robinson remembers glancing around for the Eyeball, waiting to see if she would step in and steer Gustine toward more profitable customers; but the Eye merely watched from the corner, patient and implacable.

The proprietor sets Henry's chair and sweeps out a few stray frogs before heading downstairs to perform his nightly transubstantiation of vinegar and lead into wine.

And now, dear readers, the Labour in Vain is quiet. We have it all to ourselves until John Robinson comes back to lock up and blow out the last light. Perhaps since we are finally alone, we should take this opportunity to make an apology. When the body of a story is stretched out before us, we who are new to the telling of tales sometimes don't know where to make the first cut. Which is the best way to enter? Shall we plunge deep into the heart of the matter or begin systematically with the extremities? It is clear to us now that we have opened this particular story in the wrong place. We realize now that it would have been better to have begun a month earlier, not among the jostling wicker baskets of the marketplace, nor picking our way through an explosion of river frogs that provides the ribbiting backdrop to our narrative, nor even beneath the great Wearmouth Bridge where Gustine found the means of returning to Henry. No. How much wiser to have begun a month ago with their first encounter, on a night Henry wishes to push aside forever, but one Gustine cherishes like a pressed flower. Since it is impossible to take back a cut once given, let us then trick time. Let us use this back corner table that has absorbed so many sad cemetery tales as a talisman, and learn of it the story Henry told Gustine the night of his failure, the night he brought her here and changed both their lives irrevocably. Readers, touch your hands to it like a séance table and allow it to lead us back to a dark night in September. Slowly back. Go slowly back. Do you see yourself strolling along the Church Walk, through the acclivitous shadows of orphanage on our left and workhouse on our right, down to the inevitable caesar of this grim triumvirate, the Trinity graveyard? Are you prepared to begin again with the story our table has to tell?

The moon shines eerily on a false chemical winter, the alternate night of our beginning. Emaciated box shrubs stand stiff and defiant against the white sky, the lead roof of Trinity Church gleams like quicksilver. All is cold and silent and dusted white. With the cholera scare, by order of the new Board of Health, the sexton must mix great shovelfuls of quicklime into the mounds of earth that partner all fresh six-foot troughs to corrode diseased bodies into instant bones. We may have watched him of an evening chop and turn, heave and pat, raising pure white drifts throughout the yard, and when he was done, drive the flat headstones into place like sledding accidents gone face-first into snowbanks.

The sexton's dog, who is usually left tied up to warn off intruders, who would at the skittering of a squirrel or the fluttering of a mourning dove bark until all the veins stood out on his muscular neck, died two weeks earlier from gnawing a brick of unbroken lime. The sexton himself is down with the 'flu he periodically picks up from the bodies he handles and is sleeping it off at his sister's house. It has been two hysterical years since Burke and Hare were caught; the town has calmed down; the graveyard, no longer patrolled, is once more the exclusive domain of its tenants. On the alternate night of our beginning, as Henry creeps across the town moor, crunching through shimmering floes of broken glass, skirting the ghostly skeletons of dumped cattle given their last rites by rats, his is the only ghost that stirs.

(Later, at the Labour in Vain, Henry will tell Gustine that the laudanum he took to calm him for the task had, in fact, the opposite effect. Once he had leapt the cemetery wall, he had the sensation of skiing wildly through the night, of trees and stones and shadows rushing too fast past him, of time itself speeding downhill. He carried a burlap sack, a shovel, and a crowbar; he could feel the sweat running down the back of his neck and realized his arms were shaking from clenching the crowbar. Henry later told Gustine that he made an enormous effort to slow his racing heart.)

Despite the frozen look of the land, it is not cold. The soil gives off a damp chill from the previous night's rain but the warm air soups a lazy white fog in the hollows between mounds. Henry moves efficiently through the thicket of last century's gravestones, barely glancing at the names. There had been no feared epidemic to frost these graves with lime, and Henry moves past them quickly. He needs to select his grave as he would a fresh fish, and he knows that a young woman, first cousin to the couple who took the back table at the Labour in Vain that night, was interred this morning. The couple looked so wretched he doubted they could have afforded a sturdy coffin. Probably the cheapest of nails and few enough of those. He wants only to finish this awful thing, to slap the wet body onto the slab and say to his students, Here, I have done it. That I may not ever again be accused of conspiring with murderers, I have dirtied my own hands with grave soil, I have carried the dead weight of a body on my own shoulders. That I may never again be accused.

(Have you ever taken laudanum? he will ask Gustine later, sitting with his elbows on the same back corner burying table where earlier he had narrowed fragments of that grieving couple's conversation into a point on the map of Trinity's graveyard, a brilliant patch of earth buzzing as though freshly sifted with cocaine, underneath which sleeps a pale first cousin. No, she will shake her head. I never have.)

Henry is so dizzy he hardly knows how his shovel makes connection with the soil or how the first clod of earth comes to hit his boot. It rained the night before and the dirt is heavy, pregnant with earthworms and busy black pill bugs, but he digs and digs like a man possessed. At last, he is doing it. He is the teacher now; he is doing what Sir Astley Cooper never had the guts to do, what Knox would rather pay professional murderers to do. Time moves in fits and starts as he digs deeper and deeper, not the required six feet, barely four, when his shovel strikes home. He flings it aside, wedges the crowbar beneath the floor on which he stands, prying back the coffin's lid with a loud crack of splintering wood. At last. At last, he kneels, looking upon his prize. Shrouded in a length of filmy linen from which a few strands of long brown hair escape over her shoulders, she sleeps on her right side, dreaming of angels and hot cups of tea and a comfy seat at the sandal of God, the usual poor person's dream of Heaven. He can reach in and touch the rounded curve of her hip, embrace her narrow shoulders. He could climb in beside her and pull the dirt over them both like a blanket.

He gently rolls the girl onto her back and reaches around her waist to draw her up. But barely has he gotten his arms around her when he feels this girl is spongy underneath, her winding sheet wet and reeking. Mary Paterson? he whispers, breathing in the unmistakable smell of cheap whiskey. I left you behind in Edinburgh.

Henry drops the body sharply against the coffin and scrambles back to the surface. This isn't happening. Calm down. Calm down, he tells himself. Men far less competent and careful than you have dug up bodies and not been driven mad by it. Reach in, feel under her armpits. Pull. Yes, this is not the smell of rye, but merely a ripening body not yet preserved in salt. This heaviness I understand; it is not a frantic pulling back to the grave but the purely scientific phenomenon of blood pooling in the extremities. He lies flat on his belly and tugs the young woman free of the earth. Now that he has her above ground, he sees she looks nothing like the one for whom he almost mistook her. By laudanum moonlight, the similarity in height and hair coloring had been uncanny, but it was a momentary terror; he has composed himself now. He eases his bag over this first cousin as gently as he might help a lady into her cloak. I have only to fold her gently into this sack, replace this earth, climb this wall, and fly across the town moor. I have only to secure seven more first cousins for my students before the school year is out.

> Knox holds the purse strings
> Chiver saws the bow
> With hearts as black as sin
> And hands as white as snow. . . .

One of the many songs the balladeers wrote during the trial coupling his name with Knox's is stuck in his head. He works quickly to refill the grave, sending shovelfuls of earth into darkness. His hands, he realizes, have become uncomfortably hot, and when he looks down, to his dismay, they *are* white as snow. Henry could shake himself for his stupidity. Even the most witless hireling would have thought to wear gloves before he dug around in a poison-laced graveyard. Henry wipes his raw, quicklime corroded hands on his white powdered jacket. He tears open his contaminated frock coat, pushing against the cool white shirt, and leaves

44   *Sheri Holman*

hot bloody handprints against his chest. He needs to wash this off fast; his hands—his surgeon's hands will be eaten away. He frantically refills the grave, but there is no time. Flinging aside his shovel, Henry lunges for the bag of first cousin—they must get out of here. But when he lifts his hard-won prize, the burlap sack runs with clear yellow whiskey.

No! Henry cries, flinging the bag back into the half-filled grave. He pushes hard against the chemical snowdrifts, stumbles and falls on a hard stone marker, cracking his lip, instinctively touching his searing hands to it and igniting his mouth. *Stay away!* Just behind him he hears a stampede of stumbling, heavy footsteps, he feels the heat of breath against the back of his neck, reeking of filthy rags, sweet drugged-gin, yellow-tongue, headachy anger. It overpowers the putrescence of the graveyard, coming closer and closer, the fetid breath that hid in the mouths of all sixteen corpses delivered to Dr. Knox's school. He scrambles up and over the high brick wall, leaving far behind cousin, crowbar, and bag. He looks back and finds himself face-to-face with whiskey-bloated Mary Paterson and the furious, limbless gang of sixteen.

(They had followed me, you see, he will say to Gustine later at the Labour in Vain, watching pass over her thin intent face the masks of those beggars, all murdered over two years ago in that cheap Edinburgh boardinghouse, crept up upon and suffocated while passed out drunk, consigned not only to haunt the living forevermore, but to do it with crippling, bloody, eternal hangovers.

How could I have not known they were murdered? he will ask her as if expecting an answer. When Burke and Hare brought bodies so fresh that blood still foamed at the mouth and dripped from the nose? Why didn't I ask the question we all had on our lips when six-toed, cauliflower-eared Daft Jamie, beloved by all boys and organ grinder monkeys for his liberality with cashew nuts, went missing from the street, just at the time a headless, footless corpse appeared on Dr. Knox's dissecting table? Or go to the police the night they arrived with a grandmother and a twelve-year-old boy folded into a pickle barrel, whose bodies had so obviously set into rigor mortis while inside that we had to smash the barrel before we could free them? Or cry out when they presented us with the naked body of a prostitute I'd been with only the night before—giddy and beautiful and very much alive— folded inside a tea chest, franked with threads of moldy black pekoe? She is almost too beautiful to cut, Dr. Knox had said, calling in an artist to paint her as a cadaver odalisque, preserving her in a trough of whiskey for three months so that his students might explore her perfect musculature. How could I deny Mary Paterson? Would you have kept silent, Justine?

Gustine, she corrects.

Would you?)

Henry falls running from the wall and never looks back.

It is at the town moor communal pump that Gustine finds him as she is heading home from a long night's work. She stops by the pump as she does most nights to wash away an evening's accumulation of gentleman callers and finds a man slumped over at the watering trough, running cold water over his hands and face. He is staring at her so strangely she thinks surely she must know him from somewhere. Henry sobs through the cascade of icy pump water when he sees the pale blue vision advancing on him. *I didn't know. Leave me alone.*

Had we only chosen this night as the night of our beginning, we might even have ended our chapter conveniently here at the Labour in Vain, where Henry took Gustine once he realized that she was not Mary Paterson—how could she be—but in fact one of her kind, a creature who might, more than anything else, help him erase this awful night from his mind. Another girl already had a customer upstairs at John Robinson's, so they waited at the burying table, and while they waited Henry found himself telling this strange blue girl everything about himself. He poured it all out to her: how he fled Edinburgh after Burke and Hare were arrested rather than face the public's wrath, how doctors must constantly battle stupid, stupid superstition when people should just donate their bodies to Science damn it like he was going to do, like the valiant Jeremy Bentham had done, and how he was a goddamned failure, yes he was, having to face his students empty-handed, and all because he couldn't secure them a body. A damned dead body. She listened carefully, barely sipping her gin, and when she finally spoke, she surprised him.

Funny, she says through her sugar, I come across dead bodies all the time. Would you like it if I brought you to them?

Says Henry, pausing long enough to make sure he understands her, You would do that?

Yes, says Gustine, if it would help you. And in return, she continues, in return you will let me ask you a favor.

Her tone of voice has changed. She is not the gentle listener of a moment before, but a flinty businesswoman. Over her shoulder, he sees the couple come downstairs from John Robinson's upper room. The woman's face is red and rough from the man's two-day stubble and both look tired and drunk. Henry is gripping Gustine's hand hard in his own. Her nails, in contrast to her dress, are ragged and grimed with red clay. At least he thinks it's clay. The gin and the laudanum hit him the same time as the realization that he has confessed his deepest, most damning secrets to a total stranger. She is in a position to demand almost anything of him. And what does he know of her?

Gustine cuts her eyes to the staircase. That's us, she says.

Henry swallows hard and tries not to be sick in the bar. For the first time he notices that this girl's dress is the color of mercury against a syphilis sore.

I think I should go home to bed, he says to Gustine. The bar has emptied out. Only an old one-eyed woman and John Robinson are left. Gustine looks crestfallen and a little reproachful.

I lost money coming here with you, she says. My landlord is going to be mad.

Oh, of course, says Henry, reaching into his pocket and finding a silver crown. Thank you for the company.

Gustine's eyes brighten at the sight of so much money.

I'll find a body for you, she says. Don't worry.

He rises and sees her out the door. The old woman trails out behind her and he wonders if Gustine notices. In another hour Henry is passed out in bed; in another day, he is forced to read about an aborted body-snatching at the Trinity graveyard and how the victim's ghost terrified the thieves away.

It's strange with some stories that no matter where you begin, be it in the crowded marketplace or in the lonely grave-yard, among the living or with the dead, you are fated to end up in the same place. If we lift our hands from the back cor-ner séance table, and rub our eyes, behold—here we are, still at the Labour in Vain. So, it seems it made no difference, dear reader, where we cut into our story. Had we begun a month earlier instead of tonight, we might have taken a different path, but we still would have ended up here, in a lonely bar, watching John Robinson bolt the door behind us, and blow out the last remaining light.

III

THE MORGUE

Sod me," says Gustine, "it was right here."

The rain has stopped and the frogs, to whom any down-pour is forty days and forty nights, have sent forth their raven and dove. The waters lie upon the land beneath the Wearmouth Bridge in great continental puddles of tidal flooding: a Deluge to the croaking population of Sunderland, a nuisance to Gustine, who must lift her skirts and wade to where she found the body at what was then low tide. She splashes back and forth in the shadow of the bridge, churning up glassy silt dumped by Horn and Scott's Bottle Works next door. She swears this is the spot. Could he have floated out with the tide? No, it is not that deep yet. Gustine retraces her steps up the steep bank and stomps angrily back down.

"Just come down here a little farther," Gustine commands. "It must have been under here."

That marvel of the modern world, our Iron Bridge, perched upon its two masonry abutments on either steep bank, looks cold and imperious and unforgiving at night. It arches high above, casting its austere shadow now upstream, now down, depending on which of its flanking glasswork fur-naces are firing. Upstream it darkens the ballast mountains of sand used by the Sunderland Bottle Works; downstream, frowns upon a line of free standing four-story warehouses and the muddy flats that lead to the Iron Foundry.

Beneath the bridge, our black river lies fallow; flat-bottomed lighters that at high tide would have been moored in the middle of the channel waiting to ferry corn, timber, stone, and cloth are leashed loosely along the shore. When the rising tide knocks them together, they answer hollowly as if in sympathy with the empty bellies of their owners, men who have not earned a living wage in months. The barge drivers, too, are suffering. And the man who pilots the harbor's single steam tug, a machine that could turn ships around in six days when before they might have dallied six weeks waiting for a good wind. All the river men sit idle now, playing cards in drafty rooms up and down the quay, cursing the Board of Health and laying bets on when they'll pass an edict forbidding the very tides from turning. There is no one out to be happy he will not have to row in the rain, to pull no matter what the weather against the choppy Wear water and risk capsizing in the wake made by the churning, tireless steam tug. There is no one out at all.

Henry follows Gustine deeper into the shadows, along the bank lambent with milky bits of buried glass from the bottle works. He hugs the masonry abutment of the Great Bridge, trying to keep above the tide. When he looks up, he is staring into the longest expansion carcass in the world. Bowed iron ribs are ball-and-socketed together by hollow joints of straining metal. Thermal expansion has warped the bridge's sunniest side, creating a ferrous boil in the infrastructure that requires twelve horizontal splints to pull it back into shape. Underneath, the gulls of Sunderland have shat the bridge's spandrels skeleton white.

She is leading me to be murdered, Henry thinks grimly, inching around the abutment. Her pimp will come at me with

one of those heavy-bottomed bottles. He will bring it crashing down upon my neck, rifle my pockets while Gustine keeps
watch and his terrier sniffs my pant leg. Henry looks around
for anyone who might hear if he calls out. Four powerful men
on the opposite bank feed blocks of stone into the sparking
open turret of the Sheepfold Lime Works. Roasting great
hewn blocks from the Fulwell Quarry into quicklime for use
as fertilizer and glassmaking flux and burning Board of
Health cemetery snow, they couldn't possibly hear him. No
one could hear.

"Maybe down here?" Gustine wades up to her ankles in
black river mud and impatiently beckons him to follow.

Beyond her, the glowing cones of the bottle-work furnaces
strain at their seams, oozing orange threads of molten glass
where the mortar is compromised. They sigh carbon dioxide
and groan enough flame to throw crazy reflections onto the
black surface of the river, scorching the patent slips where
half-built schooners are mirrored mouldering crookedly on
stilts; touching off the steep tiled rooftops peeping upside
down from Bridge Crescent and Matlock Street; even playing
the pyromaniac with the reflection of that great iron
Narcissus arching above their heads. Gustine moves in and
out of shadow, now lit by infernal light at the water's edge,
now swallowed by the moonless dark. Henry steps on something soft and leaps back. Beneath his shoe, a river rat, slick
and silver and gaudy with glass dust, darts into the water and
quickly furrows upstream.

When he looks up again to find Gustine, a half-lit man is
looming in front of him.

"Jesus Christ," Henry shouts.

Gustine wheels around at the sound of his cry while
Henry, in a single fleeting thought, wonders if he can reach

the rig he left tethered up the bank before he bleeds to death.

"Will you help us, please?" she pleads.

The man steps out of the shadows and Henry, to his great relief, sees it is no pimp after all, but an old waterman with a wide triangular torso, bowed legs, and a face like a brown puckered apple. He is one of a dying breed of passenger ferrymen who thirty years ago was put out of business by the Great Bridge and has since then spent every night haunting his old competitor.

The old man leans on his ferry pole and doffs his wool cap to Gustine.

"What's a nice young lady doin' down a' the stinky river a' this hour?" he asks kindly, showing a mouthful of black teeth.

Gustine puts her hand on his arm.

"Oh, sir! My husband and I have had terrible news. Someone claimed he saw my brother's body down by the riverbank. My husband bade me stay at home, but I insisted on coming. Please, have you seen him?"

There's that voice again. Where on earth did she learn to speak this way? From penny novels? Henry doubts she can even read. From the theatre? Her accent, gone. Her cadence, articulation perfect. In that dress, with that pure, distraught voice, she could have stepped out of the finest house on Fawcett Street. She could be Audrey's next-door neighbor.

"Y' should've made 'er stay in, sir," the waterman scolds Henry. "'Tis a dangerous place for a lady."

"I know," says Henry, awkwardly. "She insisted."

The waterman nods to Gustine and draws Henry aside.

"I did see some lanterns round here 'bout an hour ago," says he. "You might try Mag Scurr's down the Quay. But take this lady home first."

"I will," says Henry.

"It's no place for her."

"I know," fumes Henry, annoyed to have this water person think him capable of bringing a real lady to the stinking river bottom at night.

"God bless you," calls Gustine in her Fawcett Street voice as Henry tugs at her.

He can't get away from this dark, lonely place fast enough. On the road above, he sees his team's impatient breath curl against the fog, hears the creak of the carriage settling in the damp cold. This is ridiculous. He is chasing a corpse that he does not even know exists. His students are probably even now at his house, being offered sherry by his befuddled valet, wondering where the hell he can be. He will just have to face them. He will refund their tuition and apologize to his uncle Clanny. He and Audrey will be married quietly and he will move her as far away from Edinburgh and London and this awful town as he can get. To America, where a man might start over and make money with no honest profession whatsoever. Climbing into the carriage, he is so full of dull disappointment that he barely realizes Gustine has hopped in beside him.

"Gustine." He turns to the eager girl settling the lap robe over her dress. "I will drive you wherever you would like, but I am going home now."

"The old man told us to try Mag Scurr's. I know where that is."

"We don't know that the body was taken there," Henry says. "Even if it was, how on earth are we supposed to get it now?"

The horses stamp testily, churning the fog with their tails. Gustine sits in silence, picking at a loose thread on her tartan lap robe.

"I am going to drive you home now," he repeats. "Please tell me where."

"Mill Street," replies Gustine tersely.

Henry turns his horses toward the East End and gives them a sharp switch. The oil lanterns swinging from each side of the rig light a thick wall of fog, punctuated every few blocks by the misty blue halo of a street lamp. It is getting darker and darker the farther he pushes east; the streets begin to spiral back on themselves like a knot of baby snakes. Next to him, Gustine sits with her eyes straight ahead, her lips pressed into a tight suture.

"Why are you angry?" he asks roughly. "We spent a few hours together over a month ago. I forgot all about it. Why have *you* been looking all this time?"

"You asked me to," she says.

"Do you do everything someone asks you to?" he snaps.

"Mostly."

He urges the horses faster. From the moment she came into the bar, he'd felt a thin sheen of sweat break out upon his brow, as if she were calling some fever out in him. Down at the river bottom that same oily contamination spread over his chest, down his shirt, and between his legs; now he can hardly wait to get home, draw a hot bath, and wash this whole evening away. But of course, he can't go home and take a bath—his students will be there.

"There is practical anatomy and contemplative anatomy," she quotes his own words back to him, singsongily, as if had she memorized without fully understanding them. "The first we learn by experience, the second we learn from the teacher. The first looks at structure, the second at cause. How is a teacher to teach the cause when there is no body from which to learn the structure?"

"You remember that? From a month ago?"

"Yes."

"You are far ahead of my students, then," says Henry, subdued.

"You said it was impossible to become a doctor without the study of the human body and that every body you examined made you a far better doctor," Gustine reminds him.

"I did say that. But what do you care?"

"I care because one day I may need you to be the best doctor you can possibly be."

"Why? What's wrong with you?" he asks.

"Why do you assume I need help for myself?"

"Who then?"

"I will get you this body, tonight," Gustine says, ignoring his question, "if you promise that one day you will let me call on you for help. As soon as I saw you, down at the pump, I knew you were the only one I could trust. Now, how badly do you want to be a good doctor? How badly do you want that body?"

How badly does he want that body? He didn't realize how badly until he knew it was lost. Henry thinks of going home to face those four boys, waiting with their dissection kits on their laps like wide-jawed baby birds. His speech obviously impressed Gustine; so why does he find it so difficult to believe it himself?

"We'll try Mrs. Scurr's. If he's not there, that will be the end of it," Henry says abruptly, and, taking a sharp left, heads for the wharves and timber cranes of the Low Quay. This is a mistake, he is thinking. Perhaps she is trying to blackmail me. Perhaps this is all a setup. So be it. I can go on no longer teaching solely from books.

"Good," says Gustine. "I hate to be wrong about people."

*

Margaret Scurr is Sunderland's East End Renaissance
woman. A philosopher in the higher math of pawnbroking,
she is equally accomplished in the lesser known art of corpse
display. Her shop off the Low Quay brings her myriad talents together under one roof: in front, her prosperous pawnshop is crammed with stale clothes, framed oil paintings of
the Wearmouth Bridge, and, since the Quarantine, a wealth
of tin compasses and barnacly purloined anchors left by desperate sailors; while in back, she keeps a single spotless
room. Into Mag's back room the constables of Sunderland
bring all the bodies they fish from the River Wear, and while
Mag gets nothing like the traffic of the famous Paris
morgue, the lure of anonymous bodies in back does draw a
bit more business in front. When the curious and bored
come in to see what the tide has washed up, who is to say
they won't stay to browse a bit? And for her generous services
rendered, services for which she is paid a paltry shilling per
corpse by the vestry, which one of us would begrudge Mag
Scurr the clothes off those bodies that remain unclaimed to
sell out front?

When the Wearmouth Bridge night toll taker on his way
to work stumbled upon the same deceased male as Gustine
and dutifully reported it to the constables, they brought the
body, not even an hour ago, here to Mag Scurr's. No, she
said, she did not recognize him, but if she laid him out in
the back, someone surely would. She had another body
brought in last week. Once she'd picked the sea crabs off
that one's face, brushed what was left of his beard, and
worked her magic, one of her regular customers had made a
positive identification. The body belonged to a decrepit
drunk called merely Old Fist, who had no one living to

claim him. The constables came back and carted him off to the Trinity pit.

The first thing Mag does when she receives a body is strip it and check for distinguishing marks. This man should be easy to place. He has a twisted left leg, shorter by about two inches than his right. On his right arm he sports a heavy tattoo of the hero of Camperdown, Sunderland native Jack Crawford, climbing the mast of the HMS *Venerable* to nail up the Admiral's colors. He's a sailor, certainly, with those bulging forearms and brown, muscular back. Mag dispatches her boy with a description to the Life Boat pub, where a good number of sailors spend their Saturday's pay. With all these clues, it should be only a matter of hours before someone steps forward to identify this one.

Her second order of business is to assist whichever physician the constables send over to rule out foul play. She likes to strip the body before the doctor arrives, just in case there is a bit of money about the pockets. No need to have rich, greedy doctors finding it when they have more than they know what to do with anyhow. She keeps a keen eye on the sawbones those constables send over—usually Dr. Haselwood, but sometimes kindly Dr. Clanny. She wouldn't leave a corpse alone in a room with one of them any more than she'd leave her boy alone with a hungry wolf. Doctors are always waiting for you to turn your back or step out for a moment; looking always for a chance to disappear with a poor man's remains and make their infamous experiments upon it. No, Margaret Scurr watches the doctors very closely; she waits in the room for them to write out the death certificate and assures them she'll fill in the name as soon as it's known. In the early days, before Dr. Haselwood knew what she was about, he on more than one occasion hinted that a clever morgue keeper might earn a pretty penny by not trying very hard to find the next of kin. Just write "Unclaimed" here on the death certificate, he said, and send for me. She gave him a piece of her mind that night, for sure, and the next time he was summoned by the police to Mag Scurr's place, he claimed his wife was ill and suggested they tap Dr. Clanny.

When the doctor finally goes and she is alone with the corpse, then Mag may put her true talents to use. She began this extra service several years ago when bodies were going unclaimed more often than not, due mostly to her neighbors' lack of imagination. You see, it's difficult sometimes for us to recall a face or a figure that we knew in the specificity of life after it has been claimed by that great leveler Death. Even bodies not bloated or in a state of decomposition or half-eaten by scavengers are difficult to peg, taken out of context. So Mag began studying each body long and hard, divining from subtle clues its former walk of life, its likes and dislikes, what it might have aspired to, had it only lived. Then, trusting her instincts entirely, she would walk to the front of her shop, rummage through her pawned items, and find a blazon or two for her anonymous guest. She had guessed the man last week might have been a drunk by the stippled, sanguine bulbosity of his nose, so she leaned him against the wall, shut his eyes, and put a dented flagon in his hand. That very day, a man who had already been in and felt certain he'd seen the pale, flaccid body somewhere before, just couldn't for the life of him figure out where, burst into tears and knew immediately it was his drinking buddy Old Fist on Mag's table. It's the tankard, he cried. I'd never seen him before without a drink in his hand.

She's done the same for the sad, too frequent Wear suicides. Arranged a poor girl's hair in a style a little unbecoming, as a distressed woman would have taken no great pains over it. From the victim's hunched spine and the calluses on her fingers, Mag has known to lay a bit of lace-maker's tatting in her lap. Nearly every one of these girls has been pregnant, according to the doctor's death certificate, but it's not often the boyfriends who step in to claim them, nor is it the father. It is usually a shagged-out, beat-up mother, or maybe a fallen friend who sidles through the front pawnshop, stopping to finger a shiny pink rag of dress hanging up, nodding slowly when shown the body. What the Wear has taken away, Mag gives back—an object, a look, the smallest aids to identity. She even takes a liberty or two with the remains made completely unrecognizable by the river. If she learns a distraught wife has been three months looking for her missing sailor husband, she'll tuck a hank of knotted rope under a skeletal arm. If a lighterman has disappeared, she might lay a lump of flesh atop an oar. What's the harm in reuniting lost and found? thinks Mag. The living have something to bury, the dead have someplace to go.

No foul play, tonight's doctor says, a heart attack, but he can't be sure unless he performs an autopsy. No? Well, that's your prerogative, but perhaps the next of kin will want—No? Mag speaks for the whole East End on this matter. Town's in an uproar since the attempted body-snatching at Trinity last month, and even less likely to allow such a thing. She's watching him fill out the death certificate when the front bell rings. Who would be ringing at this time of night? Unless it's her boy back already with the next of kin.

The bell jangles again.

Mag fixes the doctor—at least it's the kindly one—with a warning eye and makes her way through the dark pawnshop. She raises the latch and opens the door on two rich people: a handsome man, if a bit skinny inside a sable-trimmed coat, and a young lady shivering inside a fantastic blue ball gown. He should give her that coat, Mag thinks.

"Are you Margaret Scurr?" asks the man, gruffly.

"I should say so," answers Mag.

"Do you have the body of a man, aged approximately forty-five, who was found beside the river tonight?"

"Why do y' care t' know?"

The young lady pushes into the store. Now that she sees her up close, Mag realizes she's not quite as well-off as she first thought. Oh, she might fool some, but a pawnbroker can spot the difference. The flimsy tulle gathered up all around the wide skirt is patched in places with cheap white netting, and she can see that the gorgeous blue dress is not properly held up underneath. She hasn't pawned twenty-five years' worth of fashions not to know a thing or two about frames. You must build these dresses from the inside out, layering petticoats, cinching corsets, tying flaring wicker cages around the arm's eye to support the gigot sleeve. The *gros de Naples* gown, though obviously of good quality, conceals a practi-cally naked body underneath. You're not fooling me, Mag thinks. Exactly what we can't see is what gives you away.

"Please, we want him," Gustine says.

"Is that the next of kin, Mrs. Scurr?" the kindly one calls from the back. The sound of his rich Irish voice causes the gentleman in the doorway to step back in alarm.

"Come along, darling," the gentleman nervously com-mands the blue dress. "We obviously have the wrong place."

But Gustine shakes off his hand. She is looking around, trying to take a measure of the place: the racks of dirty clothes, the hodgepodge stacks of nicked china and stained bed linen, the rows of little children's shoes lined up as if marching off to Sunday school. Mag's shop, she sees, is a shrine to hope: hope that a family will be able to buy back their eldest child's shoes before their youngest child has out-grown them, hope that sheets will once more be needed when the mattress is gotten out of hock. The pawned items have grown moldy with hope, Gustine can see; Mag's stacks have grown higher and higher until hope leaves barely an inch of room left to walk to the back. He must be back there then, in that cold final room where, alone in the store, no money is required for a reclamation. She walks purposefully toward the lighted doorway at the back of the shop.

"Darling," says the gentleman angrily, backing out. "Let's go."

Gustine pauses in the doorway. Mag's back room is scrupulously clean, furnished with two wooden tables, the first sporting a blazing nickel candelabra. A middle-aged man—the doctor, he must be—stands over the second table, using what remains uncovered as an impromptu desk. He has his left hand resting paternally on the thigh of a corpse—*her* corpse—and with his right is filling out a form, dipping his expensive pen in a pot of cheap ink. Gustine had not counted on anyone else being here, had expected to lay quick claim to the body and be gone. Now if she is to get Dr. Chiver his body she must be careful. Who is this man? What will he want to hear?

Though she has never been to school nor learned to read, those who know Gustine will tell you she possesses a certain uncanny intelligence, hard to quantify but not so unlike Mag Scurr's. What Mag practices on the dead, Gustine applies to the living, and were the two to become friends they might trade any number of miraculous stories. Mag might tell

Gustine of the time she placed a pawned trumpet in the hand of an unrecognizable corpse, only to discover when he was identified that the selfsame man had, amazingly enough, two years previously placed that very instrument with her. Gustine could appreciate that story, because Gustine too has a gift. She might lean in to pug-faced old Mag and whisper a little secret. She might tell her that she can see through clothes.

It's true. Before a man has opened his mouth, Gustine can tell what sort of poke he'll be after. Just from the shape of his body she can tell whether he will strip down or unbutton only his trousers; whether he will take her in a dark alley or bed her in a brilliantly gaslit room. Well-made men, she knows, will fuck her slowly, watching themselves reflected in a darkened window or in the mirror over the bed at John Robinson's; they will come with excruciating slowness, and then will be most miserly with their spunk as if unable to bear parting with it. Ugly men will fuck her slowly, too, but when they are about ready to ejaculate, will pull out and blast her in the face like an artist smearing the canvas with white paint to erase a hated subject. The key to some men, she has learned, lies buried under layers of jackets, shirts, and waistcoats. Let him walk with his hands in his pockets and she will know he'll want to see those hidden hands on every part of her body. Let him wear his ascot wrapped too tightly and he will want to choke her. She knew a man once who constantly rubbed his sore elbow through his coat sleeve. She guessed he made it sore from obsessive frigging and sure enough, he could not finish except in that way.

Now when a man approaches her, Gustine finds herself mentally undressing him, looking for the defect on his naked body that will make him vulnerable to her. If she finds it first, she wins: he is in her power, not she in his. If she does not find his one seat of shame, Gustine's experience has told her, men's little humiliations have a strange way of rebounding on the women around them. It is best to be prepared.

What, then, is the key to this doctor? She checks his head. His white hair is brushed forward, with no attempt made to cover his scrubbed pink pate—no, he is not self-conscious about going bald. She glances at his face: a straight, unbroken Irish nose, clear brown eyes. Nothing there. But what is this? Ah, look how the fabric of his jacket throws a crooked shadow between the left sleeve and the lapel, mark how his Cross of India medal (which she recognizes because her landlord, too, wears one, though his was taken in exchange for a week's rent from an erstwhile hero fallen into drink) hangs as if disturbed below by a knot of uneven skin. Why, this doctor has been wounded in the shoulder. She sees now how he favors his left arm, by resting it gently on her corpse. That must be it. He straightens at the sight of her in the doorway. Without a moment's hesitation, Gustine walks forward and lays her head upon the crook of his shoulder.

"Here. Here," exclaims Clanny, taken aback by this unlooked-for display. "What's this?"

She is not yet sure what to say; it will come to her, just as whatever dirty words men want to hear bubble up out of instinct. Already she can feel his scarred flesh pulse around her face as if to enfold it. He has a daughter her age, she would lay money on it, and he blushes when she climbs up on his lap, too old for that sort of thing, and rests her cheek against the very same spot.

"Miss. Please," Dr. Clanny stammers, paralyzed with surprise and something like shyness.

Gustine out of instinct remains quiet. She cuts her eyes to the naked body on the table. Her body, the one she found, lies just out of reach. That pug Irish nose, that twisted bullying leg. He would nail her standing up just to prove he was no damn cripple.

"Are you related to this man?" asks Clanny, awkwardly patting her back with his free right arm. Damn if this girl is not fastened to him like a vine.

Gustine looks up into his flushed face, barely lined, though she can tell he's at least fifty. She puts her hand to the joint of his shoulder to keep her place there, and can feel his heart thump heavily like he's been climbing stairs. Yes, he has a daughter her age—she can tell by the sad confusion in his caresses. Should he hug her like a child or pat her cautiously like a woman? Let him stay confused, she decides.

"He was my father," Gustine whispers.

That labourer, father to this dress? Clanny finds it hard to believe, but no less than Mag Scurr, who has followed Gustine into the back room, certain, in her deepest bones, that this chit is up to no good.

"Tha' man's no Da to the likes o' you," scoffs Mag openly.

Gustine ignores her and places her head once more against the doctor's chest. Gently she fingers his silver Cross of India medal. Her landlord has much to say on the troops in India. He reads aloud from the newspaper every night, working himself into a rage over a government that cares to waste its money on curryfied brown gits when it might better feed starving Christians back home. This doctor's medal shows not a breath of tarnish—it must be very important to him.

"My father left for India in 1816, a month before I was born," Gustine says. "His whole troop perished of cholera there. My mother to the day she died never gave up hope he survived and would return to us."

"And you believe this is he?" asks Clanny. "Without having ever seen him?"

Gustine nods. "She said I might recognize him by . . ."

The girl trails off, and Clanny can see she is overcome by emotion, running her eyes wistfully over the naked body of her own lost father. They come finally to rest on his monstrous tattoo.

"She said, 'You will know him by the tattoo on his right arm.'" Tears come unbidden to Gustine's eyes. "Of his best mate Jack Crawford. Hero at Camperdown!"

Among the less charitable of Sunderland, Mag Scurr's flat round face has been compared to that of a palsied English bulldog. Now in her undisguised disbelief at Gustine's story, her black eyes bulge, her jowls quiver, making her look, if possible, even more pugnacious.

"If your Da was such great mates with old Jack Crawford," says Mag, "enough to get him tattooed, let's call Jack over to second the identification. He lives in a cheap lodging house down the street. I've got his Camperdown war medals in pawn for drink."

"How cruel you are, Mrs. Scurr," Dr. Clanny chides. "Can't you see this poor girl is dissolved in grief?"

Gustine, certain now of victory, hides her smile against the doctor's coat. I will have that body and I will give it to Dr. Chiver and he will become the best doctor he can possibly be. Clanny chucks Gustine under the chin, and she raises her tear-roughened face.

"Have you anyone to help you?" he asks.

"My husband." Gustine looks around the empty room. Where the hell is he? Mag Scurr has not seen the gentleman who accompanied her since Dr. Clanny first called from the back. What sort of husband leaves his wife to cry on the shoulder of a stranger, when he has two capable ones himself? What honest husband would even think to bring a woman to a place like this?

"My husband is driving our carriage around," Gustine says.

"I'll send for the constables and let them decide the matter," Mag says firmly.

"We have no need of the constables, Mrs. Scurr," Clanny says, stroking Gustine's damp blonde hair more confidently now. "Let them get on with the business of arresting the thieves and prostitutes of this city. I'll release this body upon my own authority." With a little reluctance, he detaches Gustine from his frock coat and offers her a clean linen handkerchief. As Gustine gratefully blows her nose, Dr. Clanny reaches for the death certificate he was drafting when she arrived and dips his pen in ink. "What was your father's name?"

His name? Gustine looks over at the corpse. Mag Scurr has discreetly positioned his hands over his private parts; stiff, swollen, filled-with-cold-black-swamp-water fingers and two huge padded thumbs eclipse whatever he might have had down there. But look at that hideous tattoo. Jack Crawford, British Hero, with his legs wrapped around a thick black pole. If Gustine knows anything about men, she knows what an oversized tattoo means.

"Dick Liss," Gustine says without even the shadow of a smirk. Dr. Clanny dutifully writes it down.

Henry has made four trips to his rig and back, determined each time to abandon Gustine to her fate. Of all the bloody luck, to nearly run headfirst into his uncle Clanny. To have his respected uncle learn how he spends his time—cavorting with prostitutes and sniffing around back alleys for corpses like a pig after slop. What if Audrey found out? He paces feverishly up and down the wet, cobbled street. He must have been mad to put his school, his reputation, the reputation of his innocent fiancée in Gustine's filthy hands.

Calm down, my boy, calm down. Lean your head against the wall, take a deep breath. Henry closes his eyes and tries to still his furious, unreformed heart. This pounding monster in my breast is nothing but an organ; knowable, controllable. Look, now I enter the great venous system bound for the right auricle of the heart. I move to the ventricle, from the ventricle to the lungs, from the lungs to the left side of the heart, and from thence to the general arterial system to be elastically sped through the entire body. Uncle Clanny did not see me, he thinks, flushing his panic down a million tiny capillaries until it is so broadcast and attenuated it is easily absorbed. Gustine will not betray me. All will be well.

That is better, he thinks after a few minutes, feeling his agitation drain until he is calm enough to crave a cigarette. He strikes a friction match and cups it around the hand-rolled tobacco paper he's removed from the case Audrey gave him as an engagement present. It is awkward with his bandaged hands; his fingers are bound tightly together like flippers, and twice he drops the match. He flings the cigarette to the ground and unwraps his left hand, unfurling a long white streamer of gauze. His palm is pink and tender, but the blisters healed weeks ago. He'd only continued to wrap his hands as a precaution, and now, he realizes, as an excuse. If he could not hold the scalpel, he could not cut. If he could not cut, he would have no need of a body. Impatiently, he releases his other hand from its soft prison. Tonight, perhaps. Tonight will decide it.

He lights another cigarette, leans against the wall, and slowly smokes it. He can only imagine what Gustine is saying to his uncle Clanny. He knows he should have turned to his uncle months ago, when the trouble first began, but he could not bear to do it. Uncle Clanny has been so generous already, and Henry is not even his flesh and blood. He is Dr. Clanny's wife's sister's son, the fearful, introverted only child of a widowed mother. He wants—no, he needs—to prove to his uncle (and to Audrey and to all of Sunderland) that he can make it without assistance. He wants to prove it so badly, he has thrown in his lot with this bold, blue prostitute. She is in there now, doing what he was not man enough to do.

He extinguishes his cigarette and flexes his restored hands. Henry is a little vain of his tapered fingers, long and white like the winter-stripped limbs of a birch tree. He stretches them out before him and peers at Sunderland through their thicket. On the bank, severed fish heads gape at the muddy feral cats who snatch them up and streak away. Stunted sea crabs pick at what the cats leave behind. Our fog, finger-proud itself, curls upstream, filching the cooking fires of poor beggar families along the piers. It is an accomplished thief, this fog, for stray cats, derricks, and even entire houses disappear as it moves past. Henry watches the fog's progress up and around Crach Rock, where the Wear makes a sharp bend and widens into the tidal harbour. If he could see far enough, he'd spy a pug-faced little boy leaving the Life Boat up there on Pottery Bank, dragging behind him a short, suety sort of woman. It would be Mag's boy he sees, who spent his evening shaking the coattails of every labourer and

labourer's wife in the crowded Life Boat pub, doggedly recit-
ing his description, until at last he was passed on to an
angry, barely sober laundrywoman. She'd spent a full hour at
the Life Boat tap, railing against her no-count Irish drunk of
a husband who'd not come home with his paycheck *again*;
probably out with his mate Jack Crawford, Hero of
Nothing-but-Sots as far as she was concerned, drinking himself bloody stupid; and here she was, having to go from bar
to bar to search him out, and when she found him, by God,
she would bite that damned tattoo right off and spit it back
in his face.

A very different laundrywoman Henry would see leaving
the bar. Her eyes are red and her nose is pinched and her jig-
gling arms, which only half an hour before were aching for a
melee, hang limply at her sides. The gin she drank in retalia-
tion for her husband's beering has up and gone, leaving her
with a dull ache behind her plain, wide face. She did not even
kiss him good-bye this morning when he left for another
fruitless day at the docks. She even begrudged making his
lunch.

But Henry cannot see that far; in fact, he has dropped his
hands and shrunk back into the shadows of Mag Scurr's
establishment. The door bangs open beside him and his uncle
Clanny steps out.

What has she done to him? Henry wonders. His uncle,
adjusting his hat, buttoning his coat, is humming a little tune.
He has a noticeable bounce in his usually decorous walk, and
an adolescent's smile on his respectable face. His uncle trots
up steep Long Bank, headed back toward the center of town.
Henry does not move until he sees his uncle tip his hat to a
stout lady and a little boy, out very late, and disappear around
the corner onto High Street.

He jumps when Gustine puts her hand on his shoulder.

"I got him," she says.

She got him. By God, they've succeeded! Now that it is real, Henry's mind races through the long night before him—getting the body home, preparing it, making the first cut before daybreak. His students are probably asleep by now, but he will wake them with this glorious body. So much to do! He glances down at brave Gustine, who is watching him with that searching look on her pointed, serious face. He can't help himself—he pulls her to him and hugs her tight.

She is so small in his arms, he can feel each catlike rib under its silk. She is so frail, and as cool as if she'd taken the blue of her dress into her very bloodstream. I don't care if she tries to blackmail me, he thinks. I am reborn tonight.

"Dr. Chiver," asks Gustine, murmuring against his chest. "Do you study a man from the inside or the outside?"

"Both," replies Henry.

"Do you study all of the inside?" she asks, inching her cheek across his chest, searching out the thing she suspected but could not prove. I was right, thinks Gustine. Oh God, I was right.

"Yes," says he.

"The heart?"

"I'm especially interested in the heart," replies Henry, smiling at her childish understanding of anatomy science. He releases her and takes a step away.

"I should bring the rig around," he says. "Wait here."

Gustine watches Henry sprint around the corner to where he left his horses and carriage tied up. John Robinson was wrong about Gustine—she does not have a crush on Henry Chiver, though she did feel her whole body go soft when she felt that miraculous spot. No, the young girl feels something

far stronger for the doctor, something that would make
Henry's blood run cold if he even suspected it. She thinks of
him as something like her own personal god, and as she is
barely acquainted with the one in Heaven, lays all her offer-
ings at his very mortal feet. You see, that night a month ago,
when she discovered him furiously washing his hands, blistering and singing on laudanum under the public water pump,
Gustine took the time to undress him. Before he even saw her,
she had slipped off his pants and found beneath them strong,
hairy legs branching off from a half-erect, square-dealing
penis. Without his being aware, she'd lifted away his white-
powdered jacket, checked his arms for twists and scars, crept
up his spine, and burrowed beneath his hair. Gustine had
stood back, still not showing herself, and undone each delicate ivory button of his bloodstained shirt, peeling the sheer
cotton from his shoulders, inching it down his biceps, letting
it drop around his waist, as the final button pulled away from
the last straining slit. And there, between the second and
third fastenings, before she even knew his name, Gustine had
discovered the key to Dr. Henry Chiver. Tonight she con-
firmed it. In that moment by the pump, she saw neither his
hands nor his face, noticed not whether he seemed kind or
mean; all parts of him retreated except for the key: that
shadow in his chest, the sunken hollow beauty of it. They are
a fit, she said to herself. This is the one to save us.

She hears horses' hooves clatter on the pavement behind
her and she knows he is returning. She is not prepared for the
headlights of his carriage, with their wicks turned up to cut
through the fog, and as they swing around the corner, their
sudden intensity momentarily blinds her. When her sight
returns, Gustine can hardly believe what she sees coming
toward her, trailing thick black mud across the quay like some

antediluvian creature just born from the river. It is the old
woman advancing on her, her dress steeped in mud, her
square-toed boots mud-caked, even her hair dripping mud as
if she had burrowed for miles underground only to surface in
the glare of Henry's lantern, a brown pupil born from a
blinding Eye.

False blue rat. To run so far away.

When Henry reins in his horses and calls softly for Gustine,
he cannot find her anywhere. He gets out and looks around
the corner, walks down to the water, even searches through
the bulging racks of clothes in Mag's shop, before giving up
and finally carrying away the dead body Gustine found for
him. Five minutes after he has gone, the bell jangles at Mag's
front door. She is restacking the pile of framed Wearmouth
Bridges that careless husband knocked over with the stiff
corpse's legs.

"Who is it?" she asks, thinking, Damn him, what does he
want now?

"It's me, Ma!" Mag's boy shouts through the wood. "I
found the lady. The wife of the tattoo."

Mag opens the door on a thick-waisted woman stuffed like
a sausage into a pea green dress. Her sleeves are rolled down
over chapped red arms, her mobcap flops tiredly, her face,
pitted and sallow, tells Mag everything she needs to know.

The laundrywoman says, "I've come to take my husband
home." She chokes on her words, but it is Mag who wants to
cry.

IV

9 MILL STREET

Mike's got a frog.

It's beneath his talents, Whilky knows, but goddamn it, he can't stand that ribbut, ribbut all bloody night long. Rats he could live with; they steal, they smell, but at least they let a man sleep of an evening. Frogs, though. Christ, they bring their slimy omens down upon a household and give you warts as if the ones you have aren't bad enough. God damn them, thinks Whilky, pulling the rubbery green legs from between Mike's sharp teeth. Let go!

"I've got one too, Da!"

Now Pink's got a frog. What did he do to deserve this? His six-year old daughter skittering about the house on all fours, biting after filthy creatures. She looks up at him with her glittering black, pink-rimmed eyes, reptilian-scaly from years of infection, her pink-tipped nose twitching over the flailing frog in her mouth. It's no occupation for a champion ferret, let alone a little girl.

"Drop that, you nit," roars Whilky, and the little girl reluctantly complies. The long white ferret, seeing his chance, pounces on the frog Pink dropped and bites it in half.

"Da! Look!"

"Shut up, the both of you!"

As if a man don't have enough on his mind without the dual plagues of vermin and stupidity. He doesn't know what to do with Pink. She is too daft to be sent out to work, yet she is too fanciful for him to bear having at home. He'd hoped setting her to tend the baby would settle her down, but it's only made her more intent on playing the ferret. Just look at her: down on her hands and knees, sniffing the air alongside Mike. He stretches out his arm to his prize pet and Mike scampers up on tiny feet, curling himself around Whilky's neck. Pink, watching jealously, pretends to lick her fur.

Whilky Robinson, perched on his stool before the fire, resplendent in luxurious weasel collar, laced tight with watch fobs and jangling with hocked medals, surveys with royal displeasure his little kingdom here on Mill Street. Our ruler is not so fair of face as the Plantagenets, nor does he turn so fine a calf as the Stuarts, no, sitting with his left gouty leg thrust out before him, brooding upon his subjects (Pink, his daughter; Eye, his faithful retainer); listening to his thirty lords and ladies shuffle about upstairs preparing for their day's employment, he resembles no one more closely than a burdened, pensive Henry the Eighth. He scratches his expansive belly, over which is stretched a bottle green coat giving at the armseyes. He rests his elbow on the leg of his soiled tan knee breeches that trail off into once-white stockings that terminate in scuffed oxblood leather shoes. His carroty red hair, growing behind his ears and down the back of his neck without troubling itself about the rest of his head, curls into sweaty little question marks at the nape. His brow is knit, his countenance stormy. What is to be done about this infestation?

That it's come to this, thinks he. Even Eye, methodically brushing Gustine's bit of blue frippery, has frogs worrying her thick ankles. She pays them no mind, intent as she is on her work, but our ruler is a sensitive man, and frets over the welfare of those entrusted to his care. He wants only the best for his boarders. Why, just look how he recently handled the windows. Whilky knew the view from his second story overlooking the slaughterhouse was troubling to some of his tenderhearted tenants, so without a word to anyone, he took it upon himself personally to board up all the offending windows. But then he got to thinking—how unfair it would be for him, who spends most of his day on the first floor, to have fresh air when his tenants had none. That might cause bad blood on Mill Street, and if nothing else, his is a harmonious household. To keep the peace, Whilky unselfishly boarded up the windows on the first floor as well, and if, in the process, he managed to save the window tax this bloodthirsty government has leveled on each and every goddamned pane of glass in Britain, well, so be it. His tenants come first.

So what that from the outside 9 Mill Street sags a bit along the roof, crumbles a bit along the foundation, and like a tenemental Oedipus, is blinded with cheap nails driven into mouldering shutters? So what that it appears from the outside a thoroughly condemned back alley rookery? We all know it is the inside that counts. Inside Whilky keeps a tip-top house. Mike the ferret is a championship ratter, and 9 Mill Street is one of the few boardinghouses in the East End completely (or as near to complete as an industrious ferret can make it) rat-free. It is, after its master's taste, cheerfully and tastefully decorated. The main room sports a majestic gilt-framed Wearmouth Bridge (East View) over the long table against the right-hand wall. A pastoral likeness of Dick Turpin, cutpurse, hangs to the left of it; Sunderland's own Jack Crawford, hero of Camperdown, hangs to the right. The

fireplace takes up most of the back wall, where, lined up on
its mantel in order of height, sit tasteful mementos of Mike's
exploits in the ratting ring, trophies for besting some of the
most ferocious terriers in Sunderland, and a few more
Wearmouth Bridges. Whilky has a second East View transferred onto a spittoon and a Wearmouth West View 25-Year
Commemorative stamped onto a milk pitcher. Beneath the
mantel, he makes sure, the fire always roars. Our landlord is
not cheap with his coal and, with no windows to open, the
house is snug sometimes to the point of tropicality. The
steaming laundry of his thirty tenants completes the interior
decoration; stockings and soiled underwear dangle from pins
and Mike the ferret enjoys nothing more when rat-killing is
slow than to vault up a lodger's plaid shawl and pad along the
clothesline. ·

But what gains such careful decoration if only to be
spoiled by the strewn carcasses of frogs? Whilky has been
sweeping up three dozen a day; mangled by Mike, stomped
upon by Eye, gummed by his zealous daughter Pink. It is to
drive us mad, thinks our landlord, leaning forward so as not
to scorch his august back. Another facet in the Grand Plot
that began with this summer's "census," during which the
frog eggs were insinuated, and which will culminate in this
so-called cholera morbus they've imported to eliminate us all.
Did they honestly think we wouldn't catch on?

"Da? Coffee?"

Whilky nods abstractedly to Pink as she wrestles the heavy
coffeepot onto the fireplace trivet. The price of a cup is
included in the night's rent, but if the establishment occa-
sionally forgets to put it on before the first lodgers are tramp-
ing downstairs, is it the establishment's fault they don't have
time to drink it? The tin clock on the wall is striking four-

thirty. It is Monday morning, most have to be at work by five, but spoiled by Sunday's lolling, they barely leave themselves time to get there.

Eye has heated a pan of water in the fireplace, and with careful sponging is making Gustine's dress fit for tonight. She looks up from her work as the lodgers tramp down; the bottle workers first, for they have the longest to walk, then the keelmen. A bleary-eyed mother leads her two boys off to the quay to buy fish for their baskets. They'll hawk it to the poor Irish down along Woodbine Street who haven't the gumption to walk the half a mile themselves. With each guest's descent, Whilky, not stirring from his stool by the fire, holds out a broad palm for the week's rent, payable in advance. Woe betide the keelman or glass blower who blew his salary on Saturday night. Whilky shows no mercy. He makes them march upstairs, gather their meager possessions (the trip is usually unnecessary, as they wear upon their backs all that they own), and quit the house immediately. The others have left by the time Gustine makes her way down the rickety stairs, her face buried in a small woolen bundle. She always waits for her coffee, out of principle, even if it means she has to run the whole way to the pottery.

What a difference a Monday morning makes in the appearance of our bold Gustine. Her hair, no longer apolloed and ringletted, loiters atop her head in a loose bun. Her daytime outfit, a fawn-colored shift threadbare almost to transparency from too much scrubbing, hangs loosely from her shoulders. She looks her age in these clothes, without ribbons and lace to take focus from her sharp little face. She looks like a sleepy young girl in desperate need of some coffee.

"Pink," says she. "How much longer?"

"Eeek. Eeek," replies Pink.

"In English please."

Pink hangs her head and shuffles over to the table.

"Five minutes more, perhaps."

"I'll have mine with sugar then."

Pink pulls back the blanket Gustine carried downstairs and sniffs the tiny creature inside. That's her baby, her res-pon-sib-ility for which Gustine pays Da an extra two shillings a week on top of her three shillings rent. Da says Gustine spoils that baby mercilessly, that she should save her money for it won't be alive much longer to appreciate the thought. Gustine says shut up and Pink, you know to hold this baby very, very carefully. Pink knows Don't carry it with your teeth.

Gustine rains kisses on the baby's forehead and it smiles up at her toothlessly. Baby, baby, baby, says Gustine. Baby, baby. She pulls from her pocket a bit of plum cake she bought yesterday and shoves it crumb by crumb into the baby's mouth. First thing every morning, even before Gustine's eyes are open, she puts her ear to the baby's chest. Still beating. First thing when she comes home from the pottery but before she puts on the dress, she lays her ear on the baby's chest. Still beating. Whilky says why bother—it's only a matter of time. But Gustine says I'm taking care of that, and Pink, where's my coffee?

Pink retrieves the coffeepot from the fire with a set of arm-length tongs and staggers with it back to the table. She pours a cup for all three grown-ups, one for herself, and one for Mike.

"Brother John mentioned you've been hanging about the Labour in Vain recently," says Whilky blandly. "And yet not upstairs."

"What of it?" answers Gustine, sipping her scalding coffee.

"'M not paying you to socialize."

"You're barely paying me at all."

Mike the ferret leaps from Whilky's shoulder to lap the cup of coffee Pink has placed on the floor for him. She puts hers down beside his and laps away as well.

"How d' you expect to afford all those extras for the babby?" asks Whilky. "Woolen blankets and such like? Booties and wee jumpers? You were barely earning enough at the pottery to keep *yourself* together."

"I give you money, don't I?" asks Gustine, turning the baby over to burp it. She doesn't lay it over her shoulder like most mothers, but holds it away from her body and pats its back gently.

"I'd like to know how yer gettin' it. And if yer holding out."

"I am not holding out," says Gustine pointedly. From the corner, gray old Eye looks up. She is elbow-deep in the blue dress, sponging off the mud from where Gustine fell down the Wear embankment. I dare you to say something, thinks Gustine at the old woman. Gustine is to give Eye whatever she makes and Eye punctiliously reckons up with Whilky. Out of the money she earns, Whilky takes her expenses and those of the baby's, then of the eight she usually brings home a night, pays her four shillings over a week. Until now, Gustine has never been bold enough to cheat the Eye.

"Let's see that you don't waste time. We don't want our dress lodger evicted from her digs? Eh, Eyeball?" Whilky wheezes. The old woman narrows her single eye at the landlord, then goes back to work.

Next to Mike's unrivaled record, nothing swells Whilky's chest more than the knowledge that he alone was responsible for the importation of dress lodging into Sunderland. Obvious in its simplicity, yet strangely unknown outside of London, dress lodging works on this basic principle: a cheap whore is given a fancy dress to pass as a higher class of prostitute. The higher the class of prostitute, the higher the station of the clientele; the higher the station, the higher the price. In return, the girl is given a roof over her head and a few hours of make-believe. Everyone is happy.

Like any pioneer, Whilky had his share of unforeseen setbacks. His first girl got greedy and made off with her dress, though whether she sold it for drink or pawned it to maintain a preferred childlessness, he never discovered. *Her* shadow was a washed-out old bawd who lay facedown in a bar the night First Girl absconded with the dress. He went through another set, with the same result. Not until two years ago, with diligent Gustine and incorruptible Eye, did he hit upon the perfect remunerative combination. The last thing he wants is for Gustine to ruin it.

"Pink!" Gustine drains her coffee and stands up to leave. "Come take the baby."

Pink jumps up from her cup and scampers to the table. It's time for her to be a Good Girl.

"You remember how to hold it?" Gustine asks the same question every day, laying the baby carefully in the little girl's thin arms. Support the head, cradle the bum. Whatever you do, don't ever—never, never ever—put the baby down on its chest. Or set anything, even a folded blanket, there. Or kiss it too hard in that spot. Or jokingly poke it. Are you a good girl?

"Yes," answers Pink.

"And you will remember these things?"

"Yes," answers Pink, thinking, Don't carry it with your teeth.

"And don't let *her* touch it," says Gustine, casting a dark look at the Eye. It is daytime now and she owes the relentless shadow nothing. "Don't let her near this precious baby."

"Right," says Pink.

Gustine gives the smiling infant one last kiss and draws her shawl off the clothesline. She won't be home from the pottery before seven o'clock and then Eye will have the dress waiting the moment she steps in the door. She has such a short time to love and protect this poor child. But she will see it survives. No matter what it takes.

Gustine pauses in the doorway to make sure Pink and the baby are as far away from Eye as the tight room allows. She doesn't know why she is so superstitious about the shadow and her baby, but she swears, if she ever catches the old woman laying a finger on her child, she'll gut her like a fish.

"And someone should check on Fos," Gustine calls over her shoulder, referring to one of her fellow lodgers, our friend the matchstick painter. "She didn't get out of bed this morning."

"Whoops," says Pink and the baby starts screaming. She picked up only the corner of its blanket with her teeth, but wriggly baby, it slipped right out.

It is noon and the blue sky has accommodated itself to the yellow sulfur clouds, providing a lovely green day for charity visiting. The temperature last night dropped precipitously and there is a crispness behind the smog that, had we only the conveyance to get twenty miles out of town, we might very much enjoy. The men and women of charity go on about their work, drawing their shawls more tightly about them or stuffing their hands into pockets. No one is concerned about the weather, except maybe the apothecaries. Their leeches, about two hours ago, started creeping up the sides of jars, a sure sign an electrical storm is brewing.

Since the cholera scare, the dogs of charity have been unleashed upon Sunderland's East End. The Methodist Ladies are distributing tickets for soup at the value of one penny "equal in quality as what is given to the military." The Friends of the Sunderland Dispensary are passing out tincture of chamomile along with their own printed tickets returning thanks to the Almighty God which must be redeemed by the grateful poor at church the following Sunday. The Indigent Sick Society has its blankets and stockings, the Board of Health its wagonloads of free lime for whitewash. They are rolling up Mill Street when Whilky Robinson steps out of his house to buy the newspaper. They are coming with their curled white papers and buckets of flour paste, slapping their lies over honest posters or Barklay's Asthmatic Candy and Sunderland Reform meetings, making Whilky so mad he could spit. The whole East End has been gummed and slathered, calcimined and blanchified with these damn white papers, a new one every other day. They figure if they scream it loud enough, we'll begin to believe, thinks he. It's just another facet of the Grand Plot.

BY ORDER OF THE BOARD OF HEALTH
All kinds of Putrid matter, decayed Vegetables,
Filth of every Description should be
REMOVED
Walls of Houses and Passages should be
Washed with hot LIME
and all Persons Bathed daily.
Dirty Hands and dirty Faces breed
THE CHOLERA MORBUS

The git who smacks this bill over Whilky's boarded-up, tax-free window gets a sharp rap on the head for his pains. Away with you, toady! And with your wheelbarrowload of lime dumped in front of my door! Whilky kicks the white mound left by the minions of the Board of Health. Whitewash the damn streets if you like but you'll not invade the house of a free man.

Mike peeks his narrow head out of Whilky's breast pocket at the disturbance. Look at 'em, Mike. Pious men and do-goody women marching up and down our back lanes. Hawking their moth-eaten blankets and donated stockings, darned six times at the toe until a man feels like he is eternally treading upon a pebble. But we're not fooled, are we, Mike? They'd rather see every one of us dead than give us the Right to Vote. Funny, isn't it, how this cholera morbus business only came up after the Reform Riots in October? Funny, too, how all the Reform meetings had to be canceled for fear of the contagion. And while you and I have tenants to spare, Mike, them that lodged in the workingman's pockets and the workingman's belly; by which I mean the staples of cash and food, Mike, have all up and fled in the face of this contrived *Quarantine*. A poor man is so busy contemplating those cruel desertions, so busy scheming how to lure cash and bread home again, that he has no time left to even think on Reform. Look there, Mike. Some of our weak-minded neighbors open their doors to these government patsies. But not us. Against our better judgment, we let the government inside this summer so that we might be "counted," and look what it's got us. Green toads and a coming plague that, conveniently enough, kills only the poor.

Whilky hesitates at the end of the lane. Maybe he ought to go back and wait them out. Pink, moronic git that she is, might open the door, and God only knows what they'll plant inside. But Whilky wants his newspaper and a tall glass of beer. And besides, John Robinson claimed a bricklayer came into the Labour in Vain last night with a Border collie rumoured to have killed sixty rats in ten minutes. Pink knows what he'll do to her if she undoes that latch. She's daft, but she's not that dumb.

Whilky ducks under the low arch and lumbers out onto the wide expanse of High Street, blissfully unaware that behind him, exactly nine houses in, a tidy blonde woman loaded down with charity is stepping over his uncovered midden (that overflows with decayed Vegetables and All kinds of Putrid matter) onto his privately owned stoop and is, even now, rapping sharply upon the sanctity of his door. His republican daughter Pink, resisting tyranny for the time it takes to set down the baby and scamper over, asks cheerfully through the wood," Who's there?"

"Audrey Place. With the Indigent Sick Society," comes the answer.

"Right," says Pink and opens the door.

Why, we know this Audrey. She's lived on Fawcett Street all her life. Her mother is good Dr. Clanny's wife's best friend, just as Henry's mother is sister to the selfsame wife. We understand Audrey's engagement is a much needed distraction at the Fawcett Street household; it's been so sombre with her father away, captain of a ship stuck in Riga, on the other side of Quarantine. Take a peek at her, there in the doorway, before she enters the gloom of Whilky's establishment. Isn't she pretty? Isn't her boot neat and her red-gold hair attractively but not showily dressed? There is a certain determination about her green eyes that sits uncomfortably in the softness of her face, but it is a well-formed face, somewhat too apple-cheeked and dimpled for elegance, but pleasing and kind. Though only seventeen, Miss Place for many years has extended her hands to the poor; and to her credit, she is more proud of her magnanimity than her manicure. Once, when she was but twelve, we witnessed her surrender her only umbrella so that a poor woman might not go without one. And the head cold she suffered in consequence, she wore like a badge of honour.

It takes a moment for Audrey's eyes to adjust to the untaxed twilight of 9 Mill Street, but slowly the room begins to take shape. Low ceiling, stiflingly hot fire, empty of furnishings save for a table, some stools, and a gigantean Wearmouth Bridge framed like a Rembrandt. She is a little short-sighted and squints down at the little girl who comes only waist-high, dressed in a grown woman's gown of faded pink gingham. The sleeves are rolled to her elbows and a deep hem has been taken in around the knees. It is still too long and the little girl trips as she backs up to let the lady in.

"Is your mother or father at home?" asks Audrey Place of the Indigent Sick Society.

"Dead," says Pink. "And Out to get a Pint."

Audrey looks around and catches sight of an old woman in the corner. She sits beneath an incongruous blue dress that hangs from two pegs on the wall, watching Audrey fixedly. "Is this your grandmother then?" she asks sweetly.

"Eek!" says Pink. "That's the Eye."

"The Eye?" Audrey wonders. "Then who might you be?"

"Pink."

"What is your real name?"

"Don't know. I've always been called Pink."

It never fails to amaze Audrey, no matter how many times she comes down here, that the children of the East End don't know their own names. They are all called Crank or Tough or Flotsam or Pink from the time they kick their way out of the womb. How can one expect them not to behave like animals if they are all named like dogs? Audrey sets her blankets and stockings down on the table and wanders the room. It has the standard close sweat and fried herring smell of most lodging houses, but is a good deal less filthy. True, its walls and ceiling are a bit fuliginous and like every other house in the East End, this family keeps a sloshing crock of urine in the corner. She has urged others to get rid of it, but they use it to wash their clothes; nothing gets grease out so well, they tell her. They save their ordure, too, in the reeking unemptied middens fouling the lane. Once every eight or ten weeks, farmers come up from the country and buy it for fertilizer. In the meantime it breeds typhus and scarletina and cholera. Or at least that's what Henry says.

"Would you like coffee?" asks Pink in her talking-to-boarders voice. This lady looks a little like Gustine except that her dress is not nearly so pretty, being gray and without any ribbons on it. She is plumper too than Gustine and her voice is lower like a dog's where Gustine's is higher like a ferret's. The lady nods yes to coffee, so Pink picks up Mike's cup and refills it from the pot on the hearth. It's not so hot anymore, which is how she likes it. The lady says thank you.

"Do you go to school. . . . Pink?" asks Audrey, sipping the ice-cold coffee.

"Neeak," says Pink, shyly.

"Do you go to work?"

"Neeak," she giggles.

"Neak? Does that mean no?"

"Eeeak."

"Let me guess." Audrey smiles into the spindly girl's red-rimmed eyes. "Are you a mouse?"

Oh the shame of it.

From the woeful expression on the girl's face, Audrey realizes immediately she's said the wrong thing. Quickly she switches topics.

"Pink," she says," I am here from the Sick Society to care for those in need. We are looking out for the cholera."

"Da does not believe in the cholera," says Pink raising her chin defiantly. "He says it's the Government's way of murdering the poor."

Audrey is taken aback by the girl's answer. How can a rational man not believe in a disease that's killed millions?

"I'm afraid your Da is mistaken," she says gently. "The cholera has been coming from around the world. We've been reading about it for months in the newspapers."

"Da says other governments are also killing their poor. It's where our Government got the idea."

"Sweetheart," Audrey says, shaking her head. "Your Government doesn't want you dead. They've established a Quarantine to keep you safe."

"Da says the Quarantine is to starve us so that their Cholera Morbus can kill us the quicker."

Audrey would like to wring Pink's Da's neck for all the lies he's telling this poor child. Instead she tries a different tactic.

"Well, I have some lovely blankets and stockings here I would certainly love to give away," she says. "I would love to give a lovely blanket to you, Pink. But first I must see if anyone sick needs them. Is anyone sick in your house?"

"Only Fos," Pink answers, looking longingly at Audrey's stack. "We call her Fos because she has the Fossy Jaw."

"May I see her?" Audrey asks, gathering up her blankets and stockings.

Pink lights a tallow candle in the fireplace and dully leads the way to the stairs. She gives a quick glance over her shoulder to Mrs. Eyeball, just to make sure she is doing the right thing taking this charity lady up to see Fos. The Eye watches them mount the stairs but does not stir from beneath the dress.

Twelve creaking steps take them up to the low room where the boarders sleep, a room in far worse shape than Audrey might have imagined judging by the fairly tidy first floor. It is noon outside, but midnight here, or 4 A. M. or 6 for all she can tell. The windows are boarded up, allowing in no light or fresh air. The walls are grimed brown and scattershot with the blood of crushed bugs. When she moves, Audrey's neat boots crunch infested hay underfoot, the mattresses of Whilky Robinson's thirty boarders, though some, unable to afford the 4*d* he charges per pitchforkful, sleep only on their spread-out coats. From experience Audrey knows that men and women lie indiscriminately up here, head to foot and back to back. The pregnancy rate among female lodgers tells you what sort of night's sleep they get.

"You can see her better without this," says Pink. With a quick puff, the little girl blows out the candle. An oppressive darkness swallows the room, hot and close and reeking of fish-infused urine. Something scurries over Audrey's foot and she stifles a scream.

"Over there," says Pink.

In the far corner of the room, low to the ground, Audrey can make out a faint glow. At first she thinks she is imagining it, but no, there is a green tinge to the darkness in the corner, like the faraway lights of the aurora borealis.

"That's Fos," Pink tells her proudly. "She glows in the dark."

Audrey quickly makes her way over to the effulgent creature in the corner, and reaches into her pocket for the packet of friction matches she keeps there. By the light of the match, she sees lying upon a bale of straw a narrow-faced woman, breathing shallowly, her eyes screwed up against the pain of even that dim flame. The right side of her face around her mouth is strangely sunken, as if she had just sucked the sourest lemon and couldn't quite release the pucker.

"Fos paints phosphorus on matchsticks," Pink explains. "Now she's got the Fossy Jaw. Da says soon it will be eaten clean away."

My God, thinks Audrey. And they call this poor woman by the disease that is killing her? She takes a blanket from her stack and lays it over the suffering matchstick painter.

"Friend," says Audrey, refusing to use the horrid name. "Friend, can you hear me?"

Matchstick painter, dear friend from Saturday night, are you truly so sick you cannot answer this helpful lady? We would never have deserted you to your solitary chats savants had we known you were so gravely ill. Yes, we had a story to tell, yes, an engagement to keep, but we are not heartless. We might have seen you home and safely tucked into your bed of hay. Might have sent around the corner for a hot lemon gin to settle the burning pain in your stomach. How were we to know, dear matchstick painter, dear friend Fos, when we chose to follow Gustine's gaudy blue thread that your dun brown one was near to being severed?

"I don't think she hears you," says Pink.

Rouse yourself, Fos. Give a word of comfort to this lady who seeks to comfort you. Give comfort to us who are shocked at this sudden and frightening change in you.

"We should send for a doctor," says Audrey grimly. "My fiancé will come."

Audrey tucks the edges of the blanket under the poor woman's legs to keep them off the scratchy hay, rises, and leads Pink back down the stairs. The stale air of the first floor is a welcome relief from the thoroughly fetid atmosphere above. How do they live? Audrey wonders for perhaps the thousandth time in her charitable career.

"I am going to send for Dr. Chiver," Audrey announces, making herself ready to go. She has said good-bye to Pink and left her with a cheerless olive wool blanket, when without warning, the woman in the corner suddenly starts up. She has her one gray eye fixed on something in the corner, piercing it to the ground like a pin through a butterfly. As if raised by her gaze, a tremendous squall issues from the coal bin.

"Oh no," gasps Pink. "The baby!"

The baby cries like Pink wants to at always being such a miserable failure. She can't believe she went and forgot the baby, left it over behind the coal bin, and now when she runs over, pushing Eye out of the way, she sees, though she remembered not to set it on its chest, though she did everything else right, a frog sitting on the one place you should never ever jokingly poke!

"Bloody shit!" shrieks Pink.

Audrey rushes over and Eye steps back. Pink is pointing to the frog hunkering on the baby's chest and mutely screaming. Mike would never have let this happen. He would have dragged the baby to safety or bit the frog into a million pieces or some smarter combination, but he would never let

Gustine's baby die. The lady plucks the frog off with two long fingers and flings it into the fireplace, where it sizzles and then in a second pops. She is picking the baby off the floor with her hands not her teeth and walking with it over to the table. Support the head and bum, Pink finds the voice to say.

Eye sits back down on her stool beneath the dress.

"Whose baby is this?" Audrey demands, color stinging her cheeks. These people, she swears, these people are simply not fit to have children.

"Gustine's," Pink whispers.

"Where is this Gustine?" she asks coldly.

"At work."

Poor baby, coos Audrey over the little mite. It is swathed head to foot in woolen blankets and having been left by the fire, its face is scalding to the touch. She calls the baby "it." Is it a boy or a girl? Audrey unwraps the blankets to take a look.

"Oh my God."

Pink throws out her arms to catch the baby, for surely this lady is going to drop it. She doesn't, though; she recovers much faster than Pink would have, and then Pink notices how everything changes—she holds the baby out from her so very carefully, like it is going to break. Like Gustine holds it. Audrey manages to speak. "Its chest. Was it born that way?"

Pink nods.

"What is its name?"

"Da said Don't give it a name, it's going to be dead soon. But it's been alive since summer."

Audrey has never seen anything like it. Never in her years of visiting. Nor in her hospital work. Not even in Henry's textbooks. She is holding a perfectly formed baby in her lap, possessor of wide blue eyes, a cap of super-fine black hair, plump, smiling, wagging its arms and legs. But where the frog had sat, there at the very center of this child's otherwise perfectly normal chest, is an enlarged bruise. A raised blue bruise shimmering under nearly transparent skin. But a bruise cannot beat, a bruise has no pulse, ribs would not recede and give way before a bruise. Audrey can barely comprehend what she holds in her lap. What she sees, what she could press down upon with her finger and still for all time is this baby's working heart, beating on the outside of its chest.

Poor matchstick painter, you are once more forgotten. You lie upstairs in your manger of hay, tossing and turning, fighting back the stomach cramps that have plagued you since Saturday night. Yes, your jaw is killing you, but something else may be killing you faster. Life is unfair, is it not, Fos? You lead such a brown constricted existence, moving between the matchstick factory and this boardinghouse, stopping every third night or so for your one glass of beer. We did not begrudge you your Saturday night's entertainment. No, we wanted nothing more than for you to be cheered a bit by those clowning cats. But it seems God in His Heaven was not so benevolent. For His entertainment, He sat you down next to a dirty old keelman by the name of William Sproat, the one who slapped his leg and laughed through his teeth, the one who even now is expiring down on the Low Quay, blue and shriveled and biting the bedsheets in agony.

And Audrey Place, the doctor's fiancée, though she means to do good is a woman in love. She knows how interested her Henry is in the human heart, knows that he studied it obsessively in school, that he slept with it over his bed in boyhood. Henry has poured out his heart to his intended and in return when she looks at Gustine's baby, dandling on her knee, her first thought is not, Poor baby, how your mother will weep when you are gone. No, poor forgotten matchstick painter. Audrey's first thought is strangely similar to Gustine's on the riverbank. Look what I have found, thinks devoted Audrey. I must tell Henry.

V

EMPLOYMENT

Across town, something is wrong at the Garrison Pottery Factory. It's a subtle thing, a matter of ten idle minutes, no more than that; barely the time it takes for Audrey to bid Pink farewell, take up her blankets, and lose herself in the next needy family. Certainly, to a girl whose day is circumscribed only by millinery appointments and piano lessons, ten minutes would not seem to be a great deal of time, but to Gustine working at Garrison, ten minutes is an eternity. A break of ten minutes is time enough to relieve oneself, to eat dinner, to fall asleep and have ten different dreams before being awakened by the crack of the foreman's strop. Ten minutes idle in the middle of the day, though, ten unanticipated minutes with nothing to do—well, any well-oiled factory worker will tell you, that is nothing short of a disaster.

Gustine is contemplating this disaster in the doorway between the grinding room and the blunging room, her muddy skirts moulded to every curve of her body, her face and arms stiff with drying porcelain. Over the years, she has developed a straight-backed, bowlegged run with her clay, like a woman might whose job consisted of rescuing cats from a house fire, but no matter how careful she is, the creamy gray slip rolls down her cheeks from the clay she balances on her head, oozes down her stomach and between her legs from the sixty-pound wedge she hugs to her chest. She spends her day creakily running between the slip house and her potter's lathe, slicing her sixty-pound wedges into two dozen identical lumps that with a ladleful of slip she feeds to her potter; and when she has run the finished pots to the center of the room and climbed the stepping stool to place each one on the high shelf unit dusted with sand to keep the pots from sticking, and her potter looks up at her with his hands shaking and empty and strangling nothing but air, she runs back to the slip house to begin it all over again.

But today, for the first time in her nine years at the factory, Gustine finds herself with nothing to do.

The ceilings of the slip house are uniformly low and braced with dry rotting beams bought cheap in 1753; the knobby walls have raised a stucco from their yearly white-washing over splattered clay; the windows, likewise, have been splashed and crusted over, leaving the rooms in perpetual twilight. In the dimly lit room next door men grind flint underwater to keep the dust down. They wear damp handkerchiefs over their mouths and noses as they shovel red-hot stones from the oven into a grinding trough of cool rainwater. The old grindstone is wearing out, Gustine overhears one say, his forehead pinkening in the steam. Don't call it to the foreman's attention, muffles an older, more experienced grinder. It happened once before that a replacement grindstone contained the tiniest trace of calcium carbonate that mixed into and undermined the flint. The only thing worse than grinding sixteen hours a day, Gustine learns, is to grind sixteen hours and not be paid because the pots exploded.

Leaning in the doorway, she is conscious of loitering; can feel, like bits of flying stone, the sharp glances the grinders chip at her. No one at the Garrison has time to lean against anything, much less watch what the others are doing. They know who she is and they know she should be upstairs right now, collecting her two heavy wedges of finished clay from the slappers, then getting along with her lazy self. What they don't know is that Gustine has already been upstairs and found a single man where there have always been four, beating the clay with his one wooden mallet to expel the air bubbles, slicing off wedges and slapping them back into the clay with a frustration born out of screaming shoulder muscles and a rising panic. He was crying when she surprised him, surrounded by oozing clay and idle mallets; said to her gruffly, It's not ready yet. Come back in ten minutes. Ten minutes. Here she is again, and she still doesn't know what to do with them.

Reluctantly, Gustine gives up her spot in the doorway and wanders stiffly through the slip house, past pairs of Garrison blungers who with great bladed instruments scythe clay and rainwater in coffin-length troughs, passing it through increasingly finer sieves until it comes out the consistency of cream. Behind them, the factory's only steam engine combines this creamy clay and ground flint into a single vat, and with its pistons and pugilist vanes, pounds it so violently the entire shoddy building shakes upon its foundation. The men plug their ears with twists of cotton and go about their business as if there were not a raging beast in their midst, but Gustine marvels at how it grunts and bellows; she is pleased to learn this creature is working as hard as any of them and is just as upset about it. Behind the engine, the previous batch of slip is boiling away in a long firebrick enclosure heated below by twenty fireplaces. Two toothless, shirtless old men stir the bubbling stuff with boat oars to make sure it evaporates evenly. When most of the water has boiled off, it goes upstairs to have prodigious farts worked out of it by

Gustine's slappers, but today it will have to wait with the last batch. One man cannot slap an entire day's worth of clay by himself.

Gustine sighs and steps into the dark courtyard. Thick white clouds have lowered the sky to the height of the ceilings inside, making a girl instinctively duck beneath them. Snow clouds, they look to be, but October is so early in the season, maybe she is mistaken. It is strangely exhilarating to be alone at work, to go about without her burdens in the open air; as unimaginable as stepping outside in the dress without the shadow weight of an Eye behind her. It is difficult to smile after a day in the pottery—a rind of clay has stiffened her face to impassivity—but if she could smile, she would now, aware as she is of being very, very bad, as only the idle might be.

When was the last time she was alone? She can barely remember. Certainly never before at the potters' house, where she shares a room with fifteen other people, nor at Whilky's, where thirty sleep upstairs tangled together like stray cats. The closest she comes to solitude is on her Sundays off, when she works neither encased in mud nor laced into the dress; when she might walk her baby to the town moor for an airing. She doesn't mind its weight at all—the baby is far lighter than the wedges of clay she carries, and warmer and certainly drier. She wants the baby to experience Nature, because she knows poets say it has a civilizing effect, and though most of the trees have been cut down and the grazing cows and sheep have gnawed away a good portion of the grass, there is still enough green to impress a child. On the town moor, Gustine spreads out her shawl and lays the tightly wrapped bundle carefully in the center. She wishes she could just strip off the blankets and jumpers, let the naked thing grip the grass in its tiny fists and root it mightily from the earth, but she doesn't dare. If she let her baby crawl bare-bottomed across the town moor like the other children, a draft might whip by or a miasma well up from the damp ground and extinguish the little blue light in its chest forever.

But, Christ, now she is truly alone and for ten minutes responsible for nothing. She has barely ever stepped outside the circuit of potters' house, slip house, and slapping room; now, with something like a purpose, she skirts the great courtyard mountains of chert and flint and coal and crosses to the high wall that separates the Garrison Pottery from its eponymous neighbor, the barracks of His Majesty's 82nd Infantry Division. Away from the blungers blunging and the grinders grinding, she can hear jangling spurs rebound off taut horseflesh, swords in unison slick out of metal scabbards and chunk back in. So they are still here. Gustine has not seen a soldier on the streets for over a week, and was beginning to wonder if they had shipped out. Her landlord had heard that their chief surgeon was in Jessore during the 1817 cholera outbreak and ordered the barrack gates locked and bolted to keep his men free of contagion. It has been harder on the streets without the welcome sight of a red coat; harder on the shop girls and lace-makers than on Gustine, whose dress might allow her entrance into better neighborhoods. She presses her cheek against the rough brick wall and closes her eyes. What a shame to lock all that commissioned male-flesh behind a wall. How clearly she sees the shiny patches made by woolen breeches rubbing the hair away from their muscular thighs; how often was she expected to ooh and aahh as their soldierly nipples sprang forth from their tightly buttoned coats. A soldier cannot wait to throw off his confining uniform, but once he is naked—she shakes her head—has no more imagination than to drop upon a girl stiff and straight as a salute.

Only seven minutes left—surely three have passed. Gustine looks down at her hands, tingling with shiftlessness. She has the whole complex at her disposal, but where to go first? The hot kilns look inviting. She could walk over and watch the seggars, stripped down from working in equatorial heat yet pale as new-hatched termites. They are loading the green-stage pots they've taken from her lodge into thick, lidded ceramic seggars for the first biscuit firing. When all the encased ware is stacked as high as it might go, they'll brick up the kiln walls and set the fires alight, raising the temperature inside gradually, over forty-eight hours, to twelve hundred degrees. Over another twenty-four hours, the temperature slowly drops, and when it reaches about one thirty, the seggars climb inside to disinter the pots. It is cold outside and her muddy shift is freezing to her bare legs. She might take her naughty, indolent self over to the kilns where it is warm, but for some reason she does not turn that way. Let me go where there are no people, she thinks, even if only for six minutes more.

To her left, Garrison's storehouse stands away from the complex, built at the end of a short track used for running carts of pots from the kilns. It too is low, but longer by half than the other buildings, and blissfully dark. Gustine's muddy boots crunch broken pottery underfoot as they take her slowly toward it, the only building in the pottery free of workers. Its clean black windows reflect the jack-o'-lantern slip and potters' houses, give back the orange-glowing cone-shaped kilns. I make these, thinks Gustine, raising up on tip-toe to peer into the dim, whitewashed room. For six years she has worked among the dizzying wheels of the potters' room

helping to make these wares, worked for the same potter, a
man she has watched go from young to middle-aged, growing
his beard longer and longer like a mud wasp's nest. At first,
when her potter had no child old enough of his own, she
turned the wheel that worked the belt that via a crank spun
his lathe. Four years she spent hitched to that wheel, walking
inside a hypnotic wonderland of circles, horizontal and ver-
tical shadow wheels thrown by candlelight, dreamy revolutions of time. Like a dog chasing her own tail, Gustine would
lose herself for hours; the foreman would call twenty minutes
for dinner and the ham she mechanically put in her mouth
satisfied like a solid wagging muscle. When the potter's son
grew old enough to take over the wheel, his wife conveniently
died, and for the past two years, beginning when she was thirteen, Gustine has worked as his assistant, ferrying clay atop
her head like a Russian bottle dancer, shrinking a few inches
every day beneath its weight. I make these, she thinks proudly,
looking down the long rows of stacked pots, rows of pink
and purple *Sailor's Tears* and *Keep Me Cleans*, waiting to be
packed with straw and transported out. Gustine recites softly
the aching poetry painted on Garrison's most popular item,
The Sailor's Tear.

> *The Sailor jumped into the ship*
> *As it lay upon the strand,*
> *But, oh! His heart was far away*
> *With friends upon the land.*
> *He thought of those he loved the best,*
> *A wife and infant dear*
> *And feeling filled the sailor's breast*
> *The sailor's eye, a tear.*

How sad the words! How true! She knows the tragic poem by heart, painted in black beneath the spout of a pink lustreware pitcher. Carefully painted bands of rosy pink edge the top rim and bottom base; a shakier line hides the seam where the spout was attached to the body with a bit of slip. Into a flattened oval on the side of the pitcher, the girls will transfer a moving portrait of a weeping seaman, turned resolutely away from wife and child and toward the Union Jack. Gustine has met some of the coy young paintresses who work in the paint shop, where nothing spins but dried pigment in tiny tornadoes when they stand up too fast, and clear syrupy glaze when they stir it before each dipping. They wear smart white aprons and know how to style their hair; they gossip over horsetail brushes, taking dainty dabs at their paint pots while plunging their arms up to the elbow in lead glaze to coat the pots for their glost firing. A paintress breathes in the color over which she works until her mouth is so filled with the sweet taste of lead, she desires no other food. For a year or so, she is the most beautiful creature alive—vivacious, pale, with eyes as deep and dreamy as the purple oxide of gold swirling in her pot. When at last she shows signs of plumbism, what the other paintresses call the wrist-drop, she is let go so that she might decline alone, to be remembered as young and fatally beautiful, rather than palsied, paralytic, extinguished.

Their second-best seller is a most discreet chamber pot, proclaiming:

> *Keep me clean and use me well*
> *And what I see I will not tell!*

Gustine's potter also specializes in these, coaxing two hundred wide-mouthed pots a day out of the gobbets of clay she slaps onto his wheel. The girls paint the motto on the outside, and on the inside bottom, a funny little man, his arms thrown over his head in alarm. To at least half of these, her potter adds an extra joke: a three-dimensional moulded green frog affixed just inside the lip, to make the unwary lady, with her skirts drawn up and drawers dropped down, scream like a girl. Gustine thinks they are a riot, and is sad that since the town's infestation they've fallen off in popularity.

The pots are backing up now, stacked in twos and threes; while the pressed plates, as many as a hundred high, are buckling like mushroom stalks, and the glossy figurines of spotted spaniels and fearsome lions are tucked pell-mell inside the extra shaving cups, stamped "A Remembrance from Sunderland." There are no ships to convey these souvenirs to America and Amsterdam, to London or even to Seaham. Gustine worries for the three men absent from the slapping room. What would have been a day's lost pay before the Quarantine may now be an excuse to let them go for good. To miss a day of work is now, more than ever, to sign your own termination papers.

It's certainly been ten minutes, and she cannot stand here idle all night. Gustine returns to the slip house, past the spastic steam engine, past the old warlocks stirring their slippery brew and the danse macabre of the scything blungers. She climbs the stairs to the slapping room, feeling the backs of her knees crack, opening and closing her mouth to loosen the mask on her face. She stands in the door and calls out to the slapper. Hello? When she receives no answer, Gustine creeps into the dim little room. To her dismay, the slapper sits in the corner, lit by a dying fire, his shoulders rolled forward, too tired to support even the weight of his massive forearms.

"I think they must be dead," he says, his heavy block hands hanging limply in his lap. "All three to be gone like this."

He has nothing for her—even after ten minutes, he has no worked clay to take back to the potters' house. And it is only five o'clock, thinks Gustine. There are two long hours left in the day.

"Mebbe the cholera morbus is finally among us," says he, searching for an answer in the dying embers of the grate.

What is she to do? She can't very well return to the potters' house empty-handed, and yet if she takes them half-slapped clay, the pots will surely explode in the oven. Gustine crosses to the mallet the slapper has left cleaving a giant's head of clay. How heavy can this be? She lifts it high over her shoulders and lets gravity bring it down with a thud, violently splattering herself with cold slip. This is not difficult. She can help slap and together they will get enough clay to finish the day's work. Gustine lifts the mallet again.

"Put tha' down," says the slapper, looking at her for the first time. Why, she's nothing but a girl, he sees; her moulded gown is showing off naught but skinny child's legs and a barely rounded bottom. She's as likely to drop the mallet on her foot as upon the clay.

She lets it crash again, savouring the impact and the spray of slip. This could be fun, she thinks, not realizing that a full day of raising the hammer and bringing it down could make a man wonder how his life is any different from a convict's swinging a pick in Australia. Well, it is better than doing nothing, thinks she. Better than staring into the fire like an old woman. She raises the mallet again and feels a pull like to yank her shoulders out of the socket.

"I said put tha' down."

The red-eyed slapper clenches the mallet she just held and

for an in stant Gustine is certain he will smite her with it. His powerful white belly heaves, his face contorts in thwarted rage, and when he opens his mouth, a warning hiss backs Gustine against the door.

"Me mates ayr dead. Wouldja go poundin' on their graves?"

Gustine shakes her head no, very slowly.

"Then get outta here," yells the slapper and pushes her roughly out the door. Gustine runs down the stairs as fast as her crusted legs will take her, out of the slip house and back to the potters' lodge. What is she going to tell them? She stops outside the door. What is she going to say?

"Where have you been?" Her potter looks up furiously when Gustine walks in, more than ten minutes late and empty-handed. "Where is the clay?"

At the cardinal points of the small room, three other teams of three, families all, stop what they are doing and look up. Young sons and daughters who would push against the handle of the wheel, wives and eldest daughters who would set perfectly sized wedges of clay on the spinning lathe, and fathers, under whose strong fingers pots would rise and fall, all sit silent and wait to hear her answer. It is so dark in the potting room, Gustine can make out only their silhouettes against the sinking fire. She hates this time of year. They come to work in the dark, they leave in the dark, the rheumy-eyed windows provide only the barest blurs of light even at noon. They have all learned to work by touch, like sightless moles.

"There is no more clay," she announces, not bothering to hide the frustration in her voice. "There is no one to slap it."

If anyone but Gustine had said this, she would have been beaten soundly for a liar. Those in the potters' house learned long ago, however, that no one takes her work more seriously than the assistant Gustine. Her potter looks down at his naked wheel, then up sharply at his young son, who, sagging in his harness, begins to whimper. The room is absolutely still except for the bronchial rustle of potters' rot coughs.

"What's wrong wi' them?" he asks at last. "Why didn't they send someone in their place?"

Gustine shakes her head. "Could be the cholera," she says, remembering the remaining slapper's stricken expression. Perhaps he's right—perhaps it's begun to rain cholera after all.

"Oh Jaisus," wails one of the potter's wives.

"Don't none of you go getting the cholera," orders Gustine's potter in his deeply accented pipe organ voice. "Anyone misses a day in these times, if he lives, he'll have no job to come back to."

They have not long to wait before the foreman, a short vulturine man with an impacted neck and peaked shoulders, pushes open the door to the potters' lodge. He carries the strop that Gustine felt more than once as a girl when she would fall asleep over her wheel, though more often her potter would strike her, to spare her the fury of the foreman. The doubled belt of leather is eager to bite into an idle someone now, but overwhelmed by the sheer number of choices, quivers miserably in the foreman's hand. Gustine has never seen the entire shop motionless like this. She has no idea what to expect.

"Go home," says the foreman. "There is no more work for you today."

He could not have caused a greater consternation if he'd announced the world had no more use for chamber pots. To be turned loose two hours early might well amount to the same thing, for though any salaried employee with blood in his veins would be thrilled to window-shop for two hours or stop in for an early pint before dinner, the workers at Garrison are terrified. They are not salaried; they are paid by the piece, and no clay means no pot; and no pot equals no food on the table. Gustine's potter pays her out of what he makes on each surviving piece; neither she nor any of the wives and children have an entry on the factory's payroll. They are no more than ghost employees as far as the management is concerned, and what responsibility does anyone owe a ghost?

"But we've na yet raiched the quota," says Gustine's potter. "How'll we be paid?"

"You will be paid for the pots already in the kiln," replies the foreman.

"That's not even half of a day's work," argues another potter who specializes in plaster spaniels. His moulds lay open before him like cracked eggs.

"Whose fault is that?"

Whose fault *is* that? they wonder, as the foreman lurches out to deliver the news to the rest of the factory. Slowly, the potters lift their aprons over their heads, the little boys and girls unlatch themselves from the wheels they turn. No one speaks, no one glances left or right. They must wait two days to learn how many of the pots they fashioned today made it through the first firing; then there is the glost, where still more could go wrong.

Will there be work tomorrow? It is the unasked question each takes with him out the front gates, where the two-hours-earlier sky is strangely white and electrically perverse enough to blast away their kiln along with the last remaining pots. Perhaps they will find replacement slappers, and all will be well. Perhaps (though no one will speak it out loud) even fewer employees will struggle out of bed in the morning and the factory will grind to a halt. Will there be work? The question takes them past the grinders and paintresses who stagger confusedly out from their own buildings (the lead-sated girls home to not eat what's set before them on the table, and the grinders making straight for the Life Boat pub) and down to the river, now whittled to a simple word—Work?—which they wear to float them neck high into the freezing Wear. The river bottom is rugged with smashed crockery and old worn bricks, the water numbs their skin; but when a single hot rinse at the public baths costs as much as an assistant's weekly salary, there is no other way to remove a day's accreted clay.

Gustine steps into the water behind her coworkers and allows the Wear to find her body beneath the statue she has become. Under the river's skilled fingers, her cotton shift slowly unmoulds itself from her thighs, her arms lose their hard white stiffness, her lashes gently separate. She arches her neck, and her hair, moulded to her skull, unmats in long cloudy handfuls. There is a deep fatigue born of gaining and losing an inanimate self, six days a week, fifty-two weeks a year, and she's come to find the restoration of her human flesh almost more exhausting than the job itself. As fast as she'd like to wash, she knows that if she is not careful, the river will leave a film of potter's clay upon her skin, she'll harden on the walk home, and wake in the morning to a body of hairline cracks.

What will she do if there is no work tomorrow? With winter coming on, her baby needs warmer blankets, a clean change of clothes, another diaper. There is almost no money to be had on the streets, what with the Quarantine and all the soldiers locked away like virgins in a tower. There must be work tomorrow, and the day after, and the day after that. How will they survive if there's none?

Absently, she scrubs the last rigidity from behind her knees and frees the freckles along her cheeks. She squeezes her hair clean of mud and braids it high on the top of her head, leaving two sections to frizz at her temples. Henry, she thinks. He will compensate her if she supplies him with more bodies. And by helping him is she not helping herself? There is a solution for every problem, she thinks, relieved to have a plan. If only she knew the addresses of the three missing slappers, she'd find him and take him there tonight.

Gustine feels her way up the dark bank and jogs down Low Quay, her wet shift slapping her legs. Jesus, but it's cold. She hugs herself for the run home, feeling her organs shrink against her spine. She passes Silver Street, once a fashionable address, now just another row of collapsing facades and bowed steps, jogs past Burleigh Street, where tenements began snuggling next to upper-class housing until even the brightly tiled roofs and glazed windows caught the contagion and wasted away. Mill Street is only four blocks farther, thank God—she can feel her hair turning to ice and her shift start to crackle as she sprints the last few yards.

Gustine pulls up short at the entrance to her narrow lane. Just look at that—Mill Street's been whitewashed. No one has taken the pains to clean up this passage since the gas company surveyed it five years ago and refused to run a jet.

Inside, at least it's warm. It is early yet for the lodgers to be home; one or two sit at the long table beneath Whilky's framed Wearmouth Bridge; the woman who sells fish to the poor Irish and her son have come home early, Gustine sees, and there is a man who was not here last night whose feet are wrapped with rags and twine, his toes protruding obscenely.

From two pegs on the wall hangs the blue dress, and below it, as usual, sits the Eye, her hands folded, her searchlight sweeping the room, taking in every thing, missing nothing.

"You're home early," Whilky observes, glancing up from his paper. Gustine ignores him and walks straight to the coal bin, behind which Pink sits with the baby in her lap. Its little face peeps out of the stiff gray blanket like a curious turtle from its shell. Come here, little one. Gustine reaches out and takes the child from Pink's thin arms. She puts her ear to its chest and kisses its curled fist.

"Were you a good baby today?" she asks.

"Oh, yes, very good," answers Pink.

"And Pink took good care of you?"

"Oh yes!" cries the girl, glancing nervously at the Eye. She won't tell about the frog on the chest or the charity visit or the new blanket Pink has wedged beneath the cupboard for safekeeping, will she? Oh God, Pink prays, please don't tell.

"And you stayed far, far away from the Evil Eye, did you not, good baby?" coos Gustine, herself casting a cold look at the old woman beneath the dress.

"Mike killed sixty-five rats in ten minutes today," Pink offers, quickly changing the subject. It's all her Da could talk about when he came home, first telling the fish woman's son and then the new man possessed of raw feet. You should have seen him, he said, acting out the scene. Da down on his hands and knees, pretending to throw rats over his shoulder, left then right. Flinging rats, flying rats, and Mike getting excited by the display, tearing at her Da's jacket sleeve. Da laughing, haw, haw, haw. Will you just look a that. Just like tha' he did! But when Pink scampered over and sunk her teeth into the other sleeve, tearing, laughing with Mike, no more haws, just Get up, and Where's yer brain, girl?

Whilky sits on a stool by the door, reading by a candle melted onto the table. His newspaper is spread out on his lap, an arm's length away so that he doesn't have to squint too hard. Curled upon Whilky's shoulder, with his tail nestled under his pointy chin, Mike the ferret naps. His owner's hand unconsciously steals up and tickles the soft white fur between his ears.

No wonder he's so smart, thinks Pink. Mike reads the newspaper. She's surprised she never noticed before. There he sits upon her Da's shoulder, pretending to nap, but she can see his small black eyes scanning the words before Da wets his finger and turns the page. Pink wishes she could read the newspaper. Something inside it is always delighting or infuriating her father, and if she could only learn what it was, she might make herself more useful to him. Mike's got the idea, she thinks with a sigh. He knows what's what in the world.

Gustine carefully passes Pink the baby and crouches next to her behind the coal bin. It really is the only place in the entire house a person might hunker and, for a couple of seconds, not be seen. She strips off the cold sodden dress and slings it across the clothesline overhead. From above, she pulls down an old moth-eaten blanket and wraps it around her naked body like a towel. Whilky says it's silly to be modest in her line of work, but she'll be damned if she'll let him sneak a peek for free.

"It's barely past five," Whilky says gruffly. "Did the pottery drop into the river?"

"They sent us home early today," Gustine replies, not wanting to go into it. "Owner's birthday."

She takes the baby over to the hearth and climbs half inside to get warm. Someone had been roasting herring and a scorched bit of the tail cleaves to the grate. With the poker,

Gustine pries it off, blows on it, and pops it into her mouth. It is so wonderfully hot in the fireplace. She closes her eyes and chews, savouring the feeling of her skin about to peel off. This is all that matters; heat and quiet and her own dear babe in her arms. She kisses the lobster pink cheeks above two faint shadows that would be dimples if only for a little more baby fat.

Gustine takes a deep sniff and loosens the tuck of blanket from under the child's chin. God forbid Pink should change you—what a rashy red mess your bum must be. She unwinds the layers of blanket to get down to the feedbag diaper she washes out every night and leaves to dry stiff before the fireplace. She has shown Pink a hundred times how to fold the diaper and pin it in place, but the girl is hopeless—

"Pink!" Gustine yells, though the little girl is sitting in the corner not three feet from her. "What is on this baby?"

Gustine has unraveled the child from its blanket bundle and holds it out in front of her. Her child, *hers*, is dressed in some sort of costume she's never laid eyes on before: a long, trailing gown of white Irish linen, smocked along the collar, drawstringed along the cuffs and hem, pulled together and tasseled like a chaise roll pillow. How on earth did this garment come to be on her child?

Pink, realizing all is lost, wishes she might squeeze beneath the coal bin and disappear into the floor. Mike, now wide awake, leaps from her father's shoulder and pads over to the hearth to sniff Gustine's scratchy new white baby.

"Pink?" Gustine demands.

"The charity lady put it on," she says softly. "After she give me a blanket."

"Charity lady?" Her father looks up from his newspaper. "What on God's bloody earth are you talking about?"

"I have to go outside now," Pink says, running for the door.

"No you don't." Whilky leaps up and hurls his bulk in front of the only way out. "Not until you tell me what brainless, unforgivable thing you've gone and done now."

Pink's small pink nose starts to tremble and she can feel her thick white tail bristle a warning. What would Mike do? She turns to the white ferret whose ten razor nails rest gently on the baby's white linen gown. Tell the truth he seems to shine with purity and light. It's the ferret's Code of Honor. Pink stills her quivering chin and speaks haltingly to Gustine.

"I let in a lady who was worried about Fos and then she saw the baby and got worried about that. She said the dress was for her cousin's baby christening but that this baby needed it worse. She is sending a doctor tonight to make Fos stop glowing in the dark."

A doctor? Oh God, groans Gustine, I hope she hasn't gone and ruined everything. What is the point of searching out the one perfect person if a foolish little girl is just going to come along and undo all her hard work? And look at this getup! Her child might as well be lying in a watered silk bassinet, choked with tulle and cosseted by fairy godmothers. I work two jobs, fumes Gustine. I need no one's charity.

"I knew I should never've left," Whilky roars from his place before the door. "Did I not say even unto my own pet: Mike, you, a ferret, I would trust not to open the door for the minions of the Government, but who is it I've left at home today? My addled daughter Pink, who would, without a second thought, betray her Da and all his property. Oh, why have the gods cursed me?"

"I'm sorry," says Pink almost inaudibly.

"You're a sorry little git is what you are!" yells Whilky, working himself up into a proper frothing rage. Before she can duck, he gives her a hard slap to the head with the rolled-up newspaper. Tears swim before Pink's eyes and she wishes now more than ever that she could read, to know which news was responsible for knocking her to the ground.

"Don't cry, Pink," Gustine says, as the girl scampers behind the coal bin and curls herself into a ball. "It's not a catastrophe."

"No doctor is setting foot inside this house," Whilky says with finality. "The only creature worse upon the planet than a charity lady is a doctor, and I won't have one poking and prodding and dispensing in this establishment."

"There is going to come a time when a doctor shall be admitted into this house," says Gustine hotly. "One is coming soon to cure this baby."

"The only thing coming for that baby is the undertaker," bellows Whilky.

"You take that back!" Gustine shouts, setting aside the baby and charging her red-faced landlord. The woman who sells fish to the poor Irish and the man of exposed toes edge about the long table and make quickly for the steps up to their room. Pink looks up from behind the coal bin and screams.

"The doctor is coming for Fos! Nobody even cares about Fos!"

Gustine pauses and in that instant the dress hits her like cold water thrown over an angry dog. She struggles, but Eye stands behind her, tugging the blue fabric down over her shoulders, forcing her clenched fists into the tight armseyes, and making fast the hooks. The blanket Gustine wore wrapped around her naked body drops to the ground and covers her bare feet like a puddle of mud.

"This dress belongs to me," Whilky says, poking her in the

chest once with the rolled-up newspaper. "You will find yourself evicted from it if I ever catch you bringing a doctor into this house."

Gustine shakes off Eye's cold-padded fingers and crosses back to the hearth where she set down the baby. It is crying, almost noiselessly, its tiny mouth opened into an O. Pink sinks back down behind the coal bin.

"The doctor was coming for Fos," she says. "Nobody even cares about Fos."

There are three times in an evening when a prosperous man wants a woman: after a hard day at the office, when he's sated on responsibility; after five courses in a restaurant, when he is glutted on food; and after a fine night at the theatre, when he's drunk on entertainment. It's a fact that rich men tend to be awfully sullen and morose after hours behind a desk, going about the business of sex as if taking inventory: two breasts—squeeze, squeeze; two lips—mash, mash; one quim—poke, poke, poke. After an evening at the theatre, they are, on the other hand, too excitable and daring, ready to drape a girl in scarves or dress her up like the beardless hero in a melodrama before they bend her over and demand her bare white bottom. Gustine most definitely prefers the after-dinner men. Then a prosperous man is more inclined to treat her like a fine cigar or a mellow glass of sherry, the final intoxicant to complement his champagne and oysters and custard and quail. She's found he's too full to thrash about much, and too gassy to take himself too seriously. Gustine does her best business outside the Bridge Inn when the plates from the restaurant are being cleared and a guest steps outside for a breath of fresh air. Then a man might catch a glimpse of her in the gaslight and elect to take his after-din-

ner drink upstairs. And if he chooses to share it with a
charming young lady, well, whose business is that?

Gustine has wandered up Sunderland Street and across
High ten times now, back and forth along the same two sides
of the block (though you might not call it a block—Garden
Street peters out into the old Quaker burial ground and none
of the other lanes cut through). The limestone hotel is bright
with four stories of paned windows and a fat gas lamp smiling over the front door. Men and women go in and out below
it, some climbing the grand staircase up to their rooms, some
turning left to take a table in the fancy dining room, which
shimmers with chandeliers and mirrors and buffed silver plat-
ters. Gustine pauses before the street-level bay window to
watch the patrons of the Bridge Inn. The women, far more
than the men, impress her; she takes careful notice of how
they hold their backs straight and erect when tucked into tall
caned chairs, how they keep their elbows lower than the table
lip when lifting a scant forkful of roe to their mouths. She
observes how they tilt their heads, so that their ringlets might
brush a blushing cheek, and how they murmur with their lips
barely open, as if everything they had to say were the most
precious secret. The room is alive with maize and *rose de par-
nasse* and Cossack green silk, bare shoulders and sleeves even
wider and more bouffant than Gustine's. Hair is worn tight
to the head, except where it has been erected with ribbons and
feathers in elaborate topknots or curled into tiers at the temple. Fashion might be slow to reach Sunderland, but when it
arrives, it arrives with a vengeance. Every middle-class daughter with a few coins in her purse flings away last autumn's
French *capote roquet* and runs after this spring's Tuscan grass
bonnet. Gustine can tell her spectacular blue dress is already
going out of style. She'll have to get Eye to take the tulle

puffs off the skirt and tack them onto the sleeves.

Gustine glances over her shoulder to where her stooped old shadow waits on the other side of High Street. She hates the feel of Eye's cold monkey fingers on her flesh, resents the backwardness of this animal locking her into her bright blue cage each night. She would have killed Whilky back at Mill Street if Eye had not stepped in, but Eye knows that the dress's very blueness numbs her, making her feel like she's moving underwater. God damn her. Why does she need this shadow? Gustine does not care that the Eye has seen her stretched to tearing around a thick stump of prick and done nothing about it, nor is she embarrassed that the old woman has witnessed many a slobbering, biting mouth upon her breasts. What she is deeply humiliated by—if humiliation can surpass that feeling of mortified exposure a girl suffers being watched night after night dressing and undressing, crouching over a chamber pot, or forcing a bit of sponge up between her legs—is that Eye still does not trust her. In her two years of dress lodging, she has never once given Whilky a reason to doubt her, never withheld money or gotten drunk or even, when requested to strip, laid the dress more than arm's length from the bed. And yet Eye watches her with an expression so suspicious and malevolent, so certain she will misstep, that she almost makes Gustine want to do it. She has no idea what the Eye would do to her if she did try to make off with the dress, and only the fear of leaving her precious baby an orphan prevents her from finding out.

One or two men dine alone, Gustine sees, turning back to the hotel; traveling businessmen who have braved the Quarantine. She spies the most likely candidate sitting near the window: a pale, balding man pushing a last bite of brandy-poached pears against his reluctant lips. Here is a man who guards against his own appetites, Gustine thinks, watching the top lip grudgingly give way and a thick tongue thrust out for the dessert. He has a furtive restlessness about him, and when he's stopped shooting glances at other men's wives and takes a second to look down onto the street, Gustine makes sure she steps out of the shadows into the hotel's bright circle of gaslight. He starts a bit when he sees her and she holds his gaze boldly for a count of ten. Any dining-alone businessman who mistakes the count of ten, Gustine thinks, is a businessman not worth the trouble.

Sure enough, the syrupy pears are pushed aside, the check is autographed, and the pale, balding man disappears from the dining room. Gustine determines to walk to the end of the block and back and see if he is waiting on the front step when she returns. If not, she'll move on to the Red Lion Inn, where the men are poorer but their appetites more dependable. For every step Gustine takes, the Eye on the other side of the street takes one, too—far enough behind her not to be immediately noticed, but close enough to set Gustine's teeth on edge. They turn at the dark intersection of Sunderland Street and Charles, a crossroads Gustine has never much liked, for it seems to contain all the contradictions of the town. Turn west onto Charles and the road broadens, coursing straight into tidy, well-lit Bishopwearmouth; turn east on Charles and it almost immediately dead-ends into forgotten courtyards and impossibly dark lanes leading nowhere. Old Quakers fester in the Friends Burial Ground and Methodists moulder on Number's Garth, where John Wesley opened his first church in Sunderland a century ago. Gustine pivots and walks back toward the beckoning Bridge Inn. Please be there, she thinks. It's cold and I would like to sit by a nice warm fire.

He *is* there. She sees him standing in a long black furlapelled redingote looking the wrong way up High Street for her. His bald head is covered with a tall Neapolitan top hat, just a bit too tight from the way it's perched, and he holds a feckless batonlike walking stick. Gustine smoothes her blue skirt, sets her head atilt after the fashion of the young ladies inside, and steps around the corner.

"Good evening," she says pleasantly, stopping in front of the Bridge Inn's marble steps.

The man jumps at the sound of her voice behind him. She catches a glimpse of bony eczematous hands before they thrust themselves into a pair of white gloves. Oh no, thinks Gustine.

"Hallo," says the man, with a faint Midland accent.

"Are you a stranger in town?" she asks, dipping her chin slightly to make her curls bob.

He nods and glances nervously over his shoulder.

"It's difficult on a man to be away from home." Gustine smiles sympathetically, feeling the chill wind stir her skirts and probe for her chapped naked legs. "But Sunderland is a very friendly town."

"That it is," says the man, rooted to the Bridge Inn steps.

Is he ever going to invite me up? she wonders wearily. It's too cold to stand here all night. The man above her on the steps wrings his hands nervously, flicking the walking baton dangerously close to her eye.

"If you'd like," she says, backing up a step," I could come upstairs and tell you about some of our more interesting sights."

"Oh no!" he yelps. "I just came out. I couldn't go back in."

Gustine sighs. One of those. If business weren't so bad, she would just walk away and abandon the man to his own flaky right hand for the night. But with the Quarantine, and no soldiers about to help out, she can't be too choosy. She takes a deep breath and gives it one last try.

"We might walk about, then," she offers. "I've got an hour before I've got to be home."

That option seems to spur the gentleman. He gives a curt nod and jerks down the steps, falling into place beside her. As she starts up well-lit High Street, he plunges down ill-lit Sunderland, and Gustine has to jog a few steps to catch up.

For a block they walk in silence. The man in the redingote takes long loping steps and Gustine trots alongside him. He has a long-jawed, skeletal face, with two reddened eczema ridges under his eyes like war paint. He also has a spoiled-milk nervous smell about him which Gustine recognizes as desire. When they get to the intersection of Charles, Gustine once more tries to lead them west, toward populated Bishopwearmouth, but the gentleman turns east, taking them deeper into darkness. Over her shoulder, Gustine sees that the Eye is turning the corner behind them. She makes another stab at conversation.

"What line of business are you in?" she asks, slipping her hand under his arm. She does not do it to be coy, but to protect her naked skin from the icy wind blowing up from the river. It really does look like snow.

"Plumbing," he says, and turns down Garden Street, toward the dark heart of the Quaker cemetery. The reflective white sky above provides the only light, and by it she can make out the evenly spaced iron pikes of the cemetery wall straight ahead. The putrid smell of old bones rushes out to meet them and Gustine instinctively pulls back.

"Here's fine," the man says, pushing her into a sagging doorway. She has time only to see the Eye over his left shoulder, stern as one of the Dissenter ghosts rising up from the grave, before his heavy black redingote is thrown over her face. The coat smells of tobacco and sweat and greasy animal fur. Her own trapped breath condenses inside the wool and drips down upon her cheek.

Well, it's not a roaring fire at the Bridge Inn, thinks Gustine while the man thrusts a flaky finger up her and digs about as if fishing a ring from a sink pipe. But at least it's warm.

Girl and shadow. Dress and Eye. They walk south on Villiers Street and east on Coronation; they walk north on Sans (past the cheap theatre where the first boys are lining up for tickets to Les Chats Savants, held over by popular demand), then east on High. Some nights, Gustine feels like she's caught the hem of her dress on a nail and that as she walks her skirt is slowly unraveling behind her, leaving a thin blue trail along the ground to mark where she's been. Sometimes when she lets her mind wander, she feels the thread drag along the gutters, snagging dead rats and bottles, chicken feathers and broken furniture. She feels the tangled thread grow heavier and heavier, tugging her back, making her strain to drag it, until at last she spins and sees that its very weight has become the Eye, a shadow called into being out of cumulate garbage much as the first woman was fashioned by God out of clay. There is no escape, Gustine thinks on nights like these. We will walk the streets forever, the Eye and I.

Girl and shadow, Dress and Eye. She's been walking for hours and has had no luck. And it is so cold tonight. She remembers last winter when her dress was newer and brighter, then almost nightly she was invited up to well-appointed hotel rooms where dinner was spread out in front of cheery coal fires. Her precious baby was conceived in one of those rooms, she is convinced, on a night when her stomach was full and her back was warm and she'd taken a sip of the champagne these men constantly force on her, as if getting her tipsy will make her somehow more willing than she already is. But this winter promises to be something else altogether. The hotels are half-full and the barracks are locked; the middle classes are afraid of contagion and the poor men are broke. What hope does she have now for an hour in a hotel? She must count herself fortunate to be half-suffocated beneath a plumber's redingote.

Gustine wraps her arms around her body and wedges her hands in her armpits. She walks briskly down George Street past the wide front window of a crowded public house full of overheated men stripping off their coats to drink in their shirtsleeves. Their hair is sweaty from laugh and drink, their broad red faces shine with blessed perspiration. Gustine pauses, trying to absorb through the cold pane of glass the heat generated by corduroy pants rubbing past each other to get to the bar. Five minutes, she thinks. Five minutes inside just to restore the feeling in the tip of my nose and thaw out my stiff, blue fingers. Gustine has her hand on the door when the shadow falls, icy and pickax upon it. She is a like-charged magnet, this taskmistress Eye, and by her very proximity repels Gustine away from the pub, down the street, back to work.

Down George Street, east on Coronation, up Spring Garden Lane. They pass a young mother muffled in shawls, cradling a hairy cow's hoof in one arm and a baby in the other. They pass a stoop upon which sit a girl and a dog and a pig, huddled together for warmth, while from inside their house come the syncopated screams of a woman in labour. Number 62, Gustine notes. If the woman does not survive the birth, she might be a fine candidate for Dr. Chiver. She is not even five houses away when she forgets the number. It's too much to think on nights like this, when the chill slows a person's brain to dull incomprehension. It's hard enough to walk when the soles of your feet have gone numb through your boots and you can barely feel the joints of your knees.

"May I help you?" Out of nowhere, a young man runs over, and Gustine realizes she's on the ground. How did that happen? She looks up at him—pleasant in an unconventional way, with cooked-sausage-coloured hair and back-raked eyebrows. His suit is wrinkled but obviously expensive, speaking more to his lack of a good butler than to a lack of income. Over it, he wears an unbuttoned wool coat.

"You must be freezing!" he cries.

Gustine is so numb with cold, she can barely stand up. She can tell he is unsure about her by the way he formally presents his flat-palmed, gloved hand. He keeps his body stiff and bent at the waist and his eyes respectfully averted from her face. Perhaps it's the shoes that give her away. It's always the shoes when someone looks close enough. When he spots them, she sees his body instantly relax and his impassive face lighten. He takes a step in toward her, allowing his hip to crush the fabric of her skirt, and without asking tucks her arm snugly in his.

"I don't suppose you'd like to come with me for a drink?" he asks, gripping her arm so securely she couldn't slip away if she tried. "I'll make it worth your while."

"I don't drink much," Gustine replies, having trouble getting the words through her numb lips. The young man laughs delightedly.

"Oh, sure you don't! This is rich!"

He leads her back the way she came, past the dog and pig

and little girl—still outside, though the screams have stopped—and around the back way to Playhouse Lane. He stops on the corner of the street in front of a brightly painted red door, behind which Gustine can hear a brass band playing and women laughing. She hesitates, even though she knows it will be steamily warm inside.

"You know this place?" the young man yells over the noise. "I come here all the time for my research."

He pushes through into a low room made closer by the blue ceiling of pipe smoke and pungent fumes of opium. At first glance, the clientele looks similar to that of the Labour in Vain, but as her eyes adjust to the smoke and one by one faces stand out, Gustine sees it is a very different sort of place. The men are heavy-lidded and unsteady on their feet, too free by far in the handling of their companions' bodies. As for the women, a meaty hand on a breast or a lingering finger upon an inner thigh they allow to pass unnoticed. Most are laughing and drinking gin; some slouch with their legs thrown apart and their stockings showing; others lie on the floor as if to fall asleep there. A brass band plays frenetically on a dais that looks to have once housed a pulpit, while couples haphazardly lurch about the floor in front of them.

"Used to be the old Methodist meeting house before they turned it into a dance hall," says the young man, pulling her inside. "Isn't that wicked?"

Gustine looks around in dismay. There is no shame in making money the way she does. Half the girls in Sunderland have sold their bodies at some point to put food on the table or to keep their families from the workhouse. It's almost a daughter's duty when her Da is between jobs to put on her bonnet, slip out onto the street, and a few hours later come back with a shilling or two. But these women are professional whores. They hang about the docks all day distracting honest men from their jobs, then join up with their pimps at places like this, half-clothed, half-drunk, and thoroughly bad. A woman Gustine recognizes from Sailor's Alley, a dolly she's seen on her knees performing like a Frenchwoman on men who like that sort of thing, waves familiarly. Gustine blushes for shame.

The young man finds them a small table away from the brass band and sits without offering her a chair. He reaches into his coat pocket and tugs out a small writing tablet and pencil.

"Don't look," he says, making a note on his pad. "But I think we're being followed."

Gustine glances over to the entrance, where the Eye has just stepped in. She stands like a rock in a river of smoke, the current eddying about her broad shoulders before flowing past her out the door. Gustine turns back without comment.

"You know that person?" asks the man, suddenly perking up. "Are you in some sort of trouble?"

"Yes, I know her." Even though they are away from the band, Gustine still has to shout over high-pitched spikes of laughter. "And no I'm not in trouble."

"Barmaid!" The man grabs at a harried servant girl's skirt as she whizzes by. "Whiskey for me. Gin with sugar for my companion. And one for Cyclops at the door!"

"I wish you hadn't done that," she says. "I don't drink." He twists in his chair and, taking up his pencil, makes a quick sketch of Eye that looks nothing like her. As if she weren't bad enough, he gives her a hunched back and crazy pubic-headed flyaway hair. Gustine feels a swift pang of sympathy for her enemy.

"So, tell me about yourself," he commands, pushing the

pad aside and leaning in with his chin in his hand. He is one of those, she sees, who shuts out the entire world when he looks at you. She is immediately on her guard.

"Are you with the newspapers?" she asks.

"Why? Because of this?" He holds up the pad and Gustine nods. "Ha! No. I am what you call a student of life. I am writing a brutally honest, unsentimentalized portrait of the British working classes. Their loves and prejudices, their labours and triumphs. I come here to speak honestly with the thieves and whores—to tell their stories and show the middle classes what their capitalist practices sow, their back alleys reap!"

A hank of cooked-sausage hair falls across his eyes and he licks his hand to smooth it back.

"See that poor creature over there?" He points to a rouged young woman, sitting with her arm thrown over her lover's shoulder. "She used to be a ladies' maid. Highly regarded, too. Son of the family caught her in the stairway one day when no one else was home. Ruined for life."

What else have these people told him? Gustine wonders. He probably believes every woman here was turned bad by Master's son, just as every hardworking man lost his job thanks to the cunning devices of a jealous foreman.

"Your dress is expensive," he remarks. "Did you steal it? I won't judge."

The barmaid sets a glass of gin and three sugar cubes in front of Gustine and a pint of whiskey and water before the Student of Life. Gustine bites down hard on the lump of sugar to keep from ordering him to Hell. We need the money, she tells herself. We need the money.

"It's my landlord's," she says.

"You mean pimp?" asks he.

By the door, the barmaid hands Eye a gin, which the old woman stares at for a second, then fists back in a gulp. It is close and smoky in the room, but it feels good to Gustine to be warm. She will just ignore the Student of Life and concentrate on the hot, heavy air thawing her legs.

"Is that *woman* your pimp?" asks he, when she doesn't answer. "I saw her following you down the street and I thought, Is that not always the way? Does not old age always dog youth? Does not monstrosity forever shadow beauty?"

His lids have too little skin for his wide-open expression and threaten to rip at the corners. God damn, thinks Gustine, can't we just go upstairs and get this over with—must I be forced to endure conversation, too? Sitting with Henry at the Labour in Vain was so different. He was sharing with her, telling her *his* secrets, not trying to pry her open.

"I think I should go," says Gustine, rising.

"No, wait!" He leaps out of his chair and pulls her back down. "I want you to tell me about yourself."

"There is nothing to tell," says she, exasperated and growing more self-conscious by the minute. "I'm just a potter's assistant."

"Potter's assistant!" He claps his hands and jots it down. "How rich!"

"Really," says Gustine flatly.

"I see. You are modest." The Student of Life reaches across the table and grabs her hand before she can draw it away. "Let me tell you about yourself then.

"You are young," he starts. "What, eighteen? Nineteen? You obviously haven't been at this long, not to know the Red Door," he continues, gesturing to the hall. "You haven't yet turned to drink, nor become hardened and bitter. You still hope for a better life. How did you fall? No! Wait!" He throws out his other hand. "Your story is written on your face. You gave your heart to a young man of property a year ago, two years ago; he put you up in an apartment, bought you beautiful things, promised to marry you—but when he grew tired of that pretty, sad face, he turned you out onto the street, ruined and friendless, to fend for yourself. You've pawned every trinket save the dress on your back. You can't get a character to become a maid or shop girl. Your parents won't take you back. You have no other option. Don't be ashamed," says the Student of Life. "You are without blame in this matter. Our society is set up to make a prostitute out of you."

Gustine stares at him in open disbelief. What in the name of God is he talking about?

"Darling," says he, "I am here to give you a voice."

"First of all, I am not ashamed," says Gustine, "of anything other than sitting here listening to you. And secondly, I work for a living. I work all day in the mud and I work all night on the streets. I do not need a voice—do you understand me? I have a quim. Now, do you fucking want to see it or not?"

The Student of Life lunges for his tablet and before Gustine knows what he's about, has sketched a girl who looks nothing like her, a cranky jaded creature with full breasts and open, voluptuous lips.

Gustine shoves back her chair and storms toward the door. She pushes past a barely conscious woman held upright by a pair of lover's hands on her ass, past the Eye, still holding her empty glass of gin, and out onto the street.

"Wait!" she hears behind her, but she does not slow down.

Outside, the sky scatters heavy crumbs of snow. The cold, coming after so close a room, brings tears to her eyes and sets her nose to running. What does he mean by giving her a voice? She has a voice. She uses it every day to ask for clay and to soothe her baby and to placate men. She uses it to cuss out the Eye and to sing when she's happy and to scream at the other lodgers when they wake her with their snores. She has a loud, unpretty, ferrety voice for day and a soft, throaty, helpless voice for night. Gustine stomps down the street, with the Eye on her heels in a matter of seconds. God damn it, she does this every time. The old woman breathes down Gustine's neck until the girl can't take it anymore. Gets up close upon her, breathing down her neck whenever Gustine walks away from money, breathing to remind her she belongs to Whilky, that she is not at liberty to pick and choose when she is inside his dress.

"Just tell Whilky and see if I care," Gustine wheels and shouts at the Eye. "You should have seen what he drew of *you!*"

Gustine storms up Playhouse Lane, pushing through the last-minute stragglers running for the ticket booth to the Theatre Royale, where the curtain is about to go up on "Cholera Morbus." She sees well-dressed men inside the lobby, tapping their watches and shaking their heads over friends who've yet to show, sees their wives gossiping in brightly colored clumps about what best gets frog blood out of Turkey rugs. Gustine is passing the door on the other side of the street when a hired cab careens around the corner and nearly runs her over.

"Jesus!" she cries, snatching the skirt of her dress away from the slush thrown up by the carriage.

Trapped between the cab and the wall, Gustine helplessly watches as a girl gets out, a young girl probably no more than seventeen, laughing at the snow that melts upon her black velvet mantle and lamé gauze turban with ostrich feather, stretching her slippered foot far over the gutter and leaping down. She looks like me, Gustine thinks, if I could ever laugh at snow. But how put together she is, how perfectly arranged. Embroidered velvet muff complements mantle and shoes; jet flowers linked with garnets in a chain about her neck match the trinity of black and red flowers in each white earlobe. To own a set of something—what would that be like? Eye steps up so close behind her, she can smell the smoked sprats the old woman gnawed for dinner. Is this my set? she wonders. Am I always to be paired with this hag as to my own death?

A man follows the lovely young lady out of the cab, stretching his own long legs across the slush. He has on tight-fitting black pants that button underneath his boots and a night green pinch-waist coat with high collar. She barely recognizes him so dressed up. His face is easy and relaxed, not tight with despair as she has memorized it. The girl of matched jewelry holds out a tidy gloved hand for him to take and as he does so, his eyes fall on Gustine.

"Potter's Assistant! Come back!" Gustine cannot believe her ears. The Student of Life is sprinting up the lane, his coat unbuttoned, his hair sizzling and popping about his brow. "I was wrong! I do want to see that quim! I do! I do!"

Audrey squeaks at the sound of the word and covers her mouth as if she'd said it. But Gustine's eyes are fixed on Henry, whose initial look of surprised confusion turns to horror and—oh god, is it fear? She watches his hand go quickly to the center of the young woman's back, watches him practically push her into the theatre, where they disappear into a sea of black coats and lamé turbans, matched earrings, necklaces, and drooping ostrich feathers. From inside they might all laugh at the snow, how it falls in sheets now, upon the bedraggled blue girl standing outside in it, on the one-eyed old woman breathing, breathing behind her, on the half-dressed Student, who on his knees begs her forgiveness—please God, dear lady, we don't have to talk. And please, dear lady, won't you please just come back to work.

VI

ENTERTAINMENT

"Do you know that woman?" Audrey asks as Henry pushes her into the crowded lobby and then stands in the door, blocking everyone's way. Men shoulder past him, women politely pardon themselves, but he cannot tear his eyes from the scene being played across the street: a well-dressed young man pleading with Gustine to come away with him, Gustine furiously shaking her head no; he seizing her hands and peering up into her face like a naughty child begging forgiveness, that old woman over her shoulder (who *is* she to Gustine?), and the girl finally relenting, letting him slowly draw her away, out of the gaslight, around the corner, back into darkness.

"Do you know her?" Audrey asks again, this time more plaintively. Henry turns back to find his fiancée's shortsighted green eyes pleading with him. He forgets how young she is, almost young enough to be his daughter. What is wrong with him?

"No, of course not," he lies. "I thought I recognized the man." He steers her through the crowd and over to the staircase that leads up to Uncle Clanny's box. They are late and his uncle is probably waiting.

"That was dreadful, wasn't it?" Audrey laughs nervously, warming to the dreadfulness of it. "I haven't heard that word since I was in school."

"You shouldn't have heard it tonight," says Henry, horrified she's *ever* heard it. "I'm sorry to have exposed you to it."

"Silly." Audrey taps him with her muff. "As if it were your fault."

But wasn't it? Did she not follow me here? Henry takes Audrey's mantle and hangs it on the peg in the vestibule, knocking on the door to their box and bowing to Uncle Clanny when he reaches over and lets them in. Did she not purposefully seek me out in my personal life? It could not be mere coincidence that she would be passing by at precisely the moment Audrey emerged from the carriage, so close that she might reach out and touch her.

Audrey settles down next to Henry's uncle and politely answers his questions on her mamma's health (better, thank you, for the calomel tablets he prescribed), the status of her father's ship (still quarantined in Riga, they were sad to learn), and where on earth she got that lovely dress. Her papa sent the material from Paris this summer and the trim came from London, she says with a smile, not adding that it pinches her awfully and she can't raise her arms more than a few inches before they go numb, or that she never would have had a dress like this made if she didn't think Henry would find it pleasing.

Henry is listening with only half an ear, ostensibly examining the gallery while he replays the scene outside over and over in his head. Gustine pressed against the wall, staring fixedly at Audrey as if to devour her. That man running half-dressed up the street screaming profanity, practically throwing himself upon her as she watches Henry with a look of—was it triumph? Oh God, groans Henry, what could she mean by that? He is so tired from working on the cadaver Liss for the past few days—getting less than two hours of sleep a night, he cannot think straight. He wanted to work tonight, didn't want to attend this play in the first place, but Uncle Clanny insisted and he knew Audrey was waiting for an opportunity to wear her new dress. And his day is far from over. He promised Audrey that directly after the play he would go see that poor family she discovered this afternoon. The woman who glows in the dark and the baby with the extraordinary heart.

"Darling? Are you all right?" she asks.

He turns to Audrey, dimly lit and lovely in the candlelight. To what ravages has he exposed this trusting creature? And did his own dirty thoughts not compel her here tonight? Has he not a hundred times in the past two days thought of the girl and remembered the feel of her tiny cat ribs? He draws Audrey's hand to his mouth and gently bites the pearl engagement ring he gave her three months ago.

"Yes." He squints at it like an old pawnbroker. "It's real all right."

Audrey laughs delightedly.

He shakes Gustine from his mind and joins Audrey in nodding to the other prominent families of Sunderland. Next to the empty box perpetually reserved for the local aristocracy the Marquis and Marchioness of Londonderry sits Sir William Chaytor, showing himself as much as possible around town with the hopes that when the Reform Bill is passed, Sunderland will elect him its first MP. Another box barely contains the Gourley family: shipbuilder John, his enormous wife Mary, and their erupting young son Edward. Cuthbert Sharp, mayor of nearby Hartlepool and renowned antiquarian, has taken up residence in the box belonging to the Vaux family of wealthy brewers, and next to him sits his placid wife Elizabeth, whose beauty twenty years ago, so the story goes, caused young Cuthbert to steal her and elope.

Audrey has been helping her mother plan a large wedding with relatives coming from as far away as London, but secretly Henry wishes he could tap upon her window one night and whisk her off to Gretna Green, where they might be married without the family's knowledge or handshakes from anyone.

Down in the pit, he sees, the people are growing restless. We are witnessing the end of British Theatre, Henry tells Audrey, when Congreve and Sheridan are sluiced away by the blood-and-guts melodramas written for these people below. When he left London, new auditorium-style theatres were popping up everywhere, designed so that as many as thirty-five hundred might gather to watch mindless equestrian shows or the cataracts of the Nile crash down upon live camels and pachyderms; where a fully commissioned civil war might be waged or love won and lost atop an erupting volcano. How humble and old-fashioned the theatres here in Sunderland are by comparison, so quaintly behind the times they are lit still by candlelight years after others have installed gas. Stagehands spend hours trimming the wicks and wiping the sooted glass chimneys, and still smoke chokes the audience and forces them to mop their brows for the heat. It is safe to say that only the ladies and Henry will regret the passing of candlelit theatres—Henry for nostalgia's sake, the ladies because candlelight is by far kinder upon the female skin than gas or sunlight; it goes gently over blemishes and pits, serving the same purpose here as it does in the market on Saturday night, by which we mean convincing those who are looking that the goods for sale are sound.

The old Theatre Royale is constructed of wood: its floor is wood, its pewlike seats wood, the back walls paneled with wood. The raked stage is widely planked and the orchestra pit parqueted; the columns that support the mezzanine and boxes, too, are wood, though painted red and in disguise. When the people below stomp down the aisles the whole building creaks like an ancient galleon, which illusion is further helped along by the salty, fishful smell caught in the net of their clothing. Smoking is strictly prohibited in this wooden tinderbox, so pipes languish until intermission and snuff is passed about. Coster boys hawk the score of tonight's performance to the musically inclined while entrepreneurial girls walk the pit wearing boxes of oranges like Gothic necklaces around their throats. A girl about Gustine's age glances up and catches Henry's eye. She holds up a plump ripe orange and mouths," Want it?"

Henry's uncle Clanny leans behind Audrey and taps him on the shoulder.

"I was going to send a note around to cancel tonight but you seemed so keen on coming. I think we've had our first indisputable case today."

"Of what?" asks Henry, tearing his eyes away from the girl.

Clanny nods to the gruesomely decorated playbill in his lap: an indigo blue devil prodding the words "Cholera Morbus; or Love and Fright."

"Haselwood called me in to consult," he says. "Yesterday, an old keel man named Sproat collapsed down at the Fish Quay. Thought he ate a bad pork chop, but the symptoms are right: low temperature, rice water stools, cramping and clenching up. Blue eye circles, blue hands and feet."

"Audrey, darling," Henry says at the mention of rice water stools. "Let's switch places so that I might talk medicine with Uncle Clanny."

They rearrange themselves and Henry puts his head next to his uncle's.

"Did you take him to hospital?" he asks.

"Wouldn't go. You know how these people are."

Henry looks down into the stalls, where a sea of These People push and shove, shout for the play to begin, and stomp the floorboards. He feels like he does at the Labour in Vain, like the empty space around These People is a net of invisible disease binding them one to the other, pulling where they pull, thrusting up to the surface where they push together. Is he going crazy or is the very invisibility of air infused with danger tonight?

"When he finally gave up the ghost," continues Clanny, "we had to threaten the widow with the constables to let us remove him for autopsy. National security, you know, but do these people understand?"

Henry looks down on These People with a renewed sense of anger. It seems to him sometimes that they exist solely to interpose themselves between a doctor and his understanding of Science.

"You might sympathize with the widow, Uncle, "says Audrey, having eavesdropped on every word of their conversation. "I cannot imagine what it would mean to part with my Henry's body, should he die before me."

"Men of Science should not be put in a position of begging for bodies," replies her fiancé more sharply than he means. "Especially when we are trying to understand a deadly disease. Do not make us more dependent on these people than we already are. We tell them we need their dead in the interest of England and still they cling to them. We tell them others will die without their help, and they wail about forgoing a wake! We cannot help them if they will not help themselves."

"If the poor are irrational," suggests Audrey hesitantly, "might we not turn to the wealthy?"

Clanny laughs long and deep. "Why not? Let's pop over and ask Lord Londonderry if he wouldn't let us carve up Lady Londonderry and see how far we get!"

Henry kisses the hand of his abashed fiancée. It is not her fault he has made himself dependent on one of These People. It is not her fault he has compromised himself—and possibly her—for a better understanding of how her dear heart beats and how her sweet lungs expand and the mechanics of how her tear ducts overflow when men are cruel. If it would help save her precious life, Henry would throw in his lot with a hundred Gustines. Still, looking down over the dirty crowd in the pit, he feels how horrible it is to be beholden to even one.

"There was a young man in Dublin," he says gaily, hoping to mollify her, "who began a subscription among the upper classes. He persuaded four hundred rich Dubliners to *donate* their bodies in the interest of dispelling ignorant superstitions about autopsy. I fear that until we can persuade four hundred Sunderland worthies to part with their carcasses, we'll never convince the underclasses or anyone else it is a thing worth doing."

"Doctor!"

Both Clanny and Henry rise up in their chairs. From somewhere in the pit, someone is calling for them.

"Hey, Doctor Sawbones!"

Jesus, Henry says under his breath. Something always happens when a play's delayed. Fights break out, children throw up, women get drunk and belligerent on dusty bottles of beer. Let them keep their turbulence to themselves, the miscreants. Audrey looks worriedly at her fiancé, but he whispers disgustedly: Ignore them.

"I see you up there! Which one of you stole my mate from

Mag Scurr's on Saturday night?"

A heavyset man in a fustian jacket and tight knee breeches stands on a bench, shaking his fist at their box. He takes an orange from the orange girl beside him and hurls it at Henry's head. The doctor ducks and it hits the door behind him, filling the box with the citrusy smell of Christmas morning.

"Sit down, you!" shouts Dr. Clanny, rising to his full height and leaning over the railing. "I was at Mag Scurr's on Saturday night and I released a man's body to his daughter. No one stole anything."

The unruly audience has quieted—boys have stopped running in the aisles, daughters and mothers ceased bickering—to watch the altercation; Henry can see them staring at him, some slack-jawed, some hostile and accusing. His thoughts speed to the body in his makeshift operating theatre, the beefy, tattooed cadaver Liss, filleted and labeled on ice, dripping into an empty tin pan beneath the table. Could any of these people put him with Gustine on Saturday night? Would Mag Scurr recognize him and turn him in?

"Mag says me mate's wife showed up an' the body was gone! You gave it to his daughter and her husband took it away! Except the man had no daughter!" shouts the red-faced man in the pit, reaching for another orange. The orange-girl pulls her box away—"Th' ain't free, you know."

"Well, how was I to know he had no daughter?" demands Dr. Clanny in a booming voice. "What reason did I have to doubt her?"

"No reason if you were in league with them!" yells the man. "Blood sucker!"

"Burker!" screams a woman from another part of the audience. "You'd murder the lot of us for your experiments!"

Henry feels all the blood leave his face. It is like Edinburgh all over again, the crowd and the shouting. Should he speak up and put an end to all of this?

"Why won't you let us die in peace?" screams the woman.

"You may, with pleasure, madam, die in peace, if you will but allow us to watch this play in peace." Clanny makes a prepossessing bow. He is used to commanding respect and as he stares down the crowd, his war medals gleaming, the weight of his education and Bishopwearmouth address pressing down upon them, one by one they slowly retake their seats. The orchestra, having sat nervously through the spat, strike up an air, effectively putting an end to it. The pit buzzes among itself but no one dares shout out again, and even the red-faced man on the bench thrusts his fist in his pocket and sits back down. Henry and Clanny had both stiffened at his mention of the pawnshop morgue; now Clanny lets out his breath and wipes his forehead.

"Damn Haselwood," he says. "Sounds like something he would do."

Clanny has been a physician so long, he has heard everything the masses can hurl at him and then some. Henry, sick at the idea of how close he came to ruin, marvels at how steady his uncle's hands are as he pulls out his watch chain and sighs over the time.

"Will this wretched play never start?" he asks.

Those who read the paper this morning know that a gouty letter was written to the *Herald* complaining of the bad taste displayed in mounting this new production when the cholera morbus might, for all we know, be rapping upon our very gates. "Is it to be endured that a visitation of the most alarming and afflicting character should thus become the subject of merriment and ridicule when the voice of public authority calls upon the nation at large to put up prayers in all our churches against the progress of the new plague throughout the land?" The letter seems to have succeeded only in filling the auditorium to twice what it would normally be on a Monday night, and what with tempers inflamed by the preceding shouting match, and anger running high toward doctors, is it any wonder that when the curtains are at last drawn back, the pit erupts with shouts of "Cholera humbug! Cholera humbug!"

Cholera humbug. Could any two words be more musical to the ears of Mr. Eliot, the play's auteur? He looks about him on the stage—at a grim Mr. Mortimer, the troupe's leader, at a crimson Miss Watson, dutifully stepping forward to curtsy to her audience. When Mr. Eliot had presented the script of what was to become "Cholera Morbus; or Love and Fright," venerable Mr. Mortimer had hung his head for shame. Miss Watson, who read the script at her dressmaker's and thus ruined the hem of tonight's green bombazine frock by repeatedly stamping her tidy foot in disgust, swore she would never lend her name to this offensive bit of drivel. It was bad enough when Mr. Eliot wrote a blood-and-guts about the Beamish Coal Mine explosion; she'd suffered through his witticisms on the Lyme Regis Ferryboat tragedy—but to make fun of a fatal disease, one that hubris might very well bring down upon her own pretty brunette head, well, she would be no part of it.

And yet here she is, dressed up as the gentle Laura, ward of the hypochondriac Gripeall. Mr. Eliot himself is playing Gripeall's servant Jeremiah—a smaller part, to be sure, but one which affords the lion's share of laughs. As the troupe's resident playwright, Mr. Eliot might compose for himself any part he wished. King of England? A flourish of the pen and it is done. Patriarch, Pharaoh, Caesar Augustus? Scribble, scribble, scribble. Done! Yet Mr. Eliot is no hog of glory: the princely parts he bestows on Mr. Mortimer, and keeps the servant roles for himself. All the better to hang back and study his work's effect.

But who could have anticipated tonight's wild response? Saturday's opening crowd sat so listlessly still that Mr. Eliot had begun to fear that in fact he had gone too far. Overnight, though, a change has come over Sunderland. "Cholera humbug! Cholera humbug!" Listen to them. They shriek the words, angry and agitated, boxing the air and stomping their feet. From the wings, he'd heard these same furious people shout down the doctors, calling them body snatchers and other foul names. He'd nudged Mr. Webster, who in the second act would portray Timothy Tug, quack physician. Look there, he'd said, nodding up to the boxes. Think you can pull off Dr. Cross of India Medal? *You may, with pleasure, madam, die in peace*, smiled oily Mr. Webster in perfect imitation of William Reid Clanny's faint Ulster brogue, *if you will but allow us to perform our play in peace.*

Two stagehands turn a crank to raise the house chandelier, and as the auditorium grows darker, the cries gradually subside. Opera glasses flash in the boxes, throats are cleared in the stalls; there's rustling and bustling and a general doffing of caps all around. Mr. Eliot cannot resist shooting one glance of triumph at the mortified Miss Watson. He'll write himself up as her husband next time and make her shower him with kisses for the lack of faith she's shown this play.

The opening backdrop of "Cholera Morbus; or Love and Fright" is that of a colonial plantation, lush with painted bamboo and twined with wide-blown tissue flowers in scarlet, violet, and gold. India is the country; the time, one year previous to *this very evening*. Upon a shady verandah are arranged Gripeall (Mr. Mortimer), his lovely ward Laura (downcast Miss Watson), and Gripeall's manservant, Jeremiah (the wiry and wily Mr. Eliot). Like a disgruntled Egyptian slave, Jeremiah, dressed in full English livery, fans his master with oversized peacock feathers, while with his free hand he shoos a native green parrot (played with avian aplomb by one "Patches"). Gripeall, a mean-tempered, miserly hypochondriac, sits wrapped head to foot in blankets, moaning under the gentle circulation of Jeremiah's fan. Cue music, thinks Mr. Eliot, and the orchestra strikes up an Easterny-sounding waltz, full of strings and Shiva-evoking clarinets. Exchange your snowy Sunderland evening, they seem to say, for a sun-drenched afternoon in Madras. Cue actors—Mr. Eliot looks down at Mr. Mortimer, who dramatically sneezes and blows his nose. Let the play begin!

GRIPEALL:

O why did I ever travel to darkest India? Tell me, Jeremiah! Why suffer the tortures of Climate? The stings of Insecta? The outrageous effronteries of Flora and Fauna? (Here swoops Parrot at his bald head.) Good God! Why have I, who am used to good English beef and puddings (in Moderation as per orders of my doctor, Sir Timothy Tug), been made to subsist on Rice, seasoned with the popular curries of this country: Typhus, Plague, Malaria, Putrid Fevers, Gangrene—

JEREMIAH:

Don't forget the Bombay Runs!

Mr. Eliot is gratified to hear thunderous laughter and applause from the audience.

GRIPEALL:

Let us speak not of these Dread Sauces, Jeremiah! You know how I fear them falling upon my food. They fright me nearly to death.

LAURA:

Come, come, dear Uncle. You are in excellent health. As for venturing to India, have you forgotten it was to fetch home poor me, whose beloved mother and father both perished in this beautiful yet unpredictable country? (Here, a Cobra—played by a Tame Garden Snake in a hood—is let loose to slither across stage.)

Mr. Eliot is cheered by Screams from the ladies in the Audience.

GRIPEALL:

Had your foolish mother, my sister, not run off with a soldier, Laura, lo those eighteen years ago, I would not be suffering in this condition.

LAURA:

Forgive her, dear Uncle. My parents were so very much in love. Would that I would ever find one to love *me* so.

GRIPEALL:

Would that you would not, wicked child. You are to nurse me for the few remaining years of my life, as was our bargain when I agreed to come for you.

LAURA:
(looking longingly away) Yes, Uncle.

While the others continue talking, Mr. Eliot sets down his peacock fan and crosses downstage to retrieve Gripeall's silver platter of pills. How he detests these old-fashioned tallow theatres with their dirty flickering candles. Critics complain that actors fall over each other to play at the edge of the stage, where, lit from below, even the sweetest ingenue appears hellish and infernal. But what are they to do? In tallow theatres center stage is a shadowy void that neither foot, overhead, nor shuttered sidelights can seem to penetrate. They must play in a straight line downstage, like prating hieroglyphics, just to be seen!

Mr. Eliot feels the heat of candles on his chin as he bends over for Gripeall's tray. He sneaks a peek at the front rows, at his people, as he's come to think of them tonight. Times *are* changing. The people, *his* people, are done with court foppery and aristocratic infidelity, finished with comedies full of words they don't understand. The new breed of playwrights, bold men like myself, thinks Mr. Eliot, thrusting his buttocks as high into the air as they will go, are writing to their tastes. He asked a man on the street just the other day—a man very like the rough gentleman in the front row who sits gnawing off and spitting out bits of fingernail—what it was the working class most wanted to see. Love and murder suits us best, sir (said the man on the street), but of late, I think there is a good deal more liking of tragedies among us.

Mr. Eliot takes a few steps upstage to Gripeall, who shivers under his mountain of blankets. Eat up, he says. The audience roars as the old hypochondriac takes a pill for each imaginary ailment, fifty-five in total—a pill to guard against Reform-itis, another to protect him from Parliamentari-osis, yet one more to ward off Old King George Cuckold Croup. With each more elaborate disease, named for scandals and popular novels, famous criminals and fallen monarchs, the workingmen and -women in the pit shriek with laughter and gratify Mr. Eliot with suggestions of their own. "How about a pill for Quarantine Ass-Ache!" yells the man in the front row. "Give us a remedy for Board of Health Ballocks Boils!" The hilarity swells until Gripeall has but one last pill left upon his tray. It is an enormous blue ball, the size of a walnut.

GRIPEALL:
Pray, Jeremiah. What is this pill for?

JEREMIAH:
Why, don't you know? It's for that most Dread Disease of all. It is for—

Mr. Eliot indulges in a huge wink to the audience.

JEREMIAH:
—the Cholera Humbug!

The pit explodes with wild applause and shouts are heard from every corner: "Cholera Humbug! Cholera Humbug!"

GRIPEALL:
Cholera Humbug? I've never heard of it. What are its symptoms?

JEREMIAH:

Well, we have it not yet in England, but abroad it has
been said to Starve the Poor, Ruin the Tradesman,
Fright the Rich, and Turn Men Blue.

GRIPEALL:

Blue, you say?

JEREMIAH:

Yes, blue. But have no fear, m' lord. It hunts only them
that are so wretched they can afford no food for their
bellies, and it kills only them poor saps who yearn to be
free men. You are already inoculated from Cholera
Humbug. You have the Right to Vote!

"Reform!" screams the audience. "Reform, not Humbug!"

GRIPEALL:

Give me the pill anyway, Jeremiah. A man can never be
too sure.

JEREMIAH:

Whatever you say, m' lord.

As Gripeall reaches for the pill, Patches the parrot swoops
down and takes it. After a series of choreographed dives, the
parrot lands on Jeremiah's silver tray, rolls onto its back with
its claws in the air, and plays dead.

Bravo, parrot! Bravo!

"Look, it killed the parrot!" screams the man who had
challenged the doctors. "Look what use their pills are!"

Listen to them, thinks Mr. Eliot, jubilantly. My "Cholera

Morbus" is an unbridled success! He glances off stage right
to where Mr. Webster is making his entrance. The portly
quack physician is decked out in a coat of saws and knives,
hung in such a way that he might not turn around without
causing the other actors to leap back in alarm. His top hat is
stenciled about with skull and crossbones, his pockets bulge
with pills, and prominently displayed upon his chest is a
hastily constructed pasteboard replica of the Sunderland
doctor's India medal! Bravo, Webster! Bravo!

"Did someone call for a doctor?" brays Mr. Webster in
Clanny's Irish lilt.

And in that instant of recognition, the audience releases a
cry that a playwright hears but once or twice in his career. It's
the subtle moment when hilarity jumps a pitch to hysteria,
when the audience suddenly hears in its own applause the
shattering of windows and the cracking of skulls. Miss
Watson glances over worriedly. She has the next line, but the
crowd is so loud she cannot be heard. Let them shout, glories
Mr. Eliot. After opening night of the ferryboat tragedy in
Lyme Regis, en masse the audience stormed a corrupt shipbuilder's and set his warehouse on fire. He can't help scanning
the boxes to note the impression his comedy has made on the
doctors. The young one, furious, is on his feet; the girl (well,
he's sorry about her) has fallen back in what looks to be a
faint. The old doctor, though—old Cross of India –wearing,
body-snatching, burking doctor that he is—sits rigidly
upright, as contemptuous and calm as if the whole theatre
did not demand his blood.

But then, just as suddenly, the shout changes again, and
now Mr. Eliot grows worried. Is it a note of panic he detects?
One woman—he can see her quite clearly, off to his left, fifth
row from the front—has leapt upon her bench in horror,

flapping her arms like a demented bird. She shrieks long after the rest of the audience has quieted in alarm, shrieks so long and loud, in fact, that her neighbors in the pit move away to clear a space for her. She is pointing to the ground, where a man lies, a man she's never met before but who was sitting beside her and who, just as Mr. Webster took the stage, vomited quietly into his cap. While the others were shouting down the doctor, he had tried in vain to struggle from his seat and make his way up the aisle, but had, to the woman's horror, collapsed at her feet in convulsions. Now his bowels have let loose and a horrible stench pervades the pit.

"Please someone help!" screams the woman. "This man is dying!"

Is this someone's idea of a joke? scowls Mr. Eliot. He looks over at fat, crestfallen Mr. Webster. The quack's saws and knives quiver, sweat runs down his cheeks and drips onto his pasteboard Cross of India medal. It is not very witty to make fun of doctors when a man is dying in the audience. He is put completely out of his part. Quick, Eliot, he hisses, what are we to do?

But Eliot too is at a loss. He turns upstage to Mr. Mortimer and Miss Watson. With a withering look at the two men, intrepid Miss Watson sweeps to the lip of the stage. She, too, had overheard the altercation between the pit and the doctors in the box, had felt for the elderly physician who had stood up to the crowd. Her father, before turning actor, had studied medicine, and as a girl at dinner she'd sat upon his medical books so that she might reach the table. Now she bends her pretty knee, stretches her white arms beseechingly up to the boxes, and calls out in her most becoming trage-dienne voice: Doctors! Oh please, is there not a doctor in the house?

*

"Don't go," says Henry sharply as his uncle rises. "They don't deserve you."

He'd watched his uncle's proud face blanch when that mincing bit of fatty tissue had taken the stage, speaking in his voice, sporting a tasteless sham of his medal, and had wanted to leap from his box to throttle the lot of them. What does his uncle owe this crowd? They need him until the moment he makes a mistake, and then they will turn on him and tear him to pieces. Henry has seen it. Back in Edinburgh, after the murderer Burke had been executed and Hare had fled, the mob came after his mentor, Dr. Knox, who had not been indicted. They hung him in effigy outside his house at 10 Surgeons' Square and, with Henry watching from the window, fell upon the doll like a pack of wild dogs. The constables came, and the crowd grew hotter, smashing the windows, hurling stones and screaming, Burker! Burker! They ran through the city, scattering and regrouping in elegant Princes Street, welling up in lowly West Port, where the sixteen murders had been committed. Back at 10 Surgeons' Square, Dr. Knox sat haughtily in broken glass, watching them try to light his greenwood trees on fire, and Henry, standing behind him, understood then—no matter how guilty you may be, it is still better to be one against the crowd.

Audrey is crying quietly in the chair beside him. He sees the other wealthy members of Sunderland society craning in their boxes, so much more excited by this turn of events than they had been by the tedious play. Down below, a hundred resentful, fearful faces stare up at him, each one mutely commanding—save him, you bloody bastard; save him or we will rip you limb from limb. Can his uncle not see it is unsafe to go downstairs? They are just waiting for us to make a mistake so that they might devour us.

"For God's sake, help him, Uncle," Audrey sobs into her handkerchief. Dr. Clanny smoothes his coattails, straightens his India medal, and walks to the door.

"Don't!" shouts Henry, throwing his arm out to block his exit. "They have humiliated you. They want to hurt you."

Clanny smiles at his young nephew. "In my day, we used to fight them at the gallows for their hanged men. The relatives bit and punched and tried to rip them out of our hands, but we had the right. I know how to handle myself with the mob, son. You must believe in what you do."

Henry steps back and watches his uncle make his way downstairs to the pit. Inside the auditorium, the men and women who only moments before were calling him burker and body snatcher step aside so that he might pass unmolested. The woman on the bench shrieks again, and now Henry can see it is because the convulsing man has hold of her ankle.

"Please, back away," Dr. Clanny commands the curious coster boys who crowd around him. The stricken man is half under the fourth row of benches, his knees drawn into his chest, his elbows striking staccato against the wooden floor. He will not release the woman's ankle and it is beginning to swell from lack of circulation, turning bulbous and blue under her white stockings. She screams and screams until Henry is sure his uncle will strike her, but instead he brings his mouth close to the patient's clinched hand and bites it— hard. The hand flexes for less than an instant, but long enough for the woman to lurch away and fall heavily off the bench behind her.

Clanny feels about for a pulse, shakes his head, and shouts up to his nephew in the box.

"Henry!" he calls. "I need you."

Henry takes the stairs two at a time; he would have leapt over the box to help, for, in truth, a deep sense of shame had come over him waiting upstairs with Audrey. The smell of the patient is overwhelming when he reaches the pit, and even accustomed as he is to the stench of decaying cadaver Liss, Henry finds it difficult to choke back his rising vomit. The sick man's face is contorted and his eyes are sunk deep in their sockets, but something about him seems familiar.

"You, you, you, and you," Dr. Clanny singles out four strong men in the audience. "Carry this body out into the lobby."

The workingmen, used to taking orders, obediently rise and lift the patient. The ill man throws back his head and groans through thin blue lips, "Put me down."

Henry unties his cravat and wraps it around his mouth and nose to keep from choking. Where has he seen this man before?

"Where ayr takin' me mate?" demands the red-faced man in the fustian jacket who had challenged Clanny earlier. He has pushed his way through the crowd and now lunges for them. "Where ayr you takin' Jack?"

"To hospital," answers Dr. Clanny.

"Over my dead body," the man says, and plants himself so that the four men might not maneuver around him. "No one who goes in there comes out alive."

"That's ridiculous," Henry sneers, though his contempt is lost beneath his wrapped cravat. "You people never come until it's too late, and then you blame us for not working miracles."

"You don't even wait for people to die in there before you cut them up," the man growls. "And when you're done, you feed what's left to your dogs."

"Stand back and let us pass," commands Dr. Clanny, nodding for the men to move forward. "If this man has cholera morbus he needs immediate attention."

"Take him to his house, then," counters Fustian.

"We don't know if this disease is contagious," says Clanny. "It could kill his whole family."

"He touched me!" screams the lady whose ankle had been grabbed. "He's killed me with his Cholera Humbug!"

"We don't know if he has cholera," Henry tries to calm her." We won' t know until we take him to hospital."

"If he's going to that hellhouse, I'm goin' with him," declares Fustian. "This man is a national treasure. This is Jack Crawford, hero of Camperdown you're lugging."

So that's it, thinks Henry. Jack Crawford. I've been looking at this man's face tattooed on cadaver Liss's fleshy left biceps for the last three days.

"You are not allowed in unless you are ill," Clanny frowns. "A hospital is not a circus."

"They won't let you go, Bob," yells the woman who called Dr. Clanny a burker, "because they're using this cholera as just another excuse to hack up our loved ones!"

"He's not goin' if I'm not goin'." Bob, as Fustian seems to be known, bears menacingly down on Henry. Clanny looks worried, and poor Jack Crawford is groaning in pain.

"Have it your way, "Henry says at last. "Come along. If you have the stomach."

The theatre is absolutely silent. It was all too easy, and Bob, who has no desire to set foot inside a hospital, looks searchingly around the pit. He can't go there—walk all alone into their territory. There in that dark and lonely place, at the mercy of their saws and scalpels, he too might "develop" cholera and need to be taken apart limb by limb.

What if neither Jack *nor* he comes out alive?

"Witness, my friends!" he shouts with such a ringing note of pathos, the actors onstage are jealous. "I leave here a well man. Sound in mind and body, possessed of both arms and legs. Witness—my head attached. If I come not back, revenge me, friends, and revenge poor sick Jack Crawford!"

Henry motions impatiently for them to be off, and together he and his uncle lead a groaning Jack Crawford through the crowd. Red-faced, contentious, fustian Bob follows the procession with his hat in his hands, his eyes fixed straight ahead on the highwater mark of his mortality. Jesus, why can't he keep his fat mouth shut?

"Ladies and gentlemen, we have a play to perform," Mr. Eliot announces, but it is a good ten minutes before the audience ceases its buzzing and quiets down. What a demoralizing turn of events, he sighs, changing offstage into his costume for the final act. He fumbles into his blue hose and laces up his blue doublet. To have them so completely in his power and then lose them to a whiff of disease. Fickle, fickle, wretched crowd. He yanks on his blue boots and fastens the clasp of his blue cape. A few minutes more and he would have had that mob at the doctor's doorstep, dismantling his house brick by brick, banging their foreheads against his windows and tearing apart his sofa cushions with their teeth. Mr. Eliot stands before a rudely hung mirror and smears his face with blue grease-paint, wipes his hands on a shammy, and draws on a pair of elbow-length blue leather gloves. Instead, at the first sign of illness, they are begging, whinging creatures, groveling on their bellies before the gods of medicine. Through a gap between the curtains and proscenium, he can see straight up into the boxes, high above the pit, protected from the contagion of the crowd. The woman who accompanied the doctors has moved to the box of another rich family, and now wilts among them, cosseted and kissed. You will have to get used to it, he can imagine they are telling her (all the while urging sips of ripe brandy), if you plan to become a doctor's wife.

Mr. Eliot finishes his makeup and pulls on a blue cavalier hat, complete with curling blue feather. He makes his way down the narrow, dark steps to the trap below stage. Pushing his body up through the hole in the floor, he squeezes into a box, fitting his head inside the tight dome at the top. He has written the scene so that Gripeall, who has barricaded himself in his room for fear of the cholera morbus, will lift the lid from his tray of food and find upon it the head of Jeremiah, in disguise as the blue disease. There are holes cut strategically around the stage. Jeremiah as Cholera Morbus will peek in at the window. He will drop down from the beams. He will slither out from beneath Gripeall's bed and sit upon his chest, scaring him finally to death. If tonight has witnessed the humiliation of Mr. Eliot the playwright, critics in the audience will later report that this night saw a great actor born. As he hounds Gripeall to his ultimate demise, he will be all ferocity, all confusion, all unexpectedness, all death.

Mr. Eliot hunkers in the dark cramped space below stage, waiting for his cue to spring. Tomorrow the newspapers will be full of him. In the role of counterfeited Cholera Morbus, one reporter will write, Mr. Eliot so terrified us that four grown men ran screaming from the theatre, while a woman of the lower orders went directly into labour, delivered of a son, eight pounds, three ounces. *I am* Cholera Morbus, Mr. Eliot finally roars, pointing a long blue finger. *And I am coming for you!*

*

Jack Crawford wakes in a theatre.

God knows how long he's been unconscious; he remembers only laughing at a fat doctor dressed up in saws, and then nothing until he opened his eyes on a glass-fronted cabinet full of the same implements, directly in front of him. It is a shadowy, close theatre he finds himself in, with eight or ten tiers of benches arranged in a circle about him. The stage floor has been strewn with sawdust, the walls hung with strange skeletal and muscular backdrops of the human body. Two players move slowly, performing stage business with tubes and beakers, pausing every once in a while to pour a kettle of steaming water into a tub next to him. He is at center stage, is Jack Crawford, and it takes him a minute to realize he must be starring in a play about his own life. Oh yes, it's all coming back now. The premise—unlikely as it may be—is that Jack Crawford, sot of Sunderland, climbs the mast of the HMS *Venerable* with a marling spike to nail up Admiral Duncan's colors when the Dutch attack off the coast of Ireland. The Hero of Camperdown, as he is now called, is presented at court for his bravery and awarded thirty pounds a year. Back home they begin to paint him on pots and stencil him onto pearly pink pitchers; soon he finds himself on nearly every mantelpiece in the East End and shipped off for export to Norway and America. But then the years begin to pass, and over a pint (and then another) Jack contemplates his own fraudulence. Jesus Christ, he never wanted to be on the HMS *Venerable*. He was grabbed by the Press Gang on the way to a pub on Pottery Bank and pointedly invited to join the Royal Navy. Aboard ship, he was whipped and sodomized, threatened with court martial and practically pushed up that pole with the colors between his teeth; then, when the smoke cleared and Admiral Duncan realized improbably that he had won, young Jack was raised up shamelessly as a hero. He knew he was naught but a shill for George's government, a working-class hero to gain sympathy among the poor for a most unpopular war. Will the audience be surprised, then, when thirty years and however many pints later, poor Jack Crawford finds less solace in his heroism than in the drink?

And here he is in Act V of his life, a tragic end for a tragic hero. His performance must've stunk, for he sees he's driven the entire audience away, all except one man, who slouches in the second row with his great wide head in his hands.

The younger player leans over him and places a cool tube of glass under his tongue. Jack falls asleep again, and when he wakes the bit of glass is being removed and the player is shaking his head.

"Eighty-four degrees," Henry says. "And the external temperature has dropped to seventy."

"Let's get him in the bath," sighs Doctor Clanny.

"Jack," Henry says, clasping the old man beneath the shoulders. "We are going to lift you now. Can you grab hold?"

"May I go home?" the old hero croaks, and his breath is icy against Henry's cheek.

"Not quite yet."

"He wants to go home! Did you hear him?" The lone audience member leaps up from the second row. How long are they going to keep him in this fiendish operating theatre? Hung round with skeletons and pictures of skeletons—it's enough to drive a perfectly healthy man to his grave, much less poor liquor-soaked Jack Crawford. "He asked to go home!"

"Not yet," says Clanny over his shoulder. "He's still too ill."

They have been working on Jack Crawford for a good eight hours now, trying first to restore his circulation and then to ease his stomach spasms. His symptoms were most severe the first few hours, when the old hero was convulsing at a clocked rate of once every ten minutes. Nothing Henry had ever seen had prepared him for this disease, and its progress has been almost unbearable to watch. In great heaving waves the old hero would vomit basinfuls of gruely white flocculent matter, the color of soap in hard water. Sometimes he would collapse back into sleep, sometimes the purging would start anew. Over the course of his convulsions it became less violent and more pathetic, just a helpless oozing of white jelly-like pus from the buttocks. His uncle collected it in a pan and when they sniffed it for clues, neither could come up with a word to describe it. "Fusty" was the closest Henry got. It had the distilled aroma of every dilapidated back lane lodging house he had ever visited, a damp, mildewy smell, as if the man were spoiling from the inside out.

But the tetanus spasms were what finally drove them to banish Robert Cooley (as they learned Bob, formerly Fustian, was more properly called) to the benches of the operating theatre. They were horrible to behold. Like panicked mice running the length of his body, the contractions would start at the sick man's toes and race up the legs to his groin; would start in his fingertips and flee down the arms to his chest. Faster and faster they'd try to outrun each other until poor Jack Crawford became one anguished, protracted spasm, jack-knifing across the operating table, only the top of his head and his heels touching the surface. Clanny and Henry would fall on him, trying to hold him in place, while his friend,

Robert Cooley, screamed every profanity known to working-men. Henry's own calves would start to cramp in sympathy— he could feel the long muscles charley-horsing into knots as he watched his uncle pour medicine down Jack Crawford's constricted throat. *You are poisoning him!* Robert Cooley banged the table. *What are you giving him?* Laudanum and brandy, you misbegotten creature. Now go sit down, you are tormenting this patient.

Jack Crawford is now in the third and usually final phase of the disease, what the doctors who first studied cholera in India termed "the cold blue stage." Henry had read of it, but never thought it would manifest itself so literally. The disease has pummeled Jack's face, leaving it a bruised black-and-blue; the old hero's hands have gone from a freckled white to a deep indigo; his feet have turned blue as if stained with woad. With no fluid to keep it plump, his skin has shriveled and his dry eyes have receded into his head. The constant spasms have so contorted his back and spine that he has become like a hunched old man. It is the most horrible aspect of the disease. Cholera has aged Jack Crawford forty years in a few short hours and turned him into his own grandfather before their very eyes.

"Here we go," says Clanny, gently lowering the sick man into the steaming tub of water. If they can only get his temperature up, he may have a chance. But Clanny and Henry barely have him an inch into the bath before he cries out pathetically.

"It's torture!" Jack Crawford wheezes.

"Acid! You're putting my mate in a vat of acid!" Robert Cooley leaps up and crashes over a row of benches to get at the doctors. "It's his bones you want, isn't it? You only care about his bones!"

"Damn it, man!" Henry roars, struggling to support Jack's dead weight above the surface of the water. "You saw us fill this tub with that very kettle. You saw me pour a pot of tea from it not even an hour ago and drink it. Your friend cries out because he is so cold, even tepid water will feel like a thousand degrees to him. We need to elevate his body temperature or he will certainly die."

Robert Cooley looks uncertain, but, unwilling to test the acid water on his own beefy forearm, he sits sullenly back down.

The doctors ease England's whimpering hero of Camperdown farther into the bath and set his arms on either side of the tub to keep his head from going under. We can leave him in for fifteen or twenty minutes, Clanny says. Let's rest ourselves by the fire.

Henry shovels a few more coals onto the brazier and pulls a hard, cane-backed chair next to his uncle's. Robert Cooley sits all alone in the shadowy operating theatre, where many a surgeon-to-be has dozed through lectures on the palmaris brevis of the hand or the thirty pairs of nerves that originate in the backbone's dorsal medulla. The man looks like he could use some sleep, but Henry knows that, for fear of having a plaster slapped across his nose and mouth, Cooley won't shut an eye. It's strange. Henry has practically grown up in rooms like this, has never thought of an operating theatre as a fearful place, but he can see how to a simple man like Robert, a suspicious man, this auditorium must appear a house of horrors. Is he more frightened of floating fetuses in specimen jars arranged neatly on bookcases, Henry wonders, or of the human skeletons, dark brown and oily-looking, suspended by delicate cords of silk? The paneled walls are decorated with prints by the master dissector/illustrator

Albinus, of bug-eyed muscle men flexing their exposed tendons in front of felled Corinthian columns, of animated skeletons (front and back view) posed before grazing rhinoceroses. Henry has always looked at them and seen the Lesser sciatic notch, the Occipitalis, the Flexor Hallucis Longus, isolated muscle and bone he would have to identify on a test. Seen through Robert Cooley's eyes, though, the engravings are rather macabre—all these flayed reanimated carcasses cavorting through Arcadia. No wonder he's afraid to go to sleep.

Henry reaches out for the ceramic cup of tea he left on the hearth after their last break. The handle has stayed hot next to the fire, but the liquid inside is cold. Having worked two solid days on the corpse Gustine procured for him, and now staying up all night with Jack Crawford, he is on the point of collapse. It is hard to keep from shaking as he drinks his cold tea.

"We need to alert the Board in London," Clanny says, leaning back in his chair with his eyes closed. "I would imagine they'll lock us down even tighter."

All summer the debate over Quarantine had raged. The merchants and landowners led by Lord Londonderry argued against it—self-servingly saying that a suspension of trade could only further bankrupt the poor and drive them more rapidly to their deaths. Clanny and a good number of the other doctors, backed by the London Board of Health and thus His Majesty, claimed it was their only protection. They'd all read the numbers in the newspaper: thirty thousand dead in Cairo in twenty-four hours, five hundred cases a day in Saint Petersburg, anti–doctor poison riots in Hungary, Paris, and Berlin. Cholera morbus must not be allowed into the realm. This was a disease to enrage the peo-

ple, to bring down governments, and with Reform Riots
already flaring in Nottingham and Bristol, His Majesty
decided it in the country's best interest to quarantine all
incoming vessels.

"What do you think they'll do?" asks Henry. His uncle
shakes his head.

"Did you read the latest Sanitary Code? 'It may be necessary to draw troops around infected areas, so as to utterly
exclude the inhabitants from all intercourse with the rest of
the country.'"

"Londonderry will never stand for it. He needs to sell his
coal."

"Then let him take responsibility for the pestilence."

Clanny stretches his long legs toward the fire. "Do you
remember back in August when Dr. Dixon called me in to
look at that keelman Robert Henry? We thought he had the
summer diarrhea, but twenty hours later, he died of it. And
earlier this month, that girl . . . what was her name—
Hazzard? Only twelve years old and dead after twelve hours.
I think the cholera has been here since the summer. I think
it's been moving among us for months.

"For that matter, who knows how many of them have died
without our even knowing it?" Clanny continues. "They don't
trust us, so they don't send for us. Our behaviour is as responsible for the spread of this disease as anything else."

Henry looks over at Robert Cooley, sitting watchfully in
the second row. Why *would* they trust us? We bully them, con-
fuse them, experiment on their kidney stones in hospitals no
respectable person would consider entering. We dig up their
bodies, steal them from their parlours, hire desperate men to
murder them while they sleep. It is a wretched business being
a doctor, thinks Henry. But what else are we to do?

"I have a theory," Clanny interrupts his meditations. "On why they turn blue."

"What is it?"

"Too much carbon in the bloodstream." Clanny sits up when his nephew doesn't answer. "Think about it. Blood changes from bright red to blue when carbon swallows all the oxygen. All summer and into the autumn it was so humid— now it is cold, but still damp. Atmospheric pressure forces the free carbon back into the body where it cannot be properly expelled. It's why we are so languid and unnerved in July and August."

"So you think it is atmospheric rather than contagious?" Henry asks, slightly confused by his uncle's theorizing.

"I'm not saying it's *not* contagious. But it may not be imported. The atmosphere in Sunderland could be responsible for its generation; men could be responsible for its spread."

"I don't know, Uncle."

"I don't know either," says Clanny, "but I'm certain of one thing. I'm going to sleep with the doors and windows cracked at least an inch until this passes over."

Henry smiles at the old man and puts his feet up on the bags of bran they have warming before the fire. Clanny likes to blame everything from gout to broken collarbones on the weather. Henry's seen the long, cramped lists he keeps in his office here in the Infirmary, pages and pages filled with discourses on climate—*Saturday, the 15th: much lightning, wind from the WSW. Sunday, the 16th: cloudy and mild*. Henry would not deny carbon might well play a part—it's as good a hypothesis as any other—but he can't help feeling it's exactly the sort of ungrounded, theoretical guess a doctor of Clanny's sort would make. He and his uncle were trained so very differently, after all. Clanny, studying to become a high-paid physician, took most of his education from books. He read the classics, observed in hospital wards, studied his materia medica to prescribe pills. If he took any anatomy at all, it consisted of sitting once or twice in a lecture hall while a demonstrator held up a brain and pointed to the medulla oblongata. Henry, coming up fifteen years behind him, took a radically different course of study. He knew he would never make as much money training as a surgeon, but he couldn't help feeling anatomy was the way of the future. You would not expect to know how a clock works merely from studying its face; you would need to open its door, examine the complex interaction of springs and gears, observe how, in the telling of time, it releases its tightly wound tension. But you might take a million clocks apart and have no one weep for them. Taking apart a poor man was another matter.

"Mr. Cooley?" Henry turns around in his chair. "Would you like to join us by the fire?"

Mr. Cooley looks up startled. Neither of them have said a word but to yell at him for the past eight hours. Why the sudden pleasantry?

"I'd like to sit with my friend," he says at last.

"You may stand by the tub," Clanny consents. "But don't say a word that might disturb him."

The awkward man in his fustian jacket and too tight knee breeches struggles down from the observation benches and walks over to his friend. Jack's naked body is dim under the water, but thin—as thin as Starvation himself. If Bob hadn't come in here with them, he would've sworn the sawbones had swapped his mate for this horrible old man in the tub. His skin is wrinkled and an awful mottled color; his hands, dangling over the edge, are turned in on the wrist and clenched into claws. His eyes are closed, but his lids are so weirdly sunk, you might see the very hollowness of the sockets like them that's on the skeletons hanging about this awful place. Aw, Jack. First Reg taken from old Mag Scurr's down on the Quay, and now you. Who's left for a man to lift a pint with?

"There's no need to cry, Mr. Cooley," Clanny says, coming over. "You must stay optimistic. Doctors are always optimistic; it's why we rarely catch the diseases we treat."

The old doctor slips a thin tube of glass under Jack's tongue and studies his pocket watch. At the prescribed time, he removes the glass and squints at it.

"It's barely come up five degrees," he announces sadly. "And he's chilled the water. Let's get him under the bags."

"Mr. Cooley." Henry taps the woebegone friend on the shoulder. "You may be of help by ferrying those sacks of bran from in front of the fire. When we lay your friend on the table, place them immediately on top of him."

The doctors reach into the tub and lift the slippery eel of a hero out and back onto the table. Obedient Robert carefully covers him with hot bags of bran, while Henry retrieves the rest and builds a steaming barricade around him. Working beneath the bags, the doctors bind Jack's still twitching calf muscles with clean white handkerchiefs and apply a mustard poultice to his chest. Like shall cure like, says Clanny, feeding him his hourly dose of ipecacuanha in brandy to induce vomiting and expel the poison more quickly.

"It's time to bleed him again," he says. "Maybe there will be some change."

The tiny lancets they used to prick him stick like feeding metal mosquitoes in the tabletop. Henry tugs one out and prepares to make a small incision in the vein that runs from the left leg to the abdomen. As blood letting is one of medicine's most powerful remedies, and hemorrhage one of its worst calamities, this important art must be exactingly executed. A patient should be bled to the point of fainting syncope without accidentally being brought to dissolution. He must never be bled in a horizontal position, but always upright, for as long as the head remains above the heart, fainting will occur before cardiac failure, and thus alert the surgeon that enough blood has been taken. Take too little blood and nothing is gained; take too much and the patient sinks even unto death.

While his uncle arranges the warm bran sacks to support the head, Henry feels about for the vein. He cuts sure and deep, holding the cup to catch the spurting fountain of red. But to Henry's astonishment, where he'd expected warm blood to gush, only a black trickle weeps from the cut. The blood that does flow from the vein wanders in two streams, side by side. One, dark as treacle, is thick and tenacious; the other, bright and of thinner consistence, runs along with greater velocity. Henry has never seen anything like it

"Take these off!" Jack Crawford startles them all by suddenly lashing out at the hot bran bags that cover him. He kicks so hard, Henry's lancet flies through the air and clatters across the wooden floor. What strange turn is this? The hero of Camperdown, only moments ago in a complete state of collapse, is struggling off the table, trying to get to his feet. He is striking out at Henry, at Clanny, who rushes over to calm him. "I feel fine," Jack rasps. "Is there nothing to eat in this bloody place?"

"Jack!" Robert Cooley pushes the old doctor aside and gathers his friend in his arms. "Ach, God, I knew you'd get better."

"Help me home," the old man begs.

"This is a trick of the disease," Clanny declares, trying to draw the patient back onto the table; but Robert Cooley has gotten his shoulder under his friend's armpit and is pulling him toward the door.

"You tried, you bloody burker," shouts Robert, supporting the weak-kneed hero. "You tried to kill him. But he is too strong."

"Look at his eyes," Clanny shouts back. "Look at his tongue."

The corneas of Jack Crawford's dry eyes are albumin-dull and cloudy, it is true, and the red vessels frizzing out from the iris are engorged with blood. The veins terminate abruptly, having no network, just a tangle of crazed dead ends. When Clanny grasps his chin and forces his mouth open, the old hero's tongue is woolly with white fur. Still, would a dying man cry out for a pork chop as Jack does now? Would he bellow for a pint of beer? Robert will not risk it.

"You will kill him for sure if you move him!" Henry rushes the pair, but Robert Cooley throws out a fist that sends him sprawling.

"C'mon, Jack," he whispers to his friend. "We'll get you to yer own bed, and get 'cher wife t'fry up a chop or two. You'll be better in no time."

"Mr. Cooley!" Clanny shouts, but the man has already dragged his friend through the door and halfway down the cold marble hallway. Clanny snatches up a lamp and runs after them. Henry grabs his bag and is fast on his uncle's heels.

The hallway is as cold as a tomb and smells of lemon oil and sawdust—and something else that bothers Robert Cooley as he rounds the corner and searches for the marble steps to the first floor: the fresh iron smell of blood. He knows the smell; his house overlooks the slaughterhouse on

Queen Street where the still pumping hearts of cattle are cut from their chests and sold, wholesale, to the sugar refinery. Does blood fill every one of these rooms? he wonders, turning away from the dark lecture chambers that open off the main hallway and branch off into more raked amphitheatres. The evenly spaced wall sconces shine only enough light into the rooms to coax operating tables into the shapes of wild beasts whose hearts beat to the rhythm of Robert's frantic footfall. Come on, Jack, he thinks. Help me. You are too heavy.

But he knows it—even before he finds the steps and jolts his friend down to the first landing—he knows as the naked body slides from his arms, as white and languid as the snow settling on the windowpane beside him: the doctors have won. His friend hardens upon touching the ground, like a puddle of warm white spittle turned instantly to ice; his legs snap straight, his arms strain to break their bones, even his cock—Jesus Christ—stretches like a piece of India rubber, explodes onto his belly, and quivers back into place. The doctors have won.

Clanny sets the lamp on the landing and both men fall to work on the old hero. Clanny is fumbling in a leather bag, pushing a set of bellows into Jack Crawford's mouth and making his chest inflate and deflate, inflate and deflate like a jerky machine. Henry is listening. Listening. Goddamn it. The man probably would have died anyway, but at least he wouldn't have to die naked in a stairwell like some raped and abandoned housemaid. After a few minutes more, Henry lifts his head from the old man's straining chest.

"He's gone," Henry says, kneeling helplessly back. Robert Cooley watches, also on his knees, his fists pressed against his mouth to keep back that low wail building up inside him.

As for Jack Crawford, he's had about as much playacting as he can stand. He's sick to death of performing his part over and over for this meagre audience. Here he is again clinging to the mast while cannons fire all around him. The admiral's blue flag snaps in his face, is nearly ripped from his hands by the fury of the wind. He doesn't want to climb; his thighs cramp fiercely from grasping the pole, his arms are in knots from clutching the marling spike. All he wants is a pint. But Admiral Duncan's second in command has a musket trained on him—*They shot away our mast, lad. We mustn't let the Dutchies think we've hauled down our colors. We are no cowards!*

We are no cowards, thinks brave Jack Crawford, trembling around the pole. He shimmies higher and higher, until he's above the smoke and can see the enemy ship parallel to them. Dutchmen swab the mounted cannons and load them with heavy nicked balls. Officers raise their sabres and shout commands. Fire! Down below, the world seems so dark and confused, but up here above it all, the sky is an improbable brilliant blue. It is a crisp October afternoon, one that back home might have inspired a long walk to Fulwell's Windmill and a lazy picnic beneath its white canvas wings. He should be lifting a bottle of beer to his lips right now, looking up through the slowly revolving panels at the empty sky, thinking about his next bottle of beer and the chuckball game on Sunday. If only the smoke would not obscure the blue, everyone might think of home, and point their cannonballs at the sea. But this flag is meant to replace the sky. It is what the men will see, when wearily they look up; the admiral's colors instead of God's blue heaven.

What am I doing up here? Jack suddenly wonders. He looks down at the two doctors and his friend Bob kneeling on the deck of the HMS *Venerable*; then they are lost in the fog of cannon fire. Why am I still holding on? What's to keep me from letting go—like this—and falling, falling through the sky, past my friend Bob and those two befuddled doctors? What's to keep me from dropping—like this—into the comforting bosom of the blue sea below?

The wintry waves take the old hero's breath away as they break over his naked head. It's colder than he thought, this sea, but it was good to let go. Who gives a bloody rat's ass for some rich admiral's colors, anyway? Left up to Jack Crawford, he's just as happy to surrender.

VII

DUTIES

It is dark again by the time Henry rolls over in his childhood bed on the third floor of his rented house on Nile Street. His grandmother's cane rocking chair sits by the window, his mother's chest-high chiffonier rests against the wall by the door. Besides an Austrian cuckoo clock (an engagement present from the Clannys), the only ornaments hung on the whitewashed walls are two framed engravings. A stern line drawing of reformer Jeremy Bentham, Henry's hero, is fixed at eye level by the door, so that his might be the first face Henry sees upon waking; and above the bed, protecting him like the crucifix he discarded years ago, hangs his childhood Sacred Heart. He has grown so accustomed to that old picture that he scarcely sees it anymore. Certainly, when he's married, he will have to stow it away with this single bed and the rest of his familiar boyhood things. Audrey will rock their first child in his grandmother's chair, where he has spent hours by the window intently reading his medical journals. Won't he resent her sitting in his seat by the window, sunlight falling upon an infant forehead rather than a clean white margin? Won't he want to pick up a medical saw and grate her bowed head from her very shoulders?

Jesus Christ! Henry starts awake to the mechanical bird ducking in and out of the cuckoo clock. Seven o'clock? He sits up confused. Seven o'clock at night? His valet must have come in, for the trousers he wore to the theatre a full twenty-four hours ago are neatly folded over his chair and his jacket hangs from a peg by his hat. He fell asleep in his stained shirt and tightly wound cravat, which would explain the fitful feeling of choking he had all night. He promised Audrey he would go see her charity family on Mill Street and instead he's slept the entire day.

The wood-plank floor is freezing cold when he sets his bare feet upon it and scurries over to the basin and jug of water his servant left on the dresser. Henry tries not to go to bed with other men's blood on his body, but studying himself in the pier glass, he sees that his face and hands are streaked with Jack Crawford's. As if losing him to that illness weren't bad enough, they spent an even more harrowing time trying to persuade Robert Cooley to relinquish his friend's body for autopsy. They scolded. They threatened. It is of the utmost scientific importance, they pleaded, tugging on the old hero like schoolchildren would a puppy. You saw how horrible the disease is—how are we to find a cure if we cannot learn how it attacks? But nothing would move red-faced, grief-stricken Bob. He clung to the corpse ferociously, shaking his head, sobbing more pitifully than Henry had ever seen a grown man. In the end, nothing they could say would persuade him. He threw the naked hero over his shoulder and ran screaming from the hospital like a madman.

Henry quickly scrubs the dried blood from his face and hands, pulls on the trousers he wore to the theatre, and opens the bedroom door to the hallway. Ugh! With the door closed, he had forgotten about the smell. Ferment from the cadaver Liss wafts up from the second floor like ghoulish bread baking.

"Williams!" Henry calls, breathing through his mouth.

"Bring a cold supper to the library, will you?"

The smell is even worse in the library, but Henry's nose soon adjusts. It is one of the drawbacks of having a home practice, Dr. Knox had told him years ago. The stench of death worms its way into your book bindings, your sock drawer, your bread larder. What's worse, Knox told him, is how quickly you get used to it. You learn to mind death in the room no more than you would a pesky housefly.

The converted operating theatre is not large, and he was forced to clear out the furniture to maximize space; only a glass-fronted cabinet, a long, waist-high trough with scale, and a teakwood lectern, holding his Albinus, remain. Recessed bookcases line the room, their shelves holding not books, but round jars sealed with pigs' bladders and red wax. Before leaving Edinburgh, Henry had been a great collector, and his specimen collection would still rank among the best in the Northeast. Along his top shelves are rows of pulpy brains, brains eaten away by syphilis, brains lacking frontal lobes, and a lengthy digression on the brains of dogs, cats, and squirrels. Next come four severed female breasts representing the lymph system, each having had mercury injected into the nipple. How sleek and modern they look, veined with silver, like automaton wet nurses built for suckling in this new Age of Machines. Eyes are next—fat human oculi, up to ten floating in the same tall jar—then livers, kidneys, and lungs. The cadaver Liss's red heart sits on a bookshelf with others of its sort, the only muscle not bleached of its color by preservative. It makes a startling punctuation at the end of the row, but it will be only a matter of weeks before it becomes waxy and white like the others. Henry hasn't had the leisure or the inclination to collect since he's been in Sunderland. He's felt that filling his shelves while his students went without teaching cadavers would be like satisfying a letch for hothouse peaches when his children were crying for bread.

Damn it, Henry swears. While he slept the day away, the ice in which the cadaver was originally packed melted, and now he floats in a long trough of lukewarm water, drowned all over again. Bietler made such a mangled mess of the abdomen trying to extract the intestines, flesh that might have kept for another two days billows uselessly in the water. It is the second betrayal of death, this rot, forcing medical science to hurry along at the speed of decomposing flesh. Well, the arms are still good. And the legs. With a sigh, Henry picks up his hacksaw and digs in at the shoulder joint. Swollen with water, but still completely distinguishable, a young Jack Crawford clings to his mast on cadaver Liss's bicep. Henry hesitates with the saw, staring into the inky face of the man he's just lost, a dead man tattooed on a dead man's arm. He doesn't have the heart for this right now.

"Your supper, sir," Williams's muffled voice comes through the closed door. His servant is not allowed in this room—not that the stench does not warn him away.

"Leave it in the hall, please," Henry says, setting aside the saw. "And Williams, bring up an old sheet and my shovel."

When his servant is gone, Henry retrieves the tray of artichokes, cold chicken, and sherry he left, takes it to the hearth, and kindles a fire. He's kept the room purposefully unheated since the cadaver's arrival, but there seems little point in that now. Mr. Liss is useless; Henry will have to dispose of him before he decays further and alerts the neighbors. He drags an artichoke leaf over his teeth and flips it into the fireplace. Having devoted all his energies to securing this single corpse, he has given little thought to finding another. He could have had Jack Crawford's if not for his friend's obstinacy. What a coup to have made the first dissection of a cholera patient in England.

Henry plucks his artichoke leaves automatically, gnawing off the meat and listening to them sizzle in the fire. Perhaps he might—No. He cuts off the thought before it has a chance to form. It was stupid. He was about to let himself consider the possibility of seeking out that girl Gustine. He has been blameless in the entire affair—both times they have met, she has sought *him*, he has never searched out *her* help. It's just that, circulating through the city as she does, she's sure to have heard of cases, if there *are* cases, and perhaps for a bit of money she might help him—But there he goes considering again. He couldn't possibly turn to a woman for help in these matters; he's thoroughly ashamed as it is of how he came by the cadaver Liss. It was bad enough in London and Edinburgh associating with the scum of the earth, the most depraved resurrection men, and then to have unknowingly consorted with Burke and Hare. He will not be responsible for drawing a woman—not even a woman: a young girl— down into that darkness.

And yet. Did she not show her true colors last night outside of the theatre? Was she not perfectly comfortable with the vilest profanity, accepting embraces from the most abandoned of men? Henry has forgotten that he himself contemplated securing her services the night of his failure at the Trinity graveyard. Now he remembers only that she dared come near his Audrey, that she shamelessly placed herself in his fiancée's line of vision, flaunting her wickedness for all of Sunderland to see. Is it even possible to further corrupt a girl like that?

"Your shovel, sir," Williams says through the door.

Henry rouses himself, setting aside his untouched chicken and half-eaten artichoke. He is thinking craziness. Of course he cannot seek out Gustine. A man might easily become contaminated by the bad company he keeps, and he will not be the agent through which ugliness ever touches Audrey's life again. He'll find another way to secure bodies for his students; sooner or later, the family of a cholera victim will give in to reason. Now he needs to pay a visit to Audrey's charity family as he promised, and see what service he can be to those in whom she's taken an interest.

But first, he has an unpleasant task. Taking up the sheet Williams left in the hall, he fills it with the remains of cadaver Liss. Some of his colleagues, he knows, would toss the body in the fire when it was of no more use, or drive him out to the North Sea and fling him over a cliff; but Henry still has enough courtesy (he won't call it superstition) to want to do right by the man. He takes up his shovel and his bottle of sherry and drags the bundle down the stairs, then out into the backyard.

Brain-coral permafrost cracks underfoot as he makes his way to his neighbor's fence, as far from his own back door as the diminutive yard allows. His neighbor's hungry black mutt scratches the wooden wall furiously, barking his excitement, as he has every other time Henry has come out here to bury rabbits or cats or his canine compatriots, all the dumb vivisected beasts who have given their lives for the betterment of Science. I give you another one, dumber perhaps than all the rest, thinks Henry, leaping upon his shovel to cut through the sod and a trespassing root from his neighbor's chestnut.

Back in Edinburgh, Henry was the only instructor willing to dig a pit for the gristle and scraps of the school's dissected corpses. By moonlight he dug in Surgeons' Square's courtyard, planting what was left of the pickled old woman and her grandson, of headless, footless Daft Jamie, of lovely Mary Paterson—though not so lovely when Knox was through. Henry pauses in his digging to take a swig of sherry. Of all their faces, hers alone he will never forget—shorn of her hair, jaundiced from months of floating in whiskey, her stained yellow eyes staring unblinkingly as he snuffed them with the first shovelful of dirt.

There's blood on yer sleeve, tight rounded Mary had slurred the night before she died, rolling up his cuff to uncover a brown stain. *Which are you? A doctor or a killer? We've vowed not to go with doctors anymore, for we don't want to end up on one of your tables. But if you're only a killer, you're all right by me.* He had found Mary Paterson in Canongate with her friend (Janet Brown; he was later to learn her name when she testified at the murder trial), beyond jolly and well onto drunk. Janet cackled as Mary threw her strong arms around Henry's neck and kissed him with a slick tongue of juniper. Maybe it was the stench of gin, maybe it was her friend's airless laughter, but Henry felt himself suffocated by this woman's flesh. *Ach, yer no killer,* disappointed Mary called as he disentangled himself and pulled away. *You'll slay no woman's heart with that attitude.*

According to Janet at the trial, the next morning friendly William Burke invited the girls into his lodging house, where he introduced them to his friend, William Hare. Before ten o'clock, Mary had made the acquaintance of two more bottles of gin and passed out drunk. Janet, who was lured outside for a walk by dour William Hare, never saw her friend again. Henry could pick up the story from there: by two o'clock, he and Dr. Knox were lifting Mary Paterson's naked body from a tea chest at Surgeons' Square and setting her to steep in a trough of whiskey. *How did one so young and healthy come to die?* he demanded of Burke, even as he handed over the money. *I saw her only yesterday and she was fine.* She died of the drink, sir, said the cagey Irishman, counting his coins. Truly, 'twas a tragedy. There could be no denying foul play this time. Only last night Henry had kissed the same lips he was now destined to dissect.

Next door, the neighbor's black dog won't stop barking. Be quiet! Henry snaps, digging his shoulder into the shovel and thrusting deeper into his backyard. The hole he has roughed out is deep enough and he tumbles the cadaver Liss from his sheet into the earth. Dig them up. Put them back in. Dig them up. Put them back in. He didn't go to medical school to become a grave digger. He stops and takes another long draw from his bottle, wipes his brow, and offers up a short prayer for the dead man. *Lord, take this your son over to the Great Majority,* he prays, while next door the neighbor's dog barks loud enough to wake the whole block. *And Lord, if Thou art merciful, go easier on the Earth's future doctors.*

There is no number on the door, and with the windows boarded up, he's unsure if he has the right address. But it's nine houses in from High Street and the stoop is as slick with rotting vegetables as Audrey described it. A thin dusting of snow has melted into the runny whitewash left by the Board of Health, and someone has sunk one of the agency's abandoned paint brushes into a mound of hoary night soil, as a warning. This is not a house friendly to health, Henry decides, rapping gently on the door with his knuckles. No answer. He knocks louder, then gives the door a little push. It is unlocked.

No lamps are lit, and it is dark inside except for a low fire in the grate. In the half-light, he sees bundles of dirty laundry sagging against a long wooden table, abandoned in the corners, and strewn along the floor before the hearth. Near the stairs leading up to the second floor, a box is balanced on two split cane chairs. It is close in the room and stifling hot, and Henry detects the familiar odor even before the pile of laundry on the floor jumps up and scampers over to him.

"We have a death in the house, so please be respectful," it says in a whisper.

Henry looks down on a little girl in an oversized pink dress. Conjunctivitis is ruining her eyes and her neck seems too stingy to support her large head. In her spindly arms she carries another smaller bundle, wrapped in a blanket. This must be the little girl Audrey told him about.

"Is your name Pink?" Henry asks gently.

The pile of dirty laundry leaning against the table looks up. It speaks with a slurred husky voice.

"Doan't speak t' him, lass," the pile says. "Yer Da won't like it."

"Yes, my name is Pink," the little girl answers hesitantly. "Do you want a room for the night?"

"I'm the doctor sent by the Indigent Sick Society." He squats to equalize their heights and sees the bundle in her arms wriggle. "There is a woman here who is sick?"

"Fat lot o' good you do 'er now," says a feminine pile in the corner. She is haunched by two smaller heaps of rags, sacked out from hawking fish all day to the poor Irish.

"We expected you yesterday," Pink says. "She was sick yesterday."

"I'm sorry, I was unable to make it yesterday," he says. "May I see her now?"

Pink walks with her bundle over to the foot of the stairs

and stops before the plain wooden box. "Here she is."

The box, stenciled "Property of Sunderland Parish," is a rented coffin with a trapdoor that will be leased by the town's poor until it has worn down to splinters. Inside, a shriveled woman is wrapped head to foot in white cambric, with only the pinched oval of her face showing. A cambric chin strap keeps her jaw from dropping, a sprig of rosemary has been tucked inside as an age-old token of remembrance, and two copper pennies have been placed on her eyelids. This must have been the woman with phosphorus poisoning, Henry thinks. But that is besides the point now. Jesus. Beneath the pennies, her skin is a deep indigo.

"How long ago did this woman die?" Henry demands of the room.

"Last night," answers the pile that leans against the table.

"We must get her out of the house as soon as possible." Henry slides the wooden lid over the woman's face. "I'll send someone around for her."

"You'll do no such thing," counters Pile. "She's being waked."

"She has died of cholera morbus," Henry says imperiously. "Her clothes and bedding must be burnt and she must be buried immediately. She will infect you if you keep her here."

"Fos had the Fossy Jaw," says Pink. "There's no such thing as cholera morbus."

"I'm afraid there is, sweetheart. And it's here in town," Henry says. "Don't go near that coffin until I can get her out of here, do you understand? And keep this baby far, far away from it."

Henry lifts the baby out of Pink's hands before she knows what he's about. The baby, like the woman in the coffin, is wrapped so that nothing but its face shows. What did Audrey say about this child? Only that it had an extraordinary heart. Henry takes the baby to the hearth, where there is light enough to examine it.

Pink hovers worriedly. "Be careful," she says. "Don't poke it."

Henry holds his finger before the child's face and moves it from side to side. Its large blue eyes follow easily. He claps his hands by each ear and the baby turns its head slightly toward the noise. Not blind or deaf. This is a remarkably good-looking baby, he thinks, to be born into such poverty. It is thin, but not nearly so malnourished as most East End infants he sees. It has brought its focus back to Henry's face and now gives him a bubbling smile which Henry can't help returning.

Slowly he unwraps the blanket, releasing the baby's pink fists and legs. This must be Audrey's doing, this Irish linen christening gown, for no mother in the neighborhood could afford such a thing. The baby squirms, happy to be free of its tight swaddling. Henry cups one of its tiny red feet and the baby pushes hard against his hand.

"Seems healthy," he says. The girl Pink chews her lip nervously beside him, watching as the doctor pushes back the gown. Up it goes, past the baby's flailing legs and dimply knees, inching up its blue-veined baby belly to reveal its ab-sol-ute orig-in-ality, as Gustine calls it.

Just like the charity lady, Pink thinks when the doctor gasps. That look on his face.

"Where is this baby's mother?" Henry demands, his voice cracking with excitement. *My God. I am holding a medical impossibility.*

"She's at work," answers Pink.

Does she know what she has created? he wants to shout. *Does she realize this baby should never have been born?* He looks wildly about the room for someone, anyone, who might appreciate the marvel in his lap. A child born with its heart on the outside of its body! A working, pumping, four chambered heart, beating under a thin layer of skin. He has read of children born with four legs, of children born with a twin growing from a rib, of a boy from Bengal who grew a head on top of his own head that blinked and breathed and did everything but speak. No one would have thought he could have survived, but he lived until age four, when he was bitten by a cobra. The miracles of science are endless, but they happen to other people, in places far away.

"Who the hell is this?"

"Eeek!" Pink leaps from the hearth and runs for the coal bin. Henry looks up to see a thick-faced, red-haired tough stomping down the stairs toward him. On his shoulder a startled white ferret digs in its claws to remain upright.

"Who let a bloody sawbones into my establishment?" the man roars.

Henry rises, holding the baby carefully against his chest. "I am Dr. Chiver, sent by the Indigent Sick Society."

"I am Whilky Robinson," says Whilky. "And you are trespassing."

Whilky has been upstairs with a prospective lodger, a nice young chap with a cheery bottle of brandy. He's been fluffing Fos's vacated straw for the man, not minding if he did have a drop, thank you; no harm in starting the wake early. Whilky and the young man were discussing the rumours of cholera that had been floating around the town since Jack Crawford was carted out of last night's performance. The prospective lodger had lifted a pint with Jack's shaken mate Robert Cooley earlier that day, and heard all about how they plunged poor Jack in a vat of acid, and how they'd run after Robert with their scalpels to take the skin from his very body. An enemy to the poor man, that's my definition of a doctor, said Prospective Lodger before he passed out on Fos's vacated straw. Dastardly followers of Malthus every last one of 'em.

"Mr. Robinson," says Henry, "I am here to help."

"Help? How? By planting more frog eggs in my house?"

Henry cups his hand over the baby's head protectively. "I have come at my own expense to care for that woman and this——"

"You won't rest easy until every poor man is dead or in the workhouse! You politicians and medical men flaunting your laws of population!" interrupts Whilky. "You think I've not heard of Malthus?"

"What are you talking about?" asks Henry, completely confused.

"Using your goddamned cholera morbus to winnow out the poor! You think I'm not onto you?"

Why does he bother with these people? Henry looks into the ignorant faces of 9 Mill Street: the obstinate, jowly stupidity of this half-drunk landlord, the slack bundles of filthy laundry, slumping across the table or spreading slatternly in the corners. He wishes he did have the cholera in his power— he would thrust it straight down Whilky Robinson's throat.

"And who said you could hold that baby?" Whilky abruptly snatches the child away, causing it to set up a terrible howl. He thrusts it in the direction of the coal bin, where Pink darts out long enough to take charge of it, then disappears again.

"Sir, do you understand how special that child is?" shouts Henry, realizing he does care about one inhabitant of this godforsaken place. He's barely had a chance to examine it.

"I understand it's a drain on my already daft daughter to

look after it when she might be out earning an honest wage. I understand it's bankrupting its foolish mother, who should've let it starve months ago. And I understand it's keepin' you in my house long after I've ordered you to leave!" Whilky strides to the front door and flings it open.

"Let me take it to my house where it will be safe," Henry pleads, hating the sound of entreaty in his voice.

"I'd as soon toss it in the garbage as look at it," Whilky says sourly. "But I'll not be held accountable for the fury of its mother should she come home to find it gone."

Henry picks up his bag and storms to the door. He bangs his shin on the split cane chair holding poor indigo Fos in her box.

"You have a cholera body in your house," he says, advancing on Whilky. "I'll have the Board of Health come around if you don't get her in the ground."

"Get'er in the ground so that you can dig 'er up, you mean?" laughs Whilky. "Not on yer life."

The landlord gives Henry a shove with his shoulder and slams the door behind him. It is cold and dark in the lane and Henry is shaking with fury. Bloody barbarian! He steps off the stoop and into a stream of coursing whitewash, splattering his good pants and ruining his shoes. Bloody bastard! Henry looks around for the paintbrush thrust in night soil, wrenches it free, and plunges it into the paint. It gives him great satisfaction to scrawl the word across that bloody barbarian bastard's front door.

SICK, Henry paints in big dripping letters. And flings the brush away.

He wasn't looking for her when he turned off Mill Street onto Sailor's Alley, a low passage where women leaned in doorways, their legs crossed at the ankle, their hands on their hips, watching him beneath hooded lids—women who murmured as he stormed past, Four shillings, sir, clothes off for five. He wasn't looking for her on the Church Walk, in the crotch of the young girl who startled him by lifting her skirt to display milk white thighs and a thatch of brown hair. He was not looking for her outside the theatre where he'd seen her last night, nor down by the bridge where she had taken him a week ago; but by the time he reached the Labour in Vain, shaking, exhausted from walking the city not looking for her, he was exceedingly relieved to find her.

"I have been insulted."

She was sitting with another gentleman, a nervous, thin man who jumped up the moment Henry arrived and bolted through the front door. Henry took his seat and began speaking, low and angrily. There is a man, he told Gustine, an ignorant, obstinate, cretinous landlord who keeps a low lodging house. In his parlour a woman lies dead of the cholera, poisoning his lodgers. It is unsafe. It is wrongheaded. But nothing I said would convince him of his error. "*He threw me out of the house!* I want that body, Gustine. For the lodgers' sake, I mean, it must be removed."

Gustine looks startled to see him, as startled as he is to be here. After what happened outside the theatre, she thought never to see him again. "Tell me what happened," she says.

Where to begin? Maybe he should he start with last night when Robert Cooley ripped naked Jack Crawford's body from their hands and ran off with it screaming, *You'll never carve him, bloody sawbones, you'll not cut him up!* Or earlier that evening when a corpulent common actor insulted his uncle, a pillar of the community? No, certainly his case against Whilky Robinson begins back in Edinburgh when the mob burned Dr. Knox in effigy and ruined his mentor's distinguished career. When have the ignorant poor not set themselves against him?

"It is the insolence of willful ignorance I cannot abide," he says. "He is so proud of his house. I'll show him how safe he is in his house."

"Where does this landlord live?" asks Gustine.

"Mill Street—9 Mill Street."

Henry is so on fire with his plans, he fails to notice the nervous look she throws over her shoulder at the bartender, John Robinson, her landlord's brother.

"Let's go upstairs," she suggests, rising quickly. "We can speak more privately there."

Beside the bartender, he notices for the first time the old woman with whom he always sees her, watching them intently. Her enormous gray eye fixes on him, and for a split second he feels she can see his heart beating, like that baby's, his clenched, angry heart pumping bile through his veins. He doesn't like the idea of being mistaken for one of Gustine's customers, but perhaps it is safer to speak privately.

"We can take her while he is sleeping," Henry says under his breath, following her up the stairs. "From under his very nose. And if we get caught, I will say I am operating under the authority of the Board of Health. This woman is a nuisance, she is a pollutant. I am only thinking of the other lodgers."

Gustine unlocks the second door down the hall and automatically slips the ribboned key around her wrist. A small Argand lamp sits on the floor next to a calico-covered straw mattress. This is Gustine's usual room at the Labour in Vain and John Robinson, out of friendship to his brother, keeps it a little bit cleaner for her. Henry looks around. There is no place but the bed to sit.

"Last night I came across a woman dying in childbirth," she offers, settling herself carefully on the edge of the mattress. "Not far from here, on Spring Garden Lane. Shall we not take her instead?"

"Gustine," says Henry angrily," you are not hearing me. I must have that woman. From Mill Street."

"Why do you need her in particular? Is it only to make the landlord angry?"

Henry bristles, annoyed she would think him so petty. "I don't need that woman," he says," but she is a contaminant, Gustine. Her clothes and winding sheet are vessels for the disease itself, her rotting body is putting out who knows what sort of miasmas, and the whole lodging house is in danger unless she is removed. A child lives in that house, the most amazing child I've seen. For the child's sake, if no one else's, I should take that body."

"You saw a child?" she asks, surprised.

"A prodigy. How he has survived in that squalid tenement is beyond me. His parents should be taken out and shot for their irresponsibility."

"Why do you call them irresponsible?" she asks, concerned.

"They should have immediately alerted the medical community. I have read of only one other case of a surviving *ectopia cordis*, back in 1671. In most cases the ectopia is complete and the heart is born naked. No child could survive that severe a deformity. But in the older case, as in this one, the ectopia was partial, with the heart being herniated and covered by the thinnest layer of skin. With proper medical care, that patient lived into his seventies. I know I could preserve this child's life, too, if I could only get to it."

Into his seventies? Though she has understood nothing else Henry has said, she's grasped that last: with his help, her child could outlive her. She nervously passes the key around and around her wrist. Here the doctor is saying what she most longs to hear, that he might cure her child, and yet she hesitates. Speak, Gustine, she commands herself. Now is the time: throw your child upon this doctor's mercy and beg his help. But he called her irresponsible and claimed the child's parents should be taken out and shot. Nor has she forgotten the look of horror with which he regarded her outside the theatre. It kept her up in tears last night thinking that all her plans were ruined.

"I must get back to work," she says at last, hearing the old woman move on the other side of the door. "Go to Mill Street between two and three; I will see the door is left unlocked so that you may remove the woman."

"Thank you," Henry says, nodding solemnly.

What he has proposed is far more dangerous than claiming a body from the morgue or resurrecting one from the cemetery, and Gustine is suddenly afraid. She is about to allow a thief into her own home, to invade her landlord's cherished privacy and take what belongs to him. She has her doubts, but for her child's sake, it must be done.

"Gustine," Henry says, embarrassed, watching her fit the key into the lock. "Do you have to go so soon? Downstairs they'll think we—they'll think I couldn't—of course, we wouldn't—'

Gustine turns back in surprise. With a few words, the stern surgeon of moments before has been transformed into a blushing schoolboy. She smiles at him from the doorway before slowly refastening the lock. I have nothing to fear from you, thinks she gratefully, watching his cheeks redden. You need me as much as I need you.

"Will ten minutes do?" she asks with a grin. "Most don't even last that long."

VIII

FOS

Though Whilky took what little you possessed—2*s* 10*d* sewn into a handkerchief, a handful of matches with their powdered glass friction sheet, the ticket stub to Les Chats Savants, a charity blanket, a comb, a well-thumbed Bible inscribed with pencil, "The Meak Shall Inherit the Earthe" —you have left a legacy for 9 Mill Street. Your first beneficiary, Whilky's prospective lodger, who in passing out removed all eventuality from his situation, right now is having a vivid, drunken dream in which a bare-breasted glowing woman appears at his bedside. Between her long fingers she holds up a match for him to blow out; but when he tries, the alcohol on his breath, instead of extinguishing the match, causes it to flare. He watches helplessly as the match falls upon his bed, screams as the straw combusts in cold blue flame. He doesn't know it, but five more men in the coming weeks will try to blow out that same match, each with identical results. The sense of humour that eluded you in this earthly life seems destined to be yours in the Great Hereafter.

Sleet rattles on the roof and drums against the boards covering the windows. It is three o'clock in the morning, and the lodgers of 9 Mill Street have gone to bed. Some, like your heir, cramp fitfully in their straw; some, like Whilky downstairs in his cellar apartment, snore obliviously. The younger boys, only pretending to be asleep, are pushing their pelvises up against the younger girls, who are only pretending a need to stretch so that their backsides touch the hard quivering muscles behind them. The dirty old men's hands move under their coats, the dirty old women's fingers flurry. The hard workers sleep as dreamlessly as their babies, half of whom have had sleep guaranteed them by laudanum drops. An unemployed sailor gets up to pee in the cold fireplace.

You have your own private room now, narrow and tight, but gloriously all yours. You rest comfortably with your sagging chin wrapped tightly and two cold coins on your eyes— no need to fear a sleepwalking boy will step on your arm in the night, or wake you with his bad dreams. How often did you and the thirty other lodgers start awake, sweating and paralyzed, at three in the morning merely because some troubled child screamed out, Stop! It's eating me! It's true, the wolf that was eating you was different from the alligator that was eating your neighbor, which in turn differed from the enormous rat that was eating the little boy, but crowded together how could you not all share the same terror? That's the trouble with lodging houses: all of their nightmares eventually became your nightmares.

Downstairs, though, the room is still, disturbed only by the occasional snap of methane hidden in an ember of coal and the hiss of sleet on the windowsill. Across from your wooden box, you are being watched by Whilky's daughter Pink. She leans against the warm brick hearth and the heat from the dying fire cups her cheeks like a mother's hands. Her heavy head drops to the side, bobs up, drops to the side, bobs up. She slits her eyes at you—yes, you are still dead—and then they close again. She and Eye were the only ones willing to sit up all night and make sure you didn't accidentally come back to life. Don't laugh; it's been known to happen: young mothers have fallen into comas and been buried alive with their stillborn infants, grandmothers have groaned and rolled over just as the nails were about to be hammered in. Three days of watching and waking are sometimes still not enough. Just look at that pretty Italian girl in that play—Juliet—look what became of her. Pink knows how young mothers have been known to fall into comas and get buried with their stillborn infants. She dreams intermittently about the mother whom she barely remembers, who had kind eyes and a fluffy white tail peeping from under her skirt. Her mother walked upright on her hind legs and licked Pink's face when she was sick. She barely remembers watching and waking her mother and baby brother those three long years ago. All she clearly remembers is the wedge of yellow cheese a neighbor brought her, and the smell it left on her fingers.

At the foot of your box, the old fixture Eye sits on her stool where the blue dress, hanging on its pegs above her, caps her head like a frivolous ancien régime hairdo. The laudanum drops Gustine slipped into her coffee earlier tonight are beginning to take effect, and things are bit by bit losing their shape. Take Pink, for example, leaning against the hearth. To Eye, the figure of sleeping Pink seems to contain the shadowy outline of another little girl, one that Eye wants to forget. That girl sits above a hole, watching the chain that disappears down into it. Eye sees the chain jump, knows something heavy is hanging from the bottom of it. She sees a rat dart by, and the girl leap up to chase it. She sees the chain rush down the hole. The old woman snorts and blinks her one gray eye. Her lid has barnacles growing on it tonight and it is betraying her.

Glow rat's in the box.

She sees you, the smudged firefly glister of your exposed

face and hands against the piece of white cambric she helped Gustine wrap you in last night. Rat glows. Dead rat. But damn that shadow world again. Flickering beneath you, she sees a younger, prettier lady missing her arms and legs, wearing her chest open like a vest, sleeping with her chin thrown back. It is a disturbing shadow and Eye rolls her eye away. She looks up into the bell skirt of the dress above her, through the waist, all the way to the neck. She imagines squeezing through a tight underwater tunnel, clean and cold and blue. When she comes out the other side, she will be in that two-eyed younger place before the hole and the chain, before the rat. Eye stretches up, kicks her thick club feet, has almost reached the surface when a sound outside causes her to freeze, sputter, and back out. She rolls her stern gray eye to the door and trains it like a slingshot on the latch.

In the cellar that might be accessed by a door beneath the front stoop, Whilky Robinson sleeps in an actual bed with a furry white ring nestled under his chin. The landlord's apartment is a small, damp room that floods several times a winter, encouraging spores on the quilts and mud on the earthen floor. The seepage has left a child's growth chart around the room, with different color lines of mildew marking each advancing year. Pink, when she's not watching a dead lodger, sleeps next to the coal shoot in the low trundle bed her mother brought to the marriage along with the bedstead Whilky and Mike now sleep in. Whilky rarely dreams of his wife who died in this bed; he's more likely to be caught dreaming of some Figure of Oppression: a Lord Londonderry, for instance, or a William Pitt, the Younger. It took Whilky a long time to fall asleep tonight. He ground the insults of that doctor between his teeth until he gave himself a nasty indigestion, and then his stomach troubles kept him up. It is difficult being a freedom fighter, more difficult than anyone sitting at home reading a book can imagine. To stand up to men wealthier and more powerful than yourself and send them flying from your house? It takes guts. And Whilky, if nothing else, has no deficiency of guts.

Cholera in my house? he mumbles in his sleep. Cholera in *my* house? At last the minions of the Government have made a mistake. They should have picked as their patsy Jack Tanner up the block or credulous Tim Downs. You could have told either of those two that the Hindoo Hullabaloo was in town and they would have willingly spread the news, found symptoms in themselves, and dutifully died of it. Whilky rolls over and punches his pillow. Ask for the right to vote and just see how the Government answers: with doctors and poisons and frogs; with poor laws and anatomy acts and Thomas Malthus.

The poor, because they are starving, will by necessity feel themselves on the verge of extinction, Malthus wrote. A species threatened with extinction procreates wildly to save itself. Exponentially (and Whilky is not quite sure he completely understands the word, except to know it is like a shaken fist in his face) the undesirable poor will reproduce, to the detriment of worthier citizens, spreading misery and sloth until every inch of the planet is contaminated. But what is to be done? Feed and clothe the wretched poor? No! Of course not—then they will have no incentive to work hard and prosper. Lock them away in poorhouses? Separate husbands and wives? Pass laws that give their bodies to surgeons if they are unable to afford burial? Now that sounds better. Wretchedness will always exist on this earth—the arithmetic says so; allow poverty to equal death and dissection and the poor will, out of common sense, choose prosperity.

Pox on common sense, Whilky mutters. I only wish I'd gotten ten children on my wife before she died, instead of two. And only the daft daughter surviving. Who knows what torment to her father she is even now letting into his house? *Do come in,* she is saying to a reverend man in long black robes who knocks upon the door. Held in place by that strange gravity one is subject to in dreams, Whilky sits helplessly upon his stool as Pink escorts the gentleman through his house. *Here is where my Da keeps his silver,* she says, pointing out the loose floorboard beneath which Whilky secretes a pouch of tableware. *Here is where he keeps his lodging and dress money.* He had no idea Pink knew of the strongbox in the wall behind Wearmouth Bridge East View. *Oh, look here! Here's how he cheats His Majesty's tax collectors,* says the little girl, spreading her arms to include the windows. The stranger has the sour countenance of a schoolmaster as he strides deliberately to Whilky's boarded shutters and, to the landlord's amazement, with the strength of his white teeth alone tugs from them every single nail.

Who are you? demands Whilky, transfixed upon his stool. *What are you doing?*

Sunlight floods the dark corners of 9 Mill Street, exposing long black spider cracks in the plaster and caked dirt between the floorboards. Whilky sees that his daughter's face is black with grime except where tears have washed two pink tracks down her cheeks. *Come, I'll show you where our lodgers and their babies live,* she says, reaching up trustingly to the stern old man she's let into the house, placing her small dirty hand in his broad dry palm. As he moves to follow her, Whilky sees peeping from his back pocket *The Laws of Population.*

I know you, Thomas Malthus! shouts Whilky. *Stay away from my daughter!*

Why, you are a little bit of overpopulation, says the gentleman, looking softly down at the trusting girl. In nightmare time, Whilky feels his own chest contract as Pink's heart stops beating and she drops to the floor.

What have you done? he cries. *What have you done?* But that lawgiver of Population merely smiles a mouthful of nails.

Mike has suffered Whilky's thrashing with as much patience as a dutiful ferret may, but his sleep once too often has been rudely interrupted. In the dark underground room, the creature stretches and yawns widely, showing pink spotted gums and two rows of sharp teeth. He looks casually around. His enemy the frogs he has vanquished—not a croaking soul remains in the basement—but wait, what is this? An old familiar scent causes him to sit up and sniff the air. On four pink paws he pads across the bed and leaps to the floor. Sniff. Sniff. The fur on the back of his sinewy neck stirs. Sniff. It is coming from above. Mike takes the steps up to the front stoop and wedges his nose beneath the door. While Whilky sleeps, a low growl builds in the throat of his prized ferret. There is no mistake about it. Mike smells a rat.

If Gustine has a dream it is this: that her baby will live. There is nothing complex or especially overweening about her dream: she does not wish for her child to become an altar boy or a businessman; she cares not whether he learns to read or write or play a sport. She is elementary in her singular desire. Life for her child. Would any parent call such a modest hope avarice?

Baby, baby, baby, coos Gustine. Baby, baby. She is stretched out on her side with her unbundled baby before her. The lodgers' fireplace is not lit, but with no exposed windowpanes to divert it, the heat from downstairs makes their room snug enough. She reaches out her fingers to the child and he grips them firmly. Pull, whispers Gustine, drawing him to a sitting position. His head lags behind, but at the last moment, he manages to drunkenly snap it forward. Good baby! Gustine laughs and the baby laughs, a gargling, gassy sort of wheeze, but a laugh nonetheless.

Shush! a neighbor commands. There is the scratchy sound of bodies turning over in straw, a barnlike restlessness to the lodging house that Gustine hates. Across the room in Fos's place, the new lodger tosses fitfully: The flames, he moans, the awful blue flames. One of the dirty old men grunts and sheepishly wipes his belly with his blanket. The sailor who got up to pee now can't stop coughing. With thirty people in a tight room, and no more space between them than the width of your foot, there will be no such thing as a silent night. There are only the deeper sounds of unconsciousness after the more deliberate gossip and chatter and flirting have died out.

Gustine pushes aside the straw and presses her eye to the gap between the floorboards. It is her secret—that the crack beside her bed puts the Eye in her direct line of vision. Now it's my turn to watch you, you old monster, Gustine scowls. She cannot see Fos in her coffin from here, only Pink's feet protruding from her faded gingham gown and the Eye on her stool. She presses the lightest kiss against her baby's chest and he twines his fists in her loose blonde hair. At first Gustine had not even known she was pregnant. Hungry girls often skip their monthlies, and she'd looked on it as a blessing— not to have to bind herself with rags and miss nights of work. The lacer of the blue dress caught on, though; that canny Eye seemed to know it almost immediately. Gustine would catch her watching her belly like a cat at a mouse hole waiting to pounce on whatever peeked out. We might pity Gustine her ignorance, for you must remember, she was only fourteen years old when she conceived her child, she had no mamma to turn to, no aunt or sister to ask advice. So few customers ever asked her to strip that none who might have set her straight took notice of her condition, and even if they had, would only have considered themselves fortunate not to have to worry about withdrawing at that moment when men most love to stay put.

But when the baby was born Gustine realized how foolish she had been. It was clear to her now what the old woman had been trying to accomplish with her constant staring; it was clear to her now that the Eye had intended to draw out from her baby's body its very heart and leave the poor thing dead inside her. She pulled and tugged with all her might, and with her malevolency managed to call his heart to the outside, but Gustine's miraculous child was too strong for the old woman. He survived, and breathed at birth, and wore his heart as a badge that good shall always triumph over evil. Gustine never told anyone what she believed, but she lived its truth. She gave up all extra money to buy her special child wholesome food; she purchased, though they were clearly beyond her means, fine woolen blankets and little booties, yarn to knit him jumpers when at last she would find the time to learn to knit. She kept her baby far away from the evil Eye so that she might not be able to finish what she had started. And every night, she went back onto the streets, hoping to find in some new part of Sunderland the man who could help them. You might think she would have been looking for a husband, but no, having lain with so many men made her disinclined to become the property of any one.

Gustine watches the Eye's eye for any movement, for the

slightest twitch to give away Henry's arrival. He believes he can save us, she murmurs, kissing the baby again. How that salvation will be manifested is as murky to her as the image of the saviour formerly had been. Perhaps he will hollow out a little area so that the heart might be tucked back in; or maybe he will build a bower of bone above it. Gustine does not pretend to know how the human machine works, but surely Henry knows what to do.

Downstairs, Eye's eye cuts to the latch, and Gustine rolls onto her back, lifting her baby high overhead. Fly, little baby, fly. His arms and legs flap happily, his blue eyes catch fire in their sockets. He swoops down to kiss his mamma, and then he's off again—back up into the air, soaring above his mamma's head, squealing with delight. Shush! hisses a neighbor, but Gustine still holds him aloft. Fly, fly! No one present at his birth doubted that this baby was born merely to soar straight back to Heaven, to molt away his deformed flesh and speed like a liberated bluebird from his mother's hands. But the fates who spun him so short a thread did not reckon on Gustine for a mother. The only thing she regrets is having had to surrender poor Fos; and if she'd known who Judas was, she'd be feeling thoroughly Judas-like right now. But what must be done, must be done. Give us a kiss, little baby. Gustine brings his lips even with her own. Body by body, your mamma is mortgaging a life for you.

But what do all these dreams signify to you, coin-lidded Fos? What do you care for the Eye's shadowy visions, or the enmity of Thomas Malthus, or the future of a baby whom you will never see again? Is it not an annoyance having the dreams of the living crowd the great storehouse of the Uncon scious, making you and the rest of the cramped dead wish for nothing more than morning? Come, Fos, you have earned a little selfishness. Why should you have to concern yourself with anything in this house tonight beyond that soft creak of the floorboards coming toward you.

A careful footfall usually announces one of two types of men: lovers and thieves. You've had your lover, don't deny it, back when you worked on your cousin's farm in Hartlepool, sleeping in the hayloft during the summer months. You were part of a giggling heap of sweaty breasts and legs back in those days, teasing along with the rest of the girls about babies and how to come by them, taking turns on the outside so that your chosen favorites might visit. But on the night of your turn outside, Ned Turner came so softly upon you, you almost didn't hear him. He was like an unexpected apparition in the moonlight, a spirit to summon rapture in a stunned devotee before disappearing back into Heaven. The next day he smiled at you in the field, no more, but that acknowledgment has been good enough to live on these thirty-two years hence.

But what if, on the other hand, this is no lover's footfall at all? What if the creak is a thief? Will not Pink jerk awake and shriek? Can you not depend on the vigilant Eye to leap up from her stool and drive him from the house? Think first to tear Whilky's daughter away from the furry white lap of her ferret mother, where she has finally fallen into a rare and peaceful sleep. Think then to pierce the drug-induced fog confounding the frustrated, blinking old woman. Never having taken laudanum (or had it visited upon you), you cannot appreciate the profound inertia it insists upon. Eye is no more capable of leaping up to drive away a thief than she is of wrapping the gray shawl that's slipped to her waist back around her shoulders. She stares angrily at the shadow creeping across the floor, unable to move, conscious of only one thing—if it comes too near the dress, she will find the strength somewhere to hurl her limp body and pin it to the ground.

Unlucky for you, Fos, the creak-shadow stops far shy of the dress. It hesitates before the Eye, wavering and uncertain, then makes a quick wide circle between Pink and your box. The wind blows a sheet of sleet against the house, and the floor trembles. Pink's cold feet twitch under her faded gingham dress. The shadow stands over your private box for what feels like a very long time before a hand reaches under your back and another slips beneath your knees.

Why am I being taken from this house?

Can you really not yet know, Fos?

Tell me!

We all have a job to do, and ours has been to undertake the telling of this story. Still, there are days in any job when you want to turn away, to leave unfinished what must be done, to leave unsaid what must be known. We will tell you, then, that it is not yet time for you to rest. You have baled hay, you have painted matches, you helped narrate the beginning of our story, but you are being put back to work one last time, Fos. Your body still has some use in it.

I do not understand.

If you will know, then, look ahead with us an hour. See that clumsy black dog digging furiously under the fence separating two backyards on Nile Street? He scratches down a few inches, thrusts his muzzle in to measure, paws more red soil, snorts into the hole he's made. It is too much to ask of a dog that he remain indifferent to fresh meat, especially when his master is out of town and the servant boy forgot about his dinner. He scratches and scratches until the hole is big enough—see how he wriggles through and ranges about the yard? A few perfunctory sniffs take him straight to a plot of fresh-turned, shovel-flattened earth. The dog spins in a frenzied circle once, twice, three times, then turns up his snout and howls ravenously up at the moon. At the sound, a doctor, upstairs in his library, pauses before his glass-fronted cabinet, where he has just selected his largest saw.

What does any of this have to do with me?

Ah, Fos. You will learn soon enough.

II
A HOUSEHOLD DIVINITY

"... the heart is the beginning of life ...
it is the household divinity."

—William Harvey, *The Motion of the Heart and Blood in Animals*

IX

A PETITION

"God bloody damn!" Whilky Robinson roars into the empty coffin. *"Where is she?"*

Pink's eyes fly open. From where she fell asleep before the fireplace, she scents red-eyed, sour-stomach danger in the room, but not fast enough to outrun it. Danger has her by the hair and has smashed her face against the coal bin in the time it takes to say "eek." Pink knows; she tried to say it. But the word drowned in a thick gulp of blood.

"I ask one thing! One thing!" he shouts down at the ball she's curled herself into, and kicks at its spine. "Watch a bloody dead woman. So, where is she?"

Pink inches herself toward her corner. She's never seen her Da so mad; even Mike, hissing under the table, is afraid of him. She glances up at the tin clock. Quarter to five; time for them to light the fire and fix coffee. It's coming back now. Dreaming of her mother. Fos in her coffin. But how could it be that Fos is gone?

"Did she come back to life?" Pink asks anxiously.

"Did she come back to life?" her father parrots. "Did she come back to life? Of course she didn't come back to life, you stupid little bugger. She's been stolen! From my very own house! While *you* were supposed to be watching her." Whilky rears back a heavy-booted foot and kicks a splintery hole in the flimsy Sunderland Parish coffin.

A crowd of sleepy, tousled lodgers, roused by their land-lord's shouts and Pink's screams, has gathered at the top of the stairs. Whilky spots Gustine near the front, the only one among them who looks well rested. He lunges for the dress lodger, catching hold of her wrist and pulling her down the last three stairs. "This is your fault!" he shouts.

"What are you talking about?" Gustine struggles against him. "What's happened?"

"You know damned well what's happened. That doctor who was here last night looking at your abortion of a baby came back and took—" He sputters unintelligibly at Fos's coffin. "I ordered him out—goddamned bloody body snatcher!"

"How could that be?" Gustine wrenches her arm away. "How could he have gotten in? Even if Pink fell asleep, the Eye was here. She would have stopped any doctor, and you know it."

Gustine's words bring Whilky up short. His fury had been so leveled at Pink, he'd almost forgotten about the blinking fixture on her stool. But Gustine is right: the Eye was here, and the Eye never sleeps. He walks over to where she sits, in her same place, dogged beneath the blue dress. He screws up his face and tries to summon the courage to shout at her.

"What did you see?" It comes out a whisper.

But in all the years he's never seen Eye sleep, he's never heard her talk, either. She sits with her feet wide-planted, her heavy ape arms on her knees. Her eye fixed on the floor, she sees again the rat's shadow creep out with the cheese. Poison, she thinks thickly. Eye. Have. Been. Poisoned.

"What in the hell am I asking you for?" Whilky slams his fist into the wall beside her head, startling a shiver of plaster from the ceiling. "A bunch of traitors and morons, that's what I keep in my house!" He whirls around, rushing the lodgers on the stairs. "Get out of my sight, every last one of you!"

They flee upstairs, hurriedly dressing, not caring if they reach work fifteen minutes early and have to wait outside for the gates to open. This proves it, rages Whilky. The infernal partnership between doctors and tyrants. Frog eggs were not enough—now the Government wants us to know we are not even safe in death. Why, even as he is standing here, the Tories are lobbying for a bill that would hand the bodies of them that die in the workhouse over to the surgeons for dissection. It's not enough the Government has taxed the poor man into the workhouse in the first place, has stripped him of his dignity so that he is ashamed to consort with his former friends. Now, if he dies alone and no one comes to claim him right away—or even if they do come to claim, but cannot afford a funeral—he is considered unwanted, unloved, and no more than fodder for the surgeon's knife. Used to be only executed murderers were dissected, as punishment for the most hateful of crimes. But now it is a crime simply to be poor.

But are the bloody sawbones satisfied with a bill? No! They are so greedy they will steal into a man's house and take the dead from their very coffins! One was in here last night, prying through Whilky's things, touching his possessions. God bloody damn! The landlord of 9 Mill Street ranges about his parlour like a lost child, touching his carefully chosen artworks, picking up his Wearmouth West View 25-Year Commemorative milk pitcher and placing it woefully back on the mantel.

Pink notices the change in her father from where she crouches behind the coal bin. Mike too senses it, and creeps slowly out from beneath the table. Whilky Robinson cocks his big square head and turns his palms up to Heaven, and (oh God, gasps Pink, tears!) fat tears ooze from his stinging hungover eyes. I am not safe, even in my own house, he thinks. If They can just come in here and take whatever they please, what is left for us? He drops heavily onto his stool, surveying what used to be his kingdom but which has turned overnight into a pathetic hovel fit only for a pathetic, powerless man. They have gone too far this time, he whimpers. They have gone too far.

Sucking the blood from the tooth her father knocked loose, Pink inches around the coal bin to marvel at this stranger sitting on her father's stool. He has Da's red hair and wears Da's jacket covered with medals, but where is Da's bluster? Where is his pride? Mike rears back on his hind legs, gingerly sniffing, as if he shares Pink's confusion.

She creeps out an inch more, and abruptly her father's gaze turns to her.

"*Comfort me, Pink,*" Whilky Robinson wails, reaching out his arms to his dazed and bleeding daughter. "*Yer Da has been violated.*"

Dr. Henry Chiver saws through the sternum along the median line, taking care not to nick the soft organs beneath, and skirts the bottom of the rib cage. This one's bones are frail, he thinks as the saw goes in, not much more trouble than cutting into a large dog's chest. Setting aside his saw, he takes up a scalpel and divides the intercostal muscles, separates the costal cartilages on each side from their ribs, and carefully cuts through the pleura, which he will have his students examine in a moment. By his separating the two halves of the sternum and raising the cartilages on each side down to the diaphragm, they will be able to see the internal mammary artery, the intercostal nerves, and the three serous sacs of the thoracic cavity, one for each lung and one for the heart. The lungs, Henry sees, are strangely shrunken in their sacs and lie farther back as if pressed against the spine. Cholera lungs.

"Each sac is divided into a visceral and a parietal portion," he says, pointing with his scalpel. "The visceral portion lines the exterior of the organ, while the parietal adheres to the cavity that contains it. Both surfaces are constantly lubricated with serum so that no friction might impede the movement of the organ."

Four heads block his light and he has to ask them to step back again.

"Notice the pleura. It acts like the skin of the inner cavity. It proceeds from the sternum all the way back to the spinal column. It forms a septum, here; and here it adheres to the pericardium. Here it gathers around the root of the lung from which it extends, forming the pleura pulmonalis. This middle section, from the upper thorax, bounded by the sternum, vertebral column, and diaphragm below, is designated the 'mediastinal space.' You should be looking, Mazby, not writing."

Andrew Mazby sets down his notebook with a blush.

"These two shiny gray bands running through the middle of the mediastinum are the phrenic nerves." Henry plucks them lightly with the back of his scalpel. "They communicate with the diaphragm and the pericardium. As we go deeper into this woman's body, you will learn the inescapability of symmetry. Nature does not provide one nerve without pairing it to a second. She invests us with two lungs, two kidneys, two eyes, two ears. Even the singular brain is divided into identical hemispheres. Even the heart has two corresponding auricles and ventricles. We are paired creatures. If you take nothing else away from your lessons, understand that. We cannot exist in singularity.

"Now, moving on to the pericardium," Henry continues when his students nod blankly. "You will note this is not the pericardium of a healthy person. This albuminous film" —he rubs his fingers together, working it into a lather—"I've never seen before. And these little bruises, here, are not normal. I would imagine they are factors of the disease."

"Aren't we at risk for contagion, standing here breathing in the miasma?" asks Bietler nervously.

Henry shrugs. "It's all in your attitude, boys. If you are weak and panicky, you will become sick; if strong and resolute, almost nothing can touch you."

The four students take a step back anyway, and Henry has a good deal more light.

"This woman has no fat around her pericardium, I see," he says, prodding it with his scalpel. "Notice how the membrane is attached to the diaphragm below, and the thoracic fascia above. The left lung is excavated to fit the heart. Here you can see the external layers of the aorta, the vena cava, and the pulmonary artery."

Mazby can't help himself, and reaches for his notebook. The four boys look almost professional in their chocolate brown shalloon aprons and tied on sleeves. Their deep pockets are filled with scalpels and hooks and other dissecting equipment, which they are all itching to use. Enough talk, they are thinking, let us cut. But Henry is not about to let them mangle this body. This hard-won woman is more than an anatomy lesson; she is Jack Crawford and Isabella Hazzard and all of those he supposes will die after her. She is a study in a new disease.

"I am just going to make a longitudinal incision here, like this," he says, "and expose the heart."

Sunk deep inside the chest cavity, the muscle inside is firmly contracted in its left compartments, slightly less so on the right. The right auricle and ventricle are both filled with dark, clotted blood, while the heart in its entirety is rigid and deep red. A cholera heart.

The heavy curtains in the library billow as a cold current of air slides across the room. Henry watches his breath wreathe over the old woman's open chest, while across from him, Coombs's eyes disappear behind fogged glasses.

"Here it is, my boys," says Henry, stepping back from the body for effect. "Cut out an eye, and you will live. Injure the brain, and while intelligence may flee, function continues. You might destroy nerves and tissue and bone and fat, but puncture this organ, interfere with the working of this most primordial piece of man, and all life will cease. Look here," he says, pointing to the clenched left auricle and ventricle that speed blood to the rest of the body. "You will almost always find the left chambers contracted in a cadaver, because the last impulse of the dying body is to infuse itself with blood. The heart reaches out to the extremities. It dies fighting."

Henry stares down at the organ that has been the singular fascination of his life. He has learned a hundred reasons why the heart should stop beating—a mortal wound, strangling fat, a blockage in the arteries—but he cannot conceive of a single reason why it should start. The fetal heart emerges first from chaos, bringing with it brain, lungs, bone—but by what celestial magic does it call itself into being? If only a doctor were like a geologist, who every day finds another ancient species impressed in stone; if only Henry might lay a bit of clay over a dying heart and take a fossil of the soul, surely he could find the secret of the first heartbeat impressed upon the last.

"Except for its sunken position and the clotting, which must be due to the disease," he forces himself to go on, "this is a structurally normal organ. We might expect to find considerable fat deposits between the muscle fibers and the serous layer, but fortunately for us, this woman's heart is emaciated. You'll notice it is vaguely conical in shape, with its base looking upward, backward, and to the right side of the body, its apex facing forward, down, and to the left, resting on the diaphragm. Now, descending into the upper right auricle, here, is the vena cava. . . ."

He hears himself explain the principle vessels—aorta, pulmonary artery, vena cava decendens—yet handling this normal heart only turns his mind toward the aberration at Mill Street. He has been thinking of that child non-stop since he saw Gustine's dress hanging above that horrible one-eyed creature who follows her everywhere—there could be no two such alike dresses, certainly no two such alike old women in the impoverished East End. Why did she not tell him she lived in that house? What reason would she have for not admitting her proximity to that child? It is beyond puzzling—it is downright deceitful, when she knows how interested he is in studying it. Stop, he thinks. You are becoming greedy. Concentrate on the body at hand.

". . . And the pulmonary artery, here," he continues mechanically, "speeds blood to the lungs, where it undergoes a chemical process that changes it from a dark to a florid color. This clean blood comes back into the left auricle and ventricle, from whence it is pumped through the aorta to be distributed to all parts of the body. Now, the walls of the left ventricle are about three times as thick as those of the right—"

Henry is interrupted by a soft knock on the door. He looks up angrily. What is wrong with Williams? He knows not to disturb him when his students are here.

"It's me, Henry," a clear voice announces. "I am sorry to disrupt your lesson."

Henry and his four students look up to see a young woman neatly turned out in a brick red poplin dress. She stands in the doorway, pale with resolution, for she has never been allowed inside her fiancé's inner sanctum, and trembles now at her own audacity.

"My God, Audrey, what are you doing here?" Henry yelps. His students, blushing to the roots of their hair, instinctively shift to block the naked body from view. The blood-spattered doctor flings down his scalpel and comes around from behind the table.

She swiftly throws up her hand to stop him. "I am here only for a moment, and it is to see your students." She shifts her focus to the four boys standing shamefacedly before the corpse, looking at the sawdust-strewn floor, at the book-shelves, anywhere but at her. From the pretty silk reticule she carries, Audrey draws forth a quill pen, a little pot of ink, and a crisp piece of parchment. Careful schoolgirl handwriting covers the top quarter of the page, but the rest has been left blank—except for a single name, in the same hand, written beside the number 1.

"I have never met any of you before," she says, as though she'd been practicing the speech. "But you mustn't think of me as an excitable girl, to be disturbed by the realities of medicine. Think of me instead as a woman who shares her future husband's belief in his work—no, who even more than shares: as someone who honours it above all other professions."

But if Audrey's heart honours her fiancé's profession, her nose rebels against it. The gassy, gamy scent of flesh is so strong in the room that she is forced to lift her handkerchief to her nose or risk having her gorge rise in her throat.

"I have begun a petition to be circulated around the town," she continues. "My own name is first, and I thought Dr. Chiver's students might appreciate having their names affixed next."

"Audrey," Henry demands roughly. "What on earth are you talking about?"

She lifts her head proudly and turns to him with shining eyes.

"Like the intellectuals you spoke of in Dublin, I have begun a body donation drive. I plan to secure you and the doctors of Sunderland as many donated bodies as you need so that we might end, once and for all, that unholy practice of body-snatching. My own name, willing my body for dissection, is first."

Bietler can't help himself: he lets out a strangled nervous bleat.

"What are you talking about?" Henry shouts. "Have you gone mad?"

"I am doing it for you," Audrey says uncertainly. "There are rumours on the street today—I heard them doing my charity work—that another body has been taken in the East End. Every doctor in Sunderland is under suspicion. If people will only donate—"

"People won't donate, Audrey." Henry is so embarrassed by her behaviour, he is beside himself. "And it is certainly not a suitable cause for you to espouse. You are a woman; it is inappropriate for you to even know of such things."

"But I do know," she replies heatedly, forgetting for a moment the presence of his students. "And it does affect me if my husband is forced into immorality because of other men's superstition."

Henry steps from behind the table, determined to lead her out of the room. He is stopped by a vehement, high-pitched voice.

"I will sign."

They are all startled at Andrew Mazby's declaration. The student's face is mottled and his lips tremble. How can I disappoint this brave young woman? he thinks, his admiration overcoming, for a moment, his fear of Henry's displeasure. She is ready to sacrifice her own body for the man she respects most in this world; why should she expect any less of me? He moves to take the paper and pen she holds out, and in doing so exposes to Audrey's view the sunken-jawed face of the naked cadaver.

"You are dissecting a woman, I see," she says bravely, stepping past Mazby to observe the open body on the table. "Oh."

"Audrey, come with me outside," Henry commands.

"All the more reason for my petition," Audrey says, taking a long, woeful look at the body on the table. "Oh, Henry, then you won't have to cut up women you were sent to help."

Stung by her words, he turns away and says nothing.

"Thank you, Mr. Mazby." Audrey nods grimly at the young man as he signs his name. "Mr. Bietler? Mr. Coombs? Mr. Grose? My fiancé has spoken so often of you, I feel I might, without offense, solicit your help. Will you not, in the interests of your own profession, publicly donate your bodies for dissection?"

Why doesn't he thrust this meddling female out of the room, Grose thinks, as he sullenly takes the pen and scrawls his name under Mazby's. Bietler is equally angry at being shamed into signing away his remains. His family has a mausoleum at St. Peter's, where the Venerable Bede was laid to rest, an old and established vault into which every Bietler for the last two centuries has been interred. His father is going to kill him when he finds out. Coombs is the only one who signs blithely, completely convinced that with the speed of modern medicine, a cure for death will surely be discovered before it is his time to go.

Audrey nods to the boys and takes up her pen and paper. She throws one last unhappy look Henry's way, but he does not turn around.

"Let us hope that by example, we will lead this age out of darkness," she says simply, and pulls the door behind her as she goes. Henry waits a long few seconds before he slams his fist on the table and runs out behind her.

"Audrey! Wait!"

She is at the bottom of the stairs, being helped into her cloak by Williams. His manservant throws the frantic doctor a sly, self-satisfied look, and Henry vows to dismiss him before the day is done. Williams quickly withdraws into the parlour, leaving the two alone in the sunny foyer.

"Henry, how could you?" Audrey sobs, her brave front crumbling at the sight of him. "I promised that woman I was sending help."

"I went to honour your promise," he insists, wanting to take her hands, but conscious of the blood and gore upon his own. "She was already dead when I got there. She died of the cholera, darling; there was nothing I could have done."

"But you didn't have to steal her in the middle of the night.

You didn't have to make her naked body an object of curios-ity for young men."

"Audrey, you cannot have it both ways." Henry is so very tired, and he does not want to argue with this weeping woman before him. "You cannot sign away your own body and expect men not to look at it. It is what doctors *do*. This woman was dead, she had no more use for her body, she was a danger to others in her house, for she very well might have been infectious. Why should she not serve our purposes? Why should something devoid of life not teach us how to save the lives of others?"

Audrey has stopped crying and looks now merely miser-able. She cannot articulate what bothered her so greatly in seeing Fos upon her fiancé's table. Perhaps it was her position, prone and so very vulnerable, just as Audrey had last seen her, glowing in her straw. Maybe it was finding a roomful of men standing over a woman's naked body, and feeling that their wicked thoughts had immediately transferred themselves to her when she walked in. But more than anything else, Audrey is certain this is all her responsibility. If she had never men-tioned the glowing woman and the extraordinary child to Henry, this poor creature would not be here today. She would not be hanging open with her breasts under her armpits and her legs spread apart. She would not have been cruelly snatched from her coffin, if Audrey is to believe the rumours she heard this morning. It is all her fault.

"Did you do it, Henry?" she asks at last. "Did you take her yourself?"

He does not know what to say. He has never lied to her, but then she has never asked a question that warranted any-thing other than the truth. She places her hand over his heart and looks pleadingly into his eyes.

"I don't want to get you dirty," he says, pulling away from her.

"Just tell me you don't do this yourself," she insists.

"I have someone," he compromises on a half-truth," who knows the neighbourhoods."

His fiancée lets out a long sigh, relieved that at least he is not the monster. He is only doing what must be done until the laws might be changed; she knew that when she agreed to become his wife. "After my petition has circulated," she says, fitting her head into the hollow of his chest, "you will be able to dismiss that depraved man."

He cannot imagine what his darling might think if she knew that the "depraved man" who helps him secure his bodies is, in fact, a woman, younger even than herself.

"Don't be distressed, dearest," he murmurs into her hair. "That creature on the table is helping us understand the workings of cholera. In finding her, you may have saved any number of lives."

But Audrey's conscience is not so easily assuaged as her fiancé's. She steps back and tugs on her black kid gloves, lifts her cottage bonnet off the peg by the door and secures it under her chin. She kisses Henry on his unshaven cheek.

"I will make it up to that poor woman by getting as many names as I can. She was never given the opportunity to volunteer."

"It would please me if you did not make a spectacle of yourself, Audrey," Henry calls as she steps down into the street. "I fear we both will be gravely embarrassed."

She looks him steadily in the eye. "I wish you had as much faith in me as I have in you," she says, then turns and walks away down Nile Street, as self-possessed as any Queen of Egypt.

Henry watches her until the crowd on High Street swallows her up. A tiny coster girl, her basket stacked high with fist-sized bundles of cress, rounds the corner and smiles at Henry, but seeing his abstracted scowl and blood-soaked apron, she quickly scampers on to the next house.

"Williams!" he bellows, leaning against the shut door. "Bring me a pen and paper."

The servant materializes as instructed and Henry scribbles a brief note. Is any of this worth it? The sneaking around, lying to Audrey? He needs to know what is being said about him on the street, but it is impossible for him to leave his students right now. They will need to work all day and all night for the rest of the week to finish her, and that's if that damned Mill Street landlord doesn't take it into his head to send round the constables. "Do you know the pub the Labour in Vain?" Henry asks his servant curtly.

"Yes sir."

"Here's a shilling. Deliver this to the proprietor there." Henry hands him the slip of paper and heads back upstairs to his waiting students. "And Williams," Henry adds as the valet pulls on his coat. "It was unpardonable of you to allow Miss Place into my study. Do not bother coming back."

Williams snorts—as if all the money in the world could get him to return to this charnel house! He buttons his coat and sets off for the Labour in Vain to lift a pint to his liberation. As soon as he's out of sight of the house, he unpockets the note and reads it. *G: I am counting on your silence,* wrote his former master. *Sunday, let me take you to the country. You would like that, wouldn't you? And bring the baby. I know you are more familiar than you have said. H.*

John Robinson is on a ladder with a paint pot, touching up his shovel-and-skull street sign, when Williams passes the note up to him. The outside is inscribed "Hold for the Woman in the Blue Dress," so John Robinson, knowing full well Gustine can't read, feels it his duty to review the contents. He sits on the top step, his paintbrush clenched between his teeth, narrowly studying the doctor's letter.

"You don't understand it either?" asks Williams.

The publican frowns and rights his tipping pot of paint. "Unfortunately, sir," says he, "I fear I do."

Audrey first tried her godfather Clanny's house in Bishopwearmouth, but, poor thing, before she could even open her mouth to state her reason for visiting, Mrs. Clanny, her mother's dearest friend, whisked her inside for a cup of tea. Have you picked your dressmaker? Chosen your flowers? Orange blossoms surely, for a June wedding, and camellias. Oh, we are so proud of you, like our own daughter, you are. Audrey didn't have the heart to upset the kindly lady with her petition, so she kept it rolled up in her reticule while she nibbled an almond biscuit and listened to Mrs. Clanny's opinions on fashion. One mustn't wear a hat so large that dogs stop in the street to bark at it was the ultimate determination, and as Audrey shook hands good-bye, she vowed to keep that in mind.

She had no better luck with Dr. Haselwood's wife, or Dr. Dixon's either. Mrs. Haselwood was upstairs in bed, ill since this morning with a mysterious stomach complaint—they were all anxiously waiting the doctor's return; and Dr. Dixon's wife had been shipped off to her sister in Durham. Intrepid Audrey next set off to visit her old school friend Emily Peaverly, who was celebrating her first-year wedding anniversary with the birth of her first son. Audrey lifted the child from his mother's arms—He looks just like you!—and planted kisses on both red cheeks. She knew she couldn't possibly speak of death in the face of this promising new life, so once more she kept her petition hidden inside her reticule. She had thought it would be so much easier to bring up the subject with women, for women understand the importance of small heroic acts, and even if they would not themselves sign for fear of displeasing their husbands, they would applaud Audrey's sacrifice for her own intended.

But now it is three o'clock and she has no new names upon her petition. She has watched the other women of Sunderland drink tea, dandle babies, fret the servants with their mysterious ailments, and she has begun to worry she is less a cynosure than she is, perhaps, unnatural. Maybe Henry is right. What business does she have imagining herself dead when others are getting on with life? Her last visit (to her second cousin, who broke down in tears when she broached the subject, and begged her not to speak of such horrible things) has put her out not far from East Cross and Low Street, where among the confusion of corporation offices, her father headquarters his shipping business. Perhaps she might feel comfortable speaking to his old employees, who have known her from girlhood and might sign their names out of personal regard and loyalty to her father. Yes, she'll give it one last try. She turns her steps toward the muddy, inelegant corporation complex, where the shade falls heavy and mobs of gulls scold from red-tiled roofs.

Place Shipping, her father's company, prides itself on having the lowest ratio of shipwrecks to years in operation. Only six of its clippers have gone down in the last decade, with a loss of life amounting to 114, while Sunderland as a whole has accumulated a far worse record (the unofficial count standing at 107 ships wrecked out of 600 in the last two years alone). Most of Sunderland's overcrowded, leaking, slapped-together vessels are destroyed along the coast route ferrying coal from the Tyne and Wear down to the Thames; but all of Place Shipping's accidents have occurred in the rough waters of the German Ocean, sailing to or from Riga, where the ships take iron rails and return with large clouds of Baltic flax. Audrey's father, Captain Place, is one of the least hated shippers in Sunderland; he racks up the fewest fines for overcrowding, serves the least adulterated coffee, and has consistently had the lowest mortality from phthisis of any mogul in town. Though an owner, once every year or two Captain Place even takes command of his fleet to prove that he has not lost his feel for the sea. He set sail for Riga in late May of this year, despite reports of the cholera there, and was due back in early September. The *Audrey Eliza*, his ship, got trapped behind the Quarantine and neither the company nor the family has had news of it in over a month.

Audrey climbs the narrow stairs to the third floor, where Mr. Harrison, the company's bookkeeper, answers her knock. She smiles wanly, for of all her father's employees, including the rough-and-tumble sailors who load the ships, Audrey has always liked this man least. He has a round billiard ball face and a waxed mustache, and wears the most hideous green plaid suits.

"Miss Audrey Place!" Mr. Harrison exclaims, unctuously bowing her into the office. "We haven't had the honour of yer presence in ages."

She's only come to her father's office a handful of times, to drag him off to lunch or scold him for working too late on a Saturday. It is strange to be here without him. Four desks, three of them empty, are crowded with crates and ledger books. Cobwebs flutter from the beamed ceiling as Mr. Harrison closes the door behind her; sunlight, where it angles in from the windows, bleaches a stack of old newspapers swimming with silverfish. It smells masculine in here, but in a sour day-after-a-bender sort of way. Audrey is certain her father would disapprove.

"I am surprised to find you alone, Mr. Harrison," Audrey replies politely. "Where are the others?"

"Left early today, miss," he replies, helplessly shrugging his shoulders. "Little to do wi' yer father and the fleet still away."

"So you've had no letter either?" she asks.

"Not a word."

"Mother tells me not to worry," Audrey says with a sigh, absently removing her bonnet and gloves," but I confess, Mr. Harrison, I am growing concerned."

"I'm sure there's no need for alarm, miss," he says, taking her things and pressing her into a dusty chair. "Sit! Sit! We'll be hearing from him any day now."

Mr. Harrison pulls a chair out for himself, catching a glimpse as he does so of the bottle of mercury pills he's left sitting on his desk. That stinging in his privates had meant exactly what he feared it meant, and the apothecary has put him on yet another course of quicksilver. God damn that night under the bridge, thinks Mr. Harrison, whisking the bottle of pills into his coat pocket before his boss's daughter sees. What he wouldn't give to get his hands around that little whore's throat.

"So, what brings you down here among us working folk?" asks Mr. Harrison, scooting his chair around and crossing his legs so that one of his green plaid knees is just touching Audrey's. It's a harmless game he likes to play, and hasn't Miss

Audrey grown into a fine-looking young woman? She sits with the low winter sun behind her, igniting the red in her molten gold ringlets. Yes, indeed, how fetching the boss's daughter looks, thinks Mr. Harrison naughtily.

Certain Mr. Harrison must not realize his proximity, Audrey tucks her legs a little farther under her skirt. She glances uneasily around the office; the chairs at the other desks are dusty too, as though they have not been sat upon for days.

"I was hoping to have a word with all of my father's employees," she says, setting her reticule on her lap. "About something very dear to my heart."

"Well now, you might have a word wi' me and I'll certainly pass whatever it is along," says Mr. Harrison with a little pat to her knee.

I *will* speak of it, she decides, flinching at the pat. It is time to be brave. Audrey snaps open her reticule and draws forth the petition. She sets it on the desk before her, then folds her trembling hands primly back in her lap.

"As you probably know," she begins, colouring slightly," doctors have an imperfect understanding of the human body. They might learn a great deal from books, but it is the intensive study of physical anatomy that advances Science. How unfair it seems to me that the burden of such study must fall, as it does now, solely on the backs of the poor. . . ."

Mr. Harrison is better with numbers than he is with words, but as he labours over the handwritten petition, a strange flush comes upon him. His mouth goes suddenly dry, his groin grows hot, and he is forced to rearrange his coat so as not to embarrass himself. *To dispel superstition and light the lamp of anatomical inquiry, I hereby will my body to Sunderland Hospital for respectful dissection, so that it may be of use . . .* Be of use? He glances up swiftly at the boss's daughter. He can just imagine what sort of use a lovely body like hers would be put to—stretched out naked upon a table, alone in a room ful of men. Why, what's to stop a randy medical student from fondling those parts of hers that—from climbing up and—from doing whatever he desired, with no resistance whatsoever! To be of use? Does she realize what she is suggesting with this petition? All the names set upon it are men, he sees, except for hers.

"Miss Audrey, when did that pretty little head of yours turn so morbid?" He laughs nervously. "Your papa needs to come back and speak sense to you."

"I assure you I am in great earnest, Mr. Harrison," Audrey says, a little offended by his laughter.

"You expect the people of Sunderland to line up for a carving? Just because of this piece of paper?" He cannot look at her now, too afraid she'll read the rush of lust in his face. "I don't like to imagine those dirty little boys hacking up such a fine figure as yours. As for myself, I can think of a hundred better things to do with it."

The silence is oppressive in the empty room, broken only by a solitary gull landing awkwardly on the windowsill. My God, thinks Audrey, my father's employee is making an advance at me. His knee is pressed against her own, and when she moves, his leg follows. This is wrong, thinks Audrey, rising swiftly. I must get out of here.

"Thank you for your time, Mr. Harrison," she mutters, moving for the door.

"What's the hurry, miss?" asks Harrison, leaping up when she does.

"I made a mistake in coming here when my father was

away," says Audrey, shaking. "I'll see he's apprised of the fine
way you are conducting business in his absence."

Harrison, realizing his harmless little game might get him
dismissed, reaches out to stop her.

"Wait!" he cries. "I'd like to sign this petition of yours."
He grabs the quill off his desk, dunks it in his inkwell, and
scribbles his name next to number 6. He thrusts the petition
back at her, hoping this will be enough.

Audrey looks down at the paper, feeling soiled beyond
words. This is how she is supporting her fiancé? By submit-
ting to the advances of low and awful men? She folds the
paper and hides it in her reticule, then leaves without another
word.

"If you hear from yer Da," shouts Harrison of the green
plaid suit, "send him my very sincerest regards. Let him know
I'd do anything to help a lady. Anything at all for a lady!"

But Audrey doesn't hear him. She is halfway down the
block, fighting back her tears. Her father's employee.
Whatever made him believe he could look at me like that?
She rages, angry after the fact. If Henry were here, he would
never have dared raise his eyes to me, let alone voice his
obscene thoughts. Overhead, seagulls dart from roof to roof,
squalling at her. This world is so ugly, thinks Audrey, having
for the first time in her life snagged a thread of the world's
great tapestry of ugliness. It is impossible to do good in the
world without having it perverted.

She walks for some minutes aimlessly, following the bank
of the river. It is beginning to grow dark, but Audrey is
unaware of her surroundings, sunk in disillusionment as she
is. She wishes she'd never thought of this wretched petition,
had not made herself vulnerable with it. But how must poor
women feel, with absolutely no choice in the matter? If it is

improper for Audrey to make herself available to medical science, why do doctors think nothing of using the bodies of lower-class women? Why is there one rule for them and another for me?

Audrey looks up and finds she has been walking the wrong way. She has come to the corner of Old Bodlewell Lane and Low Street, just above the ferryboat landing. A steep flight of nearly concave marble steps leads down to the water, where a chain stretches between the East End and Monkwearmouth. The hand-cranked ferry is just leaving the other side, and the landing is deserted except for a little girl playing by the water's edge. If Audrey squints, she can make out a tightly wrapped bundle leaning against the railing, while the girl splashes up and down the bottom steps, chasing terrified green frogs. Why does this child look familiar? Audrey wonders, drying her eyes. As she watches, the little girl catches a creature's leg between her teeth, then stares off into space as it stretches and croaks and struggles to get away; she has forgotten about the frog as she watches the flat-bottomed ferry making its way from Monkwearmouth. This is too brutal, really, Audrey thinks, and runs down the steps to release the poor panicked thing.

"Please, let me have it," she says gently, cupping her hands under the little girl's chin. "You wouldn't want to be caught that way."

The little girl in the pink gingham dress looks up, the green bit of rubbery creature pushing its suction toes against her swollen face. Dear God, thinks Audrey. What happened to this child? Seeing the lady's eyes so full of kindness and sympathy, the girl slowly opens her mouth. The frog drops to the ground and quickly jumps away.

"My name is Miss Audrey Place," Audrey says softly. "I know you, don't I?"

"You gave me a blanket," replies the child, ducking her chin and looking away.

"How did you come by those nasty bruises, Pink? It is Pink, isn't it?" Audrey reaches out and gently touches her cheek, making the little girl from Mill Street shiver. The left side of her face, from her jaw up to the bare slit of eye showing, is swollen black and purple.

"Look," says Pink, reaching into her mouth. "I have a loose tooth, too."

"Were you in a fight?" Audrey asks.

Pink shakes her head. "I am just a bad watcher. I never get it right."

"You were watching someone?" asks Audrey, feeling herself about to cry again.

"A friend of mine," Pink says with a nod. "You gave her a blanket, too."

"I did indeed," Audrey whispers, feeling worse than she's ever felt in her entire young life. She looks away so that Pink will not see her tears and notices that the baby has slid down the steps until it is lying on its back, deciding whether or not to cry. Pink's eyes follow hers and she runs over to get it.

"See why I get punished?" the little girl says, exasperated. "See what I always do?"

Pink comes back and sits on the next-to-bottom step with the baby in her lap. Audrey, in her expensive brick red poplin dress, walks down and sits on the muddy step beside her. Together they watch the chain-operated ferry ratchet across from Monkwearmouth—horses hang their heads to keep balanced; mothers draw their children close to keep them from leaping off the back. Another frog hops across the hem of Audrey's dress and this time Pink makes no move to bite it. The older woman holds out her hands and it hops up; she can feel its elastic throat swell against her fingers. Poor little frog, she thinks, you didn't ask to be a plague.

"This is nice," Pink says at last.

Why has her desire to help the man she loves gotten one woman dissected and an innocent girl beaten? It is not fair. This little girl should be watching green plants grow, bread rise, and suns set, not watching sickly babies and the caskets of her father's lodgers.

"Pink," Audrey says slowly, deciding what she must do. "If I become a wealthy matron and have a big house of my very own, would you like to come and work for me? I will have many things there that will need watching."

"I would like that," says the little girl, her pinched pink nose threatening to run with emotion. "But then who would mind the baby?"

"I have a feeling that by the time I am married, Jesus will be minding that sweet babe, dear."

"Da says Jesus is a bloody git who won't take care of no one." Pink smiles, getting her father's words exactly. "I must be better than him."

Audrey looks at Pink incredulously, but says nothing. This is how I shall make amends, she thinks. I will take this child into my house and teach her how to read and write. I will tell her Bible stories and buy her dolls and brush her hair. I will take her away from those that beat her, and raise her to be a happy and much-loved child. Henry will bless her—I am sure he will.

"What is your favorite name, Pink?" asks Audrey, determined that this girl should have a new name to go with her new life.

"Mike," says Pink.

"No, what is your favorite girl's name?"

"Auuuudrey," she whispers, giggling a little and looking away.

"That's my name," laughs Audrey. "Wouldn't you like one of your own?"

"Then . . . Geraldine," Pink whispers. "That was my mother's name."

"Geraldine it is." Audrey smiles at such a little girl having such a long name. "When you come to work for me, I will call you Geraldine."

Pink giggles wildly and the baby in her lap blows happy spittle bubbles in response.

Yes, it is in her power to stop the suffering, thinks Audrey, greatly pleased with herself. She reconsiders the petition she was about to abandon and how much it might mean one day for this little girl to know she values their two bodies the same. The *Sunderland Herald* offices are not far off. What better way to reach the entire population than to print her petition as an open letter to the town?

The sun is setting and the river has grown still as the Monkwearmouth ferry reaches the Sunderland side and everyone clatters up the steps around them. So many poor haggard faces, so many stooped and sullen sons and daughters, beaten down by their day's labours. Oh, poor tired mother, dully tugging apart her brawling children, whose bony clenched fists fly dangerously close to Audrey's head. Oh, exhausted flyblown farmer, leading your nag up the depressed marble stairs and over the skirt of Miss Place's fine poplin dress. Copperas-stained shovels and splintery crates of apples, thoughtless boots and muddy hems, have you no regard for the brave Samaritan in your midst, whose only thought is for you and how she might devalue her own body for your elevation? Elbow not her tidy hair, knee her not in your blind surge up the bank; she lives to serve you.

They come and they come, thinks woeful Audrey, buffeted and knocked until Pink flings up her arms to shield her. How can it be they see me not?

X

A HOLIDAY

Sunday, Sunderland's day of rest, comes at last.

On Friday, Gustine asked John Robinson to send word back that Dr. Chiver might find her on the town moor near the pump where they first met, since she obviously could not reply in kind. On Saturday, she worried he had not forwarded her message and asked him again, whereupon he replied that of course he had, and what did he look like, a carrier pigeon? Saturday night she couldn't sleep, petrified she had annoyed John Robinson into revealing her holiday to his brother, Whilky. She needn't have worried. John had always been the private, non-violent one of the family, preferring, even as a child, to draw pretend beer for the other boys rather than play at being Dick Turpin, cutpurse, or Robert Drummond the Sunderland Highwayman. He was no powder keg like his brother; her secret was safe with him.

Now she sits in the brown grass by the cemetery with the promise of Henry's letter in her lap, waiting for him here as only a week ago she found him waiting for her at the Labour in Vain. No one has ever written to her before—not a love letter, not a birth announcement, not a poem. Nothing. Until John Robinson passed off Henry's note, she had never experienced the simple thrill that comes from having put into one's hands a piece of paper originating elsewhere, rich with words meant only for oneself. You see, Gustine does not belong to the papered class, dashing off notes at the slightest provocation—*Jane, dear, Please come to dinner Sat. 7 P. M. . . . Dearest Mrs. M. We called today at 3, but sadly found you not at home. . . . Franklin: Cook requires butter, cheese, fresh eggs, tripe (enough for eight).* She does not yet take words on paper for granted, to be burned, as John Robinson suggested, before her landlord finds out the doctor's written her, but instead ranks Henry's note somewhere near the Rosetta stone for mysteriousness and magnitude of import. Of course she knows it would be safer to destroy an incriminating document she cannot even read, but let's be fair: who ever chooses to destroy the "first" of anything they are given? Would you have smashed the tablets of the Ten Commandments, had they come into your possession? No, you would have been weaker than Moses; we daresay that like Gustine, you too, would have selfishly hoarded your first communication from One so far above yourself.

She traces the "G" in the first line and the "H" in the last, but as for the other letters spiked across the thick and creamy paper, she has to trust John Robinson that they spell a day in the country. We are going on holiday, she tells her baby, who stripped of his blankets looks rare and important in his linen christening gown, wool skullcap, and felt booties, propped against her knees so that he might have a view of the other children playing on the town moor. On this unseasonably warm day, it seems all the progeny of Sunderland is out. Nearby, a gang of boys spanghew toads, which is the local way of saying "put them on a board upon a fulcrum, jump upon the board, and send them sailing across the moor to be smashed to a jelly." The boys whoop and dance, factor complicated configurations of frogs, unlikely anytime soon to run short of ammunition. On her other side Gustine hears a young girl patiently explain that a horse's hair, left in a puddle overnight, will turn into an eel. The girl and her friend run squealing off to seed the moor with eels from their own scalps, while the spanghewers let fly a flurry of green missiles behind them. These will be your friends one day, Gustine whispers to her child, drawing him more fully into her lap. When the doctor is done with you, it will be safe for you to kill things, too.

As if on cue, the doctor's carriage, the one he brought to Mag Scurr's a week ago, clatters to a stop beside her.

"Gustine? Is that you?" He leans out and squints, recognizing her more by the baby, she thinks, than anything else. He's never seen me out of my dress, she realizes, taking his hand, climbing up and settling herself under the lap robe he holds out for her. Last night, she called on one of Mag Scurr's competitors, where she counted out from her cache of carefully saved coins enough for a secondhand shawl to cover the stained and worn fawn-coloured factory shift. She couldn't possibly leave the house in her blue dress with out chaining herself to the Eye, and Gustine was damned if she would allow the old woman to ruin the first holiday of her life. Of course, as luck would have it, the only silk shawl she liked that was ample enough to cover all the holes in her shift was an indigo and black paisley that reminded her of a thousand watching eyes anyway.

He looks awful, Gustine thinks, taken aback by the dark circles under his watery red eyes. He has shaved for the occasion and wrapped a fresh cravat around his neck, his hair is combed forward fashionably, but nothing serves to hide the worry and exhaustion etched into his face. He looks like a very different man than he who stepped out in front of the theatre not even a week ago. But then again, she is a far cry from the lovely lady in the lamé turban who accompanied him.

"You brought the baby," Henry says, glancing over. "Good."

Gustine adjusts the child on her lap and lapses into silence. Usually, she has no trouble keeping up idle chatter with men; she's learned several safe topics of conversation: weather, chuck ball, pubs, and sex. But none of these seem quite appropriate to discuss with Dr. Chiver. As they speed along Low Street back toward the centre of town, she'd like to ask him where they are going, but even that simple question gets stuck in her throat. His eyes are fixed on the broken cobblestone street ahead, and one might assume he was alone in his carriage for all the attention he gives her or her baby. This is a strange beginning to a holiday.

"The weather certainly has turned fine today," Gustine ventures.

"Yes, it has." Henry whips the horses a little faster, anxious to get out of town. Holmes Wharf flashes by, and the steps down to the ferryboat landing; they pass the corporation offices where Audrey's father keeps an office; then they are whizzing by the dormant volcanoes of Sunderland Bottle Works. Henry hangs a sharp right and holds out a coin for the man at the little tollhouse.

Well, here is something new at least! Gustine has never been atop the Iron Bridge before, and as they fly across it now (over the spot where she found Dick Liss staring up from the mud, into the dizzying heights of blue sky, so high above the town that she can look down onto the bald heads of buildings bristling here and there with ragged terns' nests), even as she is utterly convinced that, any second, she and her child

will be bounced from the rig to their deaths, Gustine wishes
they might hang suspended here, right in the middle of the
bridge, so that she might look down on Sunderland and all
the tiny men in it, feeling for once in her life what it is to be
tall. But before she can express the thought, they are descending into the familiar gray warehouses and tenements on the
Monkwearmouth side, where Gustine, though she has never
been here before, feels depressingly at home, the slatternly
streets of Monkwearmouth being as squalid and airless as any
lane near Mill Street.

Henry seems to relax, though, the moment they cross the
bridge. He reins in the horses to a fast trot and leans back
against his seat, looking at her for the first time.

"I have much to discuss with you today," he says, thinking
it would be easier if she looked more like herself. As it is, she
is almost unrecognizable out of her blue dress, hardly whor-
ish at all, just another pale and underfed East End adolescent.
Her blonde hair falls loose around her shoulders and she
wears some sheer and shapeless undergarment that is mostly
hidden by a shawl, holding the overdressed infant on her lap
like a popish Christmas pageant baby Jesus. She looks at him
expectantly, but his own eyes falter.

"What did you want to discuss?"

No. Not yet. Why spoil it for her so soon? "It can wait
until we get there," he finishes weakly.

Gustine nods and turns her attention back to the wonder-
ful new things around her. They are quickly out of
Monkwearmouth township and headed west on wide,
straight Southwick Lane. She still has no idea where they are
going, knows only that the landscape is changing around her.
Low-lying streets distend into terraced rows of houses under
construction, houses give way to soft hillocks dotted with

winter-shorn ash and elder trees. Rows of carefully planted white globe turnips radiate out from the road, planted to feed the shorthorn cattle considered (by those whose job it is to judge such things) the most handsome in all of England. Gustine has never seen a cow anyplace but the East End, led, with the rest of its condemned herd, down the narrow lanes to the Queen Street slaughterhouse. How foreign and beautiful the white creatures seem in this habitat, their dewlaps swinging as they nuzzle browning autumn grass, their arched tails flicking when they lift their eyes to watch the carriage pass.

The only thing marring her delight is Henry's strange diffidence. She wishes he would tell her the names of these cows or what part of the county they are in, but nothing in his manner invites conversation. Why would he invite her on holiday and then punish her with silence?

"Where are we going?" she asks at last, when they have been driving without speaking for half an hour. The baby has fallen asleep on her lap, lulled by the swaying of the carriage; but she has begun to labour under an unwelcome suspicion. What if he is stealing away with them like he made off with Fos the other night? It's strange he has not spoken of that. Where are we going? She is about to demand an answer when a boxy pile of stones appears on a hilltop. They crest the next hill, and the stones resolve themselves into a building—a white, soaring building, taller than anything Gustine has ever seen. Flags fly from its top, an arcade of oak trees lead up to its door. Where on earth are they? Henry stops the rig and turns to her at last.

"I thought you might like to see a castle," he says.

Tall, turreted Hylton Castle stands halfway between

Sunderland and Washington, its neighbour to the west, Henry tells Gustine, who sits up very straight in the carriage, her eyes wide, her mouth half-open. She has never in her life seen a building so grand. Though Sunderland has grown famous for its Iron Bridge, and Washington infamous as the family seat of the first American president, Hylton Castle must not be denied its fair share of glory. Erected by our venerable William de Hylton sometime during the reign of Henry V, the fortress served its purpose up through the Border Wars, when it fell into disuse and was employed as a barn by a local farmer. The family took it up again in the seventeenth century, adding two Georgian wings in the next hundred years, replacing the battlement machicolations with modern pediment windows, and bricking in the roof troughs formerly used for the pouring of boiling oil. Upon the death of the last Hylton baron in 1746, the estate passed to a nephew, who promptly sold it to one Mrs. Bowes of Streatlam and Gibside (who, though she never lived there, added a loggia and a long row of low Gothic buildings), after which the place was leased to Simon Temple, who improved it with gardens and pleasure grounds, then to Mr. Thomas Wade, who has it now, and is once more letting it fall to ruin.

The castle's fame came from the legend of the Cauld Lad, the spirit of a young servant slain by an especially brutal lord, who haunted Hylton Castle's kitchens, washing dishes if dishes were left undone, scattering plates and food if the staff proved itself too industrious. He was an odd sort of ghost, far more home-economical than malevolent, and at length was propitiated away completely with a little set of green clothes. *Here's a cloak and here's a hood*, he was heard to say before he vanished, *the Cauld Lad will do no more good*.

"An honest-to-God castle, just like the one where King William lives and King George and Queen Caroline!" Gustine shouts over her shoulder, leaping from the carriage. "It's bigger than the Corn Exchange on High Street."

"See those three crenellated towers in the center and the old carved coats of arms over the door?" Henry says, catching up with their picnic lunch. "That's the original castle. But the two wings, north and south, were obviously added early last century; you can tell because they are very symmetrical and tidy. And look at the statues of those warriors with pikes fixed atop the towers!" Henry chuckles at the grotesquery of his forefathers' taste. "They are supposed to be keeping you out, I suppose."

"Am I not supposed to be here?" Gustine asks worriedly.

Henry shakes his head. "You have every right to be here."

"Whose are all these?" She points to the clutter of crests surrounding the Hylton Moses with horns. Henry tries to remember what his uncle told him on his first visit, almost a year ago. The rampant lion belongs to the Percy family, the three parrots to the Lumleys; the Eure of Witton, he seems to remember, has the shield with three shells. The Wassyngton (or Washington) family is represented too (a Hylton married into the clan), with their three stars and two crossbars, which was to become the pattern for the American flag. Gustine won't recognize any of the names, and he doubts if she has any idea in which direction America lies.

"Those crests belong to a gaggle of rich noblemen," he tells her. "Locals and their in-laws."

"Can we go into the house?" she asks timidly.

He would not hesitate to ask for a tour were his companion Audrey or Mrs. Clanny, but to introduce an East End urchin into a manor home? Henry hesitates. No, that is really going too far. "I don't believe visitors are allowed inside," he lies.

"Well, we can see in, at least," she says. Around back, the shutters to the first story of both wings stand open, and if Henry would give her a boost, she could just make out some of the rich and elaborate furnishings. Well, what could be the harm in that? Setting down the picnic basket, he makes a stirrup out of his hands, and raises her above the sill. Gustine could never have begun to imagine the opulence inside. Not even her peeps into the Bridge Inn dining room have prepared her.

"Look, baby," she says, holding up the child in her arms. "There's a woman's bedroom, painted pink with a white and gold ceiling. It has dainty little chairs, dunked in gold, with dark pink cushions. Look, there's a clock just like the one we make at the pottery! And there in the corner, a bed dressed as if ready to march down the aisle, all turned out in white silk and damask and panels of illusion. Dr. Chiver," she calls down, "I bet only one woman sleeps in that bed, and it looks like it could hold eight, while another forty or so could spread out on the floor. Move down one."

He chuckles and carries her over a few feet so that she might see into the next room. The bottom of her shift brushes his face lightly.

"This room is completely different," she informs him. "It's part of the old castle. Look, dearest," she again addresses the child, "there are long red and blue carpets on the wall with cone-headed women on them, and in their laps are deer—no, what do you call those white animals with the horn? In the middle of their heads?"

"Unicorns," Henry replies, straining a bit to support her.

"Yes, unicorns are on the carpets, and there's a fireplace five times as big as Mill Street's, with lions guarding it. But don't worry, they're not real. There's a long table, as long as the room almost, and dark heavy chairs. I can't imagine only one family eats at that. . . ."

"It's probably the old banquet hall," Henry tells her. The foot in his hands is so small, even in its heavy boot, it might be a little girl's. It strains against his fingers, pushing up onto tiptoe.

"Move down one," she laughs, kicking him lightly with her free foot. "Baby and I want to see."

Henry is surprised at himself. He, too, is laughing like a jackanapes, hopping down a few feet so that they might spy into another window. The mid-afternoon sun has played magician with Gustine's worn-out shift, making the sheer fabric nigh invisible. He colours a bit at his proximity to her straining slender leg, so close that he might shut his eyes and rest his cheek upon it. She is barely more than a girl, but the things she must do to her lover, to have him begging for her on the street . . . Henry pushes these thoughts away. She is utterly unlike the mocking, bawdy whores of Sunderland, which makes her all the more dangerous; a man might forget for a minute what she is, and be lost forever.

"Hullo there, you!" a strange voice shouts. Henry starts up, letting Gustine's foot slip from his hands. About thirty yards away, coming around the corner of the building, is an old man carrying a rake. He is dressed in brown homespun like a groundskeeper and wears a wide-brimmed felt hat to shade his face.

"Who ayr ye and where ayr ye from?" calls the groundskeeper, keeping his distance.

"Dr. Chiver of Sunderland and a friend," replies Henry. "We're up for a picnic."

"Take yer picnic elsewhere, m' good man. Mr. Wade wants no visitors from a plague town." The groundskeeper swings around his rake and leans upon it meaningfully. "When we care to die o' cholery morbus, we'll be sure to let you know."

"We are not infected," Henry says indignantly.

"P'raps not. But we've our orders. No chances to be taken."

To be considered a contaminant by Mr. Wade, who knows as much about disease and suffering as he does about the making of headcheese? The doctor expects prejudice from the ignorant poor, but the wealthy should know better.

"Come on, Dr. Chiver," Gustine says lightly, trying to hide her growing apprehension. "Let's take our basket down the road a bit."

"'Ope you got no cholery on the wall there." The groundskeeper gingerly prods the structure with his rake.

Gustine presses the baby closer and drags a fuming Henry back to the carriage. He lashes the horses, driving them half a mile up the road, until Gustine points out a naked linden tree where a patch of pea-coloured moss looks more or less inviting. If she cranes, she can still see the castle just over the rolling hill, small and white like a lost bone button.

"I apologize for that," Henry frowns as he spreads the yellow plaid lap robe and unpacks the picnic of cold chicken, artichokes, and sherry (being servantless, Henry'd had to plan the meal himself). "If I'd had any idea we'd be received in such an ill-bred manner, I never would have come."

"It's all right," replies Gustine.

"No." Henry shakes his head. "It was greatly embarrassing."

"I'm just so happy to have had a chance to see it," Gustine says, far more at peace with embarrassment than he. "I never knew there were such homes in the world." And Gustine is honestly happy. She does not covet that house like she did Audrey's jewelry set last Monday night outside the Theatre Royale; for the smallest twist of fate could have clasped that necklace around her throat or screwed those earrings onto her lobes, but only an upside-down world could tuck her into the pink room's fairy tale bed. "Thank you for thinking to bring me here."

Her gratitude embarrasses him, and he is happy to have the food as a distraction. Self-consciously, he arranges a plate for each of them and pours two glasses of tawny Jerez oloroso.

"No thank you," says Gustine, passing him her glass. "I don't drink."

"In your profession——?" Henry says, then breaks off. "Forgive me, I just assumed."

"My mother died of drink when I was twelve," says Gustine with little emotion. "I have no desire to follow her." She eyes the chicken hungrily but pauses before the gray-green thistle. "What is this?"

"It's an artichoke," he answers with some surprise. "Haven't you ever tried one?"

"I've never even seen one." She examines it as if it were the rarest ostrich egg. "How do you eat it?"

Her sense of wonderment, he decides, that's her charm. Peeling an outer leaf for her and one for himself, he demonstrates how to scrape away the meat." Drag it between your teeth like this," he says. "Go ahead. Try it."

Gustine closes her eyes and draws the spade-shaped leaf over her bottom teeth. She keeps her eyes shut for a very long time, savouring this taste as new as an invitation, as new as a castle. "It tastes like spring," she says.

"It's delicate."

"Is the whole thing like this? It would take a long time to eat."

"Don't be impatient." He smiles. "It's a food you have to work for."

The girl nods and bites into another leaf. "I'm trying not to worry that it's wasteful."

"The best things are," Henry laughs. "But we'll cheat a little." He plucks the sharp leaves like a lover prognosticating over a flower and, then, drawing his knife, cuts the choke away from the heart. "Eat this," he says. "It makes it all worthwhile."

Gustine could not feel more like a princess. Her castle lies over the hill, her prince feeds her a rare and secretive fruit. On her lap, her baby coos happily, reaching up to take the food from her mouth. She lets him gum a little piece of the light green bottom.

"Gustine," Henry interrupts her reverie. "Why didn't you tell me this child was yours?"

Gustine pauses over her baby's dancing legs. The time for confession is upon her, but she dreads it. She takes a peep at the doctor's sombre face, the same face she watched through the crack in the floor lean hungrily over Fos. The truth is she doesn't know herself what made her hesitate the other night, when he provided her the perfect opportunity to solicit his help.

"I need to change the baby's nappie." She evades his question, untying the other rough cambric diaper from around her throat where she's worn it as a neckerchief. "Excuse us."

Henry watches her bend over the child, shake out the soiled diaper, and deftly tie it into a knot. She removes the rough cambric scarf from her neck and slips it under the baby's chapped bum.

"I spoke to you honestly of his importance to Science," he chides. "Why did you lie to me?"

"I have my own sort of science," she says, slowly. "I was going to tell you today."

He hates the sort of overcharged talk she uses to recount her first sight of him, words like Salvation and Special Gift used in conjunction with fanciful descriptions of seeing through clothes. But as silly as he finds her outpourings, it is difficult to ignore another's appreciation of one's own worth, or pretend disinterest in the effect one makes without being aware. For whatever misguided reasons, she did fortunately light upon the right surgeon. Henry believes, as she does, that of all the doctors in this benighted down, he is the only person to whom she might have turned.

"The cadaver under the bridge, the woman in your lodging house, they were only bribes to secure my help?"

"I thought it was a fair exchange: what you want for what I want."

"What is it that you want?" he asks cautiously.

"Life for my son."

She says it so simply and with such complete confidence in his abilities, Henry is momentarily at a loss for words. Life for her son, as if she desired him to make change for a crown or pick her an apple. Henry reads in her face the same implacability her customers find when they seek to leave without paying. "Gustine," Henry shakes his head, "there are medical limitations—"

"Watch this," she interrupts, digging her fingers under the baby's ribs, tickling him mercilessly. The child wriggles, and as he squeals with laughter, his blue packet of heart spasms up and out, leaping into his neck. It appears not properly anchored in the chest, but freewheeling, like Aristotle's wandering womb. "It happens when he cries as well," says Gustine, pulling down his gown. "Joy. Pain. You can read everything he is feeling by the beating of his tiny heart. He can't survive so wide open. You must help him."

"Let me see him," Henry says doubtfully, holding out his arms for the small bundle, which Gustine happily hands over. He is unnerved by her expectant, too eager eyes and seeks refuge in case history. "Was the father in any of his parts, deformed?" he asks.

Gustine blushes deeply. "I know nothing of his father."

"Your pregnancy then," he backtracks quickly. "Did your routine change, did you see or do anything that might have affected the fetus?"

"I did nothing unusual," Gustine answers, shaking her head. "I went to the pottery, I put on the dress. I ate bread and butter like always. And a little fish when I could get it."

"But something must have happened to you," Henry insists, knowing there must certainly be a scientific explanation for this child's deformity. "Did you fall? Did you have a bad scare?"

"There was one thing . . ." Gustine begins but stops herself.

"What?"

"It's nothing I've ever said out loud."

"Everything is important," says Henry, mesmerized by the rhythmic beating in his lap. The child coos, contentedly oblivious.

She is loathe to say it, for she knows how it will sound: silly, childish, stupid to one so educated as himself. Thirteen hours of pushing and moaning in the straw of the common room; Pink fell asleep, the midwife fretted about sending for a doctor, only the Eye never budged from where she knelt between Gustine's legs. She stared and stared and would not take her gaze from that hole.

"He was given the evil eye," she says at last.

"If you are not going to be serious," Henry says, a little exasperated.

But the girl insists, "That was it. I'm sure of it. And she will finish him off if I ever give her the opportunity."

"Gustine, I can't help you if you won't at least try to be scientific." Henry holds the child out to her, but Gustine shakes her head.

"There is no science to explain how he makes you feel," she says softly. "Hold him closer. Don't you see? You fit."

Reluctantly, Henry returns the child to the hollow of his chest, feeling, oddly, the power of her words. Back in Edinburgh, he met an army surgeon whose patient's stomach was made visible through an old war wound. For years, this doctor fed his patient different foods on a string, then charted how each was dissolved, and thereby plumbed the secrets of digestion. What might Henry's career become, given the opportunity to study the heart in that way? Might he not far outstrip Galen (who would haunt the gladiator ring, waiting his chance to observe the torn chests of fallen champions), and advance Science by decades, without recourse to vivisection or the stain of the graveyard?

The heart is the beginning of life, the sun of the microcosm, even as the sun in his turn is the heart of the world, thinks Henry, remembering the words of William Harvey. He looks from the child into the trusting eyes of the mother. She does not realize that she has laid a choice in his arms. He might turn away from this sun, might live by night as he has done since first arriving in Surgeons' Square, a stunted, shrinking thief and a murderer; or—dare he dream it?—give his talents over to something beyond the grave; become the nurturer of new life instead of a carrion-feeder upon the dead. He might chart patterns of growth as opposed to decay; learn how we live as opposed to how we die. The heart is the beginning of life, thinks Henry, staring down at the babe in his arms. You could be my new beginning.

"I will do what I can for him, Gustine," he says at last. "But you realize he must remain with me."

"With you?" This she had not anticipated. "Certainly he can live with me while you treat him."

"How do you expect him to survive growing up in the East End?" Henry feels he must speak directly. "Suppose he's not killed by the next fever that sweeps through—how long do you think it will be before he is brutalized by one of the other children there? Can you protect him every hour of the day? Especially when you are working two jobs? He's not a normal child. He is special."

"I know he is special," Gustine says. "That's why we came to you."

"Then trust me." Henry cradles the baby, staring down into his bright blue eyes. "Ever since I left Edinburgh, I have been searching for something that might recall me to life. I longed to leave death behind, but I knew no other way. Now I have found this child, and with a single visible beat, his heart can teach me more than all the cadavers in Sunderland."

"It sounds like you want to put him to work," says Gustine, growing increasingly apprehensive. "He is only four months old."

"He *will* work, in a manner of speaking," argues Henry, "I will study him for the good of all mankind. And with me he will be well fed, well clothed, treated as the most valuable experiment in my laboratory. Consider it. His life would certainly be better than anything you could provide."

His words go straight to her heart. In giving her what she wants, he intends to take everything. "But he is all I have," she says woefully, feeling her arms empty and aching.

"You will not have him long if you continue to be selfish," replies Henry, matter-of-factly.

There it is again: the same casual cruelty that made her hesitate to confide in him the other night. She sees her child in Dr. Chiver's house, hooked up to wires and prodded with needles. Would his life be worth anything, forced to live like that?

"Let me think about it," Gustine responds, reaching to take back her child.

Instinctively, Henry tightens his grip. "And of course, I will recompense you handsomely," he says quickly, trying to read her impassive face. "What do you say?"

"I said I'd think about it," Gustine answers, blushing hotly. "Now give him to me."

Henry steps back, disconcerted at her vehemence. Why does she set herself against him, when he aims to help her? He is overcome with the most intense desire to shove her hard to the ground and just run across the field, run with this miraculous baby and never look back. She gave him this child—how dare she now demand it returned? Well, he won't let it go. He won't.

"Be careful!" Gustine yells. "You're crushing him!"

Henry sees he has the child clasped so tightly to his chest, the fragile heart is forced to beat sideways. God, what has come over him?

"There is no need to shout," Henry says, thrusting the howling baby back at her. "I was merely trying to benefit all involved."

"Please speak no more of it," says Gustine, practically in tears herself. Oh God, baby—she presses his hot cheek to hers—I almost lost you.

"Of course not, if it distresses you."

They stand in silence for some time, Henry choking back his rage, Gustine staring off toward the white castle. She feels the sharp edge of Henry's invitation like a viper in her pocket. And yet. There is a lovely castle in the distance. Here is a hand-packed picnic. He has given a day of his life to please her, shown her riches she'd never dreamed imaginable.

Henry silently tosses the chicken carcass that would have made enough soup to feed Gustine and the baby for a week, finishes her untouched sherry, and packs up the plates. She cradles the baby while he shakes out and neatly folds the yellow plaid lap robe, then both walk dully back to the carriage. This is a miserable ending to a picnic, Gustine thinks, remembering her trembling excitement on the moor only hours ago. She pulls her shawl more tightly around her. It is nearly seventy degrees, but to her, winter has arrived.

Henry cracks his whip and the team jolts forward. Let her slump against the side of the carriage, as far away as she can get; her petulance is wasted upon him. He cuts through the meadow to bypass wretched Hylton Castle and rejoin the Southwick Lane farther along. There is only stubble in the meadow and a scattering of trees, their branches hopping with songbirds misled by the warm weather. Henry's thoughts are dark. It has been the most insane of autumns—

snowing one day, Indian summer hot the next. All of God's creatures, not only these maniacally twittering songbirds, over-reproduced in the long warm spell, and now that the first frost has come are beginning slowly to starve. There is not enough food to appease the hordes of squirrels, deer, rats, Wearside frogs, and hunger is thinning the ranks. And as with the animal kingdom, so it goes with people. Henry is not surprised disease has come to this overcrowded, filthy town. He knows Nature, like some dissolute Roman empress, loves to binge and purge, every so often tickling the back of her throat with a feather of famine or typhus or cholera morbus.

He is just about to rejoin the main road taking them back to town when from the corner of his eye he spots a structure sitting alone in the middle of the uncleared field. Impulsively, he steers the horses toward it, marveling more and more the closer they come. How very strange. It is a tall marble temple built upon a shallow incline and guarded by an iron gate, the door to which stands open an inch or two. Above the temple grows a single plane tree, spreading its naked branches to shade those who have no more need of shade. The red earth around it looks churned and fresh trampled as if just quit of a crowd. How odd, thinks Henry. The resemblance is uncanny.

"Why are we stopping?" asks Gustine dully.

"It is a mausoleum," replies Henry. "Here in the middle of nowhere."

"I've had enough death," says Gustine, turning away. "Keep going."

But Henry drops the horses' lead and stares, transfixed. With the plane tree shadowing the false Greek temple, and the stones scattered about like ruined columns of a fallen city, this place could have come directly from one of his anatomy texts; all it lacks is an erect skeleton contemplating its own mortality. So isolated, this is surely the abandoned grave site of some old noble family that has moved its dead onto more fashionable pastures, but even knowing that, Henry cannot shake the sensation it is supposed to mean more. Why should we come across a page of my Albinus here in the English countryside? thinks he. What am I to make of this? All around the door, the earth is fresh-trod and the gate has been left half-open. Someone has been laid here since the last rain, which means a body no more than three days old. Have I been led here for a purpose? he wonders, stepping out of the carriage as if in a trance and walking toward the crypt.

"Dr. Chiver," calls Gustine. "Please take me home."

There is a Latin epitaph etched into the marble pediment, darkened into readability by the pollen from the tree above. *Et in Arcadia Ego*; I, Too, Am in Arcadia. Death follows me no matter where I go, thinks Henry, even here to this idyllic place. But I could turn away. Even if Death lays a trail of bread crumbs, I do not have to follow it. Behind him, Gustine sits miserably in the carriage. I should go back to the horses and drive her away from here, he thinks. But the tracks are so fresh, and the gate is ajar, beckoning, as if commanding him to come forward. This is her fault, he thinks irrationally. It was in her power to return me to the living; instead, she has forced me back among the dead.

He steps through the gate, crushing acorns deep into the mud. Yes, people have certainly been here. Many sets of footprints, a procession maybe; large feet, small, even the tracks of children. The person laid inside must have been highly regarded, a lord or a lady certainly, to command such a crowd and such a mausoleum. He will be no different on the inside, though, no matter how well bred; simply another map for his students, another page of notes, another few jars of floating organs.

"Please, don't go inside!" Gustine shouts.

The ironbound door squeals upon its hinges as he pushes it open and slowly steps into the mausoleum. The old greed is upon him again; he feels as he did opening the door on William Burke smirking at him, offering Mary Paterson no more than three hours dead, so fresh he had to have her. As he did only moments ago, wanting to strike Gustine and make off with the child as if he were some depraved highway robber. Henry is losing control, and it scares him. Becoming involved with this girl who draws bodies to her like a lodestone, risking exposure by breaking into houses. Now pillaging a grave of God only knows who, because the crypt reminds him of his anatomy book. Turn back now, he commands himself. Before it is too late. But of course he does not.

Et in Arcadia Ego. I, Too, Am in Arcadia. Let us see who the procession of footprints laid to rest, who was mourned inside this facsimile of Albinus, who was left for Henry to find. He hesitates in the semidarkness, reaching out to take what belongs to him. Does his troubled conscience conjure that sudden accusing smell of cheap whiskey like static electricity married to the very dust motes? Or does his fevered mind misgive?

In the carriage, Gustine slumps against the door and draws her child close. She can just make out the doctor's baffled shadow, as he turns around and around, groping blindly, alone inside the empty tomb.

XI

BOARD OF HEALTH

Last night, while Gustine wept herself to sleep and Henry brooded before the fire, someone nailed a ninety-sixth thesis to the front door of the Sunderland Corn Exchange. Hammered rudely over the medical exhortations—"Do Not Drink, Incontinence Is a Friend to Cholera Morbus"; and "Avoid Pickled Pork, Especially at Dinner" —the resistance flyer sported a noblewoman dressed in the overwrought mode of last century, her wig teased to celestial heights, her skirt barely contained by the poster's frugal margins. We should more properly say the flyer depicted half a noble woman, for only her left side enjoyed the excesses of fashion. Her right side was another creature indeed: from the roots of her hair and the seams of her dress, a hideous skeleton emerged clutching a spear. In great red letters, the caption read:

> **Cholera Morbus:**
> **Death Accusing the Rich of Tyranny.**
> **They are killing the Poor, a Duty**
> **Which belongs to Him.**

Now this morning, if you look down High Street, Death Accuses the Rich as far as the eye can see. The skeleton shakes his spear into the litigious window of Odgen and Gray, Attorneys at Law; he upbraids mammon outside the gate of

Mr. Backhouse's bank. From Place Shipping to Lamb and Co. coal owners, cholera morbus fearlessly challenges the potentates of Sunderland.

A restless crowd has gathered before the poster nailed upon the door of the Exchange, where hundreds press in to read it or have it read to them. No one knows who paid to have the posters printed or who risked prison to put them up, but you might be certain just about every poor man in the crowd wishes it had been himself; just as every poor woman dependent on his wages gives thanks it was not. But why should a crowd have gathered around this particular sign when, as we noted, they litter all of High Street? Let's just say if a perverse meteor took a fancy to strike the Corn Exchange today, the widows woefully picking through the ruins would number among the wealthiest in Sunderland. The entire social register has gathered inside; and not only the town's prominent merchants and shipowners, but even our neighborhood's offering to the House of Lords, the Marquis of Londonderry. As luck would have it, these worthies have come together to contend and vote over the exact theme posted upon the Exchange door: the Board of Health, chaired by Dr. Daun, His Majesty's emissary from London, has called a meeting to address the cholera morbus.

"Please let me through," commands an unshaven Dr. Henry Chiver, holding his breath against the stench of the crowd. "I have business here."

"He has business here," one man mocks. "They're killin' us too slowly, so a meeting's been called to speed up the poisoning!"

A young man, no older than twenty, lanky and long-faced, elbows Henry in the ribs. "Hey there, mister, I wrote a song. Listen up, ye might learn somethin'!" Henry tries to back away, but no matter which way he moves, he finds himself walled in by corduroy and chintz. The grinning young man elbows himself a space and bellows loudly in a thick East End accent:

> *My sinkers! We're all in a fine hobble now,*
> *Since the cholera com to our river*
> *Aw wadn't hae car'd if 'twas ought that one knew*
> *But the outlandish name maks one all shiver!*
> *Our doctors are all in a deuce of a way*
> *And some says they've Clannied to wrong us;*
> *But I think we'll all curse the Daun o' that day*
> *The block-headed Board com amang us*

In time to his song, he improvises a shuffling dance, laughing oafishly and slapping his bony knees. With a cheer, his compatriots fling pennies at him, calling for more verses.

"What d' ye say, sir?" he bows, holding out his cap to Henry. "Spare a penny for a poor daft singer?"

"Get out of my way," Henry cries, digging in his shoulder and tunneling toward the Exchange entrance. A nervous-looking porter cracks the door and lets him squeeze through. We've already sent word to the constables, sir, the porter announces. They should be here any minute.

Down the hall, Henry squeezes through a tight corridor of silk and brushed wool, only slightly less odoriferous than the throng on the street. He spots his uncle across the mobbed room, seated near the podium, where Death (as he Accuses the Rich) is being taken down a peg by a furious Dr. Daun.

"This is the response to our sanitation bulletins," shouts the chairman, shaking a copy of the offending poster, ripped from his own front door this morning. "Suspicion and subversion! We are failing to convince them of our seriousness."

"There you are," says Dr. Clanny when Henry at last reaches him and takes up perch on his uncle's armrest. He sizes up his nephew's ragged cheek and frowns. "I came round to your house yesterday but you weren't home."

"Went for a drive in the country," Henry replies evasively. "I needed some air."

"We could have used you. Eight more cases yesterday."

"I am sorry," Henry apologizes, and quickly changes the subject. "What have I missed?"

"Not much," Clanny informs him over the chairman's harangue. "Reading of the last minutes. Roll call. Seems everyone with more than five pounds to his name is here today."

Henry looks out upon the roiling sea of powdered wigs and romantic spit curls, the tightly trousered leg chafing against the stolid knickered one. Last century is always depressingly in attendance at meetings like this, and while Henry might wax poetic over candlelit theatres or antique furniture, his appreciation for the past does not extend to its fashions. The musty, confining old clothes trap disease like pig blankets, while the false hair breeds biting fleas and lice. Against the suffocating heat, a few men have de-wigged, and fan their flushed red faces. Score one for the old-fashioned: the modern men sweat unrelieved.

"This poster is positive proof our message is being ignored," shouts Daun, crumbling Death into a tight ball and heaving him at the floor. "If we cannot convince the poor that cholera walks among them, they will never protect themselves! And if they don't protect themselves, we are done for."

In the crowd, Henry recognizes many familiar faces from his early days in Sunderland when he was more frequently invited to dinner. Mr. Thomas Brunton, proud owner of a lime kiln, shipyard, and colliery, is here at the side of his friend Mr. William Chaytor, who escorted Audrey from the theatre the night Henry attended Jack Crawford. Old Mr. Dixon (owner of Gustine's pottery) slumps in the corner, looking ready to faint from the heat, while his son and heir has given up and sits cross-legged on the floor. In a plush chair just on the other side of the podium, languid Charles William III, the Marquis of Londonderry, observes Dr. Daun as if the chairman were one of those fascinatingly horrid animalculae beneath a microscope. The Marquis' thoughtless elegance (the tight trousered style Henry prefers, the black cashmere frock coat, the velvet cravat) bespeaks his income (or at least that of his wife) as clearly as the well-worn uniform of the chairman announces him to be an army surgeon on half-pay.

"I am confused, Doctor." John Hepple, Albion and British Ship Insurance, takes the floor. "If this disease is so damned contagious, why haven't I got it? Or you? Or Lord Londonderry there? Our grandparents, God rest their souls, many of 'em remembered the last plague, and this seems to have nothing on it. Could we not be suffering with plain old English cholera, or the summer diarrhea?"

Dr. Kell, surgeon to the 82nd Reserve Regiment, and the only one in the room who has any previous experience at all with the cholera, rises to address the question. This gentleman saw what havoc an epidemic wreaked on the troops in Jessore and wasted no time locking down the garrison as tight as a convent.

"Diseases have their nature," says Kell," but they are deeply rooted in the nature of man. This particular disease seems to shun the healthy and upright in favor of those who are dissolute and wicked. The very old and very young seem to be especially adversely affected, yet I have also known it to take out soldiers in their prime. That said, having treated the disease, here and abroad, I cannot deny that what we have in Sunderland is the same cholera that has devastated the Continent. While the symptoms are similar to summer diarrhea, vomiting, cramping, loose stool," says Kell, warming to the subject, "cholera morbus is far more deadly—it produces its own sort of rice water stool—"

"Please, please, Dr. Kell," demands Lord Londonderry, putting up his hand impatiently. "As fascinating as I find this discussion of bowel movements, I insist we stick to the topic at hand. We are here to discuss the Quarantine and how soon we might see it lifted."

"Thank you, Lord Londonderry, for recalling our attention," says Daun starchily. "As most of you know, on the recommendation of our Board of Health, His Majesty has just sent a man-o'-war to patrol the harbour and enforce a second Quarantine. It has been difficult waiting fifteen days to receive imports, and we know it will be a far greater hardship on the port businesses to wait another fifteen days to export their goods, but in light of the contagiousness of this disease—"

"Wait a minute!" shouts John Harkas, sawmill owner. "My doctor told me if everyone would just stay away from oysters and cucumbers we wouldn't number a case among us."

"There is a great debate on the contagiousness of the disease, Mr. Harkas," answers the chairman. "Our medical community is split on whether it was imported or generated on local soil. Some believe it can be transmitted from person to person and thus we need the Quarantine; others that we take it straight from the atmosphere, and no Quarantine can help."

"Seems to me if it could go either way, why penalize us?" replies Harkas. "If I can't get my lumber out, I'll go broke!"

The room erupts in agreement.

"Why should the world wait fifteen days for Sunderland's coal when they might have Wigan's in three?" pipes up Mr. Thomas Brunton of lime, shipyards, and coal. "Not to mention the extra costs to merchants when after two weeks their provisions rot and spoil, when their water turns and their meat must be heaved overboard. The Quarantine has crippled us, sir, and this Board is to blame!"

For some five minutes, the chairman cannot make himself heard over the stomping and shouting, and the cries for the Board's impeachment. "Have you no thought for your brothers and sisters in the rest of England?" shouts Daun, pounding the podium for order. "It is too late for us. We are already contaminated. But we must not export certain death to the realm because of our own greed."

Henry squirms against his uncle's comfortable chair. If the disease had targeted the rich, he knows they would not be here today, examining their consciences. The harbour would be locked tight, and the wealthy fled to the country; only because cholera preys on the undesirable do they have the luxury of debate.

"It is all immaterial now," says the Marquis of Londonderry lazily, and out of respect, the room quickly quiets. "I have taken it upon myself to write the London *Standard*, stating that any report claiming the Asiatic cholera or the cholera morbus has been introduced into this town is a most wicked and malicious falsehood. I have further condemned the measures taken by His Majesty's government requiring a fifteen-day quarantine on ships entering and now departing Sunderland as perfectly unnecessary and uncalled for, especially when unlimited communication by coach and foot is permitted in every other part of the kingdom. And I concluded my letter by assuring them the health of Sunderland has never been better, with my humble apologies for any misapprehensions caused by our overanxious medical men. I have been informed the letter will run this week."

"You have already posted the letter, my lord, without first consulting the Board of Health?" Dr. Daun can barely contain his anger. "Do you realize that if we argue cholera is not here, we have absolutely no authority to enforce the Sanitary Codes? How do you expect us to protect the poor?"

"I don't expect. I expect them to get back to work."

"I must object, sir," Daun says. "By now denying the existence of this dread disease—after we have broadcast its arrival—you have not only made us a laughingstock before the whole country, you have personally signed a death warrant for the entire East End."

"Exactly how long do you think we can keep the East End idle before it rises in revolt?" demands Londonderry, for the first time this afternoon losing his composure. "You think the cholera is killing them? Starvation will kill them quicker; and the hungrier they get, the more they'll cry for our flesh. Fully employed, they barely survive from day to day. Two weeks out of work is death to them!"

"Pardon me, sir." Henry leaps to his feet, no longer able to keep quiet. "You couch your desires in concern for the poor, yet it is you who sets their meagre wages. Is it not your own coal interests you are protecting? So long as the port is open and you make money, you do not care if they live or die."

"Young man," Lord Londonderry returns scathingly. "I am well acquainted with your history. Do not speak to me of concern for the poor. They might die in my employ, but at least I do not pay to have them murdered."

Silenced, a crimson-cheeked Henry trembles above the impassive Marquis, while someone across the room smothers a snigger. Clanny sees his nephew's hand curl into a fist and swiftly rises to diffuse the situation.

"Can we not compromise?" suggests Dr. Clanny, firmly pressing Henry back into his chair. "Can we not say a disease possessing the symptoms of cholera morbus is now existing in this town, but there are no grounds for imagining it has been imported? It appears to have arisen from atmospherical distemperature and acts in most cases only upon persons weakened by want of wholesome food and clothing. We could say the further interruption of port commerce will only extend the disease by depriving the industrious poor of their bread and thus placing their families in the depths of misery and distress."

"Clanny, just because you believe this thing sprang up from thin air doesn't mean we can ignore the fact it is almost certainly contagious," says Kell.

"I am not saying it's not contagious," Clanny argues, "but that it may not be imported. It arose naturally on English soil, helped by excess carbon in conjunction with electrical storms—"

"We are not here to debate the nature of this disease, contagionist or anticontagionist," interrupts the chairman. "We are here to discuss the Quarantine."

"So we are resolved," states the Marquis, rising and imperiously straightening his cashmere cutaway. "Let us put it to the vote. All those who say Sunderland is healthy, say 'Aye.'"

"Gentlemen, wait!" Dr. Daun implores in a final desperate

plea. "Let us imagine cholera confines itself only to the poor and never darkens the door of a single householder in Bishopwearmouth. Are you never to leave the house? Are your servants never to shop? And when your cook has gone out into the infected market, when she brushes up against one whom you, today, have cast off, will you not hesitate with the fork to your lips and fear the very food upon your plate? The lower classes are part of your town; you cannot avoid them. You cannot wish this disease away. If you will not help us enforce the Sanitary Codes for their sake, think, then, to your own."

"I don't know what my health will matter when I've gone bankrupt," says Mr. Brunton simply.

So Dr. Daun and those who believe with him that the disease is contagious stand helplessly by while every business owner in Sunderland votes away the cholera morbus. Sadly, the chairman counts the number of raised doctors' hands among them: all but five of the twenty in attendance. What, after all, did he expect? The physicians don't receive their fees from the poor.

The meeting moves on, but Henry Chiver leaves in disgust.

The constables have dispersed the crowd outside, and Death has been deposed from the door of the Corn Exchange. He shakes his spear at potato peels in the gutter now, and bares his teeth at the worn soles of Henry's shoes when the doctor absently treads upon his neck. A cold wind from the east is driving a bank of clouds into town, and the weather vane atop Sunderland Orphanage, a tall, three-masted ship, points forlornly out to sea.

Henry's thoughts run as stormily as the weather. He will never escape the stain of murder, not so long as he continues in this profession. None of his opinions will matter, his name will be forever blasted, and all because of Burke and Hare. It is time he faces up to it: he died a sort of death back in Edinburgh, and while it is possible to dress up a corpse and ship it to a new town, eventually men will comment on the smell.

His heart is heavy on the walk back to Nile Street. He watches the ragpickers and street sweepers going about their business, some of the only men in full employ, set to work by the Board of Health to keep Sunderland as refuse-free as possible. Enjoy your charge while you may, Henry thinks—you have no idea how you are about to be served up by the city's elite. He walks past a Board of Health sign, readable again since the constables ripped down most of the resistance posters. PERSONS SUFFERING UNDER A TERROR OF CHOLERA MORBUS SHOULD NOT ATTEND THE DYING. That flyer too will soon come down, for with no cholera, who should be afraid? In this funk, Henry absently passes the Black Bull pub, where, out of the corner of his eye, he notices a young man sprawled upon the stoop. At any other time, Henry would assume the lad had crawled too far into his cups and merely passed out, but after the meeting, he feels he owes it to the man to investigate. The rising miasma of stale beer when Henry turns him over seems to support his initial conclusion, but he kneels and feels for his pulse, just to make sure.

In medical school, Henry was taught two models for disease: one, predicated upon contagion, which identifies the harmful agent as an enemy attacking the self; and a second, in keeping with the native soil theory, which suggests that disease dwells within each of us, merely waiting an opportu-

nity to erupt. Plague obviously fit the first category, cancers
the second. Where on the spectrum does this new disease
fall? Henry wonders, peering under the eyelids of this pitiful sot before him. If this man led a virtuous life, attended
church, ate and drank moderately, and loved his neighbor,
would he be spared? Or is it his very fabric that condemns
him? Henry is debating whether or not to send for the
Infirmary sedan when two old women approach the bar. He
puts out his hand to stop them. "Do you know this man?"
he asks.

"Is he dead?" The first woman leans over and scrutinizes
him. "Wake up!" she shouts. "Someone's going to come
along and burke you."

"Madame, there is no need to terrify the poor man,"
Henry bristles. "That was a long time ago."

"A long time ago?" cries the old woman. "I beg your pardon, sir, but my niece just came up from London, and the
whole town's abuzz with it."

"With what?" asks Henry.

"A poor little Italian boy who showed mice for a living.
Four men burked him and sold him to St. Guy's Hospital."

"And that's not the only one," adds her friend. "A mother
held her hand over the mouth of an old woman for half an
hour, then with her husband took the old dame to the
anatomy school on Windmill Street. Two taken into custody
in one week."

"You can't be too careful when ye're one of us, sir." The
first old lady shakes the snoozing drunk, who grunts and
rolls over. "Between the cholera and the burking, we can
barely keep body and soul together."

Henry leaves the two women hauling their friend inside to
sanctuary. His history has estranged him from the lower and

upper classes alike. If he is not to spend the remainder of his
life a pariah, Henry thinks despondently, something must be
done.

A light is burning in his second-story window, but Henry
knows he would never be so careless as to leave a lamp lit
when going out. He pauses with his hand on the door, his
first nervous thought of his dismissed manservant Williams,
returned to rob him. It could not be his uncle, whom he left
behind at the meeting, nor Audrey, who this afternoon was to
be fitted for her wedding gown. Then the certainty of the
intruder's identity makes him take the steps two at a time. It
would make perfect sense: he carelessly left the door
unlocked, she let herself in.

Henry pushes open the door to his study. "Gustine?"

A gasp, sharp and girlish. Henry jumps, then sees who it is.
"Mazby. Good God. What are you doing here?"

Henry's best student, the long-lashed, quiet Andrew
Mazby, leaps back from Fos's open torso. He holds a delicate
scalpel in one hand and a pencil in the other. Beside him on
the table lies an artist's sketchbook and Henry's copy of
Albinus.

"I'm sorry to be here without your permission. No one
answered my knock, but the door was unlocked," the student
stammers. He puts down the scalpel and reaches for his
jacket. Henry sees he has been working on the chest cavity,
sketching anterior views of the heart. "I wanted to get ahead
of the other students. I should not have stayed."

Poor young man, thrusting his arms into his jacket, smearing his forehead with pencil lead as he pushes back his thin
blond hair. He is inching around behind the corpse, judging
his distance to the door. Henry strips off his coat and cravat

and flings them in the corner. Why is he so afraid of me? he wonders, but asks aloud, "Do you have somewhere else to be?"

Mazby shakes his head, caught between ambition and the sheer terror of spending a moment alone with Dr. Chiver. It's true, Henry had been annoyed with Andrew Mazby for lending his name to Audrey's misguided petition, but his desire for companionship today outweighs any residual bad feeling. He picks up the sketchbook his student left on the dissecting table and flips through.

"These are good," he says, causing the young man to blush. "The coronary sinus is out of place here, though."

"I know. I am weak on perspective."

"You are much better than the others," Henry says, hearing in his voice the same paternal tone his uncle Clanny uses when speaking to him. "You will make a fine surgeon."

Mazby shakes his head vehemently to ward off the compliment. "I can only hope one day to be half so accomplished as you."

Now it is Henry's turn to color. "I've just come from a Board of Health meeting where my position as a doctor in this town was made perfectly clear. Don't envy me, Mazby."

"What happened, sir?"

The doctor walks around the table. "Our local industrialists waved their hands and pronounced us all to be healthy. There was nothing we could do to stop them. Sorry to inform you, friend," Henry leans over the cadaver Fos. "But you died of summer diarrhea."

"But, Dr. Chiver," Mazby sputters like a dutiful student, "the death rolls today listed another twelve cut down, and I know of at least twenty more cases languishing near the quay." Mazby would go on, but Henry is tired of arguing.

"History will have the final word," Henry says simply, wanting to put this day behind him. "Now tell me what you were working on when I came in."

"I was trying to determine the effects cholera had upon her heart, to make it withdraw so deeply into the chest cavity," Mazby switches subjects just as excitedly. "I was sketching its new position and comparing it with Albinus' drawings of a normal cadaver. I am embarrassed"—the boy suddenly looks away—"but as I was working, this fell from between the leaves of your book."

Mazby hands over a twice-folded canvas of Ophelia underwater—at least that is who the naked young woman, her eyes tragically fixed upon the viewer, her hair shorn away like one ready to enter a nunnery, appears to be. But the subject of this portrait could not have been further from the novitiate. Why is everything conspiring against me today? Henry wonders, taking the painting Dr. Knox commissioned of Mary Paterson. He hasn't looked upon it in two years.

"She's lovely," Mazby says.

"Observe your teacher's guilt," Henry says quietly, folding over the naked length of the girl's body so that only her sad face remains visible. "This was the sixth victim of Burke and Hare."

Mazby pulls back in alarm, as if touching the painting had in some way stained him with the crime. Of course the student has heard the rumors, but Dr. Chiver has never come right out and confessed to any involvement. Shy, gentle Mazby feels suddenly important, and more than a little apprehensive at this sudden confessional turn of events. "I was led to believe no one from the medical school was charged," the boy says, hoping to spare his teacher the obvious discomfort he himself is experiencing. "You were not to blame."

"They would never have murdered had we not provided the market."

The doctor covers Mary Paterson's face and unfolds her torso and long legs, floating in their trough of whiskey. "I realized something about myself today, Mazby. I am no better than Londonderry or any of the others looking after their own interests. We thought only of ourselves back at Surgeons' Square; we became reckless of everything, save the object of our own pursuit. The worst part is, I feel the old sickness upon me again. If I continue in anatomy, I don't know if I'll ever be free of it."

"Please, sir, don't talk that way," Mazby cries, never before having seen his teacher so morose. "There are alternatives to grave robbing and murder."

"The Anatomy Act?" Henry laughs. "Parliament will supply us with all the bodies we need, but at what cost? No matter what, the poor cannot help but know they are worth more to us dead than alive."

"I beg your pardon, Dr. Chiver," Mazby ventures. "If you are opposed to the Anatomy Act, and you have no desire to consort with resurrection men, why were you not supportive of Miss Place's petition?"

This boy is so young; Henry sighs, feeling far older than his thirty-two years today. But Henry took a valuable lesson away from Edinburgh. Aside from his students, few of the wealthy rallied around Dr. Knox when the news broke of the Burke and Hare murders, even though his experiments upon those beggars were designed to benefit them, to teach the surgeon's knife how best to avoid the rich man's artery and least afflict the rich man's nerve. Yet everyone from Robert Christison to Sir Walter Scott condemned their former friend. The wealthy do not care how we learn to heal them; the sin lies in calling attention to our methods.

"I wish I had the strength to be a crusader, Mazby, I do," Henry says, "but there are other things I would rather concentrate on. Getting to the root of this disease, for one." He gestures to the cadaver Fos. "We have a choice: we can stop and try to change the world or we can get on with our work, as imperfect as it is, and change men's minds through progress."

Mazby nods, understanding his teacher's position, and yet feeling in some small way that Dr. Chiver's fiancée is the braver of the two. Henry returns the portrait of Mary Paterson to his copy of Albinus and carries the book to its shelf. Knox had commissioned the work for use in his classes, as the most perfect specimen of female musculature he'd ever seen. He bade Henry have it when he left town, but the young anatomist has never had the heart to frame it.

"I feel I'm standing on a threshold, Mazby," he says, surprising even himself with his confession. "On one side, my old life, stacked high with corpses; on the other, the promise of a new life, preventing disease, growth as opposed to decay."

"But you always told us one was not possible without the other."

"I always believed that," Henry says, holding his book to his chest. "But I may have found an alternative. I am negotiating with a woman to raise up her child. He was born with nearly complete *ectopia cordis*." Henry pauses as his student's eyes widen in disbelief.

"You can actually see externally——?" Mazby gropes for the words, and Henry finishes for him——"the struggles of the human heart. Yes."

"Only the mother has suddenly become recalcitrant." Henry frowns to remember Gustine's set, downcast face as he let her off near the corner of Mill Street last night. He had honestly expected to receive some word from her today.

"My uncle is a solicitor," Mazby offers, as if reading Henry's thoughts. "I'm sure if it is in the best interests of all concerned, legally she could be made to part with it."

Henry pauses in putting away his book and stares long and hard at the young man. Gustine is barely a child herself; he can't imagine that any court in the country would find her a fit mother. Why should he not apply for legal custody and settle the matter quickly?

Henry smiles honestly for the first time today and claps his student on the shoulder. "Mazby, don't let anyone say you won't make an excellent doctor."

"Here's my uncle's address," Mazby says, scribbling and glowing with delight. "I'll tell him to expect you."

"Tomorrow," Henry nods.

Mazby collects his pad and follows his teacher downstairs. Outside, the costers plying Nile Street have bundled up against a lightly drizzling sleet. One man, an apple monger, has insulated himself with contraband copies of DEATH ACCUSING THE RICH; Henry can see the high hair and red words bleeding through his thin cotton shirt.

"I deeply respect the moral dilemma you face in securing bodies for us, sir," Mazby says, turning to Dr. Chiver in the doorway. "If nothing else, these dark days could bring a little relief to that anxiety. No one can blame you for what use you make of an epidemic."

No, thinks Henry, watching his student disappear down the street. No one can blame me for that.

XII

RAT

Gustine creeps under her wedge of clay, carefully descending the dark, tabid staircase from the slappers' room back to the potting house. Below, the steam engine, alone of all the workers still bellicose and robust, feeds fresh slip to the shirtless old men, who stir it around their low-tide troughs and worry that once the bubbles settle, barely a pot's worth of clay will remain. She knows they are worried—she's stood with them ten, fifteen, as much as forty minutes at a time while waiting on the replacement slappers to take twice as long to pummel half as much air out of the clay. She is adjusting to idleness, but she doesn't like it. Having the clay balanced once more upon her head makes her feel better, almost normal again. She can wrap her arms around her second wedge as if it were a beloved child at six years old, a burden to carry, surely, but a familiar, comforting presence nonetheless.

She passes by the empty spots of fallen colleagues and notes their absence, but today her mind is on her own troubles. She slept miserably last night, kept up by broken nightmares of her child in a laboratory, trapped beneath a bell jar, his eyes big and blue, trusting in the way a puppy wearing a stone around its neck licks the hand of the boy about to toss him into the Wear. His tiny heart had grown so large it flattened against the curved side of the jar while his breath silently steamed the glass until, in torturously slow dream time, he disappeared from view. At least three times during the night, she woke crying, terrified her nightmares had killed him; but each time she drew him close, she found the baby awake and smiling, wearing the expression of utter trustfulness he'd worn in her dream.

He will be well fed, well clothed. . . . His life would surely be of a higher quality than anything you could provide. The surgeon's voice follows her across the courtyard, where at four o'clock the sun is just sinking behind mountains of chert. Last night handsome Harry Hopps, an out-of-work labourer who had lived at Mill Street almost as long as Gustine, began vomiting food he'd eaten two days ago, whole and undigested. Two hours later, she could no longer recognize him. His lips were blue, his eyes retreated deep into his skull. His hands, feet, and nails turned a deep indigo, and his full sensual mouth drew back into a death's-head grimace. Whilky, with all the compassion his lodgers have come to expect, shook his fist in the dying man's face, accused him of being a Government Operative, and threatened forms of sexual violation unknown even to Gustine. His rant was lost on Harry Hopps. The lodger expired with his own hail of expletives not even eleven hours after the onset of his first symptom.

Is this how my baby should live? worries Gustine, tightly hugging her clay. Would he not be better off with another, who would feed him well and keep him clean? These fantasies carry her stiffly between the monoliths of bony chert and across the broken oyster shells of the courtyard. The beautiful Indian summer weather of yesterday's picnic has vanished as fast as it came, replaced by low chalcedony clouds, agitated and alive, quivering with fine stinging snow. Gustine is cold inside and out. *Can you protect him every hour of the day? Especially when you are working two jobs?*

She has only been working two jobs for his sake; has cared not whether she lives or dies except that through her work, she might perpetuate him. She has scrimped and saved to buy him food, to clothe him warmly; she has paid Whilky extra so that Pink might mind him and keep him out of Eye's clutches. But to think, all this effort might be replaced with a few spare coins from Henry's pocket, shillings scattered across a dressing table or slipped unnoticed beneath the sofa cushions. What is unending toil to her is a casual offer to him.

Gustine wipes slip from her lashes and continues toward the potting house. She is being ridiculous. Pink is watching her child, and she still has her job. Perhaps her baby might have more advantages should she give Dr. Chiver what he wants, but that would mean losing him forever. And Gustine is not that strong. She shifts the weight of her clay and reaches out to open the potting house door. It is better he be with me, she thinks. But, unbidden, the doctor's words return: *Can you protect him every hour of the day?*

Back at Mill Street, Pink is playing the game where she asks, Miss Audrey, may I bring you a cup of coffee? and Miss Audrey, may I help you deliver those blankets? and Miss Audrey, may my friend Mike come and visit us sometimes? He'll be no trouble, I promise.

She sits by the fireplace brushing the disgruntled weasel's fur. Little black fleas detonated by her fingers fizz away into darkness, pop, pop. The clock says we're in the quiet time of the day, when so much nothing happens that little girls must be extra careful not to let down their guards. Pink has forgotten that important fact; she is supposed to be watching Gustine's baby, propped by the fire, but she is so lost in her

Miss Audrey game, she's let the creature slip perilously close to the embers.

"Miss Audrey," Pink is saying. "May I hold your hand?" She stands the ferret up on its hind legs and makes its paw stroke her cheek. "That is so nice," she says.

Outside, another electrical storm is brewing. The air has been so hot, then cold, lately, and lightning, rather than striking, has webbed its way across the sky in violet tangles. It shoots its silks through the cracks in Mill Street's nailed shutters, followed seconds later by hissing thunder. How close was that? Pink wonders excitedly, scooping up Mike and running over to look outside. Throwing open the latch, she is surprised to find snow instead of rain swirling hypnotically in the doorway. The wind snaps it down the lane like a woman shaking the wrinkles out of sheets.

When she goes to live with Miss Audrey, a lap will be kept warm for nights like this. When thunder cracks, the kind young lady will pat her knees and Pink will scamper over to lay her head there. Perhaps she'll curl herself into a tight ball like Mike does and look up at Miss Audrey with one grateful glittering eye. Pink is not sure how she'll break the news to Mike that she is going away. She undrapes him from her arm and places him around her neck like she's seen her father do, giggling as he stands on her shoulders and prickily stretches. They are just beginning to be friends, she and Mike, finally growing to understand each other. Now that she has someone to pet her, she does not resent the strokes he gets from her Da; in fact, she feels sorry that he'll have to stay here while she moves on to real res-pon-sib-ility.

The wind in the lane changes direction again, spinning the snow back on itself. Pink's eyes travel past the faint outline of the word SICK that her Da furiously scrubbed from the door and down the darkened lane. It is fun to look for things in the snow. If she squints her eyes, like this, and lifts her chin, thus, she sees a beautiful lady dressed all in white like a bride. And if she turns her head just so, the lady lifts her veil and stretches forth her arms. Let's go home, Pink, she says. I've had such a lovely wedding and the time has come. At her feet, a flurry of white ferrets caper in a powdery ring. They will dance Pink all the way to her new house and dance her up to bed, then dance her down to breakfast in the morning. Pink sighs deeply. She could stand in the door all night, looking for Miss Audrey in the whirling snow.

Useless pink rat.

The Eye scowls up from her sewing at the scatterbrain in the doorway. That dreamy little rat has let her charge slip closer to the fire. She knows nothing about concentration. Eye looks sharp, for she understands the dangers of this quiet time of day. She sits with the dress in her lap, petting the fabric like Pink pets the ferret. She has shaken off the confusion of Wednesday night when the room was full of shadows and glow rat disappeared. Her head felt so heavy then and her eye was not her own. Everything could have gone wrong that night, thinks she, but Eye protected you. Her arthritic hands stroke the length of blue silk; ach, another froth of bouffant has torn away from the hem. Careless blue rat. But Eye will sew you up, pulling a threaded silver needle from its hiding place in her neckerchief. Lost between her thick padded fingers, the needle jabs fleshily at the blue fabric.

What will it take to teach that careless rat? What did it take to teach you, old gray Eye? You were not always old. Staring down into the sky in your lap, the clean river of this new blue responsibility, you are so grateful for having been given a second chance. And yet, since Wednesday night, your head has been full of memories; you have been caught in a curious shadowy undertow pulling you down the long dark tunnel to your first responsibility, back when you were no older than the pink rat. You have spent nearly sixty years swimming away from that place, learning concentration, vowing that what happened there would never happen again. But now during the quiet time you feel yourself slipping down the long blue tunnel to where it comes out on the other side. Where you find yourself in an underground cave in the coal fields of Durham, a little girl sitting cross-legged, staring down into a deep black hole.

You sit alone for thirteen hours, in silence, in near total darkness. Two soft-glowing miners' lamps (for your protection, the owners said; so that we might work deeper in more hellish conditions, say the miners) provide the only illumination, and they cast the strangest shadows. Sometimes the coal outcroppings overhead throw ladies in profile wearing high-crowned leghorn hats. Sometimes they look like a line of ducks waddling across the wall; sometimes your imagination fails you, and the shadows fall like dull potatoes on the ground. It is the game you play with yourself—find the thing in the shadow—thirteen hours a day, in silence, in near total darkness, for only twice a day are you called on to do anything other than watch. Twice a day, you have to pull the lever that starts the engine that lowers men into and draws them up from the bottom of the vein. You have to watch carefully, for sometimes the engine catches and then you have to shut it off quick or the cageful of miners will fall to their deaths. Sometimes, completely unanticipated, the chain jumps, meaning: there's been an accident; turn on the engine and draw up someone hurt. It is important to watch the chain and never take your eyes off it. But it is hard to watch a chain in a hole in almost total darkness, in silence, thirteen hours a day, when you are only nine years old.

Yet, you are a good girl, and you watch diligently. It is getting late and the chain looks eager to come up, knowing the next time it reaches the top, it will stay for the night. Then the miners can go home to dinner; then, you too can go home, and fall asleep at the table with food still in your mouth. It is very hot where you sit, and sweat runs down your hair into your gray eyes. Some of the other children have had trouble with their eyes, straining in the low light until their vision becomes foreshortened and the chain and hole are no more than a fuzzy puddle on the ground. But you have perfect vision. Nothing escapes you, from the crunchy centipede that shunts up the far wall to the tiny wood spider, no bigger than an eyelash, dangling from the engine above. You take the health of the hole like a doctor reads a patient's throat, observing how it slides naturally from red to sable to black to ink, all the way down to the mysterious gullet. You are a genius of vision, even though a little girl; all the other miners say so. *Ah 'ad a bit o' candy in me pocket, an' damme if tha' girl didna spy it! What's a man t' do but give a lass a bit?* They give you candy sometimes if you are sharp enough to spot the lump in their back pockets. They give you a swig of ale at breakfast and make you feel like one of the mates.

The final hour before you pull the lever that starts the engine is the hardest of the day. You have been sitting alone for twelve hours with only the centipedes and spiders for company. You think about how you will pull that lever and the crunching sound the chain makes as it shortens up to the top. You think about the tired blue faces of the men in the cage, how they swing the door open the second it clears the hole and jump out, making it sway dangerously for the men behind them. You still have a half-hour climb up to the day-light, which will be night this time of year, and a mile walk home. You watch the chain carefully now. Any moment there will be a tug, telling you to pull the lever and draw them up. You mustn't make them wait a second, or they will be wroth with you, but draw them up right away.

But what if? What if just after the tug has come and you've leaned your meagre weight upon the lever, and the engine is filling with steam and turning, groaning to pull your men up, what if at that very moment, you spy a rat out of the corner of your eye? A gray rat, with a sharp whiplash tail and big tarry eyes, creeping away with the piece of candy one of the miners gave you before he went down the hole. Between his jaws, that rat has your sugar-crusty piece of horehound, the one you have been saving all day to eat on the long walk home when you need to be cheered the most, and he is stealing away with it, skirting the soft-glowing miner's lantern, making toward the shadows where he might blend in with the lady's profile and the ducks and the dull potato.

What if, at that moment, your eyesight gets the best of you, for though another might have missed it, you see where he goes, around the corner, quick as a heartbeat. If you can only keep him in sight, you think, then you can catch him; and though the cage is slowly ratcheting higher, you too dart around the corner, knowing this tunnel leads only up, and that there is no place for him to go.

Miners' lamps are set into niches up the corridor, but your eyesight is so good, you could see that rat even in the dark. There goes his slipper-shaped shadow along the right-hand side, searching out a break in the wall to duck into. There are none—you would have seen them; he has nowhere to hide. You run faster, pattering up the soft earth floor; the rat gallops ahead, but you have him in your sights and he will not get away. It is just you and the rat, under the earth, and he is panicked by the roar of the steam engine, lifting the men. You are gaining ground; in front of you, the rat darts left, then right, knowing he is trapped. When he darts across the tunnel again, you pounce, hurling yourself at the creature, catching him behind his tricorn skull, while his tail lashes and he struggles to bite. He draws a bit of blood from your hand, but in gnashing, drops the candy. And that's all you wanted. What is rightfully yours. You fling the rat away and he bolts up the tunnel, raising a gray cloud of dust that makes you cough. Nasty rat, you think, kneeling down to retrieve the little square of horehound.

But what if from where you kneel, shoving that piece of rat-spit candy into your mouth, you suddenly hear the most mangled crunch you have ever heard in your young life, followed by the clamour a boy makes dragging a metal pipe the length of an iron fence, but a hundred times louder and a hundred times faster, and at the end, a double crash like a cage smashing to bits and a steam engine falling on top of it? You race back to the hole to see that the whole thing is red now, inflamed with screams of agony and, worse, dead no-screams at all, and your jaw trembles so that piece of horehound candy slips through and skitters off the wall of the hole, landing God knows where. If all that happened when you were nine, wouldn't that teach you the power of concentration?

"*Mike! Stop!*"

Eye is jarred out of the cave and back to Mill Street just in time to see a blur of white leap from the pink rat's shoulders and streak through the doorway, out into the chaotic snow, leaving a skid of paw prints in the direction of High Street.

"*Come back!*" Pink shrieks in high-pitched terror, and tears off after him. "*Mike! Come back!*"

The door stands open, and—like that—they are gone: white weasel and pink rat racing after him. In their place, filthy vagabond snow shambles into the house. Yes, it is the most dangerous time of day, thinks Eye, this quiet time. A time to look down and see the crushed and contorted bodies of pitmen, like limp red leaves littering the bottom of a well. The pink rat needs to be taught to concentrate. Eye's attention slithers over to where the softly cooing heart rat has slipped too close to the fire. That was her responsibility, and she's left it. Who knows what could happen to a rat left all alone?

Gustine raises the latch and steps into the potting house. She has only been gone forty minutes, but someone let the fire die down and the room has quickly reverted to frigid twilight. Wooden-handled awls and stray bits of brass wire litter one of the tables; on another, a half-formed figurine of a lion, a roar without a body, lies toppled and forgotten.

"James?" She calls the name of her potter. "Phillip?" His son.

What is going on? There are still three hours in the work-day, and Gustine has brought fresh clay. She turns round and round looking for someone. Anyone to ask what has happened.

The wheel to which she used to hitch herself—where her potter's son usually walks—offers a small clue. It has been wrenched from its cylinder and the harness torn away, like someone fell hard to the ground and broke it. A puddle of some fluid (it has mixed too well with gray-blue clay dust to be recognizable) pools nearby, next to a log, abandoned apparently in the act of being placed on the fire. Even if her potter's son had fallen and hurt himself, why would the others be gone?

She sets her clay next to her potter's silent, motionless wheel. Without the boy to turn it, the lathe is but another dead thing, more disturbing to her even than dead Fos or Harry Hopps. A person's body may or may not be contagious, but the death of a machine is always epidemic; Gustine and her baby, along with half the pottery, will slowly starve if this wheel is not restored to life.

"James?"

What is she to do? She leans against her potter's rickety stool, lashed with lamb's wool to help ease his worsening sciatica, and fights her rising tears. Gustine has worked at the pottery since she was nine years old, turning the wheel, ferrying clay, watching; and it is this lathe and this room, not the back streets of Sunderland, that have shaped her. She could not take the nightly obliteration of dress lodging if, the following morning, she could not come here and watch things be built back up again. Objects beautiful and useful are every day coaxed from the lowliest mud; chamber pots and *Sailor's Tears*—her brothers and sisters—rise triumphant, colorful, ready to be put to use. She lets her fingers explore the beveled edges of the clay-silk circle until they fall off the end of their world into the gap between cylinder and table. We are ruined, thinks Gustine darkly, easing off the stool and giving the disk a good hard spin with her hand. The larger wheel, broken and still attached by belt, won't let it budge. Wearily, she reaches for a length of wire and sets about cutting her wedge into pieces. It is a fruit less activity, but all she can think to do.

"Yer back."

She looks up to find her potter leaning in the doorway, his

beard muddily parted down the middle into two long spades. His fixed, dead eyes tell her that whatever happened most definitely involved his son.

"Where is everyone?" she asks.

"They ran away," says he.

"Why would they do that?"

"Because the cholera morbus has come to the potting house."

Cholera has come here? Gustine starts to say no, it cannot be, but her potter is still talking, dully explaining as if he'd read the events in a newspaper. His son collapsed with the spasms, and the others were so frightened, they ran away. He passed off his boy to an old woman on the street who promised to take him home, for he knew if he dared leave the gate, he wouldn't have a job to return to the next day. Her potter is supporting his son and three-year-old daughter, along with his dead wife's mother and father; he cannot be put out of employment.

"We must work hard," he says grimly. "We're all that's left."

Why bother? thinks Gustine fleetingly. We can never work hard enough to make up for the other six—faithless cowards that they are. But then she looks into her potter's sagging face and reads desperation there, along with sick fear on behalf of his boy. And doesn't his expression mirror her own?

"We'd better get started, then," she answers.

Gustine rekindles the fire while her potter repairs the broken wheel. It is a reversion for her, to take up her childhood job once more, and she feels awkward and little again just strapping the harness around her waist. Her hands move instinctively to the shallow trough in the crank, worn smooth by years of pushing, but when she leans forward the old familiar weight of the wheel gives easily before her. Together they have resuscitated the machine, are back on the endless band of revolution. The syncopated rhythm of her potter's whirring disk falls in with the beating of her heart, guiding her smoothly back into their old groove of timelessness, that hypnotic circle world where hours get pinched in the gears and pulled back on themselves. She is ten years old again and pushing with all her might against the wheel, happy when gravity takes over and rushes it to the ground, struggling when she has to pull the crank up to her chest and push it over her head. It takes a few revolutions, but the wheel finds its own momentum and then she merely guides it, resting until her potter is done hollowing out his clay and cupping it into shape, until the chamber pot is completed and she must stop so that he can begin another. As she turns, she remembers, almost viscerally, the full-bladdered panic she used to have as a girl. Then as now, the little children who turned the wheel were only allowed to go to the privy twice a day, and she fainted once from trying to hold it in. She remembers waking up in a warm puddle, her potter slapping her hard across the cheek. Tell me next time, he growled. I'll smuggle you outside.

He has always treated her, his slave, as kindly as someone who is himself a slave possibly could. Yes, he has struck her, but to spare her harsher punishment. He has never cheated her; and when she was absent three days for her baby's delivery, he found a replacement to save her job. Even as she tries to frame a way to thank him, to let him know that somehow, together, they will get through this, the tension changes on the wheel; she feels the flyaway lightness of hands no longer pressing down. Gustine looks up sharply.

"James," she says, pitching her voice louder to be heard over the spinning.

Her potter is not at his wheel. As she watches in horror, ten fingers reach for the table ledge and strain to pull their body upright. She throws off her harness and runs around to help, but her potter's strength is already failing and he slithers back to the ground.

"James, get up," Gustine urges, bending over the contorted man. "We have too much work to do."

But he has turned in on himself like a warped pot fisted back down to clay. The spasm is horrible to behold; a racking, spastic implosion of the human body. *No, please. No, please,* he moans, though his lips are being swallowed by his eclamptic mouth. *I have a family.*

"Stand up, James," Gustine commands, growing more terrified by the second. "I need you." She tugs hard, trying to pull him upright, but he is dead weight. Damn it! What is her puny strength against the crushing insistence of this disease?

She releases her potter and he falls heavily back to the floor. This is the end, thinks she. He will die and I will be out of work. I will have only the dress with which to feed my baby. Her potter is dying and Dr. Chiver wants to take her child away. Everything is coming to an end, and she is powerless to stop it.

"I will send for a doctor, James," she says, backing out of the cottage and running toward the front gate. It is snowing harder now and she slips painfully, cutting her knees on the slick oyster shells.

"Call a doctor to the potting house," she shouts, pushing past the sentry, who has given up trying to stop the employees from fleeing. "I am going home."

It blinks in the heat of the hearth, slowly roasting like a suckling pig. Its bright round eyes and coarse gray fur; its sharp teeth for clamping down; and the obscene hairless tail she knows he hides under that blanket. She has never been left alone with the heart rat; everyone says Eye, keep away. Blue says I will kill you, Eye, if you ever touch it. But it is rolling closer to the fire, sliding closer to the coals, and soon the whole room will smell of scorched rat.

Eye cocks her head at the blinking lump that disfigured the dress for six months and kept the laces from pulling tight. She remembers watching the night it gnawed its way out; staring at the hole between Blue's legs, thinking how awful to have a rat inside you, scratching and biting to be born. And now it will sizzle and pop in the fire unless she does something about it. But what can she do? A black-edged blister melts the edge of its blanket, but everyone says Eye, don't touch.

Plunge it in the hole. The idea breathes within her. Yes. Yes, that's it. Cool it in the hole.

It was the same the night she staggered home after the accident, disfigured and bruised from her beating, unable to see from her bloody left eye. She had knelt to cool her face in the stream when she saw her water-slick old enemy cleaning his paws on the bank beside her. With a cry, she seized that rat and thrust him underwater, oblivious to his squeals and bites, screwing his face into the streambed, punishing him for what he did. She would kill all of them. They were all her enemy. She sees an old woman's hand now (funny how it should be at the end of her nine-year-old arm) each out to the fire to grasp that same rat's skull. Slowly. Don't startle it or it will run away. She sees the old woman's hand grab him by the back of the head, immobilizing him, making him cry; weakly at first and then in real pain. Pluck the rat from the fire. Plunge him in the deep blue hole, Eye breathes, yanking back and instantly pushing him facedown into the stream. Drown squirming rat.

Gustine's infant struggles under the Eye's thick fingers, instinctually fighting for air, coughing and growling far back in his tiny throat like a hedgehog. He has nothing to breathe but fabric; he is taking blue into his lungs, swallowing great gulps of briny silk. He thrashes and mewls, but the shadow is resolute. Back on her stool, she pushes his head deeper into her dress-filled lap. She never understood why that weasel who rid the house of all the other rats left this one to live. She has hated it for months, watching its mother pretend to love it. But now she has ended its reign of terror. The creature goes soft in her lap and Eye flips it over to see if it breathes. It must be dead by now, she thinks. So long underwater.

But the rat is not dead. With the last of its strength, it reaches up for mercy.

Naturalists tell stories of female orangutans in darkest Africa, how the most hulking and violent of beasts, creatures who would think nothing of stealing a rival's infant and dashing out its brains, are sometimes turned from murder by the innocent face of a human babe. What sense memory slips through, one has to wonder, to turn the tide of feeling? Is it mere substitution, a human baby for a lost ape child; or does it bore deeper into the ape's thick skull to touch some half-forgotten memory of being small? What would a naturalist make then of apelike Eye suddenly rearing back from the rat in her lap, as if rather than staring, it had bitten her? Could he not fill notebooks on the look of utter confusion suffusing her face as she realizes this tiny creature has not a snout, but a human nose? As she runs her flat thumbs through his silken hair and taxes her atrophied olfactory glands to take in the tiniest hesitant sniff of him? Lecture halls could be filled analyzing the wonderment illuminating her single watery eye; papers might be presented on the musculature of a heretofore unseen smile weakly extending itself across her slack face. This is a baby, thinks she. There is no fur. No sharp teeth and naked tail. Eye has never held a baby. It is soft.

She takes him up from her lap of blue like Moses from the bulrushes, and the child, no longer fighting for air, instinctively reaches out for comfort. He clasps the thin hanks of hair that slither from her bun, and though it hurts at the roots, she does not stop him. Since the day of the accident, through the remainder of her whole long life, Eye has never been touched without anger or fear. First it was the fury of the owners, beating her into unconsciousness, more for the loss of their engine than for thirty miners' lives. Then, as she grew more silent and further into herself, anyone who accidentally brushed against her pulled back in horror. Even blue rat's skin involuntarily shrinks from her fingers as she laces up the dress. But here is a baby, patting her cheek, twining his fingers in her hair as if to pull her close and whisper a secret. Eye presses the child to her heart. Blue rat's baby loves her.

"What are you doing?"

The door bangs wide and Eye jumps, so lost in the baby she missed the telltale raising of the latch. Gustine trembles in the doorway, streaked with wet clay like a statue wept to life.

"What in bloody hell are you doing?" she shrieks.

"I found him." Pink bursts through the door behind Gustine, her small chest heaving from having chased the ferret down High Street until he made a dead-end turn onto Stamps Lane. "He almost got away, but I trapped him against a wall and—*NO!*" she screams, following Gustine's horrified stare to where her responsibility rests in the crook of Eye's arm. "Oh God! Give me that!"

Pink flings aside the guilty, shivering ferret and rushes the old woman. "I'm sorry. I'm so sorry," she sobs, tugging on the Eye's arm but begging Gustine's forgiveness. "Mike ran away and I—only left for a minute."

But Gustine does not even hear. It's over. The worst has happened. She stands transfixed in the doorway while Pink bites the Eye's fleshy arm, pulling with all her might to release the baby. *The Shadow of Death has fallen upon my child,* thinks Gustine numbly. *I am too late.*

Pink tugs with all her strength, but the Eye, pressing the baby possessively to her breast, will not let it go. She shakes her head as hot tears drop from her single gray eye, though she scarcely knows what this water means. *Don't take it away. Don't take the heart baby. Eye love it.*

But Gustine has recovered herself and flies to the fireplace. She will not stand back and let the Eye destroy her child. She will not give up with out a fight. She lunges for the hot poker and wheels it around at the old woman's head, feeling the shock of connection and the satisfying sizzle of burnt flesh and hair. In her moment of surprise, Eye loosens her hold on the baby and Pink quickly snatches it away.

"I will not let you finish what you started!" Gustine screams, her sobs finally getting the best of her. "You could not kill him then and you will not now. I am taking this baby away. You will never see either of us again!" She pulls the baby from Pink's arms and rips his blanket from the swaying clothesline overhead. Her child already seems different to her, strangely cold and faintly trembling. She quickly wraps him tight.

"Where are you going?" Pink begs. "What do I tell Da?"

"Tell your Da I've broken out of his bloody jail." Gustine throws her shawl over her head and, pressing the baby close to her body, darts out into the snow. She has nowhere to go, but she will not stay here. Not anymore.

The door slams behind her, and Pink watches a comet's tail of snow slowly melt into the floorboards. She might as well melt with it, for Miss Audrey will never want her now that she's lost the baby. The pressure in her chest is greater than anything she's ever felt; worse even than last Christmas when gin-lit Da stumbled home and stepped on the straw bird-house she made him. Over by the fireplace, Mike shakes his wet fur and contentedly settles down to sleep.

And what does Eye—numb to the poker welt even now blistering on her right temple—feel? Stunned and bleeding, she has only a conception of a thought. In her new confused haze of black and red, she wonders who let the rat into her heart, to gnaw at the place Gustine's baby used to be?

XIII

QUARANTINE

Someone is pounding loudly on the door downstairs, but Henry is too involved to answer.

He squints through his microscope, set at its highest magnifying power, one eighth of an inch, puzzled by what he sees. The slide under the microscope, a culture taken from the cadaver Fos's soiled winding sheet before he burned it, teems with strange annular bodies, what look to be corpuscles, the same size as blood globules, but whose walls refract light powerfully. What are these parasites? he wonders. Are they important? He has never seen such creatures in healthy human dejecta, and as a comparison, he takes a few drops from his own chamber pot and examines them. No. Perfectly normal. On the table beside him lies Bell's just published *Cholera Asphyxia*; but if what Henry sees has any validity, Bell's latest theory will go the way of so many others. Cholera may not breed along the sympathetic nervous system, as Bell theorizes; no, it could very well be the work of a parasite, some creature smaller than anything Henry sees with his microscope. He knows his uncle Clanny is even now at home penning a monograph on the atmospheric causes of cholera, based on his weather charts and his hunch that excess carbon is the culprit. Henry wants to invite him over to observe what breeds on the slide, but he doesn't want to get into how he came by the patient.

More rapping from below. And more insistent this time. Henry storms over to the window and throws open the sash. "Leave me alone!" he shouts.

"Dr. Chiver, it's me," a high, frightened voice calls up. "Gustine. I need to speak with you."

Gustine? He peers around the drapes and sees her standing unprotected in the snow, carrying a bundle in her arms. She's come around at last, he sighs. She's brought the baby. Quickly, he washes his hands, races down the stairs, and yanks open the door.

"Come inside," he says. "And quickly, before someone sees you."

She steps into the foyer, sloughing off a skin of mud and snow. What on earth has happened to so alter her? he wonders. Filthy and wet, she shivers around the baby, whose cheeks are waxen with cold. But there is something more. He sniffs the air uncertainly. Gustine stinks of alcohol.

"I didn't know where else to go," she says, unsteady on her feet. "I had to leave Mill Street."

"Is that whiskey on your breath, Gustine?" Henry chides. "I thought you didn't drink."

"I didn't before tonight."

"Let's get you dry," he says, realizing that the only lit fire is in his anatomical study. Well, she helped him procure the bodies, she might as well know what he does with them. He opens the door that only days before he shut on Audrey, seeing through Gustine's eyes the scummy specimen jars of eyes and hearts, the cabinet of saws, microscope, brown-jointed skeletons suspended from silk. She looks dully around, unimpressed by his collection, and Henry feels vaguely disappointed.

"Here is our handiwork," he says, striding across the room and pulling away the cloth covering Fos's naked body. Why am I doing this? he asks himself when she winces. Why am I punishing her for helping me? She turns away from the body of her fellow lodger and absently takes a seat on the raised hearth, rubbing the baby's hands and feet, trying to warm him. Glassy-eyed and sluggish, the child looks unwell to Henry. She should have known better than to bring him out in this storm.

"I can't seem to get him warm," Gustine says.

"Let him rest near the fire," Henry commands. "He needs to thaw out."

He pours himself a glass of brandy and sets it on the library table next to his barely touched dinner of this afternoon. To his surprise, the dress lodger reaches for his glass and throws it back like a professional.

"That's enough," he says, taking the empty glass from her. "I don't like to see you like this."

She sits with one hand in her lap and the other on the baby's foot, massaging it mindlessly. Her muddy hair hangs over her face, so that he has to lean down to see her. He could never have imagined her like this: disheveled and drunk like some abandoned dock whore. He finds it very disconcerting.

"So, Gustine," Henry says at last to break what is becoming an awkward silence. "Have you had a change of heart?"

"I have," Gustine whispers.

"Then you would like for me to keep and study this child?"

"Yes." Again whispered.

"You've made the right choice," he says. Poor miserable girl, she is crying into her lap, made more upset, certainly, by all the whiskey she's consumed. She needn't have done this to herself, Henry thinks; it's not as if he's a monster. He will be good to the child and raise it up almost like one of his own.

"Now please, you must let me give you something in return," he says, digging into his pocket. "How much do you want?"

At his question, Gustine's head comes up proudly. She has been rehearsing this speech for the past hour, wandering from pub to pub, searching for the courage to come here. She feels the strange thickness of whiskey on her tongue and hears her own words from far away.

"I want no money from you, only an exchange of services," Gustine starts, and almost immediately falters. "I have come to make you an offer, Dr. Chiver. You may take my baby and keep him, but let me be close by, to watch over him and soothe him when he is frightened. Take me as a maid in your house. I will cook for you; I will clean and sew. I have worked a long time in the factory, so I have not mastered all the household skills, but I am a hard worker and I will learn. My potter collapsed today—"Her voice breaks with emotion, but she cannot stop before she's gotten everything out.

"And the Eye has tried to kill my child. I cannot go back there. I have nowhere to go, no way to support him. For his sake, I will give you my baby, but please don't ask me to part from him. Take me too, so that we may be together, at least until the time when he—I know you are to be married, and I swear to make a diligent and obedient maid to your new wife."

Henry has been listening in growing alarm. To even consider having her in the same house with Audrey—a street prostitute who has made her life picking through coffins for him—no, no, it is too much. He stares down at the half-naked, drunk young girl, holding her baby up to him like a sacrifice to the pagan gods, and shudders in revulsion. Why does she ask the impossible of him?

"Dr. Chiver, please," she begs. "After all I have done for you."

But her appeal to his conscience serves only to make him ashamed and defensive. Henry was prepared to offer her a good sum of money for her very painful sacrifice, but this is simply too much. Of course she can go home; that miserable one-eyed old woman has no power over life and death. Could she truly know his character so ill that she would suggest the obscene arrangement of living here? She is a prostitute, after all, first and foremost; he knows what sort of services she is offering.

"I never asked your help the first time," Henry says hotly. "In fact, I actively refused it. And as for this woman here"— he gestures toward Fos—"she needed to be removed for purposes of sanitation. Frankly, I am surprised at you, Gustine. While I know it's impossible we should be friends, I had come to think of you with affection and respect. I had never imagined you a parasite."

His words sting her far more deeply than he knows. She would never, never have come expecting charity from him. She has always expected to work, she knows no other life. What has she done to make him treat her this way?

"Oh, Gustine. Don't cry," he says, exasperated, as the fat tears she tries to master splash upon the hearth. Look at her, on her knees, suppliant, miserable. She is drunk, poor thing, and brokenhearted at the loss of her child. He is stronger than she, after all; he shouldn't be so harsh.

"Gustine." He reaches out hesitantly and strokes her matted hair. She has drunk so much even her tears smell of whiskey. He wipes them away with the back of his hand, feeling them burn, like molten drops of snow.

Like shall cure like. Henry hears the words of his uncle Clanny as clearly as he hears Dr. Knox saying to them at Surgeons' Square, It is perfectly natural to feel as you do. This perfect whore, so freshly dead. It is better to acknowledge the lust than to be so consumed by it you sneak in one night and enact something perverse. Why is he thinking about this now? Henry tries to shake off the memories of two years ago, the night they laid Mary Paterson beneath her yellow pane of whiskey. But all he can smell is Gustine's tears, sweet like the taste of gin on her lips when she kissed him the night he pulled away. He had shut his eyes and tried to think of his mother, but it had been too much for him when Knox cupped the girl's breast appreciatively, murmuring, Beautiful, isn't it, my boy? Just beautiful. For three months, he'd had to fight his feelings for a sinful, whiskey-drowned woman with her thighs parted and her mouth open, as if daring him to take her, as he didn't dare when last they met.

And if only he had lain with her, perhaps Burke would have passed her by. Chosen her friend Janet or one of the other broken-down Canongate whores. But because he ran away, she is here, looking up at him through her yellow eyes, accusing him. You could have had me, and kept me alive. Instead now you want me, and you cut me to pieces.

Like shall cure like. If a body wants to purge, supply it with an emetic to push the poison out faster. He tells himself this as he watches his hands, the same soft white hands that had been seared by grave dust back at the Trinity pit a month ago, reach out shakily and move her shawl. Tonight she could meet his depravity with depravity. They are both so wicked, so unnatural. And he wants her; he has wanted her for three long, whiskey-soaked months. Her skin is mudscurfy and cracked, except where the snow has melted it into slicks. She looks at him confused and frightened by his strange behaviour, but it is why she came, is it not? To call this out in him? His soft white hands slip into the neckline of her soiled shift and peel the fabric from her shoulders. They are just as he remembered them; he sighs, rubbing his face against her mud-sweaty breasts, smearing his cheeks with her filth.

"No," Gustine whispers. "What are you doing?"

"Mary . . . ," Henry breathes.

Gustine struggles. "Please, Dr. Chiver, my child . . ."

"He is thawing. He is thawing," Henry murmurs, pushing the skirt of her shift higher and higher up her thighs. She is naked beneath, her legs goose-pimply around the mud, and locked tight. Why does she pretend? His soft white hands pry those lying legs apart, cracking the seal of mud between. He fumbles with the buttons on his trousers, never in his life so excited and terrified at once.

Yes. With a moan, he drives into her sump, letting himself wallow, rut like the depraved animal he is. He is where he belongs, at last, splashing himself with swill. He breathes in her hair, smelling the perfume of worms and cold earth, of rotted wood and human decay. Her tiny cunt is loamy with dirt, this little whore. Henry pounds and pounds, driving six feet deep inside her. Not yet. Not yet. He moans, and from the corner of his eye sees the baby staring at him, his heart beating like a slow blue dirge. No. Henry tears his eyes away, the terror, the excitement too great to bear. The sweet, vicious stench of whiskey. The deep peaceful feeling of suffocation. She is his fever and his cure, and he is falling. Falling. He cries, and with a shudder spends as into his own grave.

When he at last rolls off, Gustine sits up and slowly pulls her muddy pottery shift around her. She is numb from lying awkwardly on the hearth, and she has lost the feeling in her right leg. But Henry, like a convalescent suddenly awakened from delirium, is ravenously hungry. His attention turns to his food from earlier today, the pale cold chicken breast and the gray green artichoke. He reaches for the plate.

"Do you always eat the same meal?" she asks.

Annoyed with her observation, he pushes the food away. "I am very sorry I can't take you on, Gustine," he says. "It would be unspeakably wicked of me to keep a lover here while my wife was in the house. I have never been that sort of man."

She is standing over the hearth, where, despite his proximity to the heat, her baby is still strangely cold. Henry follows her helplessly, wishing she would speak, recognize what just passed between them, even if neither meant it to be. But what, after all, can he expect from a hardened professional? She is silent and mechanical, stooping to lift her child, to brush her mussed, muddy hair from her eyes. She crosses to the door and starts down the steps, still not speaking.

"Where are you going with the baby?" he asks, surprised, trailing behind her down the steps. "You just gave him to me."

She picks up the wet wool charity blanket she dropped on the way in and wraps it once more around the shivering child. It is too damp to be comfortable, but it will keep the worst of the snow off.

"I made a mistake," she says.

"It's too late," he calls. "I have an appointment with a

solicitor tomorrow and I intend to seek legal custody of that child."

"You would take him from me? Without my consent?" she asks, stunned.

"It is for his own good," Henry says, growing increasingly more frustrated. "Look at you: drunk, carrying him about in the snow, bringing him here to watch——" He breaks off, for she is opening the door without listening to him. "*Gustine, wait!*"

She turns back to him with fury in her eyes. Of course, he knows why she is angry. How stupid could he be? Henry digs in his pocket and extends her a pound note, slightly moist with perspiration. "Here, take it," he says. "For the other . . . I would never cheat you."

Looking at his extended hand, Gustine realizes that her vision, which a month ago penetrated Henry's linen shirt down to his duplicitous flesh, now sears straight through to the bone. Gone are skin, pores, and hair, all the surface markers that make a man seem unique. Now all Gustine sees is an anonymous disarranged picket fence of bones. The doctor's voice echoes in a funny, flapping mandible. He stands upon two obscene codpiece patellae. Where once her vision allowed her to distinguish the difference between him and other men, she seems now only to register his white skeletal sameness. She reaches out and takes his money. At last she sees the hollow in his chest for what it really is.

Cholera morbus began its career, piously enough, as a pilgrim. It traveled the Ganges pilgrimage routes, stowing away with the elderly in litters, crawling with children, stumping with amputees, biding its time, hoping to silently ride its transport home where it might infect a village, a city, a province. Hundreds of thousands would die before it sunk back into the ground, now sloshing in subterranean pools all across India, now lying in wait for another pilgrimage or fair, any unsuspecting convocation of men. This had been the Hindoo cycle for centuries, and would have remained happily unknown to us in Europe had not His Majesty's East India troops, in their baleful march across the continent in 1816, inevitably intersected with those same routes of pilgrimage.

From that moment on, cholera marched with the army. By 1818, the disease had reached Bombay. By 1820, ferried across the Bay of Bengal with the army's provisions, it had taken the Indian archipelago island by island until it regained land at China. A new generation of cholera, perhaps struck with the same pioneering spirit that was spurring the world toward America, took sail west, gaining Persia by 1823, Moscow by 1827; and by 1830, when Gustine, then fourteen years old, first realized her belly was beginning to swell, it had reached Sunderland's main trading partner at Riga. William Sproat, the first to officially die in all of England, illicitly sold a few lumps of coal to the cook aboard a Riga ship stuck behind the Quarantine, but what was the harm in that? No harm at all to Gustine, had he not then sat next to her fellow lodger Fos at Les Chats Savants.

But why pause here for a lesson on the pandemic history of cholera morbus? Well, sometimes the world intrudes into a story, just like it intrudes into a town; sometimes no matter how we guard against it or pretend it does not exist, the They of someplace halfway across the globe become the Us of here and now. Tonight, the cholera morbus, bred in the East End of the very World—in Bengal, as filthy as Mill Street; in Jessore, as poor as Sailor's Alley; passed hand to hand like a pestilential Olympic torch—has come for the being Gustine loves most in the world. How unfair, it seems to us, to pit a disease fed on the deaths of millions against a single little baby.

It feels far more crowded than usual when Gustine pushes her way inside the Labour in Vain, but she quickly realizes it is only full around the edges. The tables have been pushed aside to leave a rough circle in the middle of the room, inside of which squats John Robinson erecting a wall of old red and white wooden panels. His patrons laugh and talk around him, oblivious to the hammering; a few offer advice on the construction of his rat ring, a few angle for odds on Friday night's championship match. Crown Prince of Ratters is to be decided, a final contest between Whilky's Mike and whichever mongrel wins tomorrow night. In its place of honour among the ubiquitous Garrison ware on the mantelpiece (John's own Wearmouth West View 25-Year Commemorative milk pitcher, a porcelain terrier with a trout in its mouth, and Gustine's potter's specialty, *The Sailor's Tear*) sits the Silver Crown itself, a dented tin chaplet much coveted by the rat baiters of Sunderland. Whether set upon the head of a mutt or a ferret, on Friday night, with the bestowing of this crown, Divine Right shall be recognized.

"What's wrong wi' that baby?" asks an old woman when Gustine slips into the back corner cemetery table and starts to unwrap her child's blanket. It is packed hard with snow and reeks like sour rennet. "He's discoloured."

"He's fine," answers Gustine tersely.

"If he's got the whooping cough, you should put a live trout's head in his mouth. It will suck away the disease."

"No," interrupts her friend, an equally dilapidated crone,

missing her three front teeth. "Shave his wee head, hang the hair upon a bush, an' when the birds take it back to their nests, they'll carry the disease with it."

"He doesn't have the whooping cough," Gustine replies.

"What's yer poor bairn's name, girl?" asks the first old crone, kindly. "We'll say a prayer for him tonight."

Gustine looks up at the woman blankly. Her child is dying and she never even gave him a name. She said she believed he would live, grow strong, and one day bury her; yet somewhere, in the darkest corner of her cowardly soul, she worried that everyone else was right. Perhaps if he went unnamed, unbaptized, she reasoned, God might overlook him and leave him to her care. But—oh, her heart—how wrong she was. She has been an irresponsible caretaker and God is taking back her charge. Please let him stay, Gustine pleads now, stripping off his stool-soaked blanket. I will give him a name. I will call him—I will call him William after our most beloved king, a man who certainly finds favour in Your sight; but even as Gustine thinks the name William, unbidden comes the image of William Marion, vestryman, who left a xylophone of bruises down her spine when he took her on the table of the Corn Exchange. No, William is not the right name. Let it be George then, she thinks, our previous king. But a George forced her to her knees in front of his friends, a Harold, a Buck, a Tim, and a Jerry. No, all of those names are out. Closed too are all Bobs and Bills and Bruces, all Franks, Andrews, and Charleses; and certainly not a Henry. To every name, she can fix a leering, brutal, pitiless face; hands of Dicks and dicks of Thomases.

The old women drift away as John Robinson looks up to see who has taken the back cemetery table. Well now, she is about the last person he expected to see here. John Robinson sighs deeply, for more than anything, he hates conflict, and conflict with a woman is by far the worst type. Setting aside his hammer, he takes a quick shot of gin, steeling himself for the unpleasant business.

"Gustine." He nods.

"John, please just let us sit a minute." Gustine wipes away her tears. "I need to warm him up."

The publican frowns and doesn't look at her. "Heard you left Mill Street."

She doesn't care what he heard. Warming her child is all that matters. "The Eye touched him," she says. "Look what she's done."

Unless the Eye built a time machine and sent the child eighty years into his own old age, she could never have done this, thinks John Robinson. A shriveled old man has taken possession of the infant's swaddling clothes. His dull blue eyes have shied into a pinched, dented skull. His tiny fingers and toes are curled arthritically and wrinkled as if he's spent too long in the bath. If it weren't for his slowly rustling heart, John would never have recognized the child.

"You can't stay here with that thing," her landlord's brother says.

"He'll be fine. He just needs to warm up."

John Robinson shakes his head and walks away. He can't go on protecting Gustine; it will only bring more trouble upon him. She belongs to his brother and to his brother she must return. He pulls aside the young brat who hawks the Labour in Vain's ratting events. "Fetch the Eye from Mill Street," he whispers. "Tell her where she may find my brother's dress lodger."

"I need a cup of tea, please," Gustine says loudly.

He pours a cup from the strong sugared pot boiling in the fireplace, and sets it before her. Carefully, she cools a bit in a saucer and holds it to the baby's lips, hoping to tempt him, but he makes no move to drink, just stares up bewilderedly, looking for all the world like he would cry if only he could only raise the tears. She wishes he would scream or flail about; she could bear anything easier than this fixed, mute suffering.

"What do you expect for that child, Gustine?" asks John, still standing over her. "Ye should've drowned it the day it was born, as Whilky said. It has no kind of life."

"I will give him a life," she whispers fiercely, holding his two small hands over the steaming cup of tea.

"And if he grew up, what would he grow up to be? An invalid? A monster in a freak show?"

But she has imagined a future for him, she realizes, though she's never put it in words. "He would grow up like him," Gustine says, staring at the pitcher upon John Robinson's mantelpiece: *The Sailor's Tear*, her potter's most popular item. When she stops to think about it, that is how she has always pictured her grown son. A thin, sinewy sailor, healthy enough to leave her behind. *The sailor jumped into the ship / As it lay upon the strand, / But, oh! His heart was far away / With friends upon the land.* She stands on the shore in a lamé turban with trembling ostrich feather, her matching earrings and necklace flashing in the dying sun, waving him off to war. That's her boy on deck, all grown up, his arms too long for his jacket, his pants just a bit too short. He's outgrown every piece of clothing she's ever bought him, but where most mothers would bemoan the expense, she has always been secretly delighted. Every extra inch of him has been wrested from death, every popped button and let-down hem means another year of victory.

> *He thought of those he loved the best,*
> *A wife and infant dear*
> *And feeling filled the sailor's breast*
> *The sailor's eye, a tear.*

Yes, of course he will be married and a father. It took her a while to learn to love his wife, Gustine admits, for she was pert and strong-minded and Gustine hated giving up any place in her child's affections; but at last she grew to love one who loved her own so well. Lying exposed for all to see, her son's heart had been the target of too many trifling East End girls, but the one he married never sought to break it. She treated him gently and gave him a son, exactly the same age today as he was that awful cholera winter they had the scare. Oh, Gustine can laugh about it now, but she thought she'd lost him then, so blue and cold had he lain at the Labour in Vain. She lifts his own rosy pink son and waves his chubby fist for him. Be safe! she cries, straining to be heard over the hungry gulls following the boat, but he has already turned away, his eyes averted, his hands warding off the sentiment.

She leaves him there, in the exact attitude of the Garrison pitcher, unable, she realizes, to make out his features in their deflection, or to know his body except in its turning away. She has never seen the face of the man whose life she imagines for her son. He is painted perpetually leaving her.

"Baby?" she whispers, for he has grown awfully still.

The boy John Robinson sent out slips back through the

doorway. He hisses to his master, I met her on the street. She's coming.

"Who's coming?" Gustine asks, looking up sharply.

John Robinson takes away her cup of tea, pretending not to hear her. "Who's coming?" she repeats, looking around at the old sotted women, the lightermen, the burly day labourers, who have stopped drinking and fallen silent in anticipation. *She's the one that clout the Eye. Ran away from home; now the Eye's come after. Should be here any minute.* Who needs a ratting? They are getting their fight early.

No, she must not find us here. They must get out fast, before the Shadow of Death catches up to them and finishes her business. Gustine frantically snatches up her poor sick child, pressing his shuddering body to her breast. Why did she think she could trust John Robinson any further than the rest of them? So he spoke a few kind words, so he kept her bed neat; he is still no better than a dishonest bartender and cheap brothel keeper. And her landlord's brother.

"Excuse me. *Please!*" Gustine shouts, trying to squeeze between two wooden tables. But it is too late. A girl can only lose her shadow for so long. Even as she breaks free, the door flies open, scattering those who sit nearest. When they discuss it later, no one will remember having ever seen the Eye look so fierce. Blood and snow wind down her forehead across the bridge of her flat nose, pinkly dribbling from her chin. Because the swelling from Gustine's blow has completely obscured her atrophied eye, her one good one has taken on even greater intensity. She is all vision now, all seeing single-minded vengeance. She carries the wet reproach of Gustine's dress in her arms. Climb back in, treacherous rat. Do not make me chase you.

"No!" Gustine screams, warding off the old woman. "Get away from us!"

"Gustine, it's time to go home," John says sternly.

But Gustine will not go back. She barrels into the patrons at the bar, shoving three startled labourers into the Eye. The old woman lurches off balance for only a moment, but it is enough to let Gustine through. She darts through the door and back out into the furious snow.

No! No! We will never go back there. Gustine races down Union Lane and up High Street, while overhead green lightning fires through the low snow clouds. No stalls decorate High Street tonight, no candles gutter in hollowed-out turnips to light her way. The streets are bitter and desolate, emptied of people by the unnatural electrical snow and the contagious fear of disease. She must find someplace to hide. She must find someplace—Oh, please, please! She bangs on a still lit milliner's window, where deep inside a woman counts money behind a counter. The tidy shop girl screams in horror at the raving muddy apparition, and clutches the day's receipts for dear life.

"Please help me!" Gustine cries, abandoning the shop. Across the street, a middle-aged man is fumbling with his umbrella and house key. "Sir!" She races over and tugs his sleeve. "Please, I will give you all the money I have if you will let us come in and stay the night." He throws her off and she skids across the snow. Taking a panicked glance over her shoulder, she sees that the Eye is right behind. Relentless. Automatic. A machine built solely to destroy her child.

She tears down High Street, pounding on doors indiscriminately. Inn keepers take one look at her child and slam their doors shut. No vacancy. "I have money!" she shouts against vibrating wood. "I can pay!" But the doors do not open.

Gustine is running blindly now, following the silhouette of the river, escape being the only thing keeping her lungs inflated, keeping her screaming legs moving. A string of great smoking tar barrels—set up by the Board of Health to purify the air of pestilence—burns at the intersections of High and Queen Streets, High and Gray, George, Sans, all the way to the corner of High and Villiers. Gustine, like a soldier caught in the line of fire, races to each barrel, pausing long enough to catch her breath before the noxious fumes overwhelm her child, making him gag and cough.

"I am so sorry," Gustine sobs, when at Bridge the street runs dry of burning barrels. Her baby is shuddering horribly and he sucks in air in raspy gulps. How small and helpless he has become, no bigger than a corncob doll.

Round-eyed gulls, plumped with cold, look down from their roof perches as Gustine paces the final tar barrel, rocking her child and crying. Please be strong, she begs. Please. Up ahead, lightning strikes the great Wearmouth Bridge and grounds to the water, crazing floes of hard black ice, sending unlucky river rats swirling to the bottom. Behind her she hears the Eye breaking the skins of puddles that splash icily behind her, never far behind no matter how fast Gustine runs. She darts right on Lower Bedford Street, then cuts across an alley onto Bridge Crescent. Skidding down the dark muddied embankment, she stumbles over the shadow of the Iron Bridge, nearly landing on her limp child.

On her bare hands and knees, Gustine crawls to safety beneath the ferrous arch. She is so cold, she's lost the feel of him; so blinded by tears, she can barely make out his shape against the snow. But neither tears nor frostbite nor utter physical collapse can erase Gustine's old ability to see through clothes. Beneath the baby's sodden christening gown, something stirs; and in the moment of her darkest despair, the miracle for which she has fervently prayed every night of his short life at last is granted. His troubled eyes close, his arms relax, and as Gustine watches, her child's soft blue heart gently ebbs into his chest and slowly comes to rest. She places her cheek upon the smooth flat landscape of rib and skin, as normal as that of any other child of any other mother.

A long shadow falls across Gustine as she kneels in the snow. She does not need to look up to know who is approaching. She was young and foolish when she first agreed to wear the dress. Eye held out the fantastical blue gown, and Gustine dove into it like a mermaid, surfacing with her arms caught in the sleeves and the laces tight around her rib cage. In the background their landlord was saying to the old woman, I am paying you to keep an eye on that dress. If she steals it, I'll come after you both. And Pink was saying, You look so pretty. Oh, Gustine, you look so pretty. But once outside, Gustine realized that like a mermaid, she had no voice on the streets or down through the lanes; was barely able to speak above a whisper to the first man, or the second, third, fourth, or fifth of that first night. She called out only once, to the Eye, but her words went unheard, as though she'd never uttered them. *Don't watch this*, she begged. *Don't watch me.*

"Please go away," Gustine pleads, struggling to her feet.

But still the old woman advances. Like God commanding Eve to step outside her naked skin and into the shameful life of clothes, she squares off against the girl and thrusts out the dress lodger's blue gown.

"You need to watch? You always need to watch?" the dress lodger sobs, spinning on the hateful old woman. "*Then look what you have done!"* And with a cry caught up on the cruel east wind, Gustine counters the body of the dress with a body of her own. That of her precious only child. Cold. And still. And blue.

An appeal to the enlightened citizens of Sunderland,
by Miss Audrey Place

I come before you, my friends and neighbours, to ask your help in stamping out a medieval superstition that pervades our otherwise modern and sophisticated town. In these days of reform and progress, should we still labour in darkness where afflictions of the human body are concerned? Should we condemn our illustrious medical men, who daily risk personal safety for our sakes, to consort with criminals and degenerates because they lack material for study? You know of what I speak; I need not give offense by naming it. Simply let it be known that four hundred citizens of Dublin (a far less superior populace, I believe all will agree) found the courage to throw outdated convention aside and rally to their doctors' aid. I hereby circulate this open petition, with the hopes that our voluntary gifts will make it unnecessary to trouble the poor, who cannot understand the importance of medical discovery, and have learned, through current unlawful practice, only to fear it.

To dispel superstition and light the lamp of anatomical inquiry, I hereby will my body to Sunderland Hospital for respectful dissection, so that it may be put to use in the service of Greater Good.

Miss Audrey E. Place   James Harrison, CPA

Mr. Andrew Mazby

J. Bietler

Thomas Coombs

Mr. Lawrence Grose

XIV

NEWS

"Why didn't you simply take out an advertisement—'My Fiancé, the Body Snatcher'—for the entire town to see?" Henry rages, shaking today's copy of the *Sunderland Herald* in Audrey's pale, frightened face. "My reputation—what was left of it, anyway—is ruined. I'll be lucky if I'm not driven out of town. Why, just now a letter has arrived from Sir James Bietler, removing his son from my instruction and requesting prompt return of payment. What in bloody hell were you thinking, Audrey?"

He has never spoken to her this way; she would not have thought him capable. She desired only to be of use, but it seems she has made things far worse than they already were.

"I'm sorry," she whispers, flinching before his agitated, accusatory face. Only moments ago, he'd burst through the door like a madman, waving the paper, interrupting the quiet tea she was having with her godfather. Mother has not been well, and Dr. Clanny had just put her down with a sedative. He said it was nothing a good night's rest wouldn't cure, but with cholera in town, Audrey was dreadfully worried. Now to have her dearest shouting at her . . .

"And to leave your own name in print," fumes Henry, "in the company of those men. Who is this Harrison, anyway?"

At the mention of her father's accountant, Audrey's mortification knows no bounds. She bursts into tears and runs from the parlour, racing upstairs to the comfort of her old childhood bed.

"Weren't you a little harsh?" asks Dr. Clanny from the depths of his armchair.

"I spoke to her of it earlier, Uncle, and thought I'd made myself clear. She willfully disobeyed me."

Clanny sighs and lifts the china teacup to his lips. "It will blow over," he says mildly. "You are *not* a body snatcher, after all."

"Not anymore," Henry says with some passion, pacing before the fireplace. "After I received the letter from Bietler's father, I wrote the fathers of my other students returning their fees as well."

Clanny looks at his nephew incredulously. "Why on earth would you do that? That is more an admission of guilt than anything Audrey ran in the newspaper."

"I had wanted to handle it privately, in my own way, but Audrey's petition forced my hand." Henry stops and faces his uncle. "Death and I are finished. I am giving up my anatomy school."

"What?"

"I have been wed to the graveyard since I first laid eyes on Dr. Knox, Uncle. I have struggled with my conscience, knowing Science must be served, yet more often than not being its unwilling servant. Only now have I found something that has given me the courage to leave it behind, to step out of the shadows and into the light."

"And in the meantime, you have thrown over your practice and all you have worked for these many years?"

"They are nothing to me now, Uncle, but so many nightmares. I have come into a time of health, I can feel it—a new beginning."

Clanny sizes up his disheveled, wild-eyed nephew. Something has happened, but the elder gentleman does not know what.

"Just remember Jack Crawford, son," says the old doctor, shaking his head. "And be careful your 'time of health' is not a further trick of the disease." Clanny drains his tea, then slowly walks to the front door, where the Places' girl Crimmons is waiting with his coat. "Go make it up with Audrey," he says, winding his cravat about his neck and tugging on his gloves. "She only did it to please you."

Henry watches his uncle walk off to the Infirmary for another night's rounds. Maybe this has all been for the best. Audrey's misguided petition forced him into action, when his natural impulse is always to delay. He climbs the front staircase and follows the sobs down the hall to a small bedroom. His fiancée has thrown herself over her large feather bed and buried her face in her enormous grisette woolen sleeves. These new fashions, Henry thinks, remembering the classic Grecian lines of his early twenties; they are so melodramatic. Audrey's bedroom is much as he would have imagined: furnished with a poster bed, a writing desk, and a full-length pier glass that reflects her wallpaper of rose nosegays. A sentry of dolls, worn and much loved, guard the windowsills from any impetuous lover who might presume to hoist a ladder, while a wooden rocking horse, another loyal playmate, gathers dust in the corner. The entire room speaks of youth and innocence, and Henry feels almost profane stepping across the threshold. Her mamma is down the hall, asleep on laudanum prescribed by Dr. Clanny, and the servant is downstairs. What would they think of his entering her sanctuary?

"Dearest?" he asks, made contrite by her misery.

She jumps at the sound of a masculine voice in her room, for no man has ever come here, save her father and good Dr. Clanny when she had mild scarletina years ago. She turns her red, tear-streaked face to him, too hurt and ashamed to speak.

"May I come to you?" Henry asks gently.

She nods and sits up, trying to compose herself. How young she looks, he thinks, with her hair falling across her forehead and her cheeks hot and flushed. Henry feels so lost and awkward most of the time, he forgets that he is nearly twice her age and that he must be the one to guide her. It is his duty to teach her, to check her enthusiasms and save her from horrible mistakes like the one just made. He is as responsible for this mess as she is; for her own good, he should have insisted she rip up the petition, and he says as much, taking a seat beside her on the bed.

"I am sorry you lost your student," Audrey whispers. "I am sorry I am so very stupid."

"Oh, dearest, don't say that!" Henry pulls her close and kisses her pretty white forehead. "You are not stupid, you are just too fond."

They sit in silence for some few minutes, each awaiting more self-recrimination from the other. Audrey is sorry Henry lost a student, but after all, a gifted scientist like her fiancé deserves better than that ignorant landholder or his cowardly defector of a son. And can Henry refuse to see the courage it took to publish her own name before friends and family in support of his profession?

"We have much to learn about each other's ways." Henry gives her a chaste kiss on the cheek in deference to their unchaperoned position upon the bed, and starts to get up. Not that he would ever press an advantage, but he is a little disconcerted at not having to at least fight the impulse. He

can't imagine slinging his slop all over this pink and white little girl's room.

"Henry, wait." Audrey grabs his hand and pulls him back
down upon the bed. "I am in such dreadful need of comfort.
I am really the wickedest of girls."

He thinks at first she is being flirtatious, but then he sees
that more tears have risen in her eyes. Will he be comforting
her all night? He frowns a bit over her shoulder, for he only
meant to drop by and scold her, then go straight back to
work.

"What is it, dear?" He gathers her to him, but asks the
question as neutrally as possible, hoping to escape with the
shortest version.

"I have acted without your permission in another matter.
Just this morning, I promised a position in our household to
a poor little girl who is deeply troubled. You know her by the
name of Pink, and she is as good a little girl as I've ever
met—"

"Let me interrupt you, darling, and say that taking her in
is impossible. I have seen a solicitor this morning, and signed
papers to have that baby of Mill Street come live here with
us. Of course, I'll hire a nurse—I wouldn't dream of burden-
ing you with a foster child—but I'll want no more than one
stray around the house." He breaks off at the look of distress
on Audrey's face. Surely they will not have to fight about this
too.

"Oh, Henry, now I must tell you that what you wish is
impossible," Audrey cries.

"Audrey," he says sternly, "this is not negotiable. I will not
argue with you."

"You have no argument from me. That poor child is dead.
Pink told me this morning."

Dimly, he hears her go on about Pink, how the poor girl is devastated and blames herself. He continues to hold his babbling fiancée as she pours out her plans for that odd urchin, but his mind is racing. The child dead? He was fine when Gustine left his house, was he not? God, he'd been so bewitched by the mother, he'd barely noticed the child. But now he could shake himself when he remembers. The child was cold and shivering, with unmistakably bluish circles under his eyes; looking back, he must have been in the first stages of cholera morbus.

"Has he been buried?" he demands abruptly, interrupting Audrey's plans for Pink. She looks at him strangely.

"The child was illegitimate. I don't believe the mother was allowed a Christian funeral," she answers haltingly. "He was buried in the Trinity pit."

Gone? Henry pulls her close once more to hide his deep agitation. The solicitor this morning had all but assured him that with the proper petitions, the child was his; and on that promise, Henry had been enboldened to dissolve his anatomy school and begin to plan a new future. He stares vacantly out the window above his fiancée's blonde head, feeling the full weight of all he has lost. He tries to imagine what will come next, tries to picture going on with his work, but oddly enough, all that comes to mind is an experiment on the origins of life he once performed for his students, months ago, long before he met Gustine. He removed the shell of a four-days-incubated egg, submerging it in tepid water so that his students might observe the pulsing pinprick of blood that would one day develop into the chicken's heart. The point was so small, it disappeared completely during contraction, only to reappear during relaxation, representing that moment between the visible and the

invisible, betwixt being and nothing, that is the commence-
ment of life. Had this child not in some fashion become
that moment in Henry's own re-creation? While it lived and
he could observe it, a new life was possible; now that it has
contracted and disappeared into the ground, all of his
hopes must die with it. Whatever made him think he could
escape the graveyard? Henry hides his burning face in his
fiancée's hair. His future lies buried with that baby in the
Trinity pit.

Reverend Robert Gray plods across the churchyard, his black
cassock fluttering below the hem of his greatcoat, his heavy
boots sinking in the lathered quicklime mud that is supposed
to be scrubbing his underground congregation clean of filth
and decay. In his pocket, he carries a flask of wine, a jar of
vinegar, and a rag—the wine for strength and comfort, the
vinegar and rag to swab down her blistered knees and hands,
for poor girl, she won't stop patting the corrosive earth. As if
it were still in her power to soothe.

He has watched her from the window of the rectory—
what there was to watch, for she has not moved since early
this morning, except to press her cheek against the soil or
burn her lips with kisses. Please bury my child, she had
begged him yesterday. Everyone says you are a friend of the
poor. She was not one of his parishioners; he had never
seen her before she appeared at his door in her inappropriate blue gown, cradling her tiny coffin. Reverend Gray is a
friend to the poor, and he was instantly moved by the sight
of this poor magdalene whose eyes were swollen nearly
shut from crying, but the church has rules and it was not
in his power to break them. The best he could do for an
unbaptized bastard child, no matter how beloved, was the

pit on the dark side of the church, a pit of suicides and unclaimed paupers, murderers and drunks. She has been sitting beside that fresh-turned earth ever since, a rippling blue puddle on a chemical winter landscape. He is relieved to see that an old woman has arrived, though strangely, she has made no move to comfort the girl, has merely waited outside the cemetery gate, fixed as a severed head upon a pike.

"Hold out your hands, girl, and let me see them," orders the reverend, crouching down beside her. She mechanically presents her hands and he splashes the red, bleeding palms with vinegar. He swabs her raw cheek where she pillowed her head, and daubs at her swollen lips. "You can't continue to lie here—you'll soon have no skin left. Let's stand up," he says, pulling her by her armpits.

Her legs have fallen asleep from sitting in one position for so long, and they have trouble supporting her weight. She came early this morning and would stay through the long cold night if only he would let her.

"A friend has come to take you home, do you see?"

Gustine follows Reverend Gray's eyes back to the gray hulking Fafnir just outside the gate. She is back again today, though guarding from a far greater distance than ever before. Rejoice shadow, you have won! Gustine is back in the dress, laced into her only means of support, now that her potter has succumbed. You are a pair again, after only a brief interruption. But to be fair, Gustine feels no pleasure on the Eye's side, no triumph or even grim satisfaction. She looks at the old woman and sees only that: an old woman. A sad, defeated, maimed old woman. Since the death of her baby, they have become like twin ghosts haunting the streets of Sunderland. The girl and her shadow. The dress and the Eye.

Sheri Holman

The reverend gives her a little push. "Come on now. I have work to do. We must lock up."

"I will be back tomorrow," Gustine whispers, looking longingly at the ground.

Reverend Gray watches her wind through the mossy headstone garden and out through the iron gate, where she silently picks up her sentry. The old woman does not acknowledge her, but falls into step behind like the human shape of her own heavy sorrow. She is one of the oddest mothers he's ever seen—so seemingly devoted, and yet when he asked for the baby's name to record it in the register, she said he didn't have one. She couldn't think of a name to save him, she said; why should she give one to his gravestone?

When they are out of sight, Reverend Gray calls for his sexton to lock the gate behind him. He can spend no more time on this mother and bastard child. Cholera morbus has joined his flock, and tonight he must visit ten more who have shared its pew.

Last night she dreamed of a worm on the rim of a pitcher. Every squirm of his fat white body traced a crack until the pitcher crumbled to dust like an Egyptian mummy. Upon the heap of glass her child lay and did not bleed but slept so peacefully she hadn't the heart to wake him.

She rarely dreamed of him while he lived; she thought of him incessantly during the day and imagined how he did while she was at work, but she almost never filled her nights with him. It seems like such a waste now: four months of dreams given over to foolish things like falling and flying when she could have been keeping company with her beloved son. She wishes she had all those nights back to dream over again.

Gustine stands in the doorway of Nescham's fish ware-house, breathing in the briny oil of old halibut and mussels. The Quarantine patrol boat has left the tidal harbor and is rounding Crach Rock, sweeping its mirrored oil lamp eye along the Monkwearmouth bank. It is the same barge they use to drag the bottom when some desperate girl takes final advantage of the River Wear. Not two months ago, she watched a pair of constables haul another limp woman face-first up the quayside steps. Back then, in the first flush of new motherhood, she couldn't comprehend the impulse; now she has no trouble imagining herself laid out in Mag Scurr's back room, a lump of clay and a swatch of blue silk for blazons.

We are what we do. It is how people know us. Gustine ferried clay and called herself a potter's assistant. She bore a child and called herself a mother. She walked the streets and let men stretch her quim, but she never once thought of herself as a whore. She was a dress lodger; hers was but a rented self. Yet Dr. Chiver saw the truth. He saw she was a whore with or without the dress; and truly, have not all her other selves dropped away? She is no longer a potter's assis-tant. She is no more a mother. Only Whore remains, kept alive by the dress and the Eye and the insistence of Dr. Chiver's prying fingers. There is a reason every Wear suicide brought to Mag Scurr had a baby in her belly, Gustine now realizes. No woman kills herself for love, and rarely for shame. It is the cruelty of hope that does a woman in; for no matter how many men a woman has given herself to, she never holds her life cheap until she foolishly believed it to be valued.

It would be so easy to walk into the water. The patrol man swinging his big oil lamp eye would catch the top of

her head as it sank beneath the surface and think no more
of it than of a snapping turtle ducking under for a minnow.
She could shrug off her tired flesh as she once did her clay
rind at the pottery. And after all, why should she grow
attached to it? It is rented no less than the blue dress on her
back, and from a landlord far more cruel and vengeful than
the one she left at Mill Street. It would be so easy to walk
out and meet her sailor son. He is out there on his ship, his
eyes turned toward shore. She can almost see him bobbing
on the choppy waves, hear the plash of his wooden oars as
he lays them across his knees and stretches out his arms to
her.

Lost in her reverie, she does not see a small skiff brave the
Quarantine searchlight as it glances left to the Sunderland
side of the river, play dead like all the other empty tethered
lighters until danger had passed, and quickly make its way to
shore. A tall man, but gaunt as if he hasn't eaten in weeks,
drags his boat onto the quay, camouflaging it under some rotting net outside of Nescham's. His tattered, buttonless jacket
hangs loose, his once-tight white trousers bag about his
knees. He has a long, equestrian skull with sad, gentle eyes
and too many teeth for his small mouth. Beneath his arm, he
carries a bundle of carefully folded clothes, tied up with
string.

"Oh!" He stops short, nearly treading upon her in the
shadows. "I didn't see anyone there. Are you lost?"

Are you lost? How funny that her dream should be broken
by the same line used by Green-plaid and so many other men
of Sunderland. Gustine awakes disappointed. This tall,
storky sailor is not her son.

"No, I am not lost." She sighs, too tired to lie. "I am just
coming from Trinity Churchyard."

"Excuse me for being forward." He clears his throat. "But this is no neighbourhood for a lady to walk alone. I've been away for a while, but I know things haven't changed that much."

Neither moves from where they stand: Gustine in the doorway of the closed fish warehouse, the young sailor near his hidden rowboat. Her landlord has ordered her straight back to work, but she feels so dull and leaden, it is impossible to imagine propositioning this man. If it were only lying on her back and enduring, she might be able, but the hard work of charm and banter and intercourse . . . *Have you ever known perfect love?* she can just hear herself ask as he lifts her skirt. *Have you ever had a helpless baby bird die in your hands?* The young sailor looks nervously between her and Long Bank, torn between politeness and a strong desire to run away. I am not ready for this, thinks Gustine, sidling around the doorway past him. But she is too slow for his better nature. He has already abandoned his craft and is coming up the bank to offer his arm.

Well, it had to happen sooner or later. Now he will get a long look at her in the light, and she knows what will follow: either the proposition, the resignation, and the cold alley door against her back; or surprise, disgust, and a quick mumbled-excuse good-bye. But the emaciated sailor sees nothing untoward in her appearance. He presents his skeletal arm along with his sincerest wishes to escort her home. No, she couldn't possibly, she lies, startled; it is too far.

"Please don't trouble yourself about the distance," he says. "I am just so happy to have the earth under my feet after far too long at sea." He has a deep voice that he is shy about using, swallowing the ends of words and speaking as if through a drink of water. He looks too frail to lean upon, but when

Gustine, touched by his gallantly pathetic manner, agrees to take his arm, she finds it surprisingly sinewy and strong.

They walk in silence, eavesdropping on the fog that like a gossip gathers little bits from all over town: the faraway whistle of Sunderland Bottle Works' nightly shift change, a father shouting for his boy to come home, snatches of song from out-of-work men keeping warm on the docks.

> *The pitmen and the keelmen trim*
> *They drink the bumbo made of gin*
> *And when to dance they do begin*
> *The tune is "Elsie Marley," honey!*

It is comforting to have someone to lean on, for Gustine hadn't realized how very tired she was. He leads her slowly westward—the direction in which, she realizes, he automatically assumes she must live. Would you not like to rest? he asks more than once. No one has ever asked her that before.

"I am less tired now than before," she answers for the second time. "And I am grateful for the company."

"You've had a sad evening at Trinity?" the sailor asks after a few more blocks of neither speaking.

Gustine nods and feels her throat tighten.

"A relative?"

Another silent nod. The sailor seems to understand and share her quiet mood. "It is a dying time of year."

He does not speak like most sailors she has known. He is not coarse or drunk or profane or boastful. He speaks like a boy who might have gone to school and read books. She takes a long look at his face, not turned away or shaded like *The Sailor's Tear.* It is an open, respectful face.

"When my mother died last year, I used to go alone to the cemetery," the sailor offers shyly, worried he might be over-stepping his bounds. "My brother and sister would have gone, but I wanted my mother all to myself. I expect she enjoyed the company."

"You loved your mother very much?"

"More than any person in the world." He sighs. "It was hard putting her in the ground, but at least I knew her labours had come to an end. She worked every day of her life, worked herself to death to give my brother and sister and me a taste of something better. She deserved a rest. I'm sorry." The sailor stops suddenly and observes her worriedly. "I've made you cry."

She shakes her head, embarrassed that her tears are still so close to the surface. "No, it's nothing," she says. "The only comfort I have is that my child was spared having to work."

"Oh, it was a child you buried?" asks the sailor, looking ready to cry himself. "Then I am doubly sorry, miss." He tucks her arm a little tighter inside his and gives it an awk-ward pat.

"You've been a long time at sea?" Gustine changes the sub-ject, unable to continue speaking of loss in this unfamiliar atmosphere of sympathy. She can feel the propulsion of the Eye following close behind, and knows what is expected of her. But not yet. Not yet.

"I suppose you saw me row in?" he asks, a little chagrined. "And hide my boat?"

"Yes."

"Shall I turn myself in to the Quarantine patrol?"

"If everyone feels free to break the Quarantine, I don't know why we've had to suffer it all these months," Gustine responds matter-of-factly.

"Where I've been, I've seen the uselessness of Quarantine, miss. Something always sneaks through. I suppose I am proof of that."

They walk a few blocks more in silence, but as if compelled to explain his lawlessness, the sailor soon continues.

"Cholera took our captain and first mate a month ago, and we've been trying to get home ever since. Imagine how it feels to be in sight of home but stuck just offshore, without fresh food, without communication, without medicine. Some of us couldn't take it anymore." He swallows almost all of that last and she has to lean in to hear him.

"And I've heard it doesn't matter anyway—the cholera is already here in Sunderland," the sailor says.

"So we've been told."

"It devastated Riga, where we've just come from," he tells her. "Some say the refugees from Moscow brought it. From what I could make out, they thought they were being poisoned and broke the military cordons, scattering across the continent."

She doesn't think he is going to continue, for they walk in silence past the dark Exchange building, the burning tar barrels of Queen and High Streets, as far as Playhouse Lane; but finally, as if he found his voice among the locked and shuttered theatres, her escort begins to speak.

"I remember the night our captain succumbed," he says, looking not at her, but at his own big feet. "He was sitting on deck writing home to his family and I was sitting near him, like a dullard staring back at the smoky factories onshore, blaming him, blaming everyone for being stuck in that infernal port. We were flying our yellow Quarantine flags to show we complied with the law, but in our hearts we hated the Quarantine and would have broken through in a minute, just pulled up anchor after dark and risked the patrols. Only, our captain wouldn't hear of it. He was not used to taking risks at sea and wanted nothing other than to get home to his family in one piece, even if we had to sit off the port of Riga for a year. He was a cautious man, our captain—not really a sailor, more of a businessman—and he actually believed a country drew up laws to protect its citizens! I remember the first mate asking him exactly who it was this Quarantine was meant to protect: us from them or them from us? The Quarantine was a joke, miss, if you don't mind me saying so. We bought food off the local merchants who sailed out to us every day. They took our money and rowed back into town. It was a joke, plain and simple. Just like here."

The couple passes Sans Street, where a young boy is taking an armload of bottles to be filled at the dispensary. Judging from the collection of glass he carries, every member of his family was sick.

"Our captain was writing his family the night he succumbed," the sailor continues. "It was a lying sort of letter, written to make ladies feel comfortable. Not a word about the men and women dropping dead on the piers in horrible convulsions, or of their husbands and wives flinging themselves off the cliffs in fits of grief. Just a letter full of light news and inquiries into how his daughter's wedding plans were progressing. It had been hot and oppressive all day, but as the sun set, a cold east wind picked up, troubling his papers—I ran and caught one that blew away. As I handed back his letter, a raindrop hit the page. Miss, I can't describe what I felt when I saw that raindrop. I had been grumbling for rain—we all had—but how earnestly we now wished it back up in the sky. The rain, miss, was yellow, yellow like sulfur, and when the captain, in his amazement, held his wet bit of paper over a candle, it burned blue and fetid like sulfur.

"There was no escape after that," the sailor says quietly. "The Devil had come for us. Our captain died with that unfinished letter still clutched in his hand. Our first mate followed a day later. When they finally let us out of Quarantine, we had four dead men on our ship and another six dying. I came down with it too, miss. Oh God it was bad, but I guess the Devil didn't want me, for a few days later I pulled through. I learned one thing, though: I'll never sit still for Quarantine again. I'll fight, I'll run—but I won't sit and wait for Death to come to me. I know it will come, miss, there's no helping that. But it's going to have to chase me down."

They pass the corner of Nile and High Streets, the place where Gustine tried to outrun death for her child. She wishes she could share the sailor's determination, but cholera has taught her something completely different. She has no more belief in her own abilities.

"I'm sorry," he says, embarrassed. "I've been so busy talking, I haven't even asked where we are going."

Gustine has not thought that far either. "Oh, we are here," she says, glancing up at the marker as they approach the next corner building. "Fawcett Street."

"Then I was destined to be of service to you!" the sailor exclaims. "For I was headed that way. I must deliver this melancholy package to 38 Fawcett Street in the morning."

Gustine had forgotten all about the bundle of clothes under his other arm. "Why do you call your package melancholy?" she asks.

"I don't know what else to call a dead man's jacket and

trousers, his shirts, his unraveled socks. I think our captain's fresh widow and fatherless daughter will find it so. We buried him at sea, but we thought they might appreciate his clothes—filthy and worn as they are. Women are fond that way."

Gustine's own sadness has made her generous. She feels for the poor mother and daughter, sitting in their nice house on a nice street, blissfully unconscious of what is on its way to them. But didn't Dr. Chiver say the clothes of cholera victims should be immediately burned? That they were vessels of pestilence and the bringers of death? Perhaps it would be better for the sailor to dispose of those clothes right away.

"Maybe you know Captain Place's family, being a neighbor?" he interrupts her thoughts.

"Captain Place?" Gustine asks, startled by the name.

"I see you are familiar."

"A friend of mine—," Gustine begins, and stops herself. "Captain Place's daughter, I believe, is engaged to someone I know."

"The doctor? Captain spoke of the upcoming marriage frequently," the sailor confides. "It's a shame the old gentleman won't be here to attend."

So the beautiful girl of the matching earrings and necklace has troubles of her own. Gustine wonders if Henry will be kinder in Miss Place's hour of need than he was in hers. Certainly he will, for she is the thing he holds most precious in the world. He must feel as protective of her as Gustine felt about her beloved child.

"Go to them if you can, miss," says the sailor, interrupting her thoughts. "Mrs. and Miss Place will be in desperate need of their friends."

"I will," she lies. "This is my house." She picks a darkened mansion set back from the road, and quickly slips inside its gate. "I can make it the rest of the way."

"I am very happy to have had the privilege of walking you home." The gawky sailor bows deeply. "I know young ladies are more independent these days, but if you must go again to Trinity, I hope you will have your husband or a servant accompany you."

"Thank you," Gustine says, wishing a young lady might take a stranger's hand and press it. What kind of world is it, she wonders, where as a dress lodger she might have given that sailor her entire body, but as a young lady she is constrained from even extending her hand? Can the difference between herself and Audrey Place truly be so great, if one blue dress alone can erase it? Gustine is angry with herself. She cares nothing about the money or the things, but the kindness—oh, God, to ever feel entitled to such kindness.

Sadly, she watches the young sailor disappear down Fawcett and waits for him to be replaced by the inevitable Eye. She must get back to work. It is what her landlord expects, and it must be done if she is to earn the money to leave this place, which is now her only desire. Gustine has been granted about as long a respite as she could imagine.

But minutes pass, and the Eye does not appear. She was behind them the whole time; Gustine heard and understood her language, the familiar skitter of a rock kicked aside or the snap of an acorn meaning Let's get on with it. Gustine waits fifteen minutes more before giving up and beginning her long walk home to Mill Street. She feels oddly unmoored and vertiginous without the Eye behind her; as if she might fly off into the shadows like some crazed blue Cauld Lad. She has grown too used to surveillance not to mistrust this freedom.

Surely the Eye is lurking just around the corner or waiting like a buzzard to swoop upon her from the gutters overhead. Surely this is just a test, a cruel parody of independence lasting only until she comes home empty-handed, when Whilky might feel justified in tightening her leash. The Eye's absence only makes Gustine feel her more. Everywhere she looks a gray carbuncle flashes from the lamppost or peeps up from a sewer. The wheels of carriages are watching her, and the three round balls of pawnshops. She walks with her head down, trying not to feel she's replaced one watchdog with an entire town.

And where is the Eye? What could possibly induce the inveterate sentry away from her post? Perhaps the answer lies with the Quarantine dodger who kindly escorted Gustine home to the Bishopwearmouth. Not long after he left her, still floating on the young lady's kind words and gentle looks, he was seized with the strangest sensation. Someone was watching him. He felt the hair on the back of his neck rise, was so certain, he even spun around and drew his knife. Yet no one was there. Crackbrained paranoia, he scolded himself, and continued on, but not long after, while he was checking the address of a friend's family where he was to stay the night, he was sure he heard deep laboured breathing just over his shoulder. Once more, he spun around, ready to face the Quarantine patrol and fight for his freedom, but, lo—nothing. Only fog and shadows and darkly melting snow.

"May I help you, madam?" the lanky young sailor remembers asking when he finally turned back to find an old, one-eyed woman in front of him. Why does she observe him so strangely, he wondered, and why on earth does she reach out for the bundle of his captain's clothes?

But that is the last thing he remembers before the heavy blow knocked him to his knees and drove him face-first into the snow.

XV

A RESURRECTION

How much?" From his satchel, Whilky Robinson pulls a soiled linen christening gown and plops it on the counter for Mag Scurr's appraisal. He had Pink scrub the damned garment twice in a vat of hot water and lye, but to no avail: it will always be brown about the back. The old pawnbroker squints hard at it, turns it inside out and checks the seams. Not shabby, thinks she, but of course, communicates just the opposite.

"Four shillings." She screws up her face and hands it back. "It's the best I can do."

"For fine Irish linen?" Whilky squeaks. "It's worth ten!"

"Six, and not a ha' penny more," answers the old woman. "Who of our sort has the cash for such frivolities?"

Whilky scowls, thinking it over. A restless line has formed behind him, four thespians by the look of 'em, laden down with pasteboard and tinseled costumes to pawn. *I could use that linen for collars*, he overhears the only female of their group whisper to an elderly gentleman. *Lady Cromwell's habit is getting tatty.* Don't be ridiculous, comes her answer. We haven't the money to get to London as it is.

"I'll take the six, you greedy old hag," Whilky capitulates, then pointedly recounts the money she pushes across the counter. It's a little unexpected something, though it doesn't begin to make up for the money he's lost on his dress lodger's freaks.

Whilky fades back from the counter, watching the actors behind him and idly browsing Mag's farrago of goods for sale. He's not bought Mike a treat in what seems like an age (having already forgotten this morning's blackcurrant tart), and as today is his ferret's big day in the ratting ring, he deserves a special tidbit. There is much here for a landlord to covet: sextants and little tin anchors, sailcloth jackets and His Majesty's Royal Navy—issue caps. A couple dozen of the fleet are in pawn at Mag Scurr's, from the look of it; high tide washed them in and straight into hock. Yes, there is much for a landlord to admire, but what might a ferret fancy? That mane of black hair, hung from a peg by the door? 'T would make a fine nest, that is true, but Whilky prefers his pet to sleep with him. A grosgrain ribbon for his neck? Naw, thinks Whilky. M' boy's no dandy.

"This sword, I assure you, madame, is not some common poker, but an exact reproduction of the very weapon worn by Richard Coeur de Lion during the Sieging of Acre." The scrawny actor of the group has stepped forward to play negotiator, cutting figures around Mag's head by way of demonstration, thrusting and jabbing like to take her mobcap off. "Imagine," says he, "the heights of carnage a young boy might attain, wielding this indomitable piece of equipment."

"Ten pence," replies Mag.

"Ten for a singular metallurgic artifact, madame?" Steps the actor back in deep disgust. "You insult me."

"Eight if you keep playing," says Mag.

"We'll take it," interjects the older gentleman.

They haggle over a sorcerer's robe and a high three-fingered Touchstone foolscap; a pasteboard Cross of India medal comes out next, then Phebe's white tissue shepherdess frock, bespangled with glass beads and shot with silver. It is stained beneath the armpits and a few seams have given way, but it is a fetching dress and would surely turn the heads of many a Sunderland gentleman. Now there's a thought. . . . Whilky surprises himself with the idea. Should he? After all, Gustine's blue gown came by way of an actress down on her luck; he picked it up at one of Mag's competitors for 12s and change. This one he might get for even less, and it is as grand as Gustine's costume, perhaps grander. He's had his eye on another likely girl in the lodging house, flightier than Gustine, but more compliant, and wouldn't that white fit her exactly? The actors sell it to Mag for eleven shillings and when he steps up to ask for it, she flips it to Whilky for fourteen.

"Three shillings for sitting in your alligator hands not thirty seconds?" the landlord roars, but ultimately pays her price, because, as Mag knew, he wouldn't have hung about if he didn't seriously want it.

Despite his blustering, Whilky leaves more or less satisfied with his deal. Having cashed in the six-shilling linen gown, he technically got the dress for eight, and eight shillings is a small price to pay for expanding one's empire. It's a dangerous time to be entrepreneurial, this he knows, but the Quarantine can't last forever; he's already heard rumblings that that sot Londonderry is insisting it be lifted. He'll take the Eye off blue duty and place her on white, and the hell with Gustine, ungrateful little chit that she is. Out of the kindness of his heart, when he found out her brat had died and she'd lost her job at the pottery, he let her crawl back into the dress, but has she earned any money for him? No, she's done nothing but mope over that tiny coffin, making the whole house miserable and maudlin. At least it's finally in the ground and they can all move on with their lives.

BY ORDER OF THE BOARD OF HEALTH
Loose BOWELS are the
First Sign of
THE CHOLERA MORBUS
Call Immediately for a Doctor
All Sickroom Bedding and Clothing
must be BURNED
All Cholera DEAD must be
BURIED
TWELVE HOURS
after Death
BY ORDER OF LAW

Out front of Mag's the actors have paused directly in front of a bulletin, to confer and divvy up their money. Talk of timetables and stagecoaches engage the three men, but the lady, prim and pert of manner, looks up and down the Low Quay with unconcealed disgust. Her eyes widen at the sight of Whilky shoving into his satchel her Phebe dress, made by an old Italian widow who finally went blind stitching on the last rows of glass beads. Miss Watson had sobbed uncontrollably when ordered to part with it, for it was her favorite gown, and though exceedingly pastoral, could be made to double in a pinch as a wedding dress. But with the complete failure of the troupe's "Cholera Morbus; or Love and Fright," they were utterly destitute, and the only thing worse than surrendering the dress would have been staying in this godforsaken town. Now they have enough money to move on to London and remount the wretched production there—where it will be appreciated, in the words of the injured Mr. Eliot, playwright, who has still not forgiven Sunderland's refusal to riot.

"You've bought my dress, I see," Miss Watson calls to Whilky Robinson. "I hope you will take care of it."

"It's being put to a very special use," smirks Whilky. "Employment with a high profile, I assure you."

"Good," replies Miss Watson haughtily, suspicious of being mocked. "I've been married in it many times."

"Where're ye off to?" asks Whilky, sniffing out a stage-coach schedule in the scrawny actor's hand.

"London."

"To tread the boards?"

"Just so," replies Mr. Eliot, thinking, What a wonderfully cretinous character to punish Miss Watson with! Can I write him into my next production?

"I'm a bit of a performer myself," smiles Whilky broadly. "I pretend to give a bloody shit about my lodgers and their gittish little problems."

"Brilliant!" exclaims Mr. Eliot, slapping the landlord's back, while a thoroughly disgusted Miss Watson fights the urge to snatch her poor Phebe from this vulgarian's hands.

"M' little friend here is even more of a star," continues Whilky, reaching into his frock coat and extracting the weasel, who'd sought warmth in his armpit. "Meet Mike, who today is fighting Fat Tom's upstart collie for Crown Prince of Ratters. Ye look like betting men to me. Care to join us for a beer and a match?"

Miss Watson sniffs indignantly, but Mr. Eliot eagerly agrees. They've missed the morning coach and the next one won't be along until eleven this evening. Mr. Mortimer and Mr. Webster both look dubious, but Eliot's always going off after material for his sketches. At least they can kill time inside, out of the cold.

"Aw, do come along, miss." Whilky bows winningly.

"There's many a dainty sundry for a woman of your refinement at my brother's place."

What else is she to do? Wait by herself on the streets of Sunderland? With a shudder she takes the arm presented her, already imagining the adulterated wine and rancid leek tarts in store. "Just one last thing," says the landlord, reaching behind her lovely brown head and ripping the Board of Health sign from the wall. He takes from his bag one of his many DEATH ACCUSING THE RICH, and tacks it in its place. "Must do our part for the Health of the Nation," he smiles.

At stake tonight: the sovereign title, Crown Prince of Ratters. Last year's champion: Mike, Whilky Robinson's ferret. This year's challenger: Fat Tom Brown's mangy, half-mad Border collie, Banquo. The contest: A teeming cage of one hundred sewer rats, fifty each to be let loose in two five-minute intervals, during which time the contestants, one at a time, are to set upon them, following which the lifeless bodies shall be counted by an impartial judge and the regalia awarded to that ratter (dog or ferret) judged most mortiferous. Mike is the odds-on favorite, but Banquo, being larger and more erratically ferocious, is a true dark horse.

"Where are the rats then?" asks a curly-headed brunet gentleman of the labourer who has been explaining the event. "I see no cage of one hundred rats."

"Not here yet," replies his knowledgeable companion. "Comes at the last minute to avoid accidents."

So the brunet gentleman must sketch from imagination a cageful of ferocious, furious rodents, pushing their heads through the bars, hissing gruesomely at the spellbound audience. The reality is quite different. The capacity crowd laughs and jokes, ignoring the hastily constructed center pit,

which is filled with sand and ringed with an elbow-high wall
to keep the terrified rats inside. Here to lay wagers on the
contest are butchers who've scrubbed their hands but missed
their bloody forearms, splintery glassworkers from the Wear
Flint Bottle Works, a prim teacher of sewing and arithmetic
at Donnison's Charity School for Girls, whose father was a
rat catcher and in whose heart the blood sport holds a sentimental place. Then there are the keelmen, the recently laid-
off pottery workers, and of course those men whose job it
is to do nothing all day but complain about the Quarantine
that keeps them doing nothing all day, forming, as usual, the
main constituency of John Robinson's clientele. In the middle of this rabble sits the brunet gentleman, his burnt-
sausage-coloured locks falling into his eyes as he hastily
scribbles notes on his companions: *Woman to my left: fat, flatulent, bovine specimen. Breasts as big as my head. Wet nurse? Man beside
her: scrawny and consumptive-looking. Former R.C. postulant, now fills
his evenings with gin and rat baiting?* He has sketched in a charcoal
gray wash of humanity, a good deal more pockmarked and
boil-ridden than perhaps Nature has drawn, but after all, he
is trying to get the Flavor of the event, to show what amuse-
ments the Poor must pursue, denied the education to enjoy
a good book. Next to him, nursing his fifth beer, sits our old
friend Robert Cooley. An amazing personage, really, thinks
the sketch artist, for did you know he'd single-handedly
fought off six doctors coming after his carcass with saws and
knives?

At a commotion in the doorway, the artist turns his attention away from his companion and toward the troupe pushing inside, singularly out of place, he would say; for like him,
they appear to be people of quality. Three men: one tall and
thin, one short and fat, and one mature, accompanied by a

perfectly delightful young woman (who has the good breeding to look appalled), and rear-guarded by a portly, red-headed capital-looking fellow, holding high a white ferret. Why, this must be the owner of champion Mike. How rich! He has been hogging a table near the pit, but on seeing this fascinating entourage, he beckons them over to join him.

"There's a table," Miss Watson points out, relieved to see one genteel face in this wretched establishment.

"Take it! Take it!" Whilky shouts over the crowd. "I'll put up this dress and join you in a minute. What would you like to drink? First round's on me."

As he orders up three ales and a lemonade, the actors from "Cholera Morbus" make their way through the crowd to the free seats pit-side.

"Glad to make your acquaintance, glad to make your acquaintance," the gentleman gushes as introductions are made all around. "Couldn't help but notice that you looked a touch out of place."

"Out of place?" Miss Watson exclaims, rolling her pretty brown eyes. "If Desdemona might be considered 'out of place' among the Moors."

"You are of a theatrical bent, I see," smiles the young man, congratulating himself on his acuity. "You are perhaps thespians by profession?"

"How discerning!" Miss Watson turns to the others in amazement. "We were just on our way to London, but——"

"No! Don't tell me!" The young man throws out his hand to stop her. "Just tell me how close I come." He studies each face closely for a moment, then closes his eyes and begins.

"You are a talented troupe of players, performing in all the grand houses of England and Europe, feted by the press, toasted by your aristocratic audiences. You might play any theatre you desired, in any kingdom, for any price—but. Not content to gratify the rich and powerful only, you feel a need to take your work to the People, to give a little back to the Dispossessed of this great country, and so you come here to stage a masterpiece, something edifying and ennobling—a gift to the common crowd. But how could you know that at last you have reached a town without a soul, a town without the faintest stirring in its thick, barbarian chest? You play your hearts out, giving the performances of your lives—trying, trying to reach them—but do they appreciate you? No! They yawn and boo, too bestial to realize your transcendence. With the last of your meagre resources, you've booked passage to London, where at least intellect will come if the call be given. You've been brought here to await your coach by that man who accompanied you—owner of Mike, Champion Ratter, who is favored to beat Banquo, Fat Tom's Border collie!"

On that triumphant note, the young man finishes, to the applause of a deeply impressed Miss Watson. Except for the part about a masterpiece, this gentleman was uncannily correct. What a relief it will be to reach London and take up their work again there.

"I am amazed. Simply amazed," Miss Watson breathes. "Mr. Mortimer, has this young man not been spying on us for a week?"

"Indeed, it seems he has," replies the credulous old gentleman. "Pray, sir, what is your profession? Are you not a spy?"

The young man shakes his head. "Call me a spy if you will, sir. If so, it is only into human nature. I am a Student of Life—no more can I claim. I've come here to add to my book on the workingmen of England: their pursuits and their pastimes, their dreams and disappointments. By chance I learned of this 'event,' and knew my book would not be complete without a section on the prototypical pastime of Ratting."

"Ayr ye speaking of my Mike?" Whilky Robinson asks, approaching the table laden with drinks. "There was no lemonade, miss," he says respectfully to Miss Watson. "I got you a sherry instead. Whoever's laid no money on my Mike's got no right to speak of him."

"Let me remedy that immediately, sir," says the Student of Life gallantly. "Five shillings to win."

"Tha's the spirit," shouts Whilky, who gets part of his brother's house cut on all wagers, plus whatever pot Mike should win. "Ye're a fine lad!"

"And for my five shillings, sir, would you allow me the honor of interviewing Mike's owner?"

"Me? Fer what?" asks Whilky suspiciously. "Ayr you with the census?"

"Good God, no!" exclaims the Student of Life. "I am writing a book on the common man, so that his more fortunate brothers might know and understand his ways. I dream of a bridge spanning the great gulf that yawns between rich and poor, and hope to lay the keystone, if you will, with my humble book."

Whilky looks doubtful, but it is flattering, after all, to be put in a book, and who knows, if the book is published and people read it, they might find their way to his lodging house, and that would be good for business. With that in mind, Whilky agrees; the other gentlemen settle back to listen, but Miss Watson, wanting nothing less than to hear this cretin's life story, picks up the Student of Life's discarded newspaper and peruses the advertisements.

"Now then," says the excited Student," how old are you?"

"Forty-three," Whilky lies, being but forty-one. It is a

harmless lie, one that matters not at all, but that is why it is fun to tell it.

"And you are a ratter by profession?"

"No. I am——"

"Wait! Let me guess!" the Student of Life interrupts his own interview mid-sentence, and begins sketching as he speaks. "My new friends here can tell you how good I am with histories. Now let me see. . . . Judging from your cock-sure swagger and that scar behind your ear, I would wager you spent some time as a highwayman, am I right? A regular two-pistol, cutlass-carrying outlaw, sticking up coaches along the Great Northern Road! You were quite abandoned, don't deny it. One day, as I see it, while in the process of robbing the mail coach, your cutlass nicked the throat of a young lady and she quickly bled to death. You grabbed the basket at the poor lady's feet and immediately rode off, consoling yourself with thoughts of her riches. How startled were you then, when tearing open the basket you found not precious booty, but a sickly mother ferret, nursing four squirming young! Your murdered lady had stopped the coach not three miles back to rescue this weasel family, and was going to turn them loose on her estate. You were about to strangle the wretched creatures in your rage, when one—Mike, your future companion—looked up and licked your hand. In that moment your hard heart melted. I shall raise up these poor foundlings, you vowed, and forswearing banditry altogether, you have learned to find your thrills not on the road, but in the Ring!"

Whilky stares at the triumphant Student of Life incredulously, then down at his drawing. It is vaguely himself set upon a horse, holding a pistol in one hand and a basket of ferrets in the other. For the first time in his life, Whilky Robinson is speechless.

"Is he not amazing?" asks elderly Mr. Mortimer, having sat enraptured by the story.

"I think you'd make a fine subject for a play," interjects Mr. Eliot wickedly. "I imagine your character—played by myself—a virile highwayman and champion ratter, secretly loved by a thorny English rose of high family—naturally, played by Miss Watson—whom you spurn but ultimately enslave."

"I like it! I like it!" Whilky nods. "My late wife was the natural daughter of the vestry treasurer."

"If you want a subject for a play, here is a far more suitable one," Miss Watson interrupts, folding the newspaper to display a printed petition, and imagining herself in the role of its authoress. "Here is theatre taken from real life: a woman sacrifices herself and her own reputation for the sake of her fiancé, a struggling and misunderstood doctor. You could put one of your signature bad-taste touches upon it, Mr. Eliot, and torture it into a fine little melodrama."

"Let me see that." Whilky ungraciously rips the paper from Miss Watson's hands. *An appeal to the enlightened citizens of Sunderland, by Miss Audrey Place.* This isn't the Miss Audrey Pink has been mooning over, is it? The charity woman who is to marry the sawbones? He quickly scans the petition with its scant number of signatures and stalks away, leaving the actors and the Student of Life to wonder at his rude and abrupt behaviour.

"Give me the keys to upstairs," Whilky demands of his brother John. "I need to check something."

"There are people up there," answers John.

"Just give 'em."

John hands over the skeleton key to Gustine's former room and the two others he rents by the hour. Whilky storms upstairs and unceremoniously unlocks the door on a lace-maker's upturned buttocks and a red-faced apprentice's erection.

"I'll just be a minute," he says, and taking up the Argand lamp from the floor, sets about scanning the old papers John uses to line the walls. The lace-maker, apprentice, and Whilky are all in luck tonight, for Gustine's former room was papered some six months ago, and the engagement announcements from last April are pasted horizontally below the window. Miss Barrows to wed Mr. Kenneth Kitely. Miss George to wed Mr. Theodore Barkes. Miss Place to wed Mr. Henry Chiver, MRCS. There it is! Dr. Chiver of Nile Street, Sunderland, son of the widowed Mrs. Edmund Chiver. Well, I'll be damned.

"Henry Chiver!" Whilky bounds down the steps, waving the newspaper overhead, bellowing at the top of his lungs: "Henry Chiver!"

"Henry Chiver what?" asks John Robinson, as the bar falls silent.

"Henry Chiver's the name of the man who violated me! Henry Chiver is a bloody body snatcher!"

"He's the one who came after me with a knife," shouts Robert Cooley, far along in his cups. "Put me mate Jack Crawford in a vat of acid and looked to flay me alive!"

"I'll teach him to come into my house and take my lodgers!" Whilky roars. "I'll set the constables on him so fast he'll wish he'd never heard of Mill Street."

"Sorry to tell you, my agitated friend, but the stealing of bodies is not illegal." The Student of Life has flipped back in his notebook, and is looking over some notes. "I interviewed one of your fine constables a month back about thievery and petty vagabondage here in Sunderland, and I have a whole list of things that are and are not considered property. And a dead body is not considered property."

"You are telling me these doctors can steal our dead as they please?"

"Well," reads the Student, "you could prosecute for the theft of her winding sheet."

"God bloody damn!" shouts Whilky. "What is this world coming to?"

"Heigh-ho!" cries the Student of Life. "Here are the rats!"

Though Whilky seethes, the subject of doctors must be dropped for the moment while the rest of the bar turns its attention to Franklin Hobbs, Sunderland's beleaguered rat catcher. It's difficult to hold Mike back when he catches the aroma of panicked vermin; Banquo, too, scents his enemy, and sets up furious barking, delighting his contingency. Even Miss Watson looks up from her piece of newspaper to take a sip of adulterated sherry and watch the contestants muster. "The barbarity of it!" murmurs she to the entranced Student. "The depraved blood lust!"

"Oh, but it is a necessary evil," whispers the Student of Life, leaning in a little too close for Miss Watson's comfort. "Did you know our scientific community estimates a typically lascivious rat pair, over the course of a year, mates no less than ten times, producing in each litter an average of twelve healthy offspring. If their libertinism be not disrupted, either by the male's frenzied cannibalism of his young or through humankind's intervention, within four short years the original pair of rats could claim nearly three million progeny. Imagine! And we speak only of Adam and Eve. What of all the other Romeos and Juliets, Paolos and Francescas scampering through the sewers of Sunderland? Would they not soon overrun the earth? Rat baiting is philanthropic, miss, it is merciful; why, it ranks right up there with capital punishment for the greater human good."

Miss Watson bows to the Student's superior wisdom, but feels the topic of rat procreation too beneath her to pursue.

Meanwhile, John Robinson, as master of ceremonies, has climbed into the pit and, without fear or disgust, plunged his hand into the cage. Two at a time he pulls fifty rats out by their tails, leaving them dazed and disoriented inside the brightly lit circle. Some of the poor gray creatures wander the ring, sitting up upon their hind legs and sniffing at the spectators; some scale John Robinson's pant legs until he must shake them loose. Most surge together into hillocks, forcing the master of ceremonies to blow little avalanches apart, for rats hate nothing so much as being blown upon, and will scatter at human breath. Banquo strains against his collar, thrusting his long pointy snout between the pickets of the ring, for which liberty he is soundly bitten.

"Ladies and gentlemen! Rat fanciers and curious spectators!" John Robinson shouts, and the place falls somewhat silent. "Tonight, contending for the title of Crown Prince of Ratters, the collie Banquo, seconded by Tom Brown." (Wild applause). "And Sunderland's current champion, Mike the ferret, seconded by his owner, Whilky Robinson." ((Applause even wilder).

"Lay your wagers one and all!" calls John as the crowd tosses its meagre shillings and pennies into a corner of the ring. "Times are tight, but don't hold that against the poor contestants."

As challenger, it is Banquo's privilege to go first. Fat Tom drops him in the ring and much to the audience's delight (and his owner's horror), the posh collie immediately retreats in terror. The lights, the noise, the mound of rats: he sniffs and retreats, jerking back in alarm when several large sewer rats break from the pack and leap for his already lacerated snout. His fear lasts only moments, though. More like the Scottish Douglas than Macbeth's pitiful rival, he is soon seized by battle-madness and quickly becomes a fury of barking, yelping, lunging mayhem. At the side of the pit, his second, Fat Tom, shouts instructions—*Drop it, don't shake it like a rag doll, you damned dog! It's dead! It's dead! Move on to the next!*—until his five minutes are up. Blood drips from the collie's long matted fur, and he licks his paw where a vindictive rat locked on and wouldn't let go. Fat Tom takes his dog in his arms, rubbing his mouth with peppermint water to ward off any abscesses, while the remaining wounded rats are dispatched and pushed aside. John Robinson tallies the dog's official kill. Thirty-nine in all. It is a fair showing and the number to beat.

"Please, Mr. Eliot, Mr. Mortimer, Mr. Webster," Miss Watson pleads. "May we go?"

"Go now?" asks Eliot incredulously. "Before the Highwayman Ratter Robinson has had a chance to show his stuff? Avert your eyes if you will, Miss Watson, but I would not miss this for the world."

The dead rats swept into a corner, John Robinson counts out another fifty. All the more panicked for having witnessed their brothers' demise, these rats tear around the ring, bouncing off one another and trying desperately to scale the sides. John calls Whilky and the current champion Mike to the ring.

"You love me, boy, don't you?" Whilky demands, massaging his ferret's coarse white coat. "It's us against them, right? I want you to think of every rat like a sawbones. You get every last one," he growls, and tosses the sleek white weasel into the fray.

In squealing terror, the rats flee Champion Mike, but he, like the dutiful son, performs exactly as commanded. One doctor. Two. In seconds, ten doctors decapitated. With the ferret's first strike, the Student of Life's hand flies over his pad, but as fast as he draws, his talents just aren't up to the whiplash speed of the champion. So much closer to the rats in height, Mike does not have to stoop, but lashes forward for the strike, then is instantly on to the next. Fifteen. Twenty sawbones dispatched. Whilky shouts with glee.

"Kill 'em, Mike!"

"Crown Prince! Crown Prince!"

"Off with their heads!"

Where Banquo was all frenzy and zeal, Mike is calm precision, swiftly decapitating and moving on to the next. He spares no thought for the crowd of wildly cheering patrons, feels not the rain from their sloshing mugs of beer. A champion if there ever was one; no creature alive could be more methodical and determined in the kill. The rat is my enemy, therefore the rat must die. This is how Mike dispenses justice—with no thought and no hesitation.

The Student sketches: boggling eyes and gummy snarls. An elbow in a woman's back. A sharp knee pointing to money changing hands beneath a table. The Student sketches everything he sees. There a swinging red uvula; across the pit, flying spittle; sweat-stained armpits beside him; the arched eyebrows of the distressed actress. Like the French Revolution, so a ratting at the Labour in Vain, postulates the Student, pausing to jot a note. The poor taking their revenge on those who terrorize them. And at their center, La Guillotine Mike!

Five minutes seem like only so many seconds before the last rat concedes. All fifty destroyed! The ferret sits down in a pool of blood to calmly lick his paws. John Robinson leaps into the ring, lifting the startled white creature high over his head.

"I hereby bestow the silver crown and the sum of five pounds upon Mike the ferret," yells John Robinson over the crowd. "Long live the Prince!"

"Long live the Prince!" the shouts go up. "Long live Prince Mike!"

"Long live the Devil!" comes a hysterical cry from the front door, pitched with such vehemence, the entire bar turns to look. Red in the face from running and shouting, her hair unbraided and stays undone as if she'd been dragged from her house in the process of climbing into bed, the Low Quay pawnbroker Mag Scurr waves her arms and shouts, "The Devil moves among us! Everyone come! There's been a resurrection at Trinity Churchyard!"

"A resurrection?" The word is flung around the pub like a hot potato, and instantly, all sport is forgotten. Men knock over chairs, their wives trample the makeshift ring in their mad stampede to get out. High-strung Banquo, knowing no other frenzy but rats, shakes the poor limp carcasses until Fat Tom yanks him away and pulls him out the door, while Robert Cooley, standing upon his chair, bursts into drunken tears and sobs. "They're coming for me! Oh, dear God, they're coming for me!"

"To Trinity!" shouts Whilky, scooping up His Royal Highness the Crowned Prince and racing for the door. Maybe they can't put that sawbones in jail, but by God, just wait till he feels the fiery fist of the crowd's justice!

"A resurrection?" asks Miss Watson, alarmed. "What does that mean?"

"Means someone has been dug up from the graveyard,

miss," cries the Student of Life, snatching his pad and racing after the rest. "How rich! What else could possibly top a ratting?"

When the crowd has cleared and the barking has faded, the only patrons who remain seated in John Robinson's pub are the bemused players of "Cholera Morbus." Well, well, thinks Mr. Eliot, he has gotten his riot after all; not perhaps in the way he intended, but those who aim to stir the public conscience cannot always be particular in their methods. So long as there is turbulence, the auteur will consider himself well served. And as if to show just how very satisfied he is, Mr. Eliot leans back in his chair, snaps for the barkeep, and triumphantly orders another round.

Though it is perhaps the most inevitable of all divisions, few care to dwell on the Quarantine that separates the living from the dead. What is there, after all, to say about the Grave? On one side health; on the other, disease and death. On one side hope; on the other, inevitable certainty. You think you know which side is which, yet we ask you to look at it from our perspective. There can be no death for those already dead, and disease belongs only to flesh alive enough to support it. It is certain you will die; we might still hope for life everlasting. Just walk through any filthy modern town: are you any less crowded in your tenements than we are in our jumbled pits? Who then does this grave protect? You from us or us from you?

To every story there is a narration and there is a greater narration.

Perhaps it never occurred to you to ask who it is that tells this story, whether or not the narrators are truthful and kind or wish their characters well. Maybe one or two of you have paused and wondered at the voices behind the voice—who is this "us" who knows so much and yet claims not to know all—but most, we would wager, have given us no second thought. Perhaps by now you have guessed that this is not the inspiring story of medical heroism and scientific break-through. No one will discover the cure for or even the cause of cholera morbus here. No, there are books enough written on the great leaps forward in medical knowledge, on the ded-ication and bravery of those that cure. This is the story of those whose peace was sacrificed so that your tonsils might be disposed of and your septums no longer deviated. This is the story of those who serve.

Have you now guessed in whose hands you rest? Why, even here in our own backyard, we must make obvious intro-ductions. We are the citizens of the Trinity pit, dear reader: the murderers and drunkards, the prostitutes and unbaptized babies of Sunderland; we are those you would not conse-crate, those you buried at midnight, those you have forgot-ten. We are those who have been stolen as long as doctors have been questioning, and we have had enough. Look with us tonight, and let us show you the human face of resurrec-tion.

Gustine does not realize anything is amiss until she is almost home. Has someone been murdered? she wonders, coming upon the tumult in the East End. Grim-faced men with spades run inside squares of lantern light; screaming women race ahead into darkness; and she finds her own feet naturally quicken to keep pace with the rest. Is it a riot for Reform? In her experience only politics or homicide could turn out such a crowd. *Don't you know?* asks a middle-aged woman incredulously when Gustine puts out her hand to stay her. *Someone's been taken from Trinity Churchyard.*

Word of the resurrection leaped like a spark between houses, smoking men and women from their beds, sending them out into the cold half asleep and half-dressed, armed with shovels, axes, the poker from the hearth—anything they might use to dig. Mag Scurr, who had been braiding her hair and was preparing to snuggle down between quilts freshly placed in pawn, grabbed of all things a hammer in her rush out the door. She'd lost her twelve-year-old daughter three years before, you see, to an infection of the foot brought on by a rusty nail sticking up through the floorboards, and ever since has slept with a hammer by her bed. So the first thing she sees, she grabs up, and uses it to bang upon her neighbours' doors. *A resurrection!* she shouts. *A resurrection!* Come see if your child has been taken. Come find your husband. Your mother-in-law. See who sleeps and whose slumber has been profaned. Awake Sunderland! Look after your dead!

They are all running toward us now: women and children, men and furiously barking dogs. Sunderland's rat catcher, Franklin Hobbs, the man responsible for setting off the panic in the first place, stumbles in the middle of the pack. Having dropped off his cage of a hundred rats at the Labour in Vain, he was on his way to the workhouse to replenish his inventory when he saw a figure fall over the wall of Trinity Churchyard. It leapt up, flew across the town moor, and disappeared before Hobbs could even call out You there! which was in his mouth to say—only having once met the Cauld Lad of Hylton in the flesh, he was more terrified of addressing ghosts than were most men in Sunderland. His first instinct was to abandon the five rats he'd already caught along the Church Walk, and run directly home; but as the apparition had fled in the same direction as his house, he elected instead to collect his neighbours and see if anything had been disturbed inside. Now he runs along with the rest, hugging his rats, safe within the crowd. No ghost can touch him now that he has people to hide behind.

"Beware their knives!" cries drunken Robert Cooley. "They are desperate for your skin!"

Mag Scurr, that ferocious Jotun of a pawnbroker, runs with her hammer, knocking aside the slow and lame. Just look at this one, she snorts, as a wealthy young woman in a blue dress streaks past her, her yellow hair slipping its apollo, her face even more anguished and certain than all the others. Her grief is as ostentatious as her costume, for she runs with her eyes closed, her rich skirts gathered to the knee, oblivious to modesty or decorum. Shame on you, thinks the pawnbroker. What are you doing running among us anyway? Don't you know only the poor get resurrected?

Yet something seems familiar about this wealthy woman. Mag swings her hammer and races forward, peering into the shut, frightened face. Why, she is no woman—she is barely more than a girl. Pale and freckled and not at all suited for the dress she wears. Of course! It comes back to Mag instantly. This was one of the two who claimed poor Reg Smith from her back room morgue. Why, just look there— his laundress wife, with her bovine stoop-backed shamble, lurches ahead toward what, Mag does not know; Reg has never turned up.

"You there!" Mag cries, as the girl in blue pulls ahead and disappears into the churchyard. "You have no right here!"

She would follow the girl and hammer her into the ground for the grief she has caused, but there is Ellen to attend to first. Her daughter taken by a common nail, like those they used to hammer down her lid. Mag sees again the hideously swollen foot and the red line that ran like the seam in a pair of woolen stockings up to her knee, still tumid when they wrapped her in her sheet and laid her in the ground. Ellen, only twelve years old, her eldest child, her only daughter. The snatcher's punishment must wait, thinks Mag. I must first attend my Ellen.

Up ahead, our churchyard burns with lanterns and smoking torches. The men who arrived first attack the cold, damp earth with picks and axes, with shovels and with knives; the women race to join them, crying out to God. As on laundry day, a hundred skirts are filled with air, puff out and up, as knees sink down and two hundred hands dig like hounds, prying back the earth. They must take care with their digging, for the headstones are packed so tightly together—the unearthing of one plot must half-refill another. The bewildered sexton of the graveyard can only lean against the church wall and shut his eyes against the desecration. Reverend Gray, when he comes back, will be furious, he knows, but how could one man hold out against a determined mob?

The landlord of Mill Street had nearly forgotten he had a wife, Pink's mother, and a two-days son buried here until he ran past the tombstone Robinson, overgrown with weeds and streaked with sap from the overhanging maple. He falls upon the neglected plot with the frenzy of a zealot, snatching a stunned neighbour's shovel and jarring the ferret in his coat pocket with each leap he makes upon the shovel's blade. Surely the violation of his home was enough—Fate would not be so partisan as to strike him twice; but he digs faster nonetheless, determined that no body snatcher will have got the best of him. He did buy a cheap casket, he admits, digging down to the bowed and split lid, botulized from its base. And cheaper nails. Still, Fate would not be so cruel. Whilky does not want to look as he reaches in and lifts off the moul-dering lid. No, Mike! he shouts when the ferret leaps from his pocket. No! he cries again, when he hears the chilling scratch of nails inside an empty box.

"When the trumpet sounds they will all rise up and shed their shrouds, with eyes upturned they will mount the Stair—"shouts Robert Cooley, drunkenly leaping upon *Jane Ellman 1774 –1801*. His brush with the doctors has turned him Prophet; more than ever he awaits the Judgment Day. "—Unless they have been snatched, you see. Then the legless ones and the armless ones will roam the earth to seek their parts. Or spend Eternity crippled before their Maker!" From his vantage upon the tombstone, Robert can see who lost his and who lost hers and who lost none. There seems to be no rhyme or reason to the thefts. Bodies buried thirty years before are gone while those barely a month old blissfully remain. Across the churchyard, plots have been stricken, like random days crossed out on a calendar.

So the citizens of Sunderland are learning horribly what we, your narrators, have known all along; that this yard is honeycombed with empty coffins, bags of sand, and rotted black sprigs of rosemary left where loved ones used to be. One day you too will cross over into the Great Narration, there will come a time when you will want to rest undisturbed and unmolested, and perhaps then you will thank us for our jealous guardianship. Turn to look with us now upon the fates of two women: one irreproachable to ward us, the other who now understands she has made a grave mistake. First observe Mag Scurr, pawnbroker, morgue keeper, reuniter of the living with their dead; who with a hammer only has cleared four feet of earth, and at last has reached the lid to her daughter's cof-fin. From far away she hears the shrieking of other women who have just discovered that for years they have been visiting empty graves and whispering endearments to hollow boxes. Mag digs the claw of her hammer beneath the lid, pries back with all her strength the heavy pine top. *Oh, Ellen,* she weeps, *my daughter, my girl.* The heady perfume of corruption and rot could not smell any sweeter to a mother as, sobbing, she climbs inside the box, to couple with her eldest child and kiss her worm-blessed hair.

Now turn your attention to the dark side of the church, to our side, where the pit spreads wide, and the poor dress lodger Gustine is chopping with her boot, feeling for the plank of wood through this eternity of grubs and roots. The skin of her hands blisters but she does not feel it, any more than the searing of her naked knees as she kneels in our cemetery snow. She has not long to dig before she reaches the tiny coffin planted only two days before, now upended and barely covered over with dirt. She drags it from the ground, pulling along the unpinned fleshless limbs of an old pauper from the workhouse. She was here only hours ago—what could have happened in so short a time? Yet even before she feels the prophetic lightness of the tiny box, she knows what she will find.

In this case, we are spared the trouble of a haunting; for Mag Scurr, crawling on her hands and knees across the open plots, is spectre enough. She has her eye fixed on the faithless thief in the blue dress, the pretender, she who consorted with anatomists. Her Ellen is safe, but Mag wants vengeance for the entire graveyard, for all her wailing, violated neighbours. She reaches the thief in the blue dress, who sits like all the rest, with black dirt under her fingernails and scratches across her cheeks, staring uncomprehendingly into the empty box upon her lap.

"You were in league with them," Mag hisses into the mother's ear. "And it didn't save you. Well, how does it feel to have your own taken?"

Gustine turns to her in anguished disbelief, but Mag Scurr shows no mercy.

"How does it feel?"

XVI

RIOT

Lonely. That's how it feels.

Back in the second-story study at Nile Street, you've been relegated to a corner. Yours was not a face that drew men to it, not a body whose mysteries men wished to plumb. Never in your life had anyone lost sleep over you, or gone without eating because of you, or desired to know what you were like inside. Then *he* came along, and what he did seemed a small price to pay for such undivided attention. In the week since you were taken from Mill Street, you've almost forgotten the years spent alone and untouched in your back room match factory, you've been able to claim, at last, your rightful place at the center of your own story. You have felt wanted, necessary—in a strange way, beautiful. But now he has found some one new, and what remains of you sags in the corner, ashamed of its own ripeness. No wonder he has moved on. Just take a whiff of you. You've turned.

The yellow light of the lamp falls upon his soft white hands (that were trembling so badly he burned himself three times before he got it lit) and over his troubled face—which for the last quarter of an hour, since he came in with his muddy boots and earth-stained shovel, has been fixed upon a small bundle placed upon your old table. Like you were, this bundle is wrapped so that only a white petal of face shows, his swaddled chin wreathed with four long spines of rosemary that peep out like piney whiskers. A gentle barber, the anatomist shears the child of its herbal beard, carefully unwraps the contaminated winding sheet, and feeds it into the fire. Poor creature, you think when the infant is exposed. His wasted torso and limbs, the uneven ratio of head to trunk puts you in mind of an unfledged baby bird, but the sad truth is, his cholera emaciation will make the anatomist's job that much simpler. Without a lot of extra fat and fluid in the way, it will be easier for him to remove the unnecessary viscera and wash the veins clean with water. He unwraps the final layer, where the child's tiny hands, crossed over his chest, even in death protect his precious secret.

It is wrong to be jealous of a child, you know that, but what are you supposed to feel when you see the divine hunger in his eyes—an appetite that a week ago craved only you— turned upon someone else? He made you sound so marvelous to his students; who would have guessed to look at your gray exterior that you were composed of such lovely-sounding words as tissue and tibia and trachea; or that the ancients once believed your veins carried blood while your arteries transported spirits? Now, you feel the anatomist's absence when he goes downstairs to fetch a tub of water, and ache when he returns, pouring three bottles of hydrochloric acid into the bath, but does not glance over at you. He measures out and mixes into a separate earthen pot fifteen ounces of yellow beeswax, eight of white resin, turpentine varnish six ounces, then separately taps out three ounces of powdered vermilion, settling the whole upon a heated trivet to begin its gradual melting. From the drawers in his glass-fronted cabinet, he chooses the several sections of his brass syringe, screwing together the piston, its leather valves, and its barrel with his little key, then selects his finest-toothed saw and several scalpels. If only he would look upon you again with such intense fascination, tenderly run his soft white hands over *your hair*; if only he would treat you as anything other than just another bad smell in the room, you could bear it. But he has eyes only for the new one.

You know what he has in store for the helpless child as he rolls up his shirtsleeves and wipes the rust from his saw. He shared his thoughts with you earlier tonight, muttering to himself after he came home frantic from Fawcett Street and before he left with the lantern and the shovel, while he bundled you up into an old sheet like a tramp's belongings and set you in the corner. You know that the child who has taken your place upon the table will not be hacked up as you were—no, he is to be preserved in a manner to best set off his singularity. The process your anatomist ultimately favored is, in itself, not overly complex, though most are not gifted enough to undertake it successfully. He will perform a wax corrosion, by first injecting the infant's circulatory system with melted vermilion beeswax, then over the next few weeks slowly macerating away the bones and flesh, to leave a skein of arteries and veins, aorta, and vena cava. By the time he is done, he will have created a perfectly whole heart baby, stripped of its corrupt flesh, pared down to the perfect eternal circle of circulation. Varnished and sealed in an airtight case, what mattered of the dress lodger's child will survive as a testament to God's strange powers and its preserver's careful skill.

And yet he hesitates.

A household divinity. Your anatomist has had the phrase ringing in his skull since the first trespass of shovel to earth back at the Trinity Churchyard. Half of him feels like an impious grave robber, who with the profanation of the divinity's tomb has invited a curse down upon himself. That trembling half would like nothing more than to return to Trinity; to violate the Pit one last time and restore this pathetic creature to his bed. The fevered half, however, the half that took him to the churchyard in the first place, will hear of no such thing. That half is still furious he ever indentured himself to the dress lodger, letting his relationship to her—with its favors and sick seductions—pervert his judgment. But now it is too late. He was wallowing in swill while his salvation was dying beside him. A household divinity. He lost the living heart, but now with wax and acid, he prepares to preserve its resurrection.

You hear the faint sound of glass chattering against glass, and notice that the little yellow lamp on the table where he works has begun to shudder. At first, irrationally, you think the lamp cannot bear to watch what is about to happen, but then you realize its trembling comes not from fear but from a pounding on the door below. The doctor is so engrossed in the new one that he doesn't even look up. Had you a voice, you would warn him, but what can you really do, friend Fos: a jumble of rotting parts, tied up in a sheet, forgotten in a corner?

> *The arm that used to take your arm*
> *Is took to Surgeons' Square*
> *And both my legs are gone to walk*
> *The hospital that's there.*
>
> *I vowed that you should have my hand*
> *But Fate gives us denial*
> *You'll find it there with Dr. Knox*
> *In spirits in a phial.*

The cock it crows, I must be gone.
Dear lover, we must part;
And I'll be yours in death although
Damned Chiver has my heart!

"Dr. Chiver, open the door!"

Henry sets down his syringe, listening to the furious hammering from below. He knew she'd come sooner or later; he's made his peace with it.

Carefully he lifts the infant, takes up the lamp, and descends the stairs, pausing in the foyer, where her pounding is shaking his portrait of Jeremy Bentham crooked on the wall. He pauses only for a moment, though, on his way to the back door and the shovel he left beside it. Outside, the neighbor's black dog leaps onto the fence, barking in rhythm to the penny ballad Henry can't seem to get out of his head. He barks the whole time Henry works, and his barking follows the doctor back into the pantry, where he pumps water over his hands and rinses the mud off into the basin. Deliberately, he dries his hands and makes his way down the hall.

Henry unlatches the front door. "Gustine, what are you doing here?"

She pushes past him and takes the stairs two at a time. Before he can catch up, she has the door to his study open and is inside, flinging wide his glass-fronted cabinet, knocking his instruments to the floor. She looks behind his curtains; on her hands and knees, she feels behind his low-stacked woodpile. She spies the tramp's bundle of Fos in the corner and swiftly undoes the knot, then pushes it aside in disgust.

"Where is he?" she demands.

"I don't know what you're talking about." Henry stands in

the doorway, watching her destroy his study. He makes no move to stop her but lets her vent her rage on his books and carefully ordered journals.

"Don't play games with me," she snarls. "I want my son."

"What makes you think I have him?" he asks.

"If you don't have him, then what is this for?" Gustine takes up the syringe he prepared. "Or this" —she kicks the pot of carefully measured wax and turpentine into the fire. "Why have out your saws and your knives, if not to dismantle my child?"

Outside, the neighbor's black dog howls. Gustine flings wide his heavy drapes and stares down onto the pocked backyard. "Is it true what they say about you? That when you are through with us, you feed us to your dogs?"

"That's enough," Henry says, finally losing his composure. "You have no business here."

"You had no business taking him."

She pushes Henry aside, and bolts up the second flight of stairs to his bedroom. It is whitewashed and spartan only so long as it takes her to empty the drawers of the chiffonier, tear through his closet, and rip the bedclothes from the bed. The Austrian cuckoo clock is knocked from its shelf, his grandmother's rocking chair overturned; in her passion she pauses only long enough to glare at the Sacred Heart he has hanging over his bed before dashing it to the ground.

"That will be enough, Gustine," Henry orders, growing alarmed at her cold blue fury. "I am deeply sorry for your loss, but this tantrum will not bring him back."

"That's where you're wrong, Dr. Chiver," Gustine pants. "I know you are hiding him here somewhere. Will you tell me where or shall I tear this whole house apart?" Before he can catch her, she has sped by him again, down past the second-floor landing and into the ground-floor parlour. He hears her slamming the piano lid, ripping apart sofa cushions, upturning lamps and tables. He jogs down the stairs behind her. This has gone on long enough.

"Stop it." He grabs her arm as she lifts a Staffordshire vase to smash it.

"Don't you dare lay a hand upon me."

It is the first time he has touched her since their night together, and he instantly pulls back, for her skin, laced with cemetery snow, sears his flesh. Leaving her in disgust, he stalks to the pantry and holds his hands under the pump.

Behind him, he hears the vase hit the wall. She returns to her demolition, not even bothering to search anymore, just mindlessly laying waste to his house. He hears his fire irons hurled across the room into his writing desk, the furious crack of a capsized marbletop table. Let her get it out, he tells himself; she will soon be gone, and he will be done with her forever. He is drying his hands when he realizes that an unnatural silence has fallen in the next room. When he turns, he finds Gustine behind him in the hallway, her eyes fixed upon the muddy shovel leaning against the back door. Henry quickly moves in front of it, but not quickly enough.

"I am glad he's dead then," Gustine whispers, reading all she needs to in his flushed face. "He was a child to me, Dr. Chiver, not a laboratory rat you could bury in the backyard when you were through."

"He's gone, Gustine," Henry says, ready to use the shovel against her if she takes a step closer. "I understand you loved him, but if his future is to decay among suicides and murderers, wouldn't you rather see him of service?"

"When are we ever supposed to rest, Dr. Chiver?" she asks him, tears of rage and exhaustion streaming down her cheeks.

"While we live, we shovel your coal and cook your food and spread our legs, and then, when we have the gall to die, you tell us our work is still not done. No, we must toil for you even after Death has set us free."

"You rest when we've cured all the world's diseases," the doctor says, as exhausted as she. "Because that's when we get to rest."

"All the cures in the world are not worth the afterlife of my son."

"Do you think I enjoy this?" Henry shouts, finally losing his patience with this maddening girl. "William Harvey dissected his own father and sister after they died. He wept the whole time, but he knew he had a responsibility to science. We would know nothing of how blood circulates, nothing about the heart, without his sacrifice."

"I pity your future wife, Dr. Chiver," Gustine says. "You are faithful only to Death."

"Gustine, I wanted to stop this," he shouts. "Your child was to be my lifeline out of the graveyard." Henry's voice breaks with emotion. "If I could have raised him up and learned from him, maybe, just maybe, I could have begun to atone for a life of murder and deceit. But then you took him away. And here I am back among the damned. I am an enemy to both the living and the dead. Where am I to go? What can I do but continue on this path I seem unable to forsake? And whether its end shall be in Heaven or in Hell, I do not know."

"I cannot fight you anymore," Gustine says quietly. "My child deserves better than this. One day, I promise, you will feel what it's like to sacrifice something you love."

"If it were for the greater good, I would do so willingly," he says.

"The greater good?" Gustine shrugs. "Good and Evil are

opposite points on a circle, Dr. Chiver. Greater good is just halfway back to Bad."

There is nothing more for them to say. Gustine has turned her back on him when a rock shatters the front parlour window and skitters to a stop at her feet. "Dr. Henry Chiver!" a voice bellows from the street. "Answer to the people!"

Gustine steps to the window and draws the curtains on the glare of Death, come to accuse the body snatcher of Nile Street. Heralded by torchlight and accompanied by the crashing of tin pans, the East End has risen, armed with Whilky's posters impaled upon pitchforks and plastered on placards. TYRANNY! the posters cry, balled up and stuffed into a shirt and pair of pants to make a human figure, its head a bobbling pig's bladder, painted with the features of the gutless anatomist. *Give us back our John and Mary*, scream the men with picks and axes, their wives swinging clubs and hammers. *Release our Louisa, our Tom!* In front, that trussed-fustian idiot Robert Cooley, who fought the doctors over Jack Crawford's body, bangs a spoon upon a pot; beside him the disheveled pug-faced pawnbroker, Mag Scurr, hurls stones at the doctor's door. And leading the riot from the graveyard across town to the doctor's door, the wifeless, childless landlord of Mill Street uses today's newspaper to ignite the effigy of Henry Chiver into a sour, smoking conflagration.

Gustine looks back at Henry, standing in the foyer, at last worthy of a riot of his own. He does not follow her to the window, but stares out the back door, over his seedbed of bones, the harvest he will reap for the remainder of his life.

"You know I didn't take all those people," he says resignedly. "It's been going on as long as the poor have been dying."

The dress lodger turns back to the sickening thud of shovels and axes splitting the doctor's wooden shutters like ripe melons. Without another word, she flings wide the door and steps out as the squealing stampede of her fellow citizens races in, snorting over the doctor's furniture and rooting through his things. She hears them take their axes to his shelves of specimen jars upstairs, turning his study floor into a sick curiosity shop of broken glass and leaking spirits, eyeballs and jellied breasts.

At the corner of Nile and High Streets, Gustine stops and turns to watch the effigy burn—Dr. Chiver's ghostly twin, twisting from the branch of an overhanging tree. She stands alone and helpless beneath the naked flame of a broken gas lamp, knowing that nothing the crowd can destroy will make him feel the pain she did in losing her child. Oh, God, she rages against the cold night fog, Who will help her make this doctor suffer? God has given her the will, but with what weapon is a poor girl supposed to fight?

There is no question put to the Sunderland fog that it does not thoughtfully consider; but just as God supplies even his most devoted disciple with a displeasing answer from time to time, so the fog responds with what Gustine wants least in the world to see. Unsteady on her feet like a weaving drunk, the dress lodger's lost shadow lumbers up High Street. Oh please, no, thinks Gustine, shutting her eyes in despair. She thought the old woman was gone for good. But why would she ever imagine she could escape her fate? In her heavy arms, the Eye carries a familiar bundle Gustine recognizes even from a distance as the neatly folded clothes her sailor was to deliver to the Place residence in the morning. What is she doing with them?

The old woman stops beneath the shining lamp, and like a disaffected magus holds the bundle out to her. You desired a weapon, she seems to say; I present you with one. Take up the true arms of poverty. Claim the contamination you were born to.

Onstage when two enemies finally meet to draw swords and battle to the death, there is always a moment like this—a mutual recognition of the same fixation, an acknowledgment of what locked them in opposition in the first place. We are enemies, yes, but in all the world, we alone understand each other. The Eye, in stealing Captain Place's contaminated clothes, in handing them off to Gustine, surrenders the battle without a blow. Gustine sees in her enemy's face everything she never thought to find there: compassion, pity, sadness, regret. I pass the sword to you, her face says. Use it to defeat our mutual enemy.

Why? wonders Gustine. Why help her now, when the Eye's whole life has been set in opposition to hers? But then, as if sleep has been wiped from her eyes and she is suddenly, for the first time in two years, fully awake, the dress lodger sees and understands.

"You loved him, too? Didn't you?" Gustine asks. "You loved my child."

And in acknowledgment, the shadow, of her own free will, disengages forever, turns, and walks away.

XVII

LICE ON A CLEAN PERSON

Oh! Marrow, Oh! Marrow, Oh!
What dost thou think?
I've broken my bottle and spilt all my drink
I've lost all my shin splints among the great stones
Draw me to the shaft, lad, it's time to go home!

In the second story of the leaning house on Little Villiers Street, a blown robin's egg spins on a scarlet thread. And there, between two cobblestones, crushed by a cart into deep blue mortar, a dropped nosegay of violets. And over there, in the solemn procession of cattle led to slaughter on Queen Street, tied around the neck of that one cow whose wide eyes and white flanks are her only parts visible, while her black spots disappear into the night sky as if someone had already taken a bite out of her, a blue ribbon dangling a bell. Now that she's cut loose from the dress, the Eye sees blue everywhere. In the spores of a moldy slice of bread fought over by seagulls, in a young girl's hair, in the aureole of a streetlight. When did her vision narrow? she wonders. When did she start to see blue only in the body of a dress?

Oh! Marrow, Oh! Marrow, Oh! As to the robin's egg and the violets and the cowbell, like a distracted child the Eye is drawn to the bright navy neckerchiefs worn by a handful of unemployed pitmen singing down by the river. Her thirty colliers used to sing that song as she pulled them to the surface, back when they called her a genius of vision, when her eyesight was so sharp she could see their very words condense against the iron bars and drip back into the hole. Down by the river, a new group of colliers sing, twanging a Jew's harp and slapping their thighs. She watches them leap and clap in the orange light of burning barrels, hauntingly clean from weeks of unemployment. *Come along and jig with us, Mother,* shouts a pitman, catching sight of the exhausted old Eye. He lays claim to her arm, fitting it into the crook of his, and spins her dizzily around. *What dost thou think? I've broken me bottle and spilt all me drink!* At his touch, Eye blushes to the roots of her grizzled hair, for she has never had even the limited awakening of most old maids, whose fantasies might at least fall upon their fathers' best friends or their golden-throated parish priests. Until now, Eye's circumscribed life has not even admitted the hope of human contact, much less a pitman's hand on the small of her back or his thigh against hers in the pivot of a figure. *Kick up your heels, Mother,* laughs the pitman. *We're dancing away the cholera morbus.*

Before tonight, could the Eye have ever imagined herself dancing? Clasping hands with each collier, bowing and sashaying down the line from one to the next? And yet she does, having watched enough couples in her evenings out with Gustine to know how it's done. It is something new for her, and exhilarating, like holding the baby. Men touch her, she freely touches back. The dress lodger could not have been more wrong about her shadow—no matter what malevolent motives were assigned her (and many were certainly proven true), the Eye's touch never had the power to kill. Maim, yes, or wound; her hands, clasped inside those of her dancing partner, could have gripped the handle of a knife and driven it home; but to say her touch—or for that matter, her gentle cradling of a baby—was of itself lethal must must have been, as Henry suggested, merely superstition.

That is, before tonight.

It is one of those strange twists of fate that her break with Gustine has given the old woman the very powers the girl always feared she possessed. Now when she spins from man to man, laughing deep and throaty with the rest of them, she has no idea she is whirling each one off into cold blue agony. Or that later, when in her new mood of charity she shares her unfinished meat pie with a hungry old waterman, the munificent crumbs will go down his gullet blue and bitter, only to come back up tonight. She knows she has begun to feel queer over the last few hours—light-headed and concentrated at the same time, like an actor who, though she has no more lines, must stay in costume to take her bows with all the rest. But she has no suspicion that vengeance will be visited on object and instrument alike. Despite the heat of dancing, the Eye is strangely cold and achy, and if she were to glance down at her capering shadow on the snow, she would find that it, too, had become unmistakably blue.

Aw, don't leave us, Mother! cries the pitman, falling to his knees in mock beggary as she walks away, back up the bank. *Who will dance with me?*

But Eye cannot linger here all night. There on High Street, she sees a baker setting a blackcurrant pie on his windowsill to cool, and beyond him, a turquoise bird of paradise matted in a printer's window. As far as the Eye can see, a shining path stretches out before her. And she is a genius again, if only for a single night, who, finally freed of watching, might follow wherever the blue will take her.

*

Someone to see you, miss." The Places' girl Crimmons slips into the parlour wearing her most disapproving scowl. It is eleven o'clock at night, and long past time for callers. Who else but Henry would come by at this hour? Yet Crimmons says, No, miss, it's not him. Says she's a friend of his. A Miss Potter, but she doesn't have a card.

Audrey is sitting in her chair by the fire, where she has been taking up one of her old worsted wool pinafores for Pink. It has been packed away for years among outdated patterns and ragbags of buttons and trim, but with a few alterations and a good airing, it should suit the little girl nicely. Going through her old trunks had soothed her after the awful fight with Henry, in the way only cherished girlhood things might. She reread letters written to schoolmates about young men who were not her fiancé sighed over pressed roses from former darlings' boutonnieres and scores of crowded dance cards. Poring over these little mementos served two purposes: first to balm her bruised self-esteem with the recollection of former triumphs, and second to make her feel vaguely traitorous, so that her better side might rush to her fiancé's defense and repair the romantic treachery, even if committed only in memory. So she has spent the last hours sewing and remembering, putting Henry beneath all other lovers, then tearfully raising him up. Lost so long in dusty memories, she is quite disconcerted to be faced with a strange young lady—a "friend" of her fiancé's of whom he has never made mention—observing her from the doorway. Shortsighted Audrey squints at the pale young woman, elegantly dressed as if having come straight from a party, and blushes at her own disheveled appearance.

"Good evening, Miss Potter," Audrey offers, rising. "I fear I wasn't expecting company."

The newly christened Miss Potter, for her own part, is more than a little surprised by what she finds inside. She had expected to discover the privileged Miss Audrey Place perched upon a gold and pink chair, outfitted in her lamé turban and ostrich feather, earrings dimpling her lobes and matching necklace clasped around her long white throat; playing cards and sipping champagne maybe; or perhaps merely admiring herself in a hand mirror. Against the Audrey she constructed, it would be easy to walk in, say her piece, and leave. But the reality is so utterly different. Henry's fiancée is dressed in a simple, patched yellow wrapper (which she put on for comfort once Henry and her godfather Clanny left), with her hair combed out and braided loosely down her back. Her weak eyes are still a bit red and swollen, from crying and doing fine needlework in low light, for Audrey did not think to light the lamp with just herself in the room, and instead squinted close to the dying fire. Her slippers are worn and stitched with tiny blush roses, so she does not go barefoot around the house; nor must she wear her outdoor shoes as lodgers are forced to do. The fact that Audrey's oldest, most comfortable clothes are still so much finer than anything Gustine has ever owned herself is perhaps most disheartening of all.

"Please, do come in," Audrey urges.

The room is as casually elegant as its occupant, with muted silver and green trellised wallpaper, gray wainscoting, and cheerful floral carpets scattered about. Nautical decorations, as befits a shipping fortune, grace every blank space, with no less than five studies of the Wearmouth Bridge (West View) upon one wall and portraits of schooners hung like revered members of the family upon the other. Even the marble mantelpiece recalls the sea, carved as it is with fishes and tridents and a smooth white anchor over its keystone. Upon it, in all its sentimental glory, sits the ubiquitous *Sailor's Tear*, erupting with pink autumn mums to match the painted rim and handle.

"Let me just light the lamp." Audrey says, removing a porcelain bowl perched on the lamp's chimney and turning up the wick. "I apologize for the smell. We've been heating vinegar and cloves over it to keep away the cholera morbus."

"Crimmons said you are a friend of Dr. Chiver? You must forgive my memory, and remind me where we've met?" Audrey asks disingenuously, for now that she can see her better, this young lady, with her crushed dress and scratched face, hardly looks like someone her fiancé would know. And why the silence, why the queer timing of this call?

"We've never met," Gustine replies at last, in her most careful Fawcett Street voice. "But I thought we should speak."

"Pray, don't be mysterious," says Audrey, meaning it, for her nerves can't take much more of this. "Come sit down and take some tea with me."

Gustine had not planned to sit and make conversation. Her rage was to sustain her in thrusting out the sailor's bundle with a blunt explanation before coldly taking her leave. But seeing this girl so close to her own age, alone and vulnerable in this dim, silent room, has taken her aback a bit. With a guilty glance at *The Sailor's Tear* she accepts the chair opposite Audrey, and tucks her package behind her skirts.

"Please pardon the mess," Audrey nods to her sewing and the pillaged trunks at her feet. "I was taking up a dress for a little charity case I hope to rescue. She's been raised like a heathen, and lives among the lowest of the low; but I've taken an especial interest in her and hope to do a bit of good. Won't you have a cup?"

Miss Potter refuses with a shake of the head. "What do you have planned for your charity girl?" she asks.

"Oh, I'm not sure yet. She's fit for nothing, I would daresay, though her father gives her all sorts of dreadful tasks. I think that's half the reason I'm so attached to her. Her father is so cruel, whereas my father has always been so good to me."

Here is your opening, thinks the dress lodger. Hand her the bundle. Do it now, she wills herself.

"Now, how do you know my Henry?" Audrey asks.

Gustine would like nothing better than to tell the truth, but the truth does not fit her plan. "He cured me of a fever," she says flatly instead.

"Oh, a patient!" Audrey's relief is palpable, for she had been feeling more than a little alarmed by this pale, disheveled woman, visiting after eleven at night. "You are much better, I hope?"

"Much," replies Gustine. "We had our final consultation only hours ago."

"You've seen him tonight?" asks Audrey eagerly, then quickly catches herself. "I'm afraid we had a bit of a row earlier, and I've been so desperate to apologize. How did he look?"

Gustine remembers the effigy Henry, falling to cinders before his house. "Not especially well," she replies.

"I was afraid of that." Unbidden, tears leak from Audrey's already primed eyes, and all disloyal thoughts of other men are washed away. "My future husband is the gentlest man on earth," she says, happy to speak well of him and make amends for her rebelliousness of earlier. "He desires only to do good in this world, and so often, I don't comprehend how my careless actions might imperil his work."

"How can you say that?" Gustine asks, unable to imagine any sort of rift between the doctor and this accommodating girl. "No matter what the consequences, surely he must appreciate such an act of heroism on your part."

"You speak of the petition in today's newspaper?" Audrey buries her face in her hands and weeps in earnest now. "Please don't remind me of my wretched stupidity. I don't know what possessed me to print that!"

"You didn't mean it then?" asks Gustine.

"No, of course I meant it." Audrey blows her delicate nose on an old scrap of fabric. "I honestly believe, Miss Potter, that the poor will never follow where the wealthy do not lead. *We* are educated, *we* are the rational and far-seeing. How can we expect the ignorant to move beyond superstition if we espouse it? But Dr. Chiver has shown me how misguided my methods were."

And this poor girl doesn't know the half of it, Gustine thinks. If she suspected that her petition was responsible for the riot even now raging, she would surely perish with grief. But this will not do, Gustine thinks, giving herself a shake. She did not come here to admire or sympathize with Audrey Place. She came here to make her pay.

"Has something happened to Dr. Chiver?" Audrey pales at the grim look on Miss Potter's face.

Of course she would think of the one closest to heart and home. "No. Nothing has happened to the doctor," Gustine replies, sparing her the knowledge of the riot. This is far more difficult than she expected. She planned this all out while she cleaned the mud from her dress and repinned her disarrayed hair. Down by the river, she created a shared pain to take to Miss Place's house. Now is not the time to weaken. "I have come because you and I have something in common," she says.

"What is that?"

"Our fathers have both been long away at sea."

"Yours too?" breathes Audrey. "Is it not awful being fatherless? Where is your father now?"

"In Riga," replies Gustine.

"What a coincidence! So is mine!"

"I know. In fact, I have just tonight had news from there."

"News of my father?" Audrey starts from her chair. "I can see it in your face. Please tell me——he is trapped behind the Quarantine there, and we've had no word for months."

Gustine had practiced the speech on the way over: a dry account of Captain Place's death, interjected with cold expressions of sympathy for the writhing agony he must have suffered before finally perishing alone in a strange land and being ultimately dumped at sea. Now that the time has come, however, she finds the speech dying on her lips. Audrey leans forward eagerly, feverish to hear what this stranger has to say, but Gustine's carefully rehearsed words fail her.

"I met a sailor who was to give you the news," Gustine says helplessly, speaking as she would to a friend," but I thought it might be kinder coming from another woman."

"Oh dear God, no." Audrey shakes her head, knowing immediately from Gustine's tone and expression what is meant. "No. No!"

"I am so sorry."

"*Father!*" Audrey screams, throwing herself onto Gustine's narrow bosom. Gustine's own tears are still too close to the surface not to be affected by another's weeping, and she finds herself struggling through the story the sailor told her: of cholera coming aboard ship, of the letter home the captain had in his hand when he died, and of his crew's difficult journey back to Sunderland. The young girl but half-hears, sobbing in Gustine's arms. *Now that you have crippled her, finish her off,* the voice of vengeance speaks in her ear. *Reach down behind your skirts and present her the package. Take your delight in seeing her press the miasmic clothes to her tear-stained face, breathing in the deaths of continents. She belongs to* him; *she is one of them. Comfort not the woman you came to kill. Finish her off, Gustine.*

But it is so very, very difficult. As many times as she tells herself she cannot be called a murderer, that the clothes were on their way here with or without her, she recognizes the workings of her own assassin heart. She could have interrupted the inevitable; life and death were in her power as surely as they have always been in Henry's. And yet she has chosen death, for herself and the girl, as surely as Henry has always chosen it. *Stop thinking this way,* she wills herself. *Present the bundle. Punish them.* But even as Gustine fires herself, the tears of this poor fatherless girl dampen the flames. Were she only a little less trusting, a little more haughty; if she had only been wearing the matching earrings and necklace, the dress lodger could have gone through with it. But look at her—this girl does not deserve to die for Henry Chiver's sins. She will suffer enough being married to him.

"I must go to my mother," Audrey says, sitting up weakly and wiping her eyes. "How can I ever repay you?"

Gustine shakes her head, thoroughly ashamed of having come here. She has no more words, could not summon up the Fawcett Street platitudes of a Miss Potter if she tried. She hides the bundle behind her back, inching toward the door and the river, where she will destroy them for good. "I am sorry," she whispers in the doorway, as much to her unavenged child as to the brokenhearted girl.

"You have been so kind to me!" Audrey jumps up impulsively and throws her arms around the retreating Gustine. Against the suddenness of the gesture, Gustine raises her hands to ward her off, and as she does so her package falls to the ground.

"You've dropped your parcel." Audrey exclaims, swooping to retrieve it. "What is this?"

"Nothing." Gustine reaches for it.

"No, wait! That is my father's jacket. I sewed it myself. See here, the yellow stitching." Audrey forgets her manners and swiftly unties the packet of clothes. "These are my father's trousers. This is his shirt," she says, inventorying the contaminated items. From his shirt pocket, where it was hidden to protect it from thieves, Audrey draws out her father's gold watch and chain. She lifts it to her ear and listens as its hollow ticking fills the room. "Were you planning to leave with them?" she asks accusatorily.

"They are not safe," Gustine stammers. "Please, miss, just throw them in the fire."

"Throw out all that I have left of my father?" Audrey asks incredulously, burying her face in the sleeve of his jacket.

With a heavy heart, Gustine backs out of the parlour, leaving the girl to inhale her certain fate. It is what Gustine wanted, was it not?

Left all alone, Audrey rests her wet cheek against poor dear Papa's abandoned clothes, too numbed by grief to feel anything, let alone the tickling itch of a solitary louse that leaves the warmth of her father's pant leg for the new world of the daughter's collar. Slowly, the bold explorer makes its way up her neck, along the slope of her ear, across her tundra of skull, coming to rest in the golden wilderness of her disheveled braid. Too numbed by grief, it's not surprising

Audrey doesn't think of a silly saying we have around Sunderland, one taken as gospel by those who believe that when rooks feed in the street, a storm is at hand, or that the glass works, if not shut down once every seven years, will generate a salamander. If Gustine had been here, she could have told her what it is they say around Sunderland. Lice on a clean person spells a death. If you believe in old wives' tales.

"Are you giddy or anxious, madame? Do your fingers ache? Is there a burning pain in the pit of your stomach? Do you greatly thirst?"

The Eye stops before a bedraggled top-hatted impresario who, having set up outside the Theatre Royale to capitalize on the growing mistrust of crowds (not realizing fear had taken such hold that all events had been canceled), calls out to any passerby.

"What you need is a fine flannel cholera belt! Wrap it around your waist thuswise, to keep those vital parts warm, and cholera morbus will be stopped like the Frenchies at Waterloo. Or wait! If it's not a belt you want, try these potent little packets."

The impresario holds out two raggedly sewn calico squares that when clapped together produce a prodigious cloud of dust.

"Chloride of lime, madame," he announces solemnly. "Touch 'em to everything: papers, doorknobs, money. Hold one in your hand when you shake 'hello.' Guaranteed to kill the cholera morbus on contact."

The Eye reaches out for the packets and the cholera belt.

"Yes, the belt and the chloride will help, madame, but to be absolutely certain, you wouldn't want to leave without purchasing a bottle of cholera drops. Put them in your tea, madame, put them in a glass of water. To tell you the truth, madame"——he leans and speaks in sotto voce, as if at this hour any but the frogs might hear——"I've found they work best stirred into a bumper of brandy."

The Eye reaches out and takes the brown bottle of drops.

"I have candies, too, madame. And girdles lined with zinc. Pitch plasters for the back of your neck, guaranteed to be one hundred percent effective. Doctors use nothing else on their own mothers."

Eye ties the wide flannel cholera belt around her thick waist and shoves the chloride of lime squares into her pockets. She uncorks the brown bottle and shakes a few bitter drops onto her tongue. Awful.

"That comes to eleven shillings four pence, madame. Surely a bargain to maintain good health. Wait! Where are you going, madame? Come back——you can't take that without paying——"

But the Eye has left him payment in full, little does the impresario know. And all the remedies in the world won't make change for the cold blue currency with which she's paid.

Oh! Marrow, Oh! Marrow, Oh! What dost thou think?

The truth is that the Eye does feel rather giddy and anxious. There is a burning pain at the pit of her stomach and she does greatly thirst. It is awful to feel this way right at the dawn of understanding what has eluded her all these many years. It is especially awful because in the course of her wandering tonight, she has been as close to happy as she's ever been.

It all came clear that night in the snow, when she stood opposite the grieving mother, her own thick arms full of blue silk, faced with the mother's armful of still blue child. In that snow-falling moment, when nothing sounded but the sob of east wind, there in that moment Eye realized that to guard something too well might be as bad as not guarding it well enough. Once when she was young, she followed the rat and thirty miners perished; then when she was old, she followed the dress and look what happened—the rat snuck in and stole away the baby. Like a little piece of horehound candy. What Eye realized as the dress sobbed herself sick and snow swaddled the cold body of the only child she'd ever held was that she was not born to be either a prisoner or someone else's prison. She had failed the child, but she need not fail the mother. It was in her power to abandon her post. There are some holes better off not watched.

Oh! Marrow, Oh! Marrow, Oh! I've broken my bottle and spilt all my drink!

What would her life have been like if she'd never been set to watch a coal-mining shaft? She's rarely wondered that, any more than she's wondered what the world would look like seen through a matched set of eyes. And yet, if it was in her power to stop time in its coursing, she might pick a day, a day before any of this had ever happened, before she'd ever even seen a rat. She might pick a day when she was no older than Gustine's tiny baby, and her eyes had not yet fallen on anything but her parents' home and her mother's firm pink breast. Everything was pleasantly out of focus back then, from the brick red blur of the low hearth to the marigold birse of her thatched roof, sifting inside with each hard rain. How much nicer life would have been had her eyes never sharpened the pickax features of her coal miner father or discovered the blancmange resignation in her mother's face. If only her world had remained out of focus, what sort of myopic paradise could have been hers?

An old woman cannot stay a half-blind child, much as she

might like. But as brokenhearted as she was when the dress held out her only child, the Eye couldn't help feel the tiniest pang of envy. You will never see an ugly world, child. You will never know a rat.

I've lost all my shin splints among the great stones!

Eye doesn't believe these remedies are helping much. Her stomach thuds against the tight flannel cholera belt and the little potent packets have done nothing more than make her hands itch. It is late, and she is very tired. The heavy head upon her shoulders throbs rhythmically in time to the echo of the colliers singing down by the water. The Eye's trail of blue which began at the gray-blue dent in the snow where she left the sailor after she stole his tied-up packet (the dent from where if she had tracked the hand-prints and knee-prints would ultimately have led to a door a few streets away, where he pounded to be let in, someone had knocked him cold and robbed him, woe was him, taking his captain's clothes) has led her at last to a place she recognizes, where deep indigo letters proclaim their own inescapable truth: LABOUR IN VAIN, reads the hand-painted sign swinging in the wind. John Robinson's skull smiles benevolently down upon her; his working shovel is raised in salute. When she pushes open the door and steps inside, she sees that the place is empty, except for a group of four strangers, sitting as if waiting expressly for her. Three men and a woman—players, maybe, from the way they are dressed, all in elaborate costumes of blue, with curling blue feathers, blue gloves, blue boots. They will soon be off to London, then Exeter, Oxford, and Hull. They will catch a boat for America; play Canada, Mexico, Cuba, Peru. Before they retire their show, there won't be a country in the world that has escaped their little tragedy.

Mr. Eliot opens his arms to include their friend the Eye.

Come join us, he says. Let us buy you a drink. How good it feels to lay down your burden. To close your eyes and listen to the colliers sing.

> *Oh! Marrow, Oh! Marrow, Oh!*
> *What dost thou think?*
> *I've broken my bottle and spilt all my drink*
> *I've lost all my shin splints among the great stones. . . .*

Draw me to the shaft, lad, it's time to go home.

XVIII

LAST WILL AND TESTAMENT

It is one of the strange properties of cholera morbus that when a patient is bled, the life force comes out in parallel streams: one thick, slow, and tenacious; the other swift and light. The phenomenon can be explained quite readily by medical science: acute dehydration causes the patient's serum to separate out from his platelets, thus forming dual channels in the blood stream; but to Gustine sitting at the old woman's bedside, holding the cup while the doctor cuts, the Eye's blood flows like a pact. We have given our lives to avenge my child, thinks the dress lodger. We will always be a pair. The girl and her shadow. The dress and the Eye.

"You should be in bed yourself," Dr. Clanny says, as she catches the strange, double blood in her cup.

"I'm fine," she assures him weakly. She had sent for the doctor after she discovered the old woman passed out, alone, at the Labour in Vain. John Robinson and she managed her back to Mill Street, where Pink had been left in charge, her Da off to Fawcett Street, she said, following up a mysterious tip. Gustine is feverish and queasy, really too sick to be out of bed, but Dr. Clanny is overworked and understaffed, so when she insisted, he reluctantly agreed.

No one believes it is in the cosmic order for the Eye to die—the other lodgers can just as easily imagine a comet sweeping away the house or the ghost of Napoleon dropping in for a plate of eels. They keep a respectful distance, huddled around the fire downstairs, trading rumours that after the third telling will pass into fact. Did you know the Eye was born not of a woman, but had been secretly manufactured in a laboratory? No, no, the Eye was the chance child of poor old King George in his madness and an asylum inmate. The Eye worked for Scotland Yard; the Eye had been fed arsenic because "she saw too much." There are as many theories as ashes, yet all agree on one thing: that dress lodger—she is somehow responsible. Why else would the girl everyone knew abhorred the old woman volunteer her own pallet for a bed? Why, for hours, feed her ginger and calomel with a spoon? Why risk death herself to hold the old woman's hand through the bone-breaking tetanus spasms if not out of murderous guilt? Downstairs, by the fire, the respectful fear that for years had been the Eye's alone is slowly transferring over to the dress lodger.

I never knew you loved him too.

Gustine strokes the old woman's matted hair. Her heaves have abated and the singultus that sometimes replaces vomiting set in. It is horrible to witness the unconscious hiccuping, like obscene drunken giggles, racking the old woman's body. Earlier, her leg muscles contracted compulsively, but now the spasms have worked up to the muscles around her mouth, drawing her jawbone so relentlessly up and down that she who never spoke in life in death appears a chatterbox.

How did he do it? Gustine wonders. How was it possible an infant's touch could quicken the thready mass of sinew and bone in the old woman's chest, recall to life an organ so long still no one could remember the last time it stirred (though, it might interest Gustine to know, it was when she herself was born, a little girl small and vulnerable, herself kept from the Eye by her own mother, a worthless drunk of a whore who made every one miserable until she mercifully died). This rebirth of her heart was as close to motherhood as the Eye was destined to come. Would that it had not been such a long gestation.

"I am losing her pulse," announces Dr. Clanny. "Let's inject her with three cc. of tobacco. Maybe it will stimulate her."

Gustine sets down her cup and hands the doctor his syringe. "If this doesn't work," he says," we'll try an enema of oil of turpentine. If the body needs to purge, by God, we'll help it purge."

Unobserved by doctor or dress lodger, one member of the household remains upstairs, keeping to the shadows, trying not to get in the way. Nothing is as it should be, thinks Pink, watching her Da's dress lodger drip tears over the creature she was never supposed to touch. Gustine has the old woman's hands between her own, chafing them like she used to when her baby's were cold. Everything is upside down since the cholera came to town, what with frogs inside the house and bodies disappearing, enemies weeping over each other, and Da not even celebrating Mike's big night. She looks over at the Crown Prince, wearily sniffing the Eye's clenched, dark blue toes, and wonders if he feels as lonely and left out as she.

"Here she goes again," says Dr. Clanny, removing the syringe.

Gustine is helping the doctor hold Eye's punching arms and straw-stiff kicking legs through another attack when unnoticed, Pink scoops up her father's pet and creeps downstairs, past the gossiping lodgers with their theories of Eye's generation, over to her Da's stool where Mike's shining silver regalia lies forgotten. A Crown Prince should have a crown, she thinks, and neither politics nor newspapers should come before such a triumph. Pink stretches the strap of India rubber under the ferret's chin and affixes the crown in place. There. At least I haven't forgotten you.

Wrapping Miss Audrey's charity blanket around her shoulders like a shawl, Pink quietly lets herself and His Majesty out the door. Dawn is breaking, filling last night's churned snow with rosy light, rousing the gulls from their perches over the lintel. There is only one person in all the world who can make her feel better, Pink thinks, but walking west with the tin-crowned ferret in her arms, she fears her single solace might be in jeopardy. Ever since her Da swept in last night, to deposit Mike and call out the other lodgers, shouting triumphantly about Fawcett Street, how he'd be damned if God didn't love the poor man after all, she's been troubled in her mind. She would much rather her Da have no business on a street so near to her own heart, for if there's a way for him to destroy whatever happiness she could expect there, she knows he's sure to find it.

She makes it only as far as High Street and the corner of Nile before she's forced to duck back from the road, hide herself and His Majesty behind a lamppost, and curiously peek around. Maybe God loves a poor girl, too, for her Da is not at Fawcett Street uprooting her happiness after all; he is turning onto Nile Street at the head of a grand procession. "Today, the poor man's revenged!" shouts her Da.

Forty or more of her Da's friends, brandishing newspapers and swinging axes, tramp down the street. Though Pink knows none of their names, we might recognize among them a fagged Student of Life, all but worn out from chronicling this mess and desiring nothing more than to find a cup of coffee; Robert Cooley, the almost-flayed, hungover and miserable from last night, squinting in the bright morning sun; and Mag Scurr, who has scavenged a few items to pawn from her night's work. Behind Da, two strong keelmen drag a gentleman kicking and screaming, who to her amazement Pink recognizes as the doctor who marveled at Gustine's baby. Behind the struggling doctor, two more men follow with a sedan chair. Pink can't make out who is inside it; from behind, the only clue to the passenger's identity is a stringy, golden braid spilling from the window.

The men stop before a house that has been through a storm, by the looks of it: its shutters list from their hinges, the panes they were to have protected punched out and left like broken teeth in the snow. Without bothering to turn the knob, Pink's Da kicks open the unlocked front door. They march the doctor through his ruined parlour, sick and anemic in the dusty sunlight, with broken plaster chalking its Turkey rugs and shattered glass stuck between the keys of the pianoforte. Up the stairs, they push him to the second-floor landing, stepping over the broken banister and cracked posts, kicking in the door to his study. Oh Jesus, cry the men who joined the party late, instinctively crossing themselves if Catholic, spitting upon the ground to honor the Church of England. What sort of sick sod is this sawbones?

Mary, Mother of Christ, whistles Whilky Robinson, surveying the work his people did on the small anatomical study. All sorts of leathery, bladdery things in spirits swim about the room; who knows what they are, except that each one once belonged to a poor man—certainly there's no blue-blooded pickled parts in here. Broken-spined books: Albinus, Vesalius—who the hell? The landlord picks up Henry's costly leather-bound volumes and tosses them carelessly back on the floor. Laid out on the hearth in a respectful row are bodies they found in the study or dug up from the back yard: Whilky's lodger Fos; Reg Smith, taken from Mag's; Gustine's brat; and a jumble of miscellaneous bones—most likely dogs and cats, but one can never be too careful. Their greatest piece of luck of the night came, however, when they had destroyed just about everything they could destroy and were preparing to take the bodies away. A lady's maid came racing down Nile Street, screaming for Dr. Chiver—her mistress had been taken sick, please God come right away! She stopped in horror at the devastation all around her, babbling some story of a nighttime visitor in a blue dress and the news she brought along with the clothes of her mistress's father. Whilky understood almost immediately that this had been his dress lodger's doing, and offered to accompany the doctor to his fiancée's house so they all might be of service.

"Put her over here, lads," Whilky orders the men with the sedan chair.

And now, twelve hours later, they've all come back, conquering heroes leading their captives. Whilky left the vigil at Fawcett Street long enough to drop off his champion Mike, collect more men, and learn that both his dress lodger and her shadow were in the grip of what he'd just quit in Bishopwearmouth. He thought Gustine, no matter how sick, would rejoice to learn her child was avenged; but she didn't even crack a smile, paradoxical girl that she is.

"Now there, Dr. Chiver," larks Whilky, dancing Henry's carefully appointed skeleton about the room and gesturing didactically. "Since you like so much to cut people up, how's about getting started?"

"This is obscene," Henry spits. "You have no power to make me do this."

All jollity gone, Whilky leans in and slaps his newspaper, hard, in the doctor's face.

"She wanted it. Says right here in the public paper. Now get to work, you infernal sawbones, or I'll think nothing of taking this ax and striking that smug head right off your bony little shoulders."

Downstairs, Pink and the Crown Prince have sneaked inside the house and creep up to the second-floor landing behind the crowd of her Da's friends. Why were they dragging and shouting at Miss Audrey's husband-to-be? Surely that would make her new friend horribly upset if she found out. Pink's Da and his friends are crammed into a little room at the top of the stairs, she sees; some are turned away, holding their hands to their mouths. Others—grown men—cover their eyes and look ready to faint. Pink pushes through the press of fustian and corduroy breeches, clutching the Crown Prince for courage. What is her Da talking about in there?

"You thought nothing of taking our dead before they were even cold, as if the poor, along with being strangers to money, had no passing acquaintance with love," she hears him say. "Well, how does it feel, sawbones, to slice into someone you cared about? Where is your rationality now? How does it feel to be a poor man?"

Henry stands over the body, numb with shock and grief. His once beautiful girl, now an old hag, with a sharp blue nose and shriveled washer-woman's fingers; his beloved, still spasming a good hour after her heart gave out, whose arms, in a cruel parody of life, contract across her chest as if in prayer.

"We want to learn too, sawbones," says the infernal landlord, handing Henry his scalpel. "You taught your students on one of us. Now teach us on one of *you*."

Henry stands stupidly over the body of his dearest love, whose devotion to him put her in this place. The landlord commands him to teach. To teach! He almost laughs at the absurdity, when unbidden his words come back—the lesson he gave only the other day. Nature does not provide one nerve without pairing it to a second, he'd said. She invests us with two lungs, two kidneys, two eyes, two ears. The singular brain is divided into identical hemispheres; the heart has two corresponding auricles and ventricles. We are paired creatures, mourns Henry. He took the dress lodger's baby. She took his beloved in return. He should have realized: an eye for an eye, a tooth for a tooth. Even revenge is paired.

"Take up the knife, sawbones," Whilky commands threateningly.

Only the hardest-hearted would not be moved to pity at the doctor's deep unmanly sobs. There, there, Dr. Chiver. You can't expect to find compassion in the lodging house keeper's raw meaty face, nor forbearance in the quivering jowls of Mag Scurr, morgue keeper. But look about you—we know for a fact the crowd contains a few old friends. Don't you see, peeping over the shoulder of the Student of Life, your grinning, daft-looking chum from Edinburgh, with his extra toes and cauliflower ears? And there, to your right, just past Robert Cooley, that poor pickled old woman with her twelve-year-old grandson? We've all of us turned out for the show: those you bought from Burke and Hare, friend Fos, cadaver Liss, and that beautiful naked whore, your reproach Mary Paterson, raining a pool of whiskey upon your wasted study as she leans in to observe you make the first cut. The horror we see spreading across your haggard face makes us believe you've learned the truth at last. Though she is stretched before you on the table, your dearest stands with us now, married to you in a far more final way. Look upon your eternal family, Henry Chiver, surgeon and body snatcher. We will be with you always.

Pink has pushed her way through the crowd of men and finally is able to see what all the fuss is about. The little girl finds herself in a room straight out of her nightmares, with a dancing skeleton in the corner and the floor roly-poly with eyes. She sees her Da, standing behind Miss Audrey's fiancé, and the doctor himself, knife plunging in, sobbing like a man condemned. She sees a long yellow braid hanging over the side, she sees a limp hand, she sees . . . "Oh God!—*Miss Audrey!*"

Pink screams and screams until Mag Scurr, mercifully, leads her outside.

When Fos passed over, she consigned to the ages a few coins, a ticket stub, a well-thumbed Bible: the remains of a quiet circumscribed life. Her possessions were meagre, but riches compared with what a shadow might leave behind. With no money of her own and only the filthy brown dress upon her back, what could the dying one-eyed woman possibly have to include in her Last Will and Testament?

But now that she and the girl have come to terms, now that she has been forgiven, it troubles the Eye not to have something to leave her. She has never had much in her life beyond tenacity and gravity and an uncommon sort of vigilance. But that is something, after all. Instead of money or goods, which have never been hers, she might in this, her final hour, turn her genius of vision upon Gustine, and will the girl a future.

Dr. Clanny leans back in the straw and removes the stethoscope from his ears. "I've lost a pulse."

But Gustine, guarding the old woman as closely as she was

once guarded herself, sees the twitch of a thick-padded finger. Come closer, the Eye motions weakly, but is it a genuine
gesture or nothing more than the dumb show of cholera
tetanus? Pay no attention, the doctor warns, as Gustine leans
down and puts her ear to the dying woman's lips. It's a trick
of the disease.

I am a genius of vision, the Eye seems to say. Look with
me, girl, and know the future I see laid out for you. Eye hears
her voice inside her head already part of our growing chorus,
and for the first time in her life, it sounds rich and eloquent.

We have traveled only two weeks from this moment, the
Eye hears herself say, and we find ourselves back here in this
very house. My stool by the fire is empty, as is the straw you
laid me on upstairs, unclaimed by you or anyone else after I
added my old rusty voice to the Great Narration. Half the
lodging house is gone—dead in the wave that followed my
release, or fled as from a house of horrors, to take the cholera
onto Gateshead and Newcastle and Hetton-le-Hole. Our
landlord, Whilky Robinson, is nowhere to be seen, though
someone heard he was headed down to the Low Quay and
Mag Scurr's pawnshop. Yes, there he is, standing before Mag
(their camaraderie during the riot has not persuaded her to
raise her prices; five shillings, not a penny more, will she give
him for the ripped and stained blue dress he sets upon her
counter).

Aw, come on, it's worth eight at least, sulks he, but she will
not budge. Whilky sells for five and leaves the store before
Mag's shears come out and cut the wretched dress to ribbons.
We'll see no more of you, vows she. Of you, we've seen
enough.

But why did he sell your dress, you ask, you who almost
died in nursing me? Do you not remember falling ill inside it,

thrashing in agony for several days, crying out to your son, who stretched forth his arms, crying out for your wretched mother and even for me? But though you desired death, it was not yet time for you to come. The doctor who nursed me, nursed you more successfully, and slowly you grew stronger until you had the strength to stand up and walk, and that night you walked out of Mill Street. Don't you remember stealing out of the house in the dead of night while everyone slept around you, everyone but the little girl in the patched pink dress, whose hand slipped into yours and begged to go along? They were the first words she'd uttered since the fateful day on Nile Street when all hope had died within her.

Two weeks into the future and what a change there is. Look with me across town now, down toward the south near Coxon's Green. Do you see a tidy adolescent girl in an indigo frock, her hair smoothed back into a demure knot at the nape of her neck, her white nurse's apron tied in a perfect bow in the back? She stands on a wooden box, applying whitewash to the new fever hospital's walls, handing her brush off to the younger girl in her own simple blue pinafore, who splashes the stuff all over herself and drips it across the floor. They work in earnest, these two, as if their lives depended on a job well done. They wouldn't want Dr. Clanny's faith in them to be misplaced, nor would they want to lose the room they share with the other women who work at the hospital. Nurses are so hard to come by these days, and the doctor thinks you have a natural ability.

And some Saturday nights when you and Pink are buying sausages and coffee down in the marketplace, wiping your greasy chins and watching the crowds pass by, you are treated to a weirdly familiar sight. A pretty miss in a theatrical white gown, with her chin up and her eyes inviting, sets her slippered feet toward the Theatre Royale or the Bridge Inn. A few steps behind her shambles a broken-down drunk of a woman (her two blurry eyes barely registering the smudge of white ahead) whom Whilky pays in beakers of gin. Three Saturdays later, the white dress has disappeared from the street, you notice, and a jade green gown replaces it, with yet a third old woman, temperate, yes, but birdlike and nervous, and easily overcome by jade green's greedy punk of a boyfriend. Pale lavender watered silk is the landlord's last try; but when that one too skips town, he swears off dress lodging forever, thoroughly disgusted by the ingratitude and perfidy of women.

But can the genius of vision see even further into the future? The Eye's lips move and Gustine strains to make out any individual word. Where most women measure their lives in childbirth and miscarriages, the Eye hears herself say, you measure yours in epidemics. I can see ahead to 1848, when fifteen years later, the cholera, unappeased, comes once more for Britain. You are a matron now, happily married for the past ten years to that sailor who stepped off the pitcher and over the Quarantine. He treats you kindly and you go with him to visit his mother and your son at the Trinity Graveyard, you with no children in tow (your body was too ravaged for that) but happy nonetheless with your job as a nurse and your husband's love. All the babies you could want live down the street at Pink's house, where she is the mother of four, nearly a child a year since she married at seventeen a shortsighted, ferrety-looking young clerk who adores her. Your old skills as a dress lodger help you minister to the sick and dying. Those who cannot speak for pain turn to you, and you almost magically find the place that hurts them. It is your gift, and you have learned to use it well. Your family and Pink's both come through the new epidemic intact, but not long after, word reaches you through old Dr. Clanny at the hospital that his nephew was carried off in London, ministering to the ill in the slums of Stepney. Perhaps it was more merciful this way, says Dr. Clanny, helping you hold down yet another convulsing dark blue patient. Henry was never the same after poor Audrey passed on. Stopped teaching altogether, moved back to his mother's house. A gifted surgeon, though, his uncle says, shaking his head. Such a bloody shame.

Your skills are monopolized by cholera again in 1853, then in 1866, but when it comes for a final time in 1892, you are not around to see it. With Dr. Koch's discovery of the cholera vibrio, the disease that would define the nineteenth century is identified and conquered, just as you close your eyes and come to us. Cholera morbus has served its purpose; it has taught the rich to fear the poor, and that fear more than anything else will have led to all the subsequent reforms in sanitation. The cholera that began its westward career in the very year you were born lays down its head the year you die. You are one of the lucky ones: you die at home, surrounded by friends, of ripe old age. Yours has been the life span of a pandemic.

The Eye's lips cease to move. The genius of vision has spoken. She has foreseen as absolute truth all that shall come to pass, and imparted it as best she could. Escape, a family, and long life for Gustine. A new start, true love, and something akin to happiness. But is all this in Gustine's power to fulfill, or are these words nothing more than the ramblings of a delirious dying woman? It is all the same to the girl, who lays her head on the cold gray breast and weeps. What are you trying to tell me? she asks. I can't understand a word you say.

The Eye is tired of talking. Dawn breaks through the nailed and shuttered windows; outside it is a perfectly clear and cloudless morning, one of the rare days like those she knew as a girl, before the factories struggled out of the mud and the bridges clamped down upon the banks. No yellow smoke to smudge the windows, no soot to catch in the teeth; even the normally dun brown Wear runs with water the color of the living dress. She finds herself on the bank of the river, where on either side of her men and women throw themselves into the water, swim across, then run wet and shining to the field of green beyond. Where is this place? wonders Eye, who thought she knew every nook and cranny of the city. It is separated off by a pretty white picket fence, low and inviting, behind which stretches a dirt path leading where she cannot see.

Eye squints across the water, trying to make out a small, hand-painted sign hung on the white fence's latch. Three simple words she sees that will open the gate and allow her inside. As she watches, a baby crawls toward her across the meadow, happy and fat, its heart beating joyously. All she can hear is his heartbeat pounding in her ears. He laughs and stops by the gate, and though he is not old enough to speak, she thinks she hears him say, Come. Come to the place we have prepared for those who learn to love only in their last days.

Men and women race past Eye, reading the simple sign and entering. It seems to her that she has seen these words someplace before—yes, now she remembers. They were carved into every door and windowsill in Sunderland, like a secret code, worked into the fabric of everyday clothes and written into beads of sweat running down a pint of ale. Funny she never realized before now; the words—the blessing and the curse of all poor men and women, the words they live and die by—were everywhere she looked.

The Eye's gray lips move; the dress lodger leans in closer.

She is not talking, says the doctor, pulling Gustine back from what might be the Eye's fatal breath. It is only the spasms affecting her cheeks and lips. Look, he points out. Her feet are moving, too, like she is running. You don't believe she is really running, do you?

No, says Gustine through her tears. I don't suppose I do.

Then don't endanger yourself further by thinking she has something to say.

Gustine sits back, depleted and so very, very sick. She knows the doctor is right—it was all the cholera talking. And yet, when those dry lips moved and her breath like the soft creaking of a gate passed through them, Gustine could have sworn she distinctively heard a voice inside the hinges. The Eye saw all that was and all that was to come, and though she could not make Gustine understand, she did not wholly fail. You heard her correctly, Gustine. Take up the short sentence of your inheritance. Go and live a happier life. All the Eye foresaw can be yours, if you but remember the words upon the gate.

"Nothing without labour."

Travelling Light
KATRINA KITTLE

When Summer's promising dance career is ended by injury, she settles reluctanly into an unwanted career as a school teacher. Her long-term relationship with Nicolas becomes strained. And her beloved brother Todd may have no future – he is HIV positive.

As the virtus reaches critical mass in Todd's cells, and full blown AIDS manifests itself, Summer has to come to terms with life, death, relationships and her father's enigmatic injunction to 'travel light'. Watching her brother share a world with his partner, Summer observes the purest form of love, a love transcending the frailties of humanity and the inconsistencies of life.

But it is the fulfilment of a promise that Summer made to her brother as a child which forces her to face up to her greatest challenge. Ignited by death, Summer begins to realise the value of life.

∫

SCEPTRE

Cold Mountain
CHARLES FRAZIER

A soldier wounded in the Civil War, Inman turns his back on the carnage of the battlefield and begins the treacherous journey home to Cold Mountain, and to Ada, the woman he loved before the war began.

As Inman attempts to make his way across the mountains, through the devastated landscape of a soon-to-be-defeated South, Ada struggles to make a living from the land her once-wealthy father left when he died. Neither knows if the other is still alive.

SCEPTRE

Colour Book

ROSALYN CHISSICK

'Of course a sister is going to love a brother. But there is something else. He can't find the word for it – an edginess that sits between them, it is like still air before the beating of wings, like the millisecond before an explosion.'

Against a loveless backdrop, Pia and her half-brother Luke grow up to form a passionate bond that leads them away from home and into a wild, hand-to-mouth existence. In spare yet emotionally charged prose, Rosalyn Chissick charts a relationship that challenges society's boundaries and conventions. A shocking, poignant and poetic novel by a prize-winning writer.

SCEPTRE

A selection of other books from Sceptre

The Crime of Olga Arbyelina	Andrëi Makine	0 340 72315 9 £6.99	☐
The Nanny and the Iceberg	Ariel Dorfman	0 340 71303 8 £6.99	☐
Gorgeous	Lynne Bryan	0 340 73969 X £6.99	☐
Self-Portrait with Ghosts	Kelly Dwyer	0 340 73948 7 £6.99	☐
Cold Mountain	Charles Frazier	0 340 68059 8 £6.99	☐

All Hodder & Stoughton books are available from your local bookshop or newsagent, or can be ordered direct from the publisher. Just tick the titles you want and fill in the form below. Prices and availability subject to change without notice.

Hodder & Stoughton Books, Cash Sales Department, Bookpoint, 39 Milton Park, Abingdon, OXON, OX14 4TD, UK. E-mail address: order@bookpoint.co.uk. If you have a credit card you may order by telephone – (01235) 400414.

Please enclose a cheque or postal order made payable to Bookpoint Ltd to the value of the cover price and allow the following for postage and packing:
UK & BFPO – £1.00 for the first book, 50p for the second book, and 30p for each additional book ordered up to a maximum charge of £3.00.
OVERSEAS & EIRE – £2.00 for the first book, £1.00 for the second book, and 50p for each additional book

Name _____

Address _____

HOUSEBOUND   28/8/07

If you would prefer to pay by credit card, please complete:
Please debit my Visa/Access/Diner's Card/American Express (delete as applicable) card no:

Signature _____

Expiry Date _____

If you would NOT like to receive further information on our products please tick the box. ☐